It was a ___ ___ ___ she hadn't the right to ___ ___ ___ The phone rang and she waited for Eve to walk toward it, but the smaller woman didn't move.

"I'm not going to answer it," she said. "Not this morning. It won't be good news."

Ruthann shrugged. "I don't know who makes up those rules anyway. I mean, who says we have to answer the phone every time it rings? Or the door? It's your house. Your life. You can do whatever you want."

"I can't believe you just said that." Eve's voice sounded shocked.

"I just meant that you shouldn't feel forced to—"

"No," Eve interrupted. "You're right. Who made up all those things that rule our lives? I had that very thought this morning. Weird, huh?"

Ruthann smiled. "I've learned to pay attention to coincidences. Maybe we were meant to meet today."

❋　❋　❋　❋　❋　❋

"Like you, I await certain authors. Constance O'Day-Flannery is one of those I wait for and she hasn't let me down."

—*Barbara Critiques*

"Constance O'Day-Flannery has continued to create masterpieces of romantic fiction that are cherished by readers and reread time and again."

—*Rave Reviews*

ALSO BY CONSTANCE O'DAY-FLANNERY

Seasons

Published by
WARNER BOOKS

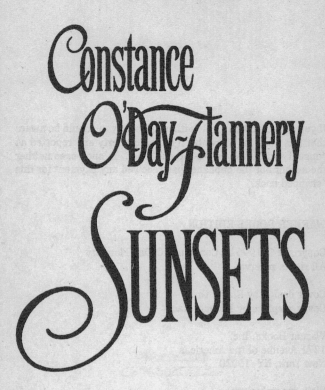

Constance O'Day-Flannery

SUNSETS

WARNER BOOKS

A Time Warner Company

WARNER BOOKS EDITION

Copyright © 1996 by Constance O'Day-Flannery
All rights reserved.

Cover design by Elaine Groh
Cover graphics by Michael Racz

Warner Books, Inc.
1271 Avenue of the Americas
New York, NY 10020

Visit our web site at
http://pathfinder.com/twep

A Time Warner Company

Printed in the United States of America

First Printing: September, 1996

10 9 8 7 6 5 4 3 2 1

Dedication

For Dale Rose Fountain, a.k.a. "Etee" . . . my dearest friend. Thanks for being my partner in crime and creating rockers that we will cherish forever. Next time around, point that finger. I promise, I'll remember.

PROLOGUE

They were seated together, as always, watching the sun go down over the City of Brotherly Love. A warm summer breeze blew off the Delaware River to the old Victorian porch, yet they each wore a sweater, for their skin had aged like fine parchment that had been left out in the rain: fragile, brittle, and stained with the tiny blemishes that come with over seven decades of life. Eve Cameron smiled as she looked down at her hand, resting on the arm of the rocker. Perhaps they were battle scars, she thought, badges of courage for surviving. For that's what the two of them were, after all. Survivors of life.

"Okay, best dancer?"

Eve turned her head, gazing with love at her friend of forty years. Together they had witnessed the turn of the century, the remarkable discoveries in science and medicine, and the infinite possibilities in the universe. She and Ruthann were as close as sisters, knew intimate details of each other's lives, and had never argued. Not really. How comforting that, at the end, they could still count on each other.

"Not now, Ruthann," Eve said in a soft voice as she touched her friend's arm. "Are you cold? Do you want me to get an afghan for you?" Although Ruthann was three years older than Eve, it was Eve who had almost always assumed the position of leadership. And how strange that was, since she had always thought she wanted someone to take care of her.

Ruthann shook her head and a tendril of white hair fell out of the knot at the base of her neck. "I'm always cold anymore," she whispered with an effort. "Play the game with me, Evie. Best dancer. Come on. . . ."

Sighing, Eve closed her eyes for a moment as she tried to think back over her life. For forty years she had played this with Ruthann. Best restaurant. Best song. Best weekend. Best Christmas. On occasion, the questions would flip to the worst. Surprisingly, and sadly, those memories still came easily.

"All right. Best dancer?" Eve smiled with remembrance. "Timmy . . . I think his last name was Hailey. Dear Lord, could he dance. Nineteen seventy-five. High school dances in Our Lady of Sorrows gym. How can that be possible? How could it have been over sixty years ago?"

Ruthann seemed pleased. "Shows your mind is still working. For me, it was Mick. Never saw a man move like that unless he was a little light in the loafers." She tried to catch her breath. "And Mick certainly wasn't."

Alarmed at Ruthann's shortness of breath, Eve said,

"Okay, enough. No more talking. And if you're too cold we'll go inside."

"No. I want to stay here on the porch. Just like we always said we would." Her mouth opened to capture air that her lungs were rejecting. "Remember? We called them rockers—the memories we could take out when we were old."

Nodding, Eve slowly rose to her feet. "We also promised to wipe the spittle from each other's mouths. Thank God that hasn't happened yet. I'm going to get you the afghan." As she walked into the interior of the house, she experienced a tightening in her chest. It felt like dread. Ruthann was eighty-two and the doctors were surprised that she had made it through the winter after that terrible bout with pneumonia. But they didn't know the strength and determination of the woman. Ruthann would probably outlive the damned doctors. Picking up the thick afghan from the arm of the sofa, Eve silently cursed the frailties of their bodies. How cruel to have the body slowly fall apart when the mind was still functioning.

She tucked the blanket around Ruthann's narrow frame and settled back onto her rocker, staring across the river to Pennsylvania.

"Best lover."

Eve sighed with exasperation. "Oh, please. Enough. I don't want to recall a lifetime. Let's just watch the sunset in peace."

"Evie? Please? This may be the last time you have to play it. For me? Do it for me?"

Surely it was senility. Why else would a seventy-nine-year-old woman be playing a silly memory game with a woman of eighty-two? Best lover . . . ? Where did Ruthann come up with these? If anyone overheard them, they would be shut away in a home. And Eve had fought too hard for her independence. Hers and Ruthann's.

"Are you thinking? It can't be *that* difficult. I didn't know there were all that many to pick from." Ruthann chuckled at her joke and then started coughing.

"Are you all right?" Eve asked with alarm.

Ruthann took a tissue from the sleeve of her sweater and wiped the corner of her mouth as she nodded. "See? I can still take care of my own spittle, thank you. Now back to you. Best lover."

In spite of everything, Eve grinned. Ruthann could always make her laugh. It was the basis for their friendship. "It's a hard one to answer," Eve whispered.

"What? I didn't hear you."

"Then turn up your hearing aid."

"I'm not wearing it. I can't stand that ringing noise it makes."

Eve rolled her gaze toward the ceiling of the porch. "Why doesn't that suprise me? If you'd had that operation the doctor suggested ten years ago—"

"Don't avoid the question, Evie," Ruthann interrupted with impatience.

"I'm not avoiding it. I said it was a hard one to answer. You're right. I didn't have many lovers, but I loved each one of them for a different reason. If I could piece parts from each, I could come up with the best."

"I'm not talking about comfort or compatibility. I'm talking about sex. Pure and primal sex."

Ruthann said the last word so loud that Eve looked around the yard, afraid someone might overhear them.

Who would believe it anyway? Two old ladies sitting around on the porch discussing great sex. But then she and Ruthann had survived gossip far worse throughout the years. They would never be nominated for matron of the year, but most of their detractors were dead and buried. That was one satisfaction in longevity.

"All right. Keep your voice down. *I'm* not the one with a hearing problem. Best lover? I'd have to say Luke."

"Hah . . . I knew it!" Ruthann was almost triumphant. "I can still picture the look in that man's eyes when you came into a room. . . ."

Eve didn't want to remember. It was too painful. "What about you?" she asked to stop the memories from rushing back at her, and she knew Ruthann was anxious to give her reply.

"Mick." Ruthann said the name with such longing that Eve turned to look at her.

"You answer Mick to everything. You didn't even think about it."

"Didn't have to."

"What? Everything begins and ends with Mick? You were forty years old when you met him. You did have a life before him."

"Doesn't seem like it to me."

Exasperated, Eve said, "I don't want to talk about sex anymore. We're too *old* to be talking about sex. Next question."

Ruthann conveniently ignored her, something she had perfected over the many years of their friendship. "Funny, when I was young I was told not to ask questions about it, so I messed it up for half my life. And now, at the end, you're telling me I'm too old to talk about it when I finally got it right?"

"If it will make you happy we'll talk about it later. Just not right here on the porch."

Ruthann looked out to the river, watching the birds at the shoreline. "All right. Next question, then. Best year."

Eve closed her eyes and sighed. Why was Ruthann doing this? Why was she forcing her to recall events in her life that were better forgotten? Who wanted to remember forty years ago, when they were in their prime? You could never recapture the past. Hadn't they both learned that lesson?

"Nineteen ninety-six," Eve said without further thought.

Ruthann nodded. "Mine too. Now, worst year."

Opening her eyes, Eve looked directly at her friend. "You're going to do this, aren't you? You're going to drag everything up again."

Ruthann's eyes watered with a thin film of tears. "I have to, Evie. One last time. If we still remember, it's—it's like paying them tribute. Now, worst year."

Eve's chin rose, almost in defiance, and for a moment her voice faltered. "The same. Nineteen ninety-six."

Ruthann reached for Eve's hand and held it with surprising strength. "Mine too," she murmured in a soft voice, thick with forty years of love. "Mine too. . . ."

CHAPTER 1

1996

Why?

She lay perfectly still under the covers and stared into the darkness of her bedroom as that question again screamed inside her brain. There was no answer, of course, and that's what tormented her day and night. She couldn't function. She couldn't sleep.

And she didn't care.

Perhaps that was the most frightening, the not caring. About anything. Nothing had meaning anymore. What was the point of getting up? Who said we had to bounce out of bed and jump into the shower? Who made up those rules? She hadn't brushed her teeth in days, and she didn't know if she was going to tomorrow. Okay, so she was probably having a nervous breakdown and somebody would eventually find her and put her away somewhere safe. The thought was comforting. What a relief it would be if her only decision were choosing cherry or lime Jell-O.

At least she wouldn't have to think anymore. For it was the thinking, the memories, that were drawing her close to the edge of sanity.

How strange that if she stared long enough into the darkness of her bedroom colored lights would appear, like a dim kaleidoscope. She remembered rubbing her eyes as a child and making it happen, but her eyes were wide open now. Maybe it was lack of sleep, or lack of food. Maybe she was hallucinating. Maybe she was dying.

Did people really die of a broken heart?

The phone rang, yet Eve ignored it just as she had done for days. Who could possibly be calling her at six-thirty in the morning? For weeks, ever since the funeral, she had withdrawn to herself. She couldn't find comfort in her friends, or her husband—which was why he had left two weeks ago. Since then she didn't answer the phone or the door.

But six-thirty in the morning? And whoever was calling was persistent, refusing to give up.

Annoyed, she picked up the receiver and said in a cautious voice, "Yes?"

"Eve! Thank God you answered. It's Molly. Are you all right?"

Eve Cameron closed her eyes and rested her head against the down pillow. "I'm fine. Why are you calling so early?"

Molly seemed to pause before continuing. "I wanted to reach you before you saw the paper this morning."

Eve hadn't read a newspaper in three months. She was

detached from the problems of the rest of the world. Somehow they didn't compare with hers. "Why? What's in the paper?" she asked without interest.

"Susan Vansciver just shot her husband."

Eve opened her eyes and leaned up on her elbow. She had a mental picture of Susan—cool, elegant, the perfect wife for a neurosurgeon. "She *shot* Doug? Why?"

"This is the part, Eve, that's so hard. . . ." Molly's voice trailed off as she sniffled away tears.

"What?" Eve demanded, sitting up. She and Molly and Susan were part of the same social circle. Wives of professionals. They were good friends, not best friends, but still . . . "Why would she do it?"

"Oh, Eve, this is going to blow the town apart. We've been deceived . . . all of us!"

"What are you talking about? Who's been deceived?"

"Us. The wives. Everybody that sent them all off to Guatemala once a year."

"Are you talking about the orphanage?" Eve asked, trying to make sense out of Molly's near-hysteria. The Rotary Club of Chelsea had adopted an orphanage in Central America. Once a year they visited and offered their services. Doctors. Lawyers. Druggists. CPAs.

"We . . . we sent them off for ten years like damned missionaries," Molly cried. "And they all have mistresses, and some even have *children*!"

"Molly, what are you saying?" Eve demanded, suddenly more alert than she had been in months.

"Susan found out Doug was keeping a mistress down there. He has been for eight years. He has three children by her and . . . and I guess Susan lost it. She shot him. My God, can you believe it?"

"Did she . . . Is Doug alive?"

Molly issued a sarcastic laugh. "Let's just say from what I understand Susan is a bad shot, but Doug won't be fathering any more children."

"I don't believe this," Eve muttered. "Susan shot Doug . . ."

"He's . . . he's not the only one, Eve."

There was a prolonged silence. "What do you mean?" Eve whispered, already afraid of the answer.

"When Stuart got the call at three this morning, I . . . I could tell by his face that he was guilty as hell." Molly started crying, and Eve closed her eyes in sympathy.

"Oh, Molly, I'm sorry," she murmured, surprised that she could feel anything for anybody.

"The little shit. I told him to leave. That I was living with a stranger. He packed his bags and left about a half hour ago. Eve? I made Stuart tell me everything, and . . . and Paul—"

"What about Paul?" Eve asked, although she knew what Susan was trying to say to her. The muscles of her empty stomach twisted painfully.

"Oh, Eve, after everything you've been through, how do I say this?"

"I'll say it for you. My husband has a mistress down there."

"They all do! Every year we sent them off with parties and tears, so proud because they were doing something noble and good . . . and . . . and they were all leading double lives! The damned hypocrites!"

"Does Paul have a child there?" Even though the thought nauseated her, Eve forced the question out of her mouth.

"I don't know. I really don't. I'm sorry, Eve. I'm sorry for all of us, but especially you. To be hit with this now. Do you want company? I can come over, if you want."

She shook her head. "No. Thanks, but . . . I don't know. I have some things to do and . . . and I'll call you later."

"Susan's being arraigned this morning. How do I tell the children, Eve? About their father . . . What do I say to them? Should I wake them for school? It's going to be in the morning paper. Damn it! I'm so angry. I know exactly why Susan picked up a gun. I have all this inside of me and no way to get it out. . . ."

"I don't know what to tell you, Molly. I'm sorry. . . . I'm so sorry. I'll call you later."

She hung up the phone and stared at it for a few seconds while remembering all those years of sending Paul off to Central America. Molly was right. The entire town thought of them as missionaries, donating two weeks of their time every spring to travel to an orphanage and do good work. The doctors would check the children's bodies and provide inoculations. The dentist would take care of their mouths. Nate Anderson would bring crates of supplies from his drugstore. Ted Schimler collected textbooks from his distributorship. And Paul . . . Paul's company supplied computers, software, and training to run the orphanage more efficiently.

And they were all screwing around.

All those years of car washes, hoagie sales, flea markets, and dinner dances to raise money . . . *for a good cause?* It infuriated her, rushing through her body like a shot of steroids. Throwing the comforter to the bottom of the mattress, Eve rose from her bed. She stepped over sweatpants, jeans, shoes, and lacy lingerie as she hurried into the bathroom and flipped on the light.

Once she had loved this bathroom. It was as large as a small bedroom, with old terra-cotta tiles on the floor and around the Jacuzzi. On the platform surrounding the large tub were ferns and plants that she had nurtured for years. Now they were dark and withered from neglect. Underwear was thrown in a pile by the shower, next to an even larger pile of towels.

Her gaze lifted to the six-foot-wide mirror over the large double sinks. Seeing her reflection, Eve stood in shock for a few moments before slowly walking up to it for a closer inspection.

Dark circles ringed her blue eyes, making her look like a raccoon. Her skin was sallow from lack of sunshine, and her hair . . . Her auburn hair was turning *gray*! She pulled it back from her temple and saw that the few silver threads she had acknowledged months ago had multiplied like mold in the shower. One day you wake up, and there it is! She drew her hand down and looked at her nails. They were chipped and dirty. *Dirty* . . .

Horrified at what she had let happen, Eve hurried to the shower and turned it on full blast. She stripped the night-shirt from her body and threw it on the pile of underwear before stepping into the hot water. Sitting down on the built-in seat, she let the water rain down on her, lowering her chin to her chest as she allowed the heat to enter her pores and burn away her inertia. She picked up the sponge and the shower gel and scrubbed at her skin, wanting to take away the sickly yellow and replace it with vitality.

Yet as she struggled to bring herself back to reality, the image of a young face raced across her mind and she cried out with sudden pain. The sound that came out of her mouth was a raw wail, a mixture of grief and anger.

Jamie . . .

How could there be any tears left? It had been six weeks he'd been gone, yet she couldn't bear to part with his things. Sometimes in the middle of the night she would get up and go into his room, smelling his clothes, remembering him when he was happy. Memories. There were so many, yet not enough. Fourteen years . . . and there should have been more.

It was so damned unfair. There should have been more!

He'd just made the varsity soccer team as a freshman when the weakness had started. He would come home from the daily practice and collapse into bed. Later, she would go up to his bedroom and try to wake him for dinner, but he was more tired than hungry. And that's when she noticed the bruises on his legs. Paul had told her not to worry so much, that Jamie was playing with the big boys now, seniors that were as developed as men, and it was expected that their son would take a few hits. But she never felt easy about it. The bruises didn't go away, and when Jamie called from 7-Eleven to ask her to pick him up because he had to sit down on the curb and rest halfway home, she took him to the doctor.

Leukemia. Such an ugly word.

She had prayed for a miracle, or at least remission so they could do a bone-marrow transplant, but God had turned a deaf ear to her and she had watched as her son wasted away in his room. She wouldn't let him die in a hospital, so she was his caretaker when they stopped the transfusions because they made him more aware of the pain. She had cleaned him, bathed him, given him morphine suppositories, encouraged him to eat, watched as his dignity was stripped away from him, like the hair on his head from the chemo. Then his young body couldn't fight anymore. He gave in . . . and gave up.

And when she needed him the most, Paul pulled away from her. In the last six months, when Jamie's condition worsened, Paul worked overtime or went away on business trips. He had always been the model husband and father. Great provider. Incredible businessman, involved with the community. Little League coach. Considerate lover. Supporter of charities. But he couldn't handle the horror, so he ran away. And she wouldn't forgive him for that. She couldn't. The son needed the father, and the father was weaker than the son.

She had so much anger inside of her. Anger at her husband for being weak. Anger at the Unholy Trinity of the AMA, the pharmaceutical companies, and the FDA. Six million dollars a day was spent on cancer research and they let big money and politics take precedence over a cure. And anger at God—that was the big one. What kind of God would strike down a child?

For years she had struggled with the God of her religion, rejecting the one of the Old Testament who was angry and vengeful. If God truly was her Father, then like a parent He would be loving and compassionate and forgiving. It was to Him that she had prayed, down on her knees, for her son's life.

In the end she had lost her son, her husband, and her faith.

It was all so damned unfair and unnatural. What was the point of getting up, getting dressed, getting on with life? What for?

Suddenly, Molly's words came into her head. They all had mistresses, and some had children. Children . . . The tears immediately stopped and she once more scrubbed at her skin. Now she had a reason to get up and get out of this house.

She had to see her husband and find out the truth.

Twenty minutes later, she towel-dried her hair and pulled it back into a ponytail. She brushed her teeth for five minutes and applied concealer under her eyes. Satisfied that she was finally clean, she went into her bedroom and tried to find clothes. She didn't have enough energy for good clothes, yet all her casual ones were dirty. Leaving her bedroom, she walked into Jamie's.

She didn't look around her at all the reminders. She couldn't. Not now. Now she had to concentrate, for she wanted to reach Paul at the company before anyone arrived. Opening the French doors to her son's closet, she pulled out a built-in drawer and picked up one of his sweatpants. She stepped into them and actually smiled as they fit over her hips. In another drawer she found a Sixers T-shirt and slipped it over her head. Before she left Jamie's room, she took his favorite Notre Dame baseball hat and stuck it on, pulling her ponytail out the back. Okay, so she might look strange, but she felt stronger wearing Jamie's things. And she needed all the strength she could find for this confrontation.

She almost didn't care about Paul having a mistress in Central America. How odd that adultery wasn't what was forcing her to finally leave her home. But she had to know the truth.

She had to know if her husband had another child.

CHAPTER 2

"You sure you got an interview this early?"

Ruthann Bucknum looked up at the security guard and
nodded. "Yes, I was told it would be first thing this morning. I . . . ah, I guess I just want to get my thoughts together before I go up." Immediately, her muscles tightened
with apprehension. Would he buy it? Would he let her sit
here for a little while?

The older man shrugged and looked down to the row of
security monitors in front of him. "Well, they're startin' to
come in now, but you'll have to wait down here until
eight o'clock."

"That's fine," she murmured as the man dismissed her.
Truthfully, she had nowhere else to go.

Sometimes she wondered if life wasn't merely this
stage where human beings worked out dramas for the
viewing interest of God. It sure felt like that as she sat in
the foyer of Palmer Manufacturing and waited to be called
for her interview. Gazing down at the run in her stocking,

she once more tried to rearrange her skirt to hide it. Lord knows, she didn't present the best picture for a job interview, but damn it, she was trying.

As soon as the thought entered her head, she mentally cringed. Her hair hadn't been washed in over a week, her clothes were wrinkled from being folded for so long. Makeup was minimal, and she couldn't afford more. She had washed and gotten dressed in the ladies' room of McDonald's and then ordered a cup of coffee, not just because she needed it, but because she couldn't stand the thought of the young kids who ran the place guessing that she was homeless. She had some pride left.

Maybe that was her downfall. Pride. Maybe that's why she found herself in this nightmare. Desperate, she had left her husband and security hoping to find happiness. All she had found so far was disillusionment. Nothing was working out as she had planned. She never expected that weeks of searching would turn into months. Sometimes she wondered if, could she have foreseen this, she would have still left.

The answer was always the same.

She would have left California. She just would have planned better.

"I called up to Personnel and they said you could go up. It's on the third floor."

Ruthann left her daydreams aside and stood. "Thank you."

Walking toward the elevator, she pushed down the rising panic and took a deep breath. She had to get this job. This was it. Her last straw. She had read about the clerical position in yesterday's paper and had used precious money to call and set up the interview. Last night, in the car, she had kept alert by praying for this position. It had to work out. She was so tired, weary of living with fear and rejection. How many times had she heard that she was overqualified for minimum-wage jobs, or couldn't come up with the dues to join a union? Everywhere she turned was a wall that she couldn't seem to climb over. She could type, file, answer phones. She would sweep floors if someone would pay her. God, she silently prayed, please let me get this one. Please don't let me go to sleep tonight afraid again. Let me know that there is a plan, that I'm not just walking about bumping my head against barriers that will never come down. Help me. Please.

The third floor came too quickly, and Ruthann smoothed down her wrinkled wool skirt before bringing her raincoat around to cover it. Maybe if she kept it on she wouldn't feel so insecure.

"Ms. Bucknum?"

She walked up to the receptionist and smiled. "Yes."

The woman seated behind the desk gave her a quick once-over and returned the smile with one of condescension. Her hair was curled in ringlets that looked damp yet somehow fashionable. Her makeup was impeccable and she wore a navy blue suit that looked fresh and businesslike. Her only jewelry was a wedding ring and gold earrings.

She was everything Ruthann should look like but didn't.

"Carol Menniger will be late this morning, so I'll be conducting the interview. If you'll fill this out, we can get started."

Taking the clipboard from the woman, Ruthann's empty

stomach twisted with dread as she looked down at the employment form. Already she had one mark against her. What next?

It was the same everywhere she'd applied. She didn't fit in, and people somehow sensed it. Looking down at the form, she filled in her name and stopped at the line asking for an address.

Lies. She had vowed to be done with them. Without further guilt she wrote down her parents' old address. It didn't matter that no one in her family had lived in the house for fifteen years. How could she tell the truth?

The rest of the form was easier. Social security number, previous experience . . . those answers were automatic. It helped her conscience, for she knew that lies were only illusions not yet revealed. Hopefully, if she got the job, by the time they checked she would have found a more permanent place to live.

She could feel the stress building up inside of her as she handed the application back with a forced smile. It would work out. It had to. She was due for a miracle.

The receptionist looked over her answers and then stood. "Let's go into Carol's office. Everyone else will be starting work, and we don't want to be interrupted."

Ruthann watched as the woman picked up the phone, pushed certain numbers, and then hung up. She figured the phone would probably automatically answer while they were in another part of the office. Following the well-dressed woman, Ruthann felt even more insecure as she adjusted the bow of her dated white cotton blouse. She had to stop this or she would blow the whole interview. She was a good person. She had some skills. She was as worthy of this job as anyone else.

"Here we are," the woman said, leading Ruthann into a large office and shutting the door behind them. "My name is Anita Collins. I'm Carol's assistant. Can I take your coat?"

"Ah . . . no, thanks. It's chilly this morning. I'll keep it on." Damn! Wrong thing to say. The woman was trying to be friendly and she was blowing it. Calm down. Sit down . . . and shut up.

Anita walked behind the desk and took the chair. Leaning back, she picked up Ruthann's employment application and again studied it. "Well, you have some office experience. You worked at this job for six years?"

"Yes. It was a small insurance office."

"And why did you leave?"

"My husband . . . he wanted me to remain home. We were trying to start a family and his position covered our expenses, so I agreed." She would never add that he threatened to leave unless she quit. Perhaps she should have let him. How different her life might have been.

"That was four years ago? You haven't worked since?"

"I worked for a few months in a video store while I sought secretarial work."

"This was in California, or here? It's not on your application."

"I'm sorry. It was here. I came back to New Jersey when my marriage ended. . . ." Why did she have to add that? What if Anita Collins didn't approve of divorce, or thought she was trying to garner her sympathy? Just answer the questions!

"Do you have any children? Any dependents?"

"No." She would not explain that one.

"When you worked at the insurance company what type of computer did you use? IBM compatible? Mac? And what software?"

The muscles in Ruthann's belly again twisted painfully. This was always the question she dreaded. "You see," she began, "it was such a small office, really like a mom-and-pop operation, and I was always able to keep up with everything using an electric typewriter. You can call to verify that."

Miss Collins placed the form on the desk and sat up straighter. "Are you saying that you don't know how to use a computer?"

"I'm a fast learner. If someone would show me, I know I could do it and—"

"I'm afraid you don't understand," the woman interrupted, shifting to a more comfortable position in the chair. "We can't train you to use a computer. We can help you become more confident with our software, but you must have a basic understanding of computers to begin with. I'm sorry, Ruthann. It doesn't look like we can offer you this job."

Desperation took hold and she found herself saying, "Please, Miss Collins. You have no idea how much I need this. If you'd just give me a chance, I swear I'll work harder than anyone and I'll learn."

Now the woman appeared uncomfortable. Shaking her head, she took a deep breath and stood up. "Really . . . you should have said something on the phone and we wouldn't have been wasting time. One of the requirements for this position is at least an understanding of word processing. I'm sorry."

Ruthann stood and her coat fell open, revealing her disheveled wardrobe. She didn't care. "Please. I'm desperate. Isn't there anything? If I can't work here in the office, what about the factory? This is a manufacturing company. There must be something."

Anita Collins again shook her head as she picked up the application. "There's a moratorium on job hiring right now while we undergo an engineering change on the factory floor. Perhaps next month."

"There's nothing?" Ruthann asked in a defeated voice. She didn't care about pride any longer.

"I wish I could help. I'm sorry."

It was on the tip of Ruthann's tongue to tell her the truth, that she was at the end of her rope, but before the words could form she saw Anita Collins's look of embarrassed resolution. It was over. There would be no sympathy from this woman.

It took a few moments for reality to sink in. Once it did, Ruthann forced a smile and gathered the edges of her raincoat around her as meager protection from the forces that seemed to be working overtime against her.

"Thank you for your time," she said, and walked toward the door with as much dignity as she could summon. Opening it, she took a deep breath and left.

There was nothing more to do. She had tried everything. If it was pride that had gotten her into this, then humility would have to get her out.

Humility. That was something she knew well.

*　　　*　　　*

Cameron Computers had been started in a small rented garage when Eve and Paul still wore bell-bottomed jeans. He distributed and franchised the major names, and she was his entire office staff. They'd invested in inventory, great stationery, a good printer, and they were in business. No one knew they were operating from a garage, and within three years they moved into a warehouse. When she became pregnant with Jamie they hired their first employee, an office manager, and the computer boom took over.

As Eve drove up to the sprawling brick building with its manicured landscaping, she glanced at the gray and black sign on the lawn. Cameron Computers. Simple. Dignified. She remembered how proud they were ten years ago when it was erected. They'd had a huge party to celebrate moving into the new building. Jamie had just started kindergarten. Thinking back, she recalled how happy she had been, how perfect her life had seemed.

How could it all have changed so drastically?

She no longer had a child; she had a husband who was a stranger. And a business that had started as just the two of them together had grown to over a hundred and fifty people working hard to make money for them. She pulled the car into a visitor's parking space, right next to Paul's beloved Jaguar. How he loved that car, catering to it like a demanding mistress. She almost laughed as she threw open the door and gathered her raincoat around her. No, Paul's real mistress was a thousand miles away.

She opened the beveled glass doors and hurried past the receptionist. "Good morning, Tracy," she murmured, not noticing the foyer that she had painstakingly redecorated three years ago.

Startled, Tracy nearly spilled her mug of coffee down the front of her blouse. "Good morning, Mrs. Cameron," she whispered in surprise.

Eve turned left and followed the short corridor to Paul's office. Even if she hadn't seen the Jag, she wouldn't have had to ask Tracy whether or not he'd arrived. Paul Cameron was always in the building an hour before his employees started their day.

He was seated at his desk, absorbed in paperwork, and he didn't notice her standing at his doorway. Observing her husband of seventeen years, Eve wondered if she had ever really known him. He had aged over the years. Despite his obsession with the gym, his waist had thickened and the skin under his chin wasn't as firm. Lines creased his face, but not laugh lines that could be endearing. The slight furrows on his forehead and around his mouth were from anxiety and pressure to succeed. Yet he was still a fairly handsome man. "Distinguished" was the way middle-aged men were described. If a woman's waist increased, if her skin wasn't as taut, if her breasts weren't as firm, and lines started to appear on her face . . . well, she was just old. Somehow it didn't seem fair, and she resented that she was comparing herself to her husband and wondering how she measured up to his mistress. *Mistress.* What did that woman think of his flaws? Did she even notice? Once, not so very long ago, each imperfection had only made her love him more—visible proof that they had endured, that they would grow old together, still united.

Sensing her presence, Paul looked up from his desk.

"Eve!" He was obviously startled to see her standing at his door. "What's wrong?"

She walked into his office, shut the door behind her, and leaned against it. "Doug Vansciver was shot last night."

"What? Doug? Who the hell would do that?" Paul shook his head in disbelief. "Why?"

"Susan shot him."

"Susan? I don't understand. . . ."

Eve couldn't walk farther into the room. She needed the door for support. "Susan found out that he was keeping a mistress in Guatemala."

Maybe a part of her was denying that her husband could be involved with it, that there might be a mistake, but Paul's face gave it all away. First he turned pale and broke eye contact with her. Then a deep red flush crept up from his neck to settle on his cheeks. Despite the cool fall morning, beads of sweat erupted on his high forehead and he wiped them away with the palm of his hand in a nervous gesture. She could feel the years of love and trust crumbling around her feet like a poorly laid foundation.

"I . . . I can't believe it," Paul mumbled, while shuffling papers around on his desk.

"What I can't believe," Eve answered, "is that all of you let us think you were decent human beings, that you were all using your talents to help others in need. We *believed* you," she added in a stronger voice. "We believed *in* you."

Defenseless, he didn't say anything. He merely continued to stare at the letter in front of him.

"Molly was right. We sent you off like you were damn

missionaries. And you let us. All those years of screwing around, of using the orphanage like that. What hypocrites. . . . It makes me sick!"

Finally, he raised his head. "Eve . . . I don't know what to say to you—"

"Tell me the truth!" she interrupted. "I know most of it already. I just want to hear it from you. I want you to tell me that you've been lying to me for ten years. That our marriage was a lie."

"It wasn't a lie. God, Eve, I love you. And . . . and it hasn't been ten years. It's eight."

She almost smiled. "Is that your defense?"

"I've wanted to tell you, Eve. It's . . . it's something that happened. It doesn't mean anything to me." His voice was filled with desperation. "I swear. But I didn't know how to discuss this with you. And then Jamie . . . I couldn't."

"What were you waiting for, Paul?"

"For you to become more stable. You . . . you're not in the right frame of mind, Eve. For God's sake, look at you! You're wearing Jamie's clothes!"

Lowering her head, she looked at her son's sweatpants. They fit. They were comfortable. And occasionally she had worn her older brother's clothes when she was growing up. It didn't seem at all odd to her. Dismissing his comment, Eve again searched her husband's face for something familiar. But he felt like a stranger, or a relative she'd known for years.

"We're getting off the subject," she finally answered. "You're very good at that, Paul. I suppose that's why you're such a good manager. But you can't manage me any longer. Now I want the truth. Do you have a mistress?"

He actually looked like he was about to cry. "Yes," he whispered as the phone rang. "We all do. You don't know what it's like down there. It just happened—damn it!" He grabbed up the receiver. "What is it?"

He listened to the caller for a few moments before saying, "I just heard about it. Eve's here. I can't talk." Hanging up the phone, he looked back at her. "Steve Canuso. He's as shocked as everyone else about Susan and Doug."

"I see the 'good old boy' network is functioning early. Trying to get your stories straight and avoid a scandal? Wait until Steve picks up the morning paper. Molly says it's going to be in it. Which means when Susan's arraigned and it becomes public knowledge, this dirty little secret will be exposed—along with every single one of you. I'm sure Chelsea will never be the same. Its most prominent citizens involved in such a juicy scandal. The newspapers will love it."

Paul briefly covered his face before rubbing his temples. "God, Eve, I'm sorry. I'm so sorry. . . ."

She felt no sympathy. "Do you have any children by this woman?" She had finally asked the question that had brought her here, and she held her breath as she waited for her husband's answer.

He slowly looked up at her, and his face appeared distorted by anguish. "One," he whispered. "A boy. But not by . . . His mother died four years ago."

She felt as if someone had punched her in the stomach, taking away her breath and her dignity. Sweat broke out over her body and bile crept up her throat. "What happened to his mother?"

"She died in childbirth and—"

"Your child? This boy?" she interrupted, sickened by the revelation.

He nodded. "That's what I was told."

"Where is this . . ." God, could she say the word aloud? "Where is your son?"

"He's at the orphanage. He's well taken care of; I make sure of it."

"I can't understand you," she whispered with contempt. "Who *are* you, Paul? The Good Samaritan takes a mistress, has a child by her, and when she dies in childbirth you put the child away and take another mistress. What kind of person are you?"

"Eve . . . if you only knew how many times I've wanted to tell you, to get rid of this guilt. That's why I pulled away when Jamie got sick. I thought God was . . . was punishing me." He started to cry, wrenching sobs that shook his shoulders. "I never intended to go back again. I was going to cut free and when you got through grieving, maybe . . . maybe we could repair our marriage and make a go of it again."

She walked up to him and, reaching across his desk, slapped his face. Her action was filled with as much anger and disgust as she was feeling. "Do you realize how self-centered you are? That everything you've been saying has been about *you*? That you only wanted to tell me to get rid of your guilt? That Jamie's illness was God's way of punishing you? What about me? What about Jamie? You betrayed me. And you failed your son—"

"Don't say that," he begged. "I'll make it up to you somehow. We can work our way through this. . . ."

She stared at him, asking in a cold voice, "When I'm done grieving for Jamie? My God! Don't you know I'll grieve for him every single day of my life, until my last breath?"

She watched the man she had lived with and loved for almost half her life unravel before her. And she felt detached. Taking a deep breath, Eve said, "It's too late for us. If you had come to me eight years ago when it first started, maybe we could have worked it out. But you were weak, and it was easier to run away from the problem than deal with it. Just like with Jamie. And I'll never forgive you for not being there for our son."

She walked to the door and grabbed the knob. Before she opened it, she turned back to the man who had once been the center of her life. "I'm going to find a lawyer and file for divorce," she said, forcing the words past the thickness in her throat.

"Don't say that, Eve," he pleaded. "I wouldn't know how to go on without you in my life."

"Don't you dare talk to me about going on. You still have a son. I have nothing left. If you want to finally do something honorable, then make your . . . son legitimate. Get him out of that orphanage."

"I could never do that," Paul mumbled in shock and desperation. "You don't understand the way it is down there, and he would never fit in here. If you'd just listen to me, Eve . . ."

She looked back at him one last time and pressed Jamie's T-shirt closer to her stomach to stop the painful cramps. "Shame on you. Where is your conscience? It might be an old-fashioned saying, but it's so true. Shame on you, Paul Cameron."

Within fifteen minutes she had parked the car and was walking toward Shop-Rite. It surprised her how calm she had remained. She felt as if she were sleepwalking, in some strange kind of trance, but she was determined to go food shopping. She had nothing in the house, not even coffee, and she wanted to smell the aroma in her kitchen again. As she approached the entrance to the store, she saw a woman standing by the door with a sign in her hand.

Automatically searching the pockets of her raincoat for change, she was about to look away when she read the words neatly printed on the white cardboard:

I will work for food. God bless you.

Eve saw a woman about her own age with red hair and freckles and great sorrow etched on her face. It was as if she recognized a kindred spirit, someone else who had been sucker-punched by life.

"I . . . I'll give you something on the way out," she muttered, finding it hard to look any longer at the tall woman.

"Thank you."

Eve nodded and entered the store. Grabbing a shopping cart, she started to throw items into it without thought. She kept seeing the woman, wrapping her dignity around her like the threadbare coat that she wore. Trying not to think, she hurried through the store and checkout line. She packed the food, making up one bag for the woman, and headed outside.

Eve approached her slowly, not wanting to hurt her feelings. "I . . . got some things, some food, and here—" She handed the woman two twenty-dollar bills. "I'm sorry, it's all I have on me right now."

"Thank you so much," the woman said as tears came into her big blue eyes. She accepted the heavy brown bag, shifted it to her narrow hip, and looked inside. "I . . . I'll have to give most of this back to you." Looking up, she muttered, "I don't have a can opener, or a place to cook this right now."

Eve backed away, desperate to get to her car. "I don't want it," she said. "Maybe you can . . ." She couldn't finish her thought. Walking away, she headed for the parking lot and the sanctuary of her car. It was too much to deal with in one morning. After her packages were in the trunk, she sat at the wheel and stared at the morning rush-hour traffic. Everyone seemed to be going on with their lives, as if nothing extraordinary had happened. Suddenly, as she turned on the ignition, tears started to run down her cheeks. The deep ache inside of her became unbearable and she banged her fist against the steering wheel with anger, anguish, and frustration.

"It's so damned unfair!" she cried, letting the sobs come. Her son was cut down in his youth. Viciously. Unmercifully. Her husband betrayed her and he had a son by another woman. And she was sitting in the parking lot of a shopping center falling completely apart.

What the hell had happened? Her life was out of control.

She remembered being a teenager, going away to college. She had lain awake wondering what her life would be like. Young. Naive. So full of hope and anticipation.

She never dreamed she would be middle-aged, alone, and miserable. That everything she cared about in this world would be stripped away from her. Looking out the window, Eve glanced at the woman with the grocery bag. Once she had been young and happy. Did she dream about her future too? Did she ever believe she would be standing outside of a store with a fucking sign saying she would work for *food*?

What the hell was happening in this world? How did we let it happen? Her entire belief structure was eradicated, and she had nothing to hold on to any longer. Her life was a lie, an open book of betrayal. Her faith was a lie. A God of love wouldn't have taken her son, or permit this terrible injustice. She couldn't stand to walk by homeless people and feel helpless anymore. Maybe it was an overwhelming problem and she couldn't help everyone, but she could make a difference with one person. Angry, wanting to fight back, she pulled her keys out of the ignition and threw open the door. Her step was determined as she approached the woman.

"I'm sorry I walked away from you," she said, wiping a tear from her cheek. "I've . . . ah . . . I've had a bad day."

The woman smiled and looked up at the sky. "Gee, it's hardly even begun."

Eve smiled back at her and shrugged. "I guess it's been a bad year. Look, if you're serious about work, I have a job for you."

"You do?" The hope in the woman's eyes was almost painful to see.

Eve nodded. "My house is a mess—"

"I'm a great cleaner," the woman hurried to add.

"I mean it's really a mess. I've sort of been preoccupied and let everything go. If you want the job, it's yours."

"I want it." There were real tears forming again in the woman's eyes. Picking up the bag of food, she stood up and held out a palm.

"My name's Ruthann Bucknum."

Eve shook her hand. It was cold. "Eve Cameron. Do you have a car?"

Embarrassed, Ruthann shook her head. "My car died last week. I've got my things in it."

"You mean you live in your car?"

"Yes."

The anger again surged up inside of Eve. "Okay. If you want to come now, I guess we can get started today."

Ruthann nodded, and as they walked farther into the parking lot, Eve thought she heard the woman whisper, "I just knew God would work a miracle today."

Eve figured God had little to do with it.

CHAPTER 3

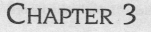

She always believed that God was watching over her, or at least a guardian angel, but her faith had taken some heavy blows in the last fifteen years. Ruthann was forty years old and at the deepest valley in her life. Cold, hungry, and homeless, she'd swallowed her pride to stand in front of that supermarket. Pride. It had kept her prisoner for almost half her life, yet she found it hard to believe that today after that excruciating interview she'd been reduced to begging. *Begging.* Dear God, how had it all happened? She'd had nearly six months of solitary existence trying to figure it out. Once she'd had a home in California. In Saratoga, a small upwardly mobile community in the wine country. She'd had a home on a hill that overlooked vineyards, a swimming pool in her backyard, a Yorkshire terrier, a BMW, a husband . . . Strangely, she missed the dog the most.

"Well, here we are," the woman next to her announced

as she pulled the car into a circular driveway in front of a large, modern home. "I warn you . . . it's a mess."

Ruthann smiled. "I don't mind work. And I'm used to cleaning."

"Oh, then you do clean houses?"

"Not really," she answered, trying to be honest. "But my home was immaculate, so I'll do a good job." No need to add that every Friday for the last fifteen years her husband would do a white-glove test before giving her the household money for the week. She knew how to clean. It was part of her survival.

Both women got out of the car and brought the grocery bags into the house. Ruthann wasn't sure what to expect, and was mildly surprised to see the condition inside the home. It wasn't dirty. It was neglected.

"The upstairs is worse," Eve announced. "I've . . . sort of been living up there the last month."

Ruthann pushed a dead fern aside and placed the paper bags on the kitchen counter. "You were sick?" she asked out of concern. It seemed the polite assumption.

"Sick?" Eve's small laugh was tinged with sarcasm. "Yes. I suppose you could say that. Listen, why don't we start by putting away these groceries and I'll make a pot of coffee."

There was something about Eve Cameron that pulled at Ruthann. She couldn't quite put her finger on it, but it seemed as if the woman was surrounded by an aura of sadness. Once again she realized that money could buy a lot of things, but happiness, real happiness, could never be purchased. Wasn't that the disovery that had sent her on this adventure in the first place?

"I'm sorry. I don't know where anything goes," Ruthann said as she took the groceries from the bag. "If you'll tell me, I'll put these away." Holding a bag of hazelnut coffee, she inhaled the scent of freshly ground beans and immediately thought back to her own home and the peace she used to find after her husband had left for work and she would enjoy a cup of coffee alone.

Was she more unhappy then . . . or now?

"Right. I'll take care of them," Eve said, pulling her raincoat off and throwing it over the back of a kitchen chair. "And you can . . . ?" She looked around the kitchen and shrugged. "I guess you can start wherever you want."

Again smiling, Ruthann nodded. It was as if she knew exactly how Eve felt. Overwhelmed by indecision. "What if I begin by making the coffee? You look like you could use a cup."

The small woman resembled the actress Sally Field. Dressed in sweatpants and a basketball T-shirt, she stared at Ruthann for a few moments and then smiled. It wasn't strained or polite, as in the parking lot of the supermarket and during the ride to this house. It was real.

"You're right. I could. It's been one hell of a morning." Eve took a deep breath and the smile slowly faded. "The filters are in the cabinet to the left of the sink."

"Great." Ruthann felt sorry for the woman. It was as though Eve suddenly remembered she hadn't the right to smile. That was also too familiar. As she turned to the cabinet, the phone rang. She waited for Eve to walk toward it, but the woman didn't move. Ruthann glanced at her employer for the day.

Eve was still staring at the phone. "I'm not going to answer it," she whispered. "Not this morning. It won't be good news."

Ruthann shrugged as she placed a paper filter in the basket of the coffeepot. "I don't know who makes up those rules, anyway. I mean, who says we have to answer the phone *every* time it rings? Or the door. It's your house. Your life. You can do what you want." She stopped speaking, took off her coat, and looked up.

Eve was clutching a box of raw sugar to her chest. "I can't believe you said that." Her voice sounded shocked.

Ruthann carefully folded her worn coat and placed it on the seat of a chair. "I just meant that you shouldn't feel forced to—"

"No," Eve interrupted. "You're right. Who made up all these things that rule our lives? I had that very thought this morning. Weird, huh?" The phone stopped ringing.

Ruthann smiled. "I've learned to pay attention to coincidences. Maybe we were meant to meet today."

They stared at each other and their gazes held for an intense moment. It had happened to Ruthann before, and she wasn't afraid anymore as the current ran through her body. When she was younger, if that same attraction had happened with a male, she would have thought it was merely that—attraction. Now it was happening with males and females, and she recognized it as a sign that the person was supposed to come into her life for a reason. But what could she possibly offer this woman who seemed to have everything except happiness?

Eve broke the gaze and started putting away the groceries, while Ruthann began bringing some order to the clutter of dirty dishes that overflowed the sink. It seemed better to keep busy than try to figure out the unexplainable.

"Ah . . . I think I'll go upstairs and bring down the laundry," Eve said while folding the empty bags. "You'll be all right down here?"

Filling the sink with hot water, Ruthann nodded. "I'll call you when the coffee's ready."

"Great. If you need anything, just yell."

Alone in the kitchen, Ruthann sighed. For six months she had been trying to rebuild her life and had met only failure. Maybe this was just a way to get out of the cold and make enough money to get a cheap room for the night. And wouldn't that be nice? Now that her car was out of commission, it was impossible to get to the airport where she had spent the nights wandering through terminal after terminal, hoping not to get thrown out by the security guards. Sometimes she'd been so tired that she'd go into the ladies' room and doze in a stall until the cleaning woman made her leave. Then she would wander again, waiting until light forced the dark loneliness of night into submission.

When she had told Ed that she'd wanted a divorce, he'd laughed at her. Told her that no man would want her. That she didn't have the intelligence to take care of herself. That she'd be begging him to take her back . . . When she had told him she had an appointment to see a lawyer, he'd reacted so fast that she still had trouble figuring out how he had managed to do it. Within five weeks she was divorced and put from her house with only her old station wagon jammed with clothes.

Banishing the thoughts from her mind, she deeply inhaled as the wonderful aroma of hazelnut coffee began to fill the kitchen.

Freedom. There was always a price.

What was wrong with her? She'd let a stranger into her home and had left her alone. The woman could be downstairs planning anything—stealing her silver, rifling through her purse. And yet . . . somehow she didn't care. There was something in Ruthann Bucknum's eyes that said she was trustworthy.

Sure. Right. As if she were a good judge of character!

Eve sat on the edge of the bed and held the box of Hefty trash bags in her lap. Her husband had been keeping a mistress for the last eight years. Correction. Mistresses. And even though she had thought of Paul as weak where Jamie was concerned, she had never thought that she couldn't trust him. She had believed that he was a man of honor. In the end it seemed she knew very little about judging character. Paul looked and acted like an upstanding citizen and husband. Who could have guessed what was in his heart?

And he had a child. A son.

She touched the basketball imprint on Jamie's T-shirt and felt her throat constrict with raw emotion. This was too unfair, too surreal. Her husband had a son somewhere in Central America. And she had . . . no one.

She wanted to lie back in bed, to again pull the covers over her head and sob out her anguish, to pretend that none of it was taking place. She felt so utterly alone. There was no one to put arms around her and tell her it was going to get better, no one to help smooth away the scars on her soul. She was alone.

Alone. The word resounded inside her head. Since Paul had left, she'd been existing here by herself, yet she had still felt connected to him if only by memories and anger. She was beyond anger, and now she saw that the memories weren't real. They were colored by deception and betrayal, making that man of her memories someone false. Yet what was reality anymore? How could you judge the present when every memory is a past lie? Where had she been? Why had she never sensed the truth? It was as if she had been away while she was married, or sleepwalking—trying so hard to do the right thing, to create a happy family—that she had forgotten about the ugliness of life. Now it surrounded her, closing in and threatening her sanity.

She immediately stood up, as if in denial, and opened the box of plastic bags. Scanning the littered room, she told herself that she needed to work and stop thinking. It was the thinking that would drive her mad. Yet as she moved about, picking up soiled clothes and dropping them into the bag, she could feel it stalk her across the room.

She knew then what it was.

Fear.

Not the kind of fear she'd felt for Jamie. Incredibly, it went beyond that. This was primal. She was afraid to be alone, to feel unconnected to society, to someone . . . anyone.

"Coffee."

Jumping at the sound of a voice from downstairs, Eve

felt the muscles around her heart tighten and radiate with heat. "Okay," she managed to yell back. Suddenly she broke out into a sweat and whispered to herself, "Get a grip. Don't let this happen."

Something inside her was pulling her back from the edge, from that fine line that marks the difference between sanity and madness. That, too, was primordial. It was survival.

Okay . . . Okay, she told herself. So your life is out of control. Temporarily. There's no one to kiss it and make it better. She had . . .

Oh, God.

It came back at her, sneaking up her legs, crawling over her body until it entered her mind and screamed that she had nothing. No one. Not husband. Not child. Not parents. Not even real friends. She was totally alone in this world.

She loved no one.

The truth reared its hideous head in front of her face and she couldn't deny it. For someone who had loved so totally, it was a near-fatal blow. She was not only unloved, but she experienced an icy numbness, as though she'd lost the capacity herself. One cannot get more alone than that. She felt as if someone had punched her in the solar plexus, taking away her ability to breathe, when she heard her name called out behind her.

"Eve? Coffee's ready. I called up, but you didn't come down."

Sitting down in a chair, she stared at the rug beneath her feet and whispered, "Yes. Thank you."

"Are you all right?" Ruthann asked from the doorway.

Embarrassed in front of a stranger, Eve nodded. "I'm fine. I'll be right down."

"Okay."

Once more alone, Eve sat back in the chair and took a deep breath. She was not going to let this happen, at least not without a fight. Somehow she would get back control.

She was alone. It was a fact. She would survive.

If only there were somewhere to turn. But she had lost all her beliefs. In God . . . family . . . community. She had herself. Barely. Was it enough?

Right now she had a woman downstairs who was waiting for her, a woman who had her own share of pain. At least she herself had shelter and food. The basic necessities. Sadly, too may people were without even that. Already she felt a bit stronger. Maybe all she needed to decide was to begin, to take the first step away from the edge.

It was an anxiety attack, that's all, she kept mentally repeating as she stood up and picked up the clothes she'd been sitting on. She couldn't have a nervous breakdown. Not today.

The aroma of fresh-brewed coffee entered her nostrils and she almost smiled. Today she was busy. First she had to have a cup of coffee. That was a beginning. Then she needed to talk to a lawyer and start divorce proceedings. And she had to get her house in order. Figuratively and literally.

"How? How did you manage all this in such a short time?"

Ruthann grinned at Eve's surprised expression. The

table had been cleaned and set for coffee. The Danish pastry Eve had bought at the store had been placed on plates. The kitchen was almost clean and the dishwasher was running. "It was good to work again. It just needed to be organized. I'll have it finished in no time and then we can get to the rest of the house."

Pulling out a chair, Eve sat down and waved her hand toward the chair opposite her. "Here. Sit down and join me. Have some coffee."

"Are you sure?" Ruthann appreciated the work and didn't want to appear pushy.

"Yes, I'm sure. We have all day to clean. Let's at least enjoy a few minutes of peace."

Smiling, Ruthann placed the dish towel on the counter and sat down. "Thank you. I can't remember the last time I did this."

"Drink coffee?"

"Drink coffee with someone. It's been . . . I've been on my own, I guess you could say."

"How long?" Eve asked, and then shook her head. "I'm sorry. I shouldn't have pried. That's none of my business."

"No. It's all right," Ruthann answered, trying to keep the loneliness out of her voice. "I left California almost seven months ago. I thought I'd return to New Jersey, but I guess it's true that you can't go home again."

"You lived here? In Chelsea?"

"In Manobao. But I'd pass through Chelsea on my way to the shore. I always thought it was a nice town."

"Looks can be deceiving," Eve muttered while placing a Danish on a plate. Handing it to Ruthann, she added, "Then your family is here in New Jersey?"

Ruthann shook her head as she accepted the mouthwatering pastry. How long had it been since she'd indulged herself in anything so sinful? It seemed like another lifetime ago. "They're all gone," she whispered, staring at the treat in front of her. She wanted to savor the moment, to draw it out and remember before she devoured it. "My parents died within seven months of each other and my brother was killed in Vietnam in 1969. After I visited their graves, I realized that I was totally alone. Scary," she whispered, no longer able to resist the Danish.

Eve looked as if she had seen a ghost. The woman's eyes were wide and staring; her jaw hung open, her body looked rigid.

"What did I say? Are you okay?" Ruthann mumbled while swallowing hard. She did not want to lose these few minutes of companionable luxury and was afraid that she had somehow insulted her benefactor.

Eve finally moved. She sort of slumped toward the table and held her head in her hands. Running her fingers through her hair, she whispered, "I can't believe you're saying that. It's too—"

"Oh, no," Ruthann immediately cut in when she realized what Eve must be thinking. "I didn't tell you that because I wanted you to feel sorry for me or anything. I don't want charity. I intend to work for my pay."

"No," Eve answered, again sitting upright. Her lips moved into a strange smile. "I was going to say that it's too incredible. I was just upstairs having those same thoughts. About being alone. And how scary it is." She held her hand to her temple and began massaging it, as if her mind were being strained. "I don't know what's going on. . . ."

"Do you want me to leave? I don't want to upset you." Ruthann pushed her chair back from the table.

"Please," Eve said, and held up her hand. "Don't go. It's just that . . . I don't know. It seems so strange that you made that remark about the rules, and now this. Both thoughts were mine earlier. But I didn't mean to offend you. And I apologize if I did."

Ruthann relaxed. "That's okay. I was more worried about your reaction. You seemed shocked. And, to be truthful, I guess I'm a little defensive. Everybody's got bad times, and people sometimes think . . ." She shrugged. "It doesn't matter."

A few seconds of silence followed until Eve whispered, "Yes, it does. It does matter, Ruthann. And . . . if you don't mind, I'd like you to tell me about yourself. You started, and I interrupted."

Ruthann stared back at the smaller woman. Eve Cameron was looking at her with an open expression. There wasn't pity, avoidance, or anger, emotions she had seen too often. There was . . . acceptance. Just that. She had a feeling that whatever she told Eve, the woman would listen and not judge. Suddenly, a spark of something nearly lost was ignited.

Dignity. She felt almost like a member of society again. Somebody was saying that she mattered.

"I was married," she began hesitantly. "It didn't work out."

"I'm sorry."

"Don't be. Even though things seem pretty dismal right now, I'd rather have my peace of mind than security."

"Really? And you have that?" Eve asked in an almost shy voice. "Peace of mind?"

"I think so. That's not to say I'm not scared. I am. Almost all the time. Every night I face the decision of how I'm going to make it through till morning. But would I rather be back in my marriage? No. Something will happen. I just have to be patient and . . . well, I guess I have to learn from this experience."

Eve stared at her for a few moments before saying, "That's a great attitude. I don't think I could be that centered. Couldn't your husband, your ex-husband, help?"

Ruthann almost laughed. "It's because I wasn't a good judge of character in the first place that put me in that marriage and eventually got me out of it with my clothes and my car. No, he wouldn't help me, and I wouldn't ask."

"How long were you married?"

"Too long. Fifteen years." Ruthann marveled at how easily and quickly two women can bond over the subject of marriage. "It was time to move on. I just needed the courage."

"But fifteen years? And you left with only your clothes and the car? What about community property?"

"When I told my husband that I wanted a divorce, he had everything put into his brother's name. Even my lawyer said there was nothing I could do after that. I should have protected myself a long time ago. I took care of the house and he took care of the finances. You see, I wasn't aware of what our finances were at any point in my marriage. I received a weekly household allowance, and he oversaw that."

Eve seemed to sit up straighter. "That's horrible. You should hire another lawyer and—"

"No," Ruthann interrupted. "I'm free of him. And, as I've said, I have my peace of mind. I was . . . it was like I was emotionally dehydrating. Does that make any sense? I felt like one of those Stepford wives. No. No more lawyers." Wanting to change the subject, she asked, "Are you married?" She had seen pictures of Eve with a tall man and a teenage boy on the foyer table when they'd entered. She assumed they were her family, but in this day and age one never knew for sure.

The woman seated across from her merely stared back for several seconds before muttering, "Yes . . . no . . . I mean . . . Good God, I guess I'm separated."

"Oh. I'm sorry." Now she understood why the house had been neglected, as well as the woman herself. Transformation. It was never an easy task.

Eve sipped her coffee slowly, as though to gain some time and some strength. Ruthann did the same, not wanting to intrude.

Finally, Eve said, "I just made the decision this morning and met you at the market after I had informed my husband— Even saying that—'my husband'—doesn't seem right anymore. I'm sorry. I must sound like a rambling idiot."

Smiling, Ruthann placed her cup back on the table. "Not at all. Considering your morning, you sound remarkably sane."

Eve actually laughed. "Thank you. You don't know

how much I needed to hear someone say that. It feels like my reality keeps shifting and I'm trying to find a balance."

Ruthann knew exactly what she meant. "I think that's the key to living on this planet: finding the balance."

It took them five and a half hours to bring order back into the house. By the time they were finished both women were tired, yet filled with a sense of accomplishment. Each found that there was something therapeutic in the physical exercise of housework. For just a few hours they could forget their problems and concentrate on simpler issues.

"I don't have enough cash on me to pay you right now, but we'll stop at an ATM and I'll get it there. If that's okay?"

Ruthann pushed her arms through the sleeves of her coat and nodded. "Of course," she answered, already sorry that the job had ended. She realized a button was loose and wished she had thought of it earlier. She was sure Eve would have lent her a needle and thread. But now it was too late. Now she must leave this warmth and return to her world. For a short while she was able to pretend, and now it was time to face her own reality. Already her mind was shifting back, trying to decide whether to spend some of her precious pay on a cheap motel room, or save it for the uncertainty of being a wanderer.

They hardly spoke while driving to the automated teller. When Eve returned to the car and gave her five crisp twenty-dollar bills, Ruthann protested. "Please. This is too much. And you already gave me forty dollars this morning."

Eve shook her head as she drove away from the bank. "Believe me, you earned every dollar. Without you, I would have been lost in the chaos. You not only clean like a professional, you also helped me in ways you'll never know. Please, Ruthann. Take the money. I would have paid twice that amount if I went to an analyst, and they wouldn't have made half the sense that you did. You were right. I need to find my balance again. Now, where can I take you?"

She gave Eve the directions back to her car. As the old Chevy wagon came into view, parked on a side street by a large apartment building, Ruthann felt the sharp ache of loneliness return. For just a little while she had felt connected to someone. "Here it is," she announced, and pointed to her car.

As Eve slowed down, Ruthann turned in the seat to face her. "Thank you so much for what you did today. You didn't have to, but you helped me, and I'm grateful for that."

"Nonsense. You helped me more than I can put into words. I think we're both grateful for the meeting. Take care of yourself, Ruthann. How . . . how can I reach you if something else comes up? I mean, I have friends that I could contact. Surely we can find some steady work for you."

"You've done enough, Eve." She opened the car door and got out. Smiling, she held the door handle and added, "Something will turn up. I just have to be patient."

Taking her car keys out of her pocket, Ruthann used her other hand to wave goodbye to her friend. For that's what it felt like. For just a few hours, someone had cared.

* * *

Eve drove back toward her home and the heaviness around her heart increased with each mile separating her from Ruthann. How could Ruthann spend the night in a *car*? How could she let her? Yet the woman had made it clear that she didn't want charity. For someone like that it would have to be seen in a different light. But what? And how? Her thoughts flitted to different corners of her brain trying to find the right answer.

A school bus going in the opposite direction stopped and Eve applied the brakes as she waited and watched. Children seemed to bounce down the steps and practically skip toward their homes. Freedom. Innocence. A sharp pain of yearning swirled through her torso. She remembered Jamie running into the house, dropping his schoolbag on the kitchen table and then proceeding to devour anything in the fridge. How many times had she scolded him for drinking milk right from the container? God, if she could only take that back. In the end, what the hell did it matter?

She was alone with just her memories. And right now they were too painful to explore. Maybe she never would. Not alone.

It was that damned fear again. Oddly, she had seen that look in Ruthann's eyes. Even though they were different women, in different circumstances, she and Ruthann were very much alike. Even their thoughts were similar.

Suddenly, as the school bus proceeded past her, she knew what to say to Ruthann. It was so simple, she almost laughed out loud. Looking for a place to turn around, Eve realized that all she had to do was be honest.

Five minutes later, she knocked on the window of the station wagon and smiled. Ruthann appeared startled, then almost happy to see her.

Rolling down the window, Ruthann asked, "Did I forget something?"

Eve placed her hands on the door and took a deep breath. "No. I forgot something. To be honest with you. Look, my son died six weeks ago. My marriage has fallen apart. My friends seem to be operating on a distant plane. I'm all alone, Ruthann. And I'm scared."

Ruthann reached out and touched Eve's hand. "Oh, Eve . . . I'm so sorry. I never had children. Never will. It must be a nightmare."

Eve wouldn't let the grief that was tightening her throat cut off her words. "Listen to me. I have that big house. Too big for one person. You can rent out the guest bedroom. Twenty dollars a week. I won't be alone, and you'll have shelter while we both try to put our lives back together. What do you think?"

They stared into each other's eyes for timeless moments, until Ruthann smiled again.

"Are you sure? I mean, you don't even know me."

"Right now I feel I know you better than my friends of twenty years. You're real, Ruthann. And I need to ground myself in some reality, because mine is certainly not too stable." She swallowed down the heavy emotion and just said it. "I . . . I need you."

The words hung in the air for a few seconds with significance and honesty.

"Then I accept, but twenty dollars a week is too little."

Eve expelled her breath with relief, straightened, and asked, "Where's your money?"

Ruthann reached into her coat pocket and brought out the small stack of bills. Eve took a brand-new twenty and shoved it into her own pocket. "There. The deal is done. At least for a week. We'll just see how it goes and play it by ear. If you want to help around the house, then fine, but let's get your stuff and get out of here. I don't know all the answers, Ruthann. But I know this is right. It's the first right thing I've felt in months."

Ruthann's eyes filled with tears as she reached behind her to unlock the back door of the car. "I knew God was watching out for me. I just knew it! This is a . . . a miracle."

Eve sighed again as she opened the door. Grabbing one of the suitcases that was partially covered by a blanket, she said, "Only one thing. No more talk about God and miracles, okay? I don't believe in either of them."

Ruthann merely smiled as she got out of the car.

CHAPTER 4

The water seemed to envelop her, wrapping itself around her body with warm liquid arms of security. She was safe. She felt safe for the first time in six months, and this was her first real bath in all that time. Six months of hurried showers or washing in public bathrooms . . . Being yelled at, threatened, pitied, or scorned . . . Yet it was that steady, concentrated glaze in the eyes of people that hurt the worst. The Great American Society wanted her invisible. For them, she didn't exist. She didn't count.

Lying back in the clean white tub, Ruthann finally let the tears seep out from behind her lids. It was okay now. She could let go—for a little while. Her mind was filled with images, scenarios that would probably haunt her for the rest of her life. The loss of self-esteem seemed monumental, and she wasn't sure how to get it back, or if it was even possible. Too many nights she had gone to sleep hungry and frightened, terrified not knowing how she would survive the week. It had seemed like a nightmare.

She had trusted people who had used her. Helped others, only to wake up and find they had stolen from her. Slept in shelters and was molested . . . The ugly scenes played on and on as the tears slid down her cheeks and fell into the steaming water.

Bringing up a hand, she covered her eyes and sighed. Still, even with all the horrors, she never completely lost her belief in the basic goodness of people. She simply couldn't. She knew it was her last thread of hope, for once it was gone there would have been no point in surviving.

And now . . . She had been right to never give up. There were still good people in this world. Eve was one. Ruthann almost smiled as she thought about both of them. They were like two wounded birds, helping each other patch up broken lives, broken dreams. And she knew she would do whatever it took to repay Eve for the kindness and trust she had shown. Ruthann considered her meeting with Eve to be almost a miracle, for she had prayed and prayed for a sign that would show her the direction she should take. It wasn't as if she expected someone to hand her a job and a place to live, and yet that's what had happened. All of it was too much of a coincidence to brush aside. Even Eve thought so.

Then and there, in the quiet of the bathroom, Ruthann pledged her friendship to a woman she hardly knew. As soon as she did it, it felt right and the heaviness around her heart seemed to lighten.

Allowing a smile to cross her lips, she picked up a bar of scented soap and began scrubbing away the first layer of her past. She began to scrub harder and harder, needing to clean away the ugliness of the world. She knew that one day she would have to reenter it. But for now it was blessing she would appreciate. Maybe it could even be a new beginning.

Eve sat in her bedroom across the hall and stared at the rug, wondering if she had finally and completely lost her mind. Surely, Paul was going to question her sanity when he heard that she had taken in a homeless person. What did she really know about Ruthann Bucknum? The woman was divorced. Living in a car. And nearly penniless. How could she explain to anyone that this woman seemed like her lifeline? That meeting Ruthann had pulled her out of her depression and forced her back into life? Hearing about the orphanage scandal had forced her out of the house, but that was only to confront her husband. Seeing Ruthann had made her angry, at society, at the damn injustice of it all, and it was the adrenaline pumping once more through her veins that had made her feel alive again.

Sighing as she heard the water being released from the tub, Eve figured it was too late now for regrets. She had offered the woman a job and a place to live for a week. There was no going back at this point. And why should she even care what anyone thought? All of her life she had played by the rules of society, and where had it gotten her? The only important things in her life were gone. Her child. Her husband. Her faith . . . in anything.

Suddenly a weird tingling sensation started in her feet and raced through her body. It wasn't scary or threatening. It was almost pleasurable, like when she first saw her husband or stared into her infant son's eyes. Or like when she had met Ruthann . . .

The sensation increased, and it felt as though her per-

ception of reality was altering. She was either losing her
damn mind or waking up from a long numbing sleep. Instantly, it all made sense to her. Those long-held, almost
treasured, rules no longer worked. And not just for her.
Scenes suddenly rushed through her mind, making her
dizzy with the kaleidoscope of images. It seemed like a
war against humanity played out against the darkness behind her lids. Flashes of senseless wars, hungry children,
homeless strangers, street violence, families torn apart by
divorce, babies born addicted to drugs—it all slammed
into her consciousness.

She wanted to scream out that *it wasn't working anymore!* Only an idiot would continue playing by those
same rules.

The silence became stronger, wrapping her in a powerful warmth that felt like the comforting arms of a
parent. . . . No, the energy was too intense, too instinctive . . .

It felt like love.

But her belief system had shut down. She desperately
tried to place the love, yet it eluded her. She didn't know
if she could ever love another human being, just as she
didn't know whether she really believed in God. Then
where was the source of this energy that filled her with a
loving calmness? The old rules told her it had to be from
someone outside herself. It must come from a parent, a
man, a child, or even a pet.

All her sources were gone. She was alone.

Eve Cameron then knew, with a truth so strong it
couldn't be denied, that in that moment her life had irrev-
ocably altered.

If she was alone, she would trust herself, her own instincts. She knew right from wrong. She knew what *felt* right or wrong. She knew about decency and compassion. She didn't need an institution—a church or a government, or even a marriage—to guide her.

For the first time in her life, she was on her own.

After a few moments, she calmly stood up and took a deep breath. As crazy as it seemed, she felt it was going to be all right. Smiling at the comforting neatness of her room, Eve figured it was a good sign that she was headed in the right direction. Her navigational equipment might be brand new, but what the hell? What more did she have to lose?

Besides, from now on she was playing by her own rules.

They met twenty minutes later in the kitchen. Eve was preparing tea when Ruthann walked in, wearing jeans, a cotton sweater, and a towel around her wet hair.

"How was the bath?" Eve asked, and saw how naturally beautiful Ruthann was. Tall, thin, striking red hair peeking out from the white towel, big blue eyes, and those freckles—she looked like a Celtic princess.

"Heavenly. Thanks. And the room . . . it's so pretty."

"Good. I'm glad you like it. It's been a long time since anyone's used that guest room." Eve smiled as she brought a basket filled with herbal tea to the table. She remembered doing it many times when her friends came for a visit. Life seemed so normal then. What did they ever really talk about? Husbands? Children? Jobs? Fund-raising? All of their lives were so conventional. No one ever wanted to rock the boat for fear of . . . what? The truth?

She knew instinctively that somehow she had separated from them. She could never look at the world through the same eyes again after what had happened in her bedroom. She was different. Not physically. A basic change had taken place somewhere inside herself.

It was as if the old Eve Cameron, the one who had been asleep, had died. She had served her purpose and was no longer needed. A new being had taken her place, someone stronger, smarter, maybe even more human.

She was tired of being afraid, of living with fear.

It was time to start living.

"I think we need to set some house rules, rules we both are comfortable with." The words popped out of her mouth without her even thinking them.

"Of course." Ruthann immediately sat down at the table and placed her hands in her lap.

Eve smiled. "Ruthann, you don't have to feel like you're in school, or at a job. Just relax. This is new for both of us. I thought we should talk about what we each expect. It's sort of like putting our cards on the table before we begin. No surprises."

Ruthann looked up as Eve spoke. She nodded. "I agree."

"Good." Eve sat in her normal chair by the window and picked out a tea bag before passing the basket to Ruthann. "I'll go first," she said, pouring hot water into her mug. The aroma of fruit and almond entered her nostrils, and she deeply inhaled before continuing.

"These will be new rules," Eve stated in a strong voice. "Our rules, not society's—it's obvious those don't work for us anymore. We'll make them up as we go along.

What feels right to us. Like, I'm not used to sharing a home with a woman. We'll both need privacy."

Ruthann put a spoonful of sugar into her tea and stirred it. "This is your house, Eve. I'm just a . . . a boarder. I'll abide by whatever rules you have."

"Don't you see?" Eve asked, shaking her head to make her point. "I don't have any rules. I guess I just want to make sure we both feel comfortable and have the respect that we each need."

"Maybe we could start by defining what you expect," Ruthann said in a low voice. "I mean, I will clean the house and cook meals and do the laundry. Is there anything else?"

Eve sat back in her chair and grinned. "I think that's more than enough. I'm not going to have the time." Again, she had no idea why she'd made that statement. It just felt like the right thing to say. She had no concept of what she was going to be doing, but she knew it wasn't caring for a home. Maybe she'd go into business again. She was intelligent, resourceful. She had years of experience. But, what . . . ? This time around it had to be fun, something that she could throw herself into and build a future.

"Once this house meant so much to me. Then it was filled with a family. Now . . ." She shrugged her shoulders. "It's far too big." Looking around her, Eve added, "And it's not me anymore. Does that make any sense?"

Ruthann lifted her mug, blew on the steaming tea, and then smiled. "Absolutely. The truth is we don't really know all that much about each other, but maybe that's a good thing, because I don't believe either one of us is the same person we were before. I think we're both going through a major transition in our lives, so it's like starting fresh. This house belongs to the old you. It doesn't . . . fit anymore."

"Exactly!" Again, she had that weird sensation of Ruthann reading her thoughts. Strange. She would put it aside and think about it later. "The old Eve," she murmured, "the wife and mother is gone, whether I like it or not. Why is change always so hard?"

Ruthann sighed as she adjusted the towel around her damp hair. "I wish I had an answer. I only knew I was on the wrong path, that I wasn't happy or with the person I should be, yet I was afraid to stay and afraid to leave at the same time. It was only when it became unbearable to get up in the morning that I knew I had to save myself and get away. I just knew something better was out there. That I deserved something better."

Eve knew she was getting real personal, yet she couldn't stop the words from pouring from her mouth. "But you slept in your car. Surely you deserved better than that."

"I didn't start out that way. I had some money when I left. Not much, but I thought it would last until I got a job back east."

"What happened?" It wasn't just curiosity. Eve really wanted to know how a person like Ruthann—intelligent, compassionate, with a good work ethic—could wind up homeless.

"Four years ago, back in California, I was secretary to a man that opened his own insurance underwriting firm. It was a little office and there was just the two of us. Mike was in his early fifties when I started and he didn't believe in computers. Thought they were the first sign that civilization was progressing in the wrong direction. Man against machine, I guess you could say. Anyway, I didn't have computer experience, only a four-year gap in my résumé. The only job I could get back here was as a clerk in a video-rental store. It barely paid enough to get by in a cheap motel room, but I was surviving. Then the family who owned the store decided to close it because they couldn't compete with the national chains, and I got laid off."

"Couldn't you get unemployment?"

"I didn't work there long enough to qualify. I went to several social agencies, but I didn't have the residency requirements and I guess you could say I sort of fell through the cracks of bureaucracy. I didn't fit in anywhere. There really was nowhere to get help."

Eve couldn't imagine the kind of life Ruthann had been living. Even though she and Paul had struggled in the beginning, at least they had food and shelter. What must it be like not to know where your next meal was coming from? Or how you would spend the night? The thought was chilling, and she was more than determined to protect her future. Tomorrow she was meeting with her lawyer for the first time. She must be strong. She had started the business with Paul, and knew its worth. She would be fair, but she would also be strong. She would not walk away empty-handed, not like Ruthann. She would protect herself, and her future—whatever that was.

Knowing she had to say something, Eve pushed the hair back off her forehead and forced a smile. "Well, that's in the past. You can spend some time here and maybe . . . I don't know, maybe you could take some computer courses at night. I could even teach you."

"You?" Ruthann stared at her.

Eve grinned back at the woman's surprised expression. "We own a computer distribution company. Before Jamie, my son, was born, I lived and breathed computers. Granted, the software changes practically every month, but I can get you started."

Ruthann appeared embarrassed. "Please. You've already done so much. I couldn't ask—"

"You didn't," Eve interrupted, wanting to make Ruthann comfortable again. "I volunteered. But that's down the road. First, let's see how this living arrangement works out."

Nodding vigorously in agreement, Ruthann sat up straighter and the towel finally parted to drop onto her shoulders.

"Oh, just leave it, Ruthann," Eve said with a chuckle. "Really, try to relax. For the next week this is your home. I don't expect you to steal the silver or attack my purse or murder me in my sleep. I do expect you to run this house as best you can and try to become comfortable with living here. After a week, we'll both decide if we want it to continue."

Eve watched as Ruthann digested her words.

"Okay," Ruthann finally said. "When do you wake up, and what do you like for breakfast?"

Eve thought about it for a few moments. "I'm not sure. I used to wake up early for Jamie and Paul, but now . . . ? I don't know. Tomorrow I have an eleven-thirty meeting, so I should get up around eight-thirty or nine."

"What would you like for breakfast?"

"I usually don't eat breakfast. Just coffee and a roll. We have Danish left over from this morning."

Ruthann took a deep breath and said in a cautious voice, "I have a suggestion. If we're starting over, new lives and everything, then shouldn't we do it right this time?"

"I suppose." How odd it was that they had come to some unspoken agreement about their lives. How odd and how simple. It was as if the two of them knew they would now be connected to each other in some way. Eve's mind was already on overload, and she filed the thought in the recesses of her brain. It was something else she would think about later.

Enthusiastic, Ruthann continued. "Okay, then we should eat a real breakfast. If we skip lunch, so be it. But maybe we could agree on breakfast and dinner. Just tell me what you like. I'm really not a bad cook, and if you have favorite recipes, tell me. I love trying new things."

"Really? I've lost all desire to cook. It's merely a chore now."

"Not to me," Ruthann said with a hint of nostalgia as she glanced about the kitchen. "It's the one thing my husband couldn't find fault with, and it's something I enjoy."

"Then cook whatever you like. I'm not hard to please."

Both of their cups were empty, and Eve considered asking Ruthann if she wanted more tea. A thought entered her mind. She needed to move their relationship to a different level, one beyond employer/employee. If they were going to live together, they needed trust. When one has little to lose, trust seems easier.

Pushing her chair back, Eve rose while saying, "This has been a long day. I didn't realize how exhausted I am. I'll lock up before I go upstairs. If you want more tea, or anything to eat, you know where it is." She took her own cup and spoon to the sink and rinsed them out. When she turned to Ruthann, she found herself smiling.

"I'm glad you're here," she said simply. "Good night."

She held her shoulders back and her head high as she walked out of the kitchen and left a stranger behind. It would be an experiment, to see if she could really trust anyone beyond herself, and yet her instincts were telling her to go to sleep. It would be all right.

And, in the words of one independent and free-thinking lady . . .

Tomorrow was another day.

"I heard from his lawyer this morning. Your husband says he doesn't want to give up the family home. He says that if you don't want the house, then he'll take it."

Holding the phone to her ear, Eve listened to her lawyer and shut her eyes briefly. The finality of it seemed to close in on her. As painful as this was, she knew she had to go through with it. Her fingers clasped even tighter around the telephone receiver as she asked, "He's agreed to the rest of the property settlement?"

Margo Sevanchik's voice was steady. "Everything else. Very soon you'll be independently wealthy. Congratulations."

Eve looked about her bedroom as once more that feeling of not belonging came over her, and her lawyer's congratulations rang hollow. "Then give him the house. It means more to him." That decision made, she quickly added, "You said very soon. How long will it take?"

"After I file the property settlement we'll be put on the docket. It could take a couple of months or be as quick as six weeks. Everything depends on the judge's calendar. Look how much we've accomplished in only a week. He's certainly not fighting you on anything."

"It's a guilty conscience," Eve answered. "But he's being fair. He can have the house. There isn't much that I want from it anyway."

"You're sure? We're sitting in the driver's seat on this one."

"I'm sure," Eve answered. "I just want to be done with all this as soon as possible."

"I know. Try and be patient," Margo said. "As far as divorce goes, this one's a dream. How's Molly doing? Have you talked to her? She came in yesterday and nearly fell apart on me."

Eve ran her hand over her eyes and sighed. "I've been so busy and I keep meaning to call. . . ." Guilt immediately settled in on her. "It must be so hard for Molly. Her children are still young."

"Yeah. And the two of you aren't alone. The town's splitting apart over this thing. Listen, Eve. . . . As your lawyer I have to inform you that *Bold Copy* contacted me to see if I would set up an interview with them."

"What! How the hell did they find out about this?"

"Calm down. It went out over the wire about Susan Vansciver, and they picked it up. She's already agreed to the interview."

"I can't believe it," Eve whispered, truly shocked. "Why would she do that?"

"Unlike the rest of the wives involved, Susan has a criminal case pending against her. I supposed she wants to garner as much public sympathy as possible before it starts. Can't say as I blame her. Anyway, I refused to talk to them—"

"Wait a minute. How did they find out about you?" Eve interrupted, horrified that a tabloid show knew about her personal life. It was surreal.

"I don't know," Margo said. "Somebody informed them that I was representing both you and Molly in your divorces. Don't worry about anyone here at the office talking to them, but you should be aware that once the divorce is final, all paperwork becomes public record."

"Oh my God, it isn't bad enough that everyone's in pain, now we have to be humiliated."

"At least you only cited irreconcilable differences. There are no direct accusations. I imagine that's why Paul isn't fighting you on anything. He's not stupid, and his lawyer has probably pointed out that this way there will be no public record of his misconduct."

"It's all so ugly," Eve murmured. "So many lives are shattered."

"I know," Margo said in a sympathetic voice. "Stay strong. The hard work is done as soon as Paul signs the property settlement. Just be patient."

Eve hung up and then called Molly. She tried to reassure her that everything would work out, but since Molly had decided to go for adultery, her divorce was even more ugly. After fifteen minutes, Eve made plans to meet for lunch and got off the phone.

Walking downstairs, she heard Ruthann singing along with the radio, and in spite of everything, Eve smiled. It was working out well for both of them. The house was spotless. Closets and cupboards were even organized. And meals . . . Eve had never eaten so well or so healthfully. Ruthann was a genius with food.

"Hey," Eve called out over the throbbing beat of Pearl Jam. Ruthann listened to the same kind of music that Jamie had, and Eve recognized the song. It was nice to hear music and have someone around who wasn't depressed.

Ruthann adjusted one of the new plants they had bought and looked up. "What do you think? Here, or next to the sofa?"

"Looks great where it is," Eve answered, and saw that Ruthann also had a flair for decorating. Gradually over the last week, Ruthann had rearranged furniture and added little touches that made the place more balanced. "Listen, don't get too attached to anything. I just spoke with my lawyer and Paul wants the house. So I gave it to him."

Ruthann straightened and pushed a stray lock of red hair off her face. "You're kidding. What will you do?"

"I'll move. I told you I was thinking about putting the house on the market, and now I won't have that headache."

"You could just walk away from it like that?"

Eve glanced around the living room and flashes of her old life passed through her memory. Jamie took his first steps in this room, she thought. The first night they spent in the house, Paul made love to her on the rug. It wouldn't be easy to turn her back and walk away, but she knew it would be harder to stay and fight the memories. "I have to, Ruthann," she said in a low voice. "I can't keep living like this."

Nodding with understanding, Ruthann walked over to her and said, "Hey . . . let's get out of here for a little while."

Eve stared at her. "What do you mean? Shopping again? We've replaced all the plants I killed. What else do we—"

"No," Ruthann interrupted. "Not shopping. Look, the sun is shining and you haven't been out of this house except to take me to the nursery for the plants. Let's go for a drive. No destination. Just get *out.*"

Eve immediately consented. She had forgotten that Ruthann wasn't in mourning, or hiding out from the world. It had been selfish and idiotic to think that anyone else would be content to live like a troll. Sunshine would be nice.

They got into the car, turned the music up and the windows down, and just drove. Eve inhaled the scents of early spring and found herself smiling as they meandered through the country roads.

"This was a great idea. I can't remember the last time I did something like this."

"Good." Ruthann was tapping her fingers on her knee as she hummed along with the music. "I used to drive for hours when I lived in California. It was my treat to myself when I finished the housework and before I had to make dinner. Even though I was alone in the house, driving seemed to connect me to the world somehow. Not to the people, but to the environment. It was also when I got my best ideas."

"Really, like what?"

"Like to leave and strike out on my own. I didn't do it standing in my kitchen and crying. I was on a back road in the wine country when I knew that if I didn't leave I would die soon."

Stopped at a red light, Eve glanced at her companion. "You would die?"

"Yeah. . . . I don't know how to explain it, but it was a feeling so strong that I just knew I had to make a change."

Continuing through the intersection, Eve nodded. "No need to explain further. I guess that's what I've been going through and why I gave up the house so easily. Even my lawyer was surprised."

"Lawyers," Ruthann muttered as they turned off the busy street onto another back road. "Don't get me started."

Eve nodded. "I know what you mean, but Margo's a good person. I've known her for years. Well, not personally, but she attended some dinner parties—"

"Not for that orphanage?" Ruthann immediately demanded.

Eve almost laughed at Ruthann's indignation. Ever since she had told her the sordid story, Ruthann's anger had been easily raised by the subject. "Yes, for the orphanage. The people who feel used and betrayed go far beyond the families involved. Oh, and guess what?"

Eve didn't wait for Ruthann to answer. "Margo said

Bold Copy has gotten hold of it and is planning to invade Chelsea. Can you believe it?"

"Oh, Eve," Ruthann whispered. "What are you going to do?"

"I'm not going to do anything. I don't have to, remember? When these vultures come, they can't prey on someone who refuses to participate. They can pick at me, but they can't devour me unless I allow it."

"You know, I've had some pretty ugly things happen to me, yet I can't imagine going on national television to . . . what? Expose my pain, or seek revenge on my husband? It's a phenomenon I can't quite understand. We're becoming a society of angry victims."

"I hate that victim mentality," Eve said forcefully as she turned onto a road that lined the shore of the Delaware River. "And that's probably why I felt so depressed. I felt like a victim, like I didn't have any say in the matter."

"It's sort of a double-edged sword," Ruthann answered. "On the one hand, some of these shows expose things we need to know. Interspersed with the dirt might be an exposé on toxic dumping. But, seriously, do we really need to know who Brad Pitt is sleeping with this month? I mean, it'll never be us, so what's the point? Perverse curiosity?"

Eve laughed. "Probably. But can you imagine what it must be like to lose all sense of privacy? To have people practically spy on you to find out details of your life? Like what food you eat and where you eat it, clothes you wear and where you buy them, friends you keep and how you found them, the lovers you take to bed and why they don't last? It must be horrible. If that's the price of fame, I think it's too high."

"I agree." Ruthann sighed. "Me? I just want to live the quiet life. Find some happiness and try to maintain it."

"Sounds reasonable. That's why I have such a problem with—" Eve quickly applied the brakes. "Hey, will you look at that?"

Eve and Ruthann sat in the car and stared at the old Victorian house with a For Sale sign on the front lawn. It was three stories high and surrounded by a wide porch that wrapped around the front. The shrubbery was old and lush.

"Isn't it beautiful?" Eve murmured, her gaze riveted on the house.

"It could be," Ruthann answered. "It looks old and needs work."

"I know," Eve said, and realized her voice sounded impatient. "Sure it needs work, but . . . it's right across from the river. Now, that's a view."

Ruthann turned and looked first at the river and then at Eve. "You can't be considering this. You said your house was too big, and this one's bigger. You haven't even started looking at anything yet. Be realistic. The paint is peeling. That porch doesn't look too strong. You don't know the condition of the roof. And that's just the outside."

Eve pulled the car over to the side of the road and shut off the engine. "I know you're right," she admitted. "But I must have been down this road fifty times in all the years I've lived here, and I never really noticed how pretty and peaceful it is. I'm going to write down the realtor." She opened her purse and found paper and pen.

"You're serious about moving?"

"I have no choice, now that I've agreed to give Paul the house. I have to find a place for us to live."

"Us?" Ruthann's voice was hesitant.

Suddenly Eve stopped writing and stared at the woman next to her. "I'm sorry. I just took for granted that you would be coming with me. Of course, you have your own plans and—"

"No, you misunderstand me. Listen, Eve, this last week has been the happiest period that I've known in a long time. I don't want to leave, but we never discussed extending it."

"Okay, let's do that now. It's working out well living together. If you're happy and I'm happy, then why not extend the arrangement? Neither one of us wants to be alone right now and I think we're good for each . . ." Before she could finish the thought, Eve broke into laughter. "Damn, this is starting to sound weird. But you know what I'm trying to say, Ruthann. I think we're friends. Honestly. You like running a house and you're good at it. It's not me anymore, yet realistically, I'm going to need someone with your skills when I make this move. Without you, it would be overwhelming."

Ruthann was staring at the house, and Eve could see her eyes filling with tears.

"Are you okay? Did I say something to upset you?"

Shaking her head, Ruthann sniffled before smiling. "It was just nice to hear that I'm needed, I guess."

Eve reached out and patted Ruthann's knee. "Listen,

lady. I'm outside in the sunshine and planning my future. A week ago I was looking forward to dying. Believe me, you're needed."

"Then can I say something?" Ruthann's voice was low and unsure.

"Of course you can. You're my friend. Closer than that. We're sharing more than just living space."

"Okay, then you have to realize there's a lot of work to be done back at your house before you can move on."

Eve shrugged. "So we'll do it together. Most of it I'll leave."

"There's something that only you can do, Eve. I'll help if you want, but it's your job."

A tightness settled around Eve's chest and her fingers gripped the steering wheel. It was as if telepathy were taking place between them. "Jamie's room."

"Yes." Ruthann touched her shoulder with sympathy. "You know you can't go on until you take care of it. I've dusted the furniture and his trophies, and vacuumed the rug, but I can't keep his memory alive like that. And neither can you. You don't need a shrine to remember him. He's in your heart, and a part of him will always be with you."

Tears were rolling down her cheeks and dropping onto her T-shirt, yet Eve didn't bother wiping them away. "It's so hard, Ruthann," she mumbled. "He was the center of my life. . . ."

"I can't even imagine the kind of pain you're dealing with," Ruthann whispered. "I'll never know what it's like to be a mother. I can't have children."

A wave of understanding passed between them. It was a timeless, instinctive sorrow shared by women.

"I'm so sorry," Eve managed to say. "Do you know this for sure? Have you gone to doctors?"

Ruthann wiped at the dampness seeping out from behind her lids. "We spent almost fifteen thousand dollars on tests and drugs before my husband gave up. I don't think he ever forgave me for not being able to conceive."

"It's not your fault."

"I know that, but he wanted to make sure everyone knew it wasn't his fault, so he told them I was damaged as a child when I was raped. God, it was so humiliating."

Eve was shocked, and her own tears quickly stopped. "Is that true?"

Ruthann nodded. "I was raped when I was twelve, but the fertility doctor couldn't find any damage to prevent pregnancy. My problem was more technical, something about low egg mobility."

"Oh, Ruthann . . ." Eve placed her hand over her friend's and squeezed. "God, I'm sorry. What a hell of a life."

Ruthann sat up straighter and forced a smile. "Hey, we're not victims, remember? We're survivors."

Eve placed her hand back on the wheel and nodded. "Right. So, as a fellow survivor, do you want to hook up with me for a while while we see what's around the next corner?"

Ruthann turned to her and grinned. "Absolutely. Instead of dread or fear, let's start looking at it like an adventure that's just beginning. Think of it, Eve. It's like we both have a clean slate. There's nothing to hold us back. We can make it any way we choose."

"I wish I had your faith," Eve said, and heard the doubt in her own voice.

"You have faith. You just misplaced it, that's all." Ruthann opened the door, while adding, "C'mon. We're here. Let's get a closer look at this place."

Eve followed her out of the car and together they walked up to the house. "You're right," Eve said. "It needs work. Look at the sagging floor on the porch. It will have to be replaced."

Standing next to each other, they stared at the old boards.

Ruthann elbowed Eve on the arm and chuckled. "Kinda like us, huh? Getting rid of the old, worn-out beliefs and starting new. Sort of like a work in progress." She took a deep breath and gazed up to the long front windows. "Now that we're standing here, I have a good feeling about this house," she murmured. "Whatever decisions you make, Eve, I'm with you. You saved my life."

"Nonsense." Embarrassed, Eve started to walk back toward the car when Ruthann's voice stopped her.

"No, please. Listen. It wasn't merely offering me a job and a place to live. You've given me trust, respect, and, most importantly, friendship. When I was at the end of my rope and ready to give up, you came along and offered me hope. You can't put a price on that."

Eve walked back the few steps and hugged Ruthann. "Don't you realize," she whispered against thick red hair, "you've done the same for me? We're in this together."

Ruthann's arms came up and tightened around Eve. "Then whaddya say we walk up there and knock on the door?"

Eve pulled back. "We can't. What will they think? They're probably looking at us right now and think we've lost our minds on their front lawn. We have to go through the realtor."

Ruthann grinned widely. "Who says? Whose rules?"

It took only seconds for Eve to pick up the challenge. "You're right. Let's go before I chicken out."

Arm in arm the two made their way to the tall wooden doors, each knowing that their friendship was now sealed.

CHAPTER 5

She figured it was only polite to wait outside while Eve, the realtor, and the owner had their third discussion. So much had happened in the last week, and Ruthann was still trying to find her proper place in all of it. On most levels she felt close to Eve, yet on something like this she was searching to find a comfort zone. That's why it had been easy to volunteer to wait outside for the contractor. A part of her was afraid to trust the new, bright circumstances in her life and the overwhelming amount of trust a virtual stranger was showing toward her. It didn't make sense. People just didn't operate like this. If the situations were reversed, she couldn't honestly say she would be as completely open as Eve. Living on the streets had altered her level of trust in her fellow man. Yet a stronger, more instinctive place was calmly saying it was all right this time. It felt safe. Incredible, but safe.

Looking out across the front lawn, Ruthann sighed and shook her head with amazement. They were going to do it. Eve was going to do it, she mentally corrected. Ruthann realized she had never in her life met anyone quite like Eve. The woman was a powerhouse of energy when she was motivated to use it. In less than two weeks Eve Cameron had decided and accomplished what might have taken other people months: She had resolved to divorce, bargained for a fair settlement and was just waiting for her court date, decided to move, gave up her house, found another, was in her third negotiation on that house, and had arranged for a building contractor to give an estimate on renovations.

Ruthann suddenly realized it took her two years just to decide to leave California and her marriage. She felt like an emotional slug compared to Eve.

It must have been all those years of being in business with her husband, because Eve sure knew what she was doing—or at least looked as if she knew. Ruthann had been so used to getting her husband's approval before making even minor household or life decisions that watching Eve was exciting and maybe a little scary.

Her gaze expanded and she smiled. This house had to be the right thing for Eve. It was so pretty and so peaceful here with the tall shade trees. Beyond the road was another small lawn that ran right to the shore of the river. Eve said she wanted to put a gazebo there. Her fingers ran over the old wooden boards beneath her touch. Together, they had fantasized about sitting on the porch in wide wicker rocking chairs surrounded by lots of plants and flowers.

Nice fantasy, Ruthann thought. You know this woman a couple of weeks and now you're lifelong rocking-chair friends? Get real. Yet hearing Eve talk about it made it seem almost real, or at least possible. And if anyone could make it happen, Eve could. She had included Ruthann in most of her discussions with the realtor and the owner, Mrs. Benning. Eve later said that offering to pay cash may have prompted Mrs. Benning's eager responses. Eve figured that in two months at the latest, probably sooner, she would receive her divorce settlement and be able to hand the woman a cashier's check. Meanwhile, she was ready to place down a deposit, get the process moving, and have the contractor begin renovations. That way, Eve explained, most of the repairs would be completed before they moved in. But Eve needed the estimate before submitting her final offer.

Could it actually be possible? Could Eve really make all this happen? And what would she, herself, ever contribute, other than being a housekeeper? So many emotions and feelings swirled around inside her, and she deeply inhaled the air coming in off the water.

Once more Ruthann gazed out to the river and the sailboats of all sizes that seemed to glide effortlessly over it. She could even see the skyline of Philadelphia downriver. A feeling of peace finally came over her, but was short-lived as a black Jeep pulled into the driveway.

The contractor.

Ruthann stood up and waited as a tall man got out and walked up to the porch. He was carrying a worn leather briefcase that reminded her of an old-fashioned schoolbag.

"Hi. Eve Cameron?"

Ruthann hesitated for a moment as she stared at the

man while mentally sizing him up, then smiled. "No, she's inside."

The man returned her smile and offered his hand. "My name's Mick Larkin. Ms. Cameron asked me to meet her at this address for an estimate on repairs."

"Yes, I know," Ruthann answered while shaking his hand. "I'll show you the way."

She led him through the front doors, past the large foyer with huge rooms on either side, beyond the center staircase into a dining room twice the size of her old one, and then into the kitchen. It was the best room in the house as far as Ruthann was concerned, and it had great possibilities.

"Eve, excuse me. The contractor has arrived," Ruthann interrupted the lively conversation taking place in the room.

It appeared that Mrs. Benning and the realtor were discussing the commission on a cash deal. Both had turned along with Eve as Ruthann and Mick Larkin entered the room.

"Hi," Eve said while standing up and shaking the man's hand. "Thanks for coming so quickly." She looked around the room to the others and, after introducing them, again addressed the contractor. "I'm negotiating to buy this home, yet we all admit it's in need of repair. What I'd like is for you to go through it and make a work list and the estimated cost. From structure, plumbing, electricity . . . whatever is needed to make this house sound for the next forty years."

Mrs. Benning coughed. "It's not exactly falling down, dear."

"No, of course not," Eve quickly answered with a smile. "But if I make this my home I intend to live here until I'm an old woman rocking on that front porch." She winked at Ruthann. "I just want to make sure it's still there."

Mick Larkin laid his briefcase on a counter and opened it. "Okay," he said, taking out a metal clipboard and pen. "Why don't I start in the basement?"

"Through that door," the realtor pointed out. "Should I go with you?"

Mrs. Benning sighed and closed her eyes briefly, as if straining for patience. "We *were* having an important discussion, John. I'm sure the man can find his way. I told my daughter I would have an answer for her by the end of the week. She needs to make her own arrangements if I'm to move out to Colorado."

Eve patted Mrs. Benning's arm in a show of sympathy, then looked up to Ruthann. "Would you mind showing Mr. Larkin the basement? You know most of the repairs we discussed, and I'll join you as soon as—"

"I have the list in my purse," Ruthann interrupted as she reached for the worn leather. "Here it is. Don't worry. I'll take care of it. You go on with your discussion." At last she felt useful.

She led the man out of the kitchen and down the old narrow steps into the basement. "Be careful," she called out. "The step next to the last is shaky."

She waited for the man to join her at the bottom and watched as he bent over to inspect the wooden step.

"It can be reinforced," he said, standing upright and

looking back up the stairs. "But I'd suggest the whole stairway be replaced."

Ruthann immediately thought of all of Eve's expenses and answered, "Mrs. Cameron only wants necessary repairs right now."

He looked at her then, really looked, and Ruthann found herself to be the recipient of a slow and damned near brilliant smile.

"We never really met," he stated. "You know my name . . ."

As his voice trailed off, she looked down to the cement floor for a few seconds before again meeting his gaze. "Ruthann Bucknum. I'm sorry. I should have introduced myself earlier."

"Well, Ruthann Bucknum, the first thing you should know about me is that I don't lie. I could say that you'll have to take my word for that, but I'd rather show you." He walked around the stairway and pointed to the top. "See this? It's got to be thirty or forty years old and the wood is rotting away. Most of the pressure on this staircase is absorbed at the bottom now, and that's what's making the step shake. It could be repaired, but it would eventually have to be replaced in a few years. I haven't been hired for that. Right now, today, my only job is to point out areas where problems exist."

He looked at her and again smiled while bringing his pen up to the clipboard. "With your permission, I'll begin my list?"

She nodded. It was all she could do. Something about the man made her want to back off. In fact, she wanted to run upstairs into the kitchen, instead of following him around in this dark basement while he checked plumbing lines. Every once in a while he would make a comment about something and she would nod or answer with a word or two. He was friendly enough, nonthreatening, and he looked fairly successful. His faded dress jeans matched the crisply ironed collarless shirt. And he wore a stylish navy blue jacket over it. He had that look of casual grace that some men possess. She could see it in the way he moved. Maybe he was once an athlete, a runner or something. Tall. Dark. Very dark. And handsome. A deadly combination for some women. He didn't wear any jewelry, so there wasn't a ring. . . .

She shook her head, as if she could also dislodge such stupid thoughts. How long would she have to stay down here?

As though reading her mind, the man announced, "Okay, I think I've got everything. Shall we go up?"

Grateful to escape the closed quarters, Ruthann said, "Absolutely," and headed for the stairs.

"Watch that step at the bottom."

She stopped and looked at him. There was a teasing grin on his face and something else . . . as if he was waiting to see if she had a sense of humor.

"You forget, Mr. Larkin, that I pointed it out to you. I happen to have a very good memory."

Okay, so her sense of humor was lost somewhere. All she wanted was to get back into the daylight. Once in the kitchen, Ruthann saw that the discussion was still in progress, so she led the man upstairs. She took out her list and pointed out the many areas Eve expected to renovate. There were five bedrooms and Eve wanted to make two of them into a large sitting room, almost an apartment with a separate entrance—which meant breaking through the outside wall to install a staircase. Knowing how expensive that would be, she had told Eve not to do it, especially if Eve was doing it for her. Eve had insisted, saying the only way the two of them could live together was if they could have privacy when they wanted it.

"Let's start with these two bedrooms," Ruthann said as she led the contractor into the larger one. "Mrs. Cameron wants to break through this wall into the next room to make it into a big living area, sort of like an apartment."

"We'll need to get a building permit for that kind of work. Maybe even a variance from the township." The man ran his long hands over the wall and then knocked on it a few times. "Seems solid. I don't foresee a problem."

"Well, she also wants to have a door put in with a stairway for an outside entrance."

"Really?" Mick Larkin seemed more interested in that proposal. He walked over to a window and opened it to get a better look at the outside wall. "We might have a problem with the trees out here."

"I don't think she wants to cut down any trees," Ruthann quickly answered. "Can't you . . . I don't know . . . redirect the stairs around them?"

He turned from the window and looked at her. Again, Ruthann felt that weird sensation pass through her body. Interpreting it as fear, she drew her shoulders up as if to put a protective wall between them.

Strangely, he merely smiled. Again she was struck by the way his entire face seemed to light up by only the movement of his lips. Weird.

"Good instincts usually tell you what to do long before your head has to figure it out. Michael Burke."

"What is that supposed to mean?" Ruthann demanded. "And who is Michael Burke?"

The man chuckled as he seemed to caress the molding around the old window. "It means that you might have instinctively come up with a way to solve the tree problem. Unfortunately, it'll also be more expensive than a vertical staircase. Oh, and Michael Burke? I'd say he was just a man with a little bit of wisdom to share with the rest of us, those who are stumbling along."

Ruthann resisted rolling her gaze toward the ceiling with exasperation. Even though she hadn't yet figured out this guy, she didn't want to insult him. "Well, Mr. Larkin, isn't it *your* job to come up with a cost-effective solution? Not mine?"

He grinned at her, as though recognizing that she was trying to put him off. She hated the idea that this man might read her so easily. Women weren't a problem, but a male gaining that kind of power over her was frightening.

"You're right. It's my job, but I'm not above listening to advice. Actually, I believe it's all around you, if you take the time to look and listen."

"Are you a preacher or something?" She didn't mean for it to come out like that. She wanted to be polite, but there was something about this man . . .

He actually laughed at her. Shaking his head, he tucked the clipboard under his arm and opened a closet. "I'm not a preacher. Sorry if I came off like that. I'm more . . . how did you put it? Or something. I'm more something." He peered into the small space before shutting the door. Turning to her, he said, "Is there an attic entrance, or pull-down steps?"

Still trying to figure out his cryptic remark, Ruthann turned toward the hallway. "It's back here," she said over her shoulder as she left the room and led him to the door at the end of the hall. "We haven't been up there yet, so I don't know what you'll find."

"Ahh, an adventure," Mick whispered as he opened the door and looked up the stairway. He turned his head and stared back over his shoulder to her. "Care to join me?"

It was the way he said it that made her stomach muscles tighten in defense. It wasn't quite businesslike, and yet it wasn't as if he were asking for a date or anything. It was friendly, almost as though they were friends already. It was also unnerving.

Who *was* this guy?

The steps creaked with age, and Ruthann wondered how many people had used them over the years. Had children run up here to hide and play? Had Mrs. Benning's weary steps brought her to this place to store boxes of old clothes and Christmas decorations? Several possible scenes played out in her mind as she ascended. When they reached the top, Ruthann felt the heat in the air that she breathed. She smelled the mustiness of a place not frequently used.

"Wow." The word slipped from her lips as she looked around at the clutter. The quaintness of the attic reminded her of a Norman Rockwell painting.

Boxes were stacked in a disorderly fashion amid an old dollhouse, weathered trunks, a dress dummy for sewing, a platform with train tracks . . . In the flash of seconds,

Ruthann's mind saw the Bennings' time in this house as a family moving through life. It seemed so normal, so unlike the last fifteen years of her own.

"Look at this," Mick said in an almost reverent voice.

Ruthann turned her head and saw him hunched down beside an old bicycle. Its wide tires looked flat and the handlebars were crooked. "It's a bike."

"Not just a bike. A 1959 Schwinn."

"So?" She couldn't see the fascination with a beat-up old bicycle.

He looked up at her and grinned. Again his face was transformed by the action. His dark eyes seemed to almost sparkle with pleasure. "This is a treasure, Ruthann. They're very hard to find."

She shrugged, not really interested. "Maybe you should ask Mrs. Benning if you can buy it. It doesn't look like she's exactly a collector of bikes." She watched the way he gently ran his long fingers over the chrome frame. "Are you?"

"A collector?" He shook his head. "Not really. I have three bikes of my own. All of them fairly new."

"You ride?" It sounded silly, as if she was asking him if he owned three bikes for the fun of it. "I mean . . . are you a . . . what do they call it? A cyclist?"

He stood up and nodded. "When I get the time. Now that spring's here, I should get more riding time in."

She'd figured he was some sort of athlete. Not a runner. A cyclist. Interesting. She watched him walk around the dimly lit attic and realized that was why he seemed so graceful. Next to him, Ruthann felt like one of the ballerina hippos in *Fantasia*. She almost cursed out loud when she realized she was comparing herself to a stranger. What the hell was wrong with her?

"Ruthann? Mr. Larkin?"

She breathed a loud sigh of relief at the sound of Eve's voice calling out to them. "We're up here in the attic," Ruthann yelled back as she walked toward the stairs. Let Eve handle this now. She'd done as she had been asked. Now she only wanted to get away, to go outside and put her feet firmly back on the ground. Whoever Mr. Mick Larkin was, it was none of her business.

Forty-five minutes later, Ruthann watched from the shore of the river as Eve walked the contractor to his Jeep. They shook hands and Larkin opened the door to his vehicle. He paused for a moment and then looked down the driveway, across the road, directly at her. She could see him smile as he raised his hand and waved.

Not wanting to appear rude in front of Eve, Ruthann waved back and then looked across the Delaware to Pennsylvania. He was just being nice, she thought. He wants the job, and maybe he thinks she might have some influence on Eve. The crazy thing was that part of her never wanted to see Mick Larkin again, never wanted to feel that insecurity, that indefinable pull. Yet, down deep, she admitted a small amount of pleasure that he had looked for her to wave goodbye. Maybe he was just a nice man.

She almost laughed. A nice man. In her experience, that was a contradiction in terms. No wonder he seemed like an alien to her; no wonder she felt uncomfortable in his presence. She shook her head as she reached down and picked a buttercup from the weeds. She'd been on the street too long. She didn't even know how to relate to nice people.

"Well, what do you think?"

Ruthann turned at the sound of Eve's voice. "About what? The house?"

Eve shrugged. "The house. The negotiations. The contractor."

Twirling the tiny blossoms between her fingers, Ruthann answered cautiously. "You know what I think of the house. It's perfect for you. Mrs. Benning seems very interested in closing the deal, and as for the contractor . . . well, that's your decision."

Eve stood next to her and watched a sailboat tack its way toward Riverton. "I just asked because you spent some time with him. I like him. He's direct. His prices seem fair, although he's getting back to me with a complete estimate. What do you think, Ruthann? I value your opinion of people."

She mentally sighed. What right did she have to discredit someone she had just met? And for what reason? Because he scared her on a level that was too deep for anyone else to understand? "He seems nice."

"What's wrong?"

Ruthann pulled herself together and smiled. "Nothing. Really. If you like him, then hire him."

"Is it because—"

"No, really," she quickly interrupted. "It's silly. He seems . . . I don't know . . ."

Eve nudged her with an elbow. "He's cute."

"Oh, please." Completely embarrassed, Ruthann threw the buttercup into the water. "Like I even noticed."

"Well, I think he noticed. He made a point of waving goodbye to you."

"He was being polite. Now, stop it. The very last thing I need in my life right now is a man, or even thoughts of a man. I don't even know where I'll be, let alone anyone else."

"I hope you'll be with me," Eve said, crossing her arms at her waist. "Are you thinking of moving on?"

Ruthann turned to her friend and smiled. "No, Eve. I won't leave you now. But who knows what the future will bring? Why, you might even meet someone and get married."

Eve's mouth opened, yet no sound immediately emerged. When it did, it sounded strangled. "Get married again? Never! I don't think I'll ever trust a man again. They operate differently than we do, I think."

Ruthann nodded. It was sad how many women were seriously damaged by betrayal. What was even more sad was that Eve had so much love to give, and nowhere to give it. Perhaps that's why she channeled so much energy into her plans for the house. The house wouldn't hurt her. "Okay, let's drop the man talk and concentrate on more important issues. Like, how does salmon sound for dinner? Mrs. Benning has fresh dill growing in the greenhouse and she said to help myself to any of the herbs."

"Salmon sounds fine," Eve said as they walked back toward the house. Before they crossed the road she reached out and stopped Ruthann. Looking at the tall Victorian, she whispered, "We're going to be happy here, aren't we?"

Ruthann felt the hope transferring from Eve to herself.

It was so strong that it was almost tangible. Staring at the house, she whispered back what Eve wanted to hear. "Yes. We'll be happy."

Yet deep within her she knew everything had a price, and she prayed, for both their sakes, that it wouldn't be too dear.

CHAPTER 6

"Eve, Paul's here."

She looked up from the box at her feet and nodded to Ruthann. "Send him up."

"Are you okay?"

Again, she nodded. She was beyond weary, and words seemed hard to form as she picked up Jamie's soccer trophy and gently placed it in the box with the others. Looking around her son's room, her throat almost closed with fresh emotion. It still didn't seem real. She knew that no matter how much time went by, it never would. A part of her was cut off; she thought of stories she had heard of amputees who still had phantom sensations. She would always feel Jamie. He had been an extension of herself that time or absence would never alter. She wondered if fathers felt the same way. Paul had never said, and he appeared to go on, conducting life and even business with the same level of focus. Was it because she had carried and nurtured life within her that she simply couldn't let go? Just packing away his things felt sacrilegious, as if by doing so she was admitting that the bond had been severed. It was unnatural. She should have gone first. She should not be sitting on her dead child's bed, packing away a short lifetime of memories.

How could everything have changed so drastically? She felt as though she were leading some other woman's life. She was already divorced, had moved into a new home that was still being renovated, and now was cleaning out her son's bedroom.

There were moments when it all seemed surreal, as if it were a long tearjerker movie that never ended. She played the part as expected, yet no matter how long or how well she did it, nothing felt natural. Would comfort and peace never come? And where was the happy ending? She didn't think she would ever find it in her lifetime.

"Eve?"

She blinked a few times, trying to bring herself back into the present. Her husband, ex-husband, was standing in the doorway staring at her. For a split second, it felt so normal, so right, and then the heaviness reentered her heart and she tried to smile.

"Thanks for coming, Paul. I thought this was something we should do together."

He entered the room and picked up Jamie's old teddy bear from a shelf in the closet. He held the treasured childhood toy in his hands and gazed at it. "Remember when we lost it in the mall and Jamie went nuts?"

Eve smiled at the memory. "You bought another one and dragged it on the driveway to make it look old. I always wondered if Jamie really believed that one was Brown Teddy."

Paul clutched the stuffed, worn bear that had been their son's sleeping companion for the first eight years of his life. "I don't know if I can do this," he murmured while scanning the room.

Eve felt the old resentment resurface. Why was it that Paul thought she was strong enough to do it alone? Even in ancient times it was always the women who handled the aftermath of death. Did he think it was her duty? That this painful task was somehow structured into her DNA because she was a woman?

"Look," she said, trying to keep patience in her voice, "I've already moved into the new house. Everything I want from here is . . . is there. This is the last room, and I didn't think it was fair to leave this for you. But it's really difficult, Paul. It has to be done. *We* have to do this, and somehow go on."

He sat down on the edge of the mattress and continued to stare at the teddy bear. "I don't know how to go on without you, Eve," he muttered. "I feel like I've lost everything. My marriage. My son. Half my business . . ." He turned to her with a tortured look on his face. "Isn't that punishment enough?"

She didn't answer immediately. Part of her wanted to put an arm around his shoulders in compassion, and yet a stronger part wanted to shake him. He had a child, a poor innocent hidden away in an orphanage. Her son was gone. He still felt as if all of this was only about *him*, how it had affected *his* life. Why wasn't he taking responsibility?

"Listen to me," she said with as much strength as she

could muster at the moment. "Nothing I have done is punishment against you. Everything I have done, everything I am doing now, is because I'm trying to go on." She felt tears threatening, and took a deep breath to stop them. "We have to go on, or die. Sometimes, I swear I think dying is easier."

He shook his head. She wasn't sure if he was disagreeing with her statement or losing patience with her. She no longer had the ability to read him accurately.

"I can understand," he finally said, "why you felt a divorce was necessary. It's an ugly situation, and you had to divorce yourself from it. I didn't fight you on that. Some scavenger from *Bold Copy* contacted my office for an interview, so I don't blame you for wanting to separate yourself from this mess. But, Eve . . . this is going to blow over, and then—"

"Enough!" Eve grabbed the edge of the bedspread with her fist. "It's done. Finished. I can't go through this again. I'm fighting for my sanity here. I won't allow you to—"

"Eve?" Ruthann suddenly appeared at the doorway. "I'm sorry to interrupt, but we have that meeting with the contractor in twenty minutes. Can I help you finish this so we won't be late?"

Paul looked from Ruthann back to Eve. Ruthann's appearance had deflated the intense discussion before it could escalate. Eve didn't remember an appointment, but felt relief that she wouldn't have to argue a dead issue again.

"Paul . . . Ruthann Bucknum," Eve introduced them, and her voice sounded weary even to her own ears. "Ruthann's going to be living with me."

Ruthann moved farther into the room, and Paul merely nodded in acknowledgment.

"We're not accomplishing anything like this," Paul mumbled, and stood up. "You need time. Just promise me you won't talk to these tabloid shows. Enough damage has been done."

She couldn't believe it. He was leaving this to her again, just as he did when Jamie was sick. Now his only concern was that his reputation not be raked even more publicly through the mud. "That's right, Paul. Run away. I'll do this last act alone. Just tell me if there's anything of your son's that you want me to leave."

His face was flushed with emotion. She couldn't tell if it was anger, grief, or frustration as he quickly looked around the room.

Suddenly he reached down and grabbed the teddy bear again. "I'll take this," he muttered as he walked toward the door. "I'll call you when you calm down."

Ruthann followed him, like a watchdog on guard duty. "I'll see you out," she said in a controlled voice.

It took every ounce of willpower to watch Paul leave and not jump up from the bed to snatch back her son's childhood security blanket. Not the teddy bear, her mind screamed as tears threatened to choke her. Not that!

Feeling sucker-punched, Eve fell back onto the bed and clutched the pillow to her face to smother her sobs. When she inhaled the faint scent of her son that still lingered, she brought it even closer to her mouth. Dear God, when would the pain end?

She felt the touch of someone and jerked her head away

from the pillow. Ruthann stood in front of her with two tall glasses.

"Here," she offered. "I made a drink. All I could find was rum and Coke. We packed almost everything else."

Sniffling, Eve sat up and took the glass. "Paul likes rum, not me. Unless it's in daiquiris." Her lips trembled with emotion. "He took Jamie's teddy bear," she whispered, trying to stop the flow of tears while staring at the dark concoction in her hand.

"Yeah, well . . . you know what I say?"

"What?"

"Fuck it."

Shocked, Eve looked at her friend. "What?"

"You heard me. Fuck it, Eve. Enough is enough, and I think we've both been through enough, especially you. You know what this is turning into? A depressing soap opera."

"I've never heard you speak like this," Eve said, turning her mind away from Paul, and even her son. What in the world had gotten into Ruthann?

"Well, it's a part of me now," Ruthann answered matter-of-factly. "I picked it up on the streets, and it takes a whole lot to make it come out. But you know what? It's more real than this polite talk we've been taught. Like that movie said, 'Sometimes you've just gotta say fuck it, and go on.' I can't watch you do this anymore. You're going to have either a nervous breakdown or a stroke. You can't keep this up, Eve. You can't treat this room like a damned shrine that you have to dismantle because your ex-husband doesn't have the balls to help. I've stood back and bit my tongue because I didn't think I had the right to speak out."

Ruthann brought the rum and Coke to her lips and drank. Catching her breath, as if she wasn't used to the taste of alcohol, she then added, "Now I believe I have the right. We're friends. I don't think this conversation is going to change that. If we're going to live together, then I have to be able to speak my mind."

"I never said you couldn't," Eve answered in her own defense.

"I know. I thought I was showing respect for you, but I wasn't. If I respect you, then I should let you know when I think you're screwing up. And you're screwing up big time now, because you're letting the past control you. Jamie's gone. He's never coming back. And you don't want Paul back. You don't have your perfect family anymore, and I'm real sorry about that. But you live either in the past or the present. That's all there is."

"I can't let it go," Eve almost cried out. "Damn it, Ruthann. The bedspread still smells like Jamie!"

Ruthann shook her head sadly. "Then we wash the damn bedspread, because this isn't your son's room anymore. This isn't even your house anymore. Your house, your future, is down by the Delaware River. Not here. We're here on a mission, your final act in this house, and I've kept out of all this until now. But you hired me to help you, Eve, and that's what I'm going to do."

She pulled out a wire drawer from the closet and grabbed a handful of underwear. With both hands full, she kicked an empty, opened box toward her and dropped the underwear into it. "Let's get out of here and end this torture. We'll take the boxes to River Road and put them in the attic. Next time you want to take a trip down memory lane, you can do it there. There's no place for you here, Eve. The past is over. Let's get on to our future, whatever it is."

Eve knew she was right. The past was over. It really was finished. Her roles of wife and mother were over. Just memories. The only thing she could cling to was the uncertain future. Even though it scared the heck out of her, it was still better than this. Suddenly, her tears stopped. The heaviness around her heart lightened. "Fuck it," she muttered, and brought the glass to her mouth. Gulping the drink, she almost coughed from the strong taste as she listened to Ruthann's chuckle. She held the glass up and made a toast as she wiped at her eyes. "Here's to the future," she said, and then added, "May it be kind to us."

Ruthann smiled as she lifted her own glass in a salute. "To the future . . . whatever it may be."

Eve put the glass on a night table and stood up. She stripped the bedding from the mattress and rolled it into a ball. "I'm going to throw this in the washing machine and then we'll clean out the room. You're right."

Ruthann's grin was wide and warm with affection. "That's the spirit."

Eve paused at the doorway. "And speaking of spirits, let's not get drunk. Not yet. On the way home I want to stop at the liquor store. I make a mean strawberry and banana daiquiri."

Ruthann opened another drawer and filled her arms with clothes. Looking up, she laughed. "You're on. We can sit on the porch and watch the sunset."

"There isn't really an appointment, is there?"

"No. I just had to step in and get him out if he couldn't help."

"Thanks."

"Hey, we're a team. Right? Let's hurry up, before the sun sets."

Nodding, Eve left to go downstairs. That was her future? Sitting on a porch getting drunk with a friend? Because she fully intended to medicate herself tonight after leaving this house forever.

She reached the laundry room and flipped open the lid to the washer. "Fuck it," she whispered to herself, feeling stronger every time she said the word that she'd chastised her son for muttering in front of her. She almost giggled, thinking of the absurdity and misplaced importance that she had put on a four-letter word. It was only a word and held no real power, unless she or society chose to attach it.

Adding the soap and setting the dials on the washer, Eve realized this would be the last time she used these machines. How many hours over the years had she spent in this room washing and folding and ironing to keep her perfect little family perfectly dressed?

"Fuck it." Shaking her head, she figured maybe she really was fighting off a nervous breakdown if obscenity was the only thing capable of bringing her comfort now.

She definitely was no longer Eve Cameron—supportive, loving wife, good mother, community volunteer. Even the last traces of that person seemed to be disappearing.

She would get drunk tonight and watch the sun set over the Delaware River. It might not be much of a future, but it was better than wallowing in self-pity.

Maybe she would even discover who she was becoming.

It was simply beautiful and seemed to fill her with peace. The sun cast a soft orange-rose blush that colored the sky with its soothing pastel hues. The clouds even appeared to absorb the glow and radiate warmth. The water on the river sparkled and reflected the sun's last phase as it began its descent behind the horizon. Even a few gulls and water birds soared in the distance. It was as if Nature created this beautiful scene as a gift for just the two of them.

"You did it, Eve. We're here on the porch and everything is just like we imagined."

She leaned her head back against the cushion of the rocker and sighed with contentment as she watched her friend lazily run her fingers over the graceful leaves of a nearby Boston fern. "You know what, Ruthann? Everything, all the work and moving, seems worth it right now . . . just to feel like this."

Nodding, Ruthann whispered, "It is beautiful, and so relaxing. Of course, we're both working on our second daiquiri here, and that may have something to do with it. By the way, where did you ever learn to make these? They're delicious."

Eve closed her eyes for a moment and then smiled. "Cozumel, Mexico. Nineteen eighty-seven. Best vacation. Best family vacation." She opened her eyes and gazed out across the river. "We found this little restaurant and it had a hidden courtyard. It was lovely. Palm trees, exotic flowers, even parrots in the walnut trees. Anyway, that's when

I found out how to make the best daiquiris in the world, as far as I'm concerned."

"Well, I'm not an expert, but I'd have to agree. You took Jamie?"

Eve nodded as flashes of scenes raced across her mind. "I'll always remember him swimming with the island boys in the surf and riding the waves in. That blond head amid so many dark ones. I could actually feel his joy. Those beautiful children accepted him immediately. I remember being filled with a sense of peace, as though I was witnessing the way it should be: innocent children playing together and it didn't matter what color they were or even if they could speak the same language."

Ruthann sighed and absently pinched a dead blossom from the huge geranium plant between them. "Great memory."

Eve turned to her friend. "What about you? Best vacation?"

It was Ruthann's turn to go inward, and she too gazed out to the water. "Five years ago. Nineteen ninety-one. Paradise Island in the Bahamas. It was supposed to be a second honeymoon. Of course, it didn't turn out that way."

"Then why is it your best vacation?"

Ruthann looked at her. "Ed didn't believe in holidays. The only other time we actually went away together was our honeymoon in San Francisco." She shook her head slightly, trying to get back to the point. "I married a true anal-retentive type. Felix Unger, without the wit or parody. He actually went to Paradise Island and brought work with him. I, on the other hand, must have birthed the first twinges of my screw-'em attitude, because I did it all. Rented a scooter, went into Nassau and ate lunch with the ladies who made straw hats, parasailed over the most beautiful water I've ever seen . . . God, I felt so alive."

Eve smiled, picturing Ruthann telling her colorless husband to screw himself as she went out and experienced life. Just as she was about to ask another question, a long white limo pulled up to the lawn across the road.

"What's this?" Ruthann asked as both women sat up straighter to get a better look. A matching limo parked behind the first.

Leaving the first car was a man in a black tux. He held his hand out to someone inside and a young woman emerged dressed in white.

A bride.

Soon Eve's little expanse of lawn was nearly filled with a wedding party that obviously had chosen to use the gazebo as a backdrop for formal pictures.

"Maybe they don't know that it belongs to you," Ruthann suggested. "It *is* across the road from the house. Maybe they think the town owns it."

Eve sipped on her daiquiri and watched as the photographer tried to arrange the wedding party. "Let them use it," Eve whispered. Once she had loved weddings, the whole ritual of two people publicly taking an oath to love and honor each other.

Raising her glass, she said, "Let's toast them. God knows, they'll need it."

She and Ruthann held their daiquiris up and quietly wished them good luck.

"Think they'll make it?" Ruthann whispered.

"They've got a fifty-fifty chance. Not great odds when you're talking about your life and bringing children into the world." She thought about it for a moment and looked at Ruthann with horror. "Geez, do you think we jinxed them? Two divorced, slightly drunk women, talking about the poor odds in making a successful marriage? God, maybe some tipsy, disillusioned woman looked at me on my wedding day and thought the same thing—some miserable fairy-godmother-type person, like in 'Sleeping Beauty,' you know? One who didn't wish me well and maybe that's why I have this curse on me now and . . . What? What are you laughing at?"

Ruthann put her glass on the wicker table between them and covered her mouth as she continued to chuckle.

"What?" Eve again demanded.

"You're drunk, Eve."

"I am not." She straightened her shoulders and pushed her hair back off her face while assuming a sober expression. At least, as sober as she could manage.

"But do you think it's possible?" she asked. Somehow it seemed very important to know if thoughts had the power to affect the future, anyone's future. "I mean, here I am watching what should be a beautiful scene and I was suddenly depressed for them. Can I jinx them by that?" She shook her head, trying to get her thoughts out. It seemed important. "Look at them. They've just performed a very serious and joyful ritual. What if years from now they look at each other and they're strangers? Do we ever really know the person we pick for our life partner?"

"Then what should we do? Install emotional detectors at weddings? Eve, *everybody's* disillusioned. I don't think people have real commitment today. Not like they used to."

She disagreed with Ruthann. "I think since the beginning of the institution very few couples have had a real commitment to loving and honoring. When we're like those two across the street we believe it. God, we *believe*. We take it for granted that it'll always be there. But it takes work, and life's more complicated now. How many times did your husband make a point of taking time to honor you?"

Ruthann's eyes widened as she stared at her. "We're talking about Ed, right?"

Eve laughed. "Sorry." She let out a long and loud sigh. "Instead of toasting, maybe we should pray for them."

"I thought you didn't believe in God anymore."

"Okay, next question," Eve said, trying to change the subject. "Let me see . . ." She searched her brain for a good subject.

"I've got it! I've got it!" Ruthann interrupted in a high voice. It was obvious to Eve that she wasn't the only person on the porch slightly drunk.

"What?"

"Best lover."

"You're kidding, right?"

"No. Enough of the vacation travelogue. If we're tripping down memory lane, let's get to the good stuff. I'll tell you mine."

Eve sipped the now melting daiquiri and shrugged her shoulders. "If you feel you must."

Chuckling, Ruthann reached out and playfully slapped

Eve's shoulder. "Oh, c'mon. You know you're dying to hear, right?"

Trying to keep a straight face, Eve concentrated on the wedding party. "Not really. I mean, why would two women who haven't had sex in . . . It's almost a year for me. What about you?"

"I thought you didn't want to know."

"Oh, shut up. I'm trying to make a point here, okay? How long?"

"About the same time."

"Okay, so why would two women who haven't had sex in over a year *and* have no hope of having it anytime in the near future want to discuss the subject? It sounds like self-inflicted torture."

"Oh, stop it. The best sex I've ever had . . . wasn't really sex."

Eve almost spit out her drink and quickly brought up her hand to check her chin for strawberry-and-banana mixture. "What the hell are you talking about? This, I've got to hear."

"It wasn't full sex. Penetration . . . you know what I'm talking about. It was before I met Ed. Nineteen seventy-six. I was twenty-two. Joe Moran. His father was French. That must have been where he got it from. Lord, but that man could make love to a woman. When he kissed you, Eve, he held your face between his hands . . . you know what I mean? Like you were precious or something. Then his kiss deepened and he slid his fingers through your hair and then down your back and brought you closer and . . ."

Her words trailed off and neither woman spoke for a few silent moments.

"And?" Eve demanded, suddenly very interested in Ruthann's sexual experience. She must be drunk, because her friend's little tale was actually stirring memories of feelings she had thought were dead.

Ruthann closed her eyes. "And he adored me. That's the only way I can put it. That's the way I felt." Her lids slowly lifted and she stared straight ahead. "I've never felt like that again. Never. Kinda cruel to experience something extraordinary and then have it snatched away."

"What happened to him? Why didn't you stay with him?"

Her smile was slow and sad. "He died after Vietnam. I heard he came back pretty messed up."

"I'm sorry." Eve touched Ruthann's arm. "And then you married Ed?"

Ruthann nodded. "After Joe, I sort of gave up and married the first man who asked me. It wasn't fair to either of us."

Eve was thinking how Ruthann's life with anal-retentive Ed must have seemed after experiencing such passion and sensuality with her Frenchman.

Ruthann must have sensed Eve's thoughts, for she quickly changed the mood. "Okay, now your turn. Best sex?"

Eve groaned. "Let me get you another drink." She started to rise, but Ruthann reached out and stopped her.

"Later. Spill your guts, lady. Best sexual experience, and it doesn't have to mean the whole enchilada."

"Now I'm turned on, and hungry," Eve moaned.

"Stop trying to get out of it."

Eve sat back and watched as the wedding party made

their way to the limos. How had this conversation taken such a bizarre turn? Two middle-aged women sitting on a porch talking about sex? And she was the one that had started this trip down memory lane!

Little did she realize that for the next forty years she would be playing it.

CHAPTER 7

The town of Chelsea had never seen anything like it in its one-hundred-and-thirty-six-year history. Citizens had prided themselves in maintaining order and balance throughout the turmoil that, at different times in the past, had affected other towns in the nation. On the surface, it appeared that Chelsea was a place out of time with the rest of the world.

It was still a haven for middle- and upper-middle-class values. The community spirit was still alive. Churches were still full on Sundays. Little League baseball was still launched in the spring with a huge picnic on Opening Day. Everyone recycled their garbage and tied their newspapers for pickup. Charitable organizations flourished, along with the landscaped gardens where the wealthier women held their monthly meetings. At any moment an observer might expect to see Beav and Wally riding their bicycles on the tree-lined streets. Taxes might be high, but no one organized a revolt because their desired way of life was, for the most part, meticulously maintained. The city council had successfully fought a battle with the state to exclude low-income housing from its township limits. The streets were clean and safe. If drugs were used it was a family problem, to be discreetly handled, not the community's. There were no homeless people, because the police would pick up any who strayed into town and deposit them beyond the city limits. Let the next town worry about them. It was as though Chelsea were existing in an invisible bubble of protection against the realities of the world. And, for a high percentage of folks, appearances were everything.

When Monty Clarke from *Bold Copy* arrived in town with his film crew and his questionable British accent, following Susan Vansciver's shooting spree, the citizens of Chelsea felt under siege from the media. The county newspapers and even the ones across the river in Philadelphia had picked up on the story and were dragging it out week by week, like jackals savoring a tasty morsel. It was open season in Chelsea, and everything and everyone was fair game. Some feared that property values might take a sharp nosedive when the latest rumor surfaced; it was said that Monty couldn't decide if the title of his exposé should be "The Misbehaving Missionaries" or "Rush Limbaughland."

Eve drove through the once quiet town and didn't immediately notice the subtle differences. Her mind was occupied.

"Listen," she said to Ruthann, and then sighed with impatience. "It's time to let go and just do it. Isn't that what you're always saying to me? If you're worried about the money—"

"Of course I'm worried," Ruthann interrupted. "I can't afford to spend anything on clothes right now."

"I'll lend it to you."

"I told you I don't want to owe you money. I already owe you so much."

"You earn your way." Eve maneuvered the car as if on automatic pilot. She had driven this same route so many times that the scenery was merely a blur as she concentrated on the two ribbons of asphalt in front of her. "Okay, how about this? Since we're almost there, we stop at the nursery first and then go to Expressions. Just to look." She glanced sideways to get a reaction.

"There's really no need," Ruthann muttered, turning her face away to look out the window.

Eve's shoulders slumped as she considered that she might be trying to manipulate her friend. Was she that controlling? She didn't think so. What was wrong with advancing her some money for clothes? She had seen in the last month how Ruthann would fuss every time they had to leave the house. It was true that Ruthann's clothes had seen better times. In fact, they were worn and faded. She didn't care about that, but she did care that the condition was causing Ruthann to be uncomfortable every time they were in public. She was constantly pulling and smoothing the material, as if by touch she could transform them. What was so wrong about wanting to help?

Turning into the crowded lot of the nursery, Eve found a parking space and they both got out of the car.

"I think the rosebushes are around the side," Eve said,

noticing an oversize van parked carelessly and taking up two spaces. As she and Ruthann continued toward the plants she observed a small group of people and a man holding a Minicam on his shoulder. "Maybe they're doing a spot on gardening for the six o'clock news."

Ruthann shrugged. "Here are the roses. Oh, look at the white ones. And the pink. The red . . ."

Both women admired the flowers and were deciding which plants looked healthiest when Eve was distracted by a commotion close to the parking lot. The small crowd appeared to be moving, as though following someone. Her interest piqued, Eve tried to see who was so important to have caused this attention.

"Is that Molly?" she asked aloud, even though she knew Ruthann had never met the woman. She was almost sure that the TV camera was following Molly Kellerman. "Following" was an inaccurate description. It appeared that whoever was trying to talk to her was also trying to keep her from leaving. Immediately, Eve's mind put it together. For weeks she had avoided even reading the newspaper because of the sensational coverage.

"It's *Bold Copy,* or one of those other vultures."

Ruthann touched her forearm. "Maybe we should leave."

Eve saw Molly put her hand to her face, as if she were brushing away a tear. In that moment, something snapped inside of Eve. She forgot about Ruthann, the rosebushes they were buying for the side of the house, her own privacy. She remembered Molly calling her almost three months ago. It was that phone call that had pulled her out of depression, that had galvanized her energies to get out of the house. That one call had changed her life.

"Come on," she urged Ruthann as she hurried toward the group of people.

"What are you going to do?" Ruthann asked in a nervous voice as she tried to keep up.

"I don't know." The words had barely left her mouth when she pushed through several people and held out her hand to Molly Kellerman.

Molly's face was flushed and her eyes were almost glazed with near-panic. Recognizing Eve, she grabbed hold of the outstretched hand.

"Let's get out of here," Eve said.

"Mrs. Kellerman, are you going to stay in Chelsea now that your husband, the president of the orphanage, has resigned?"

"Get out of our way," Eve demanded, noticing that Monty Clarke was much shorter in person than he appeared on the television screen. He actually had pancake makeup on his face and neck. Good God . . .

The man narrowed his gaze and turned his face toward the camera slightly. "Aren't you Eve Cameron? Wasn't your husband also involved in the scandal? Joey, get this. We've been looking for her," he advised his cameraman as he held a microphone in front of Eve's face.

Ruthann broke through and stood on the other side of Molly, as if she were the woman's bodyguard. "Come with us. Leave your car. We'll pick it up later."

It sounded like a good plan to Eve. All she wanted was to escape this insanity.

"What about your children?" Monty persisted, keeping

pace with them as they led Molly away. "Aren't all of you just innocent victims of your husbands' sexual appetites? This is your chance to tell the world and set the story straight. What about you, Mrs. Cameron? Don't you have anything to say?"

Ruthann put Molly in the back of the car and climbed into the front. Eve opened the driver's-side door and looked at the man.

"Have you no decency? You're a grown man. Somewhere you must have a family. Aren't you ashamed to make money off other people's misery?"

She got into the car and backed it up, not caring if she mowed down the cameraman. Monty pulled his assistant's shirtsleeve to get him out of the way as Eve shifted into drive and slammed her foot down on the accelerator.

No one spoke until they were racing down the road and well away from the infamous intruder.

"I can't believe it! What a jerk!" Ruthann turned to face Molly in the backseat. "Are you okay?"

Eve looked in the rearview mirror. Molly's head was slumped down to her chin and she was covering her eyes with her hand as she wept. She nodded in answer to Ruthann's question, yet didn't look up.

"I'm sorry this happened," Eve murmured in sympathy. "It's crazy."

"They won't leave me alone!" Molly's voice sounded tortured. "They've even gone to the school. The police had to come and make them leave." She finally raised her face, while wiping at her cheeks. "Oh God, why is this happening? Will it never end?"

Anger rose sharply within Eve and her fingers tightened on the steering wheel. "There's something sick with society when shows like *Bold Copy* are feeding our perverse curiosity."

"But, Eve," Molly almost pleaded, "why are they doing this to us? Isn't it enough that we're all holding on by a thread? Why this torture?"

Eve's gaze caught Molly's and she recognized the anguish reflected in them. She'd been there herself. Unable to stand it anymore, she looked back to the road and realized she was driving to her house. She slowed down to five miles over the speed limit and finally relaxed her fingers. They weren't being followed.

"Molly, we're going to my house so you can pull yourself together. Don't worry."

"But they know where we all live. They're everywhere!"

"I've moved," Eve answered. "I don't live in Chelsea anymore."

"You moved?" Eve could hear the surprise in Molly's voice.

"I live by the river now. I don't think the buzzards have gotten wind of it yet. Paul's living in the old house now. They must follow him around. Oh, by the way, Molly . . . meet Ruthann Bucknum. She's living with me."

Ruthann smiled and extended her hand.

Molly wiped hers on the skirt of her jumper and shook it. "Thanks for rescuing me."

"My pleasure. Never liked Monty Clarke and his show. Who watches that stuff?"

Eve began to relax as she drove down her street. "Lots of people, or they wouldn't be on the air."

"But we're not celebrities," Molly persisted. "We're just ordinary people."

"They don't care," Eve remarked as she pulled the car into the driveway behind the contractor's trucks. "It's gossip. And it's juicy. I don't mind the newspapers so much, but this TV garbage is too real. If we refuse to talk to them, they'll eventually go away when something else catches their attention."

"This is it?" Molly whispered as she looked at the old Victorian, newly painted in a soft white with teal trim. A graceful wisteria wreath hung on the front door. "Eve, it's beautiful."

"Thanks. We've been working really hard to get it in shape." They got out of the car and walked toward the front steps. When they were on the porch, she turned to Molly. "How about a cup of coffee?"

"Coffee sounds great. Can we sit out here?" Molly looked from the wide porch out to the river. "It's so peaceful."

Eve smiled. "That's why I bought it. I had the same feeling." Just then she heard the sound of electrical tools coming from the back of the house, and she grinned. "Well, usually it's quiet. We're still not finished with repairs."

"I'll get the coffee," Ruthann volunteered. "They're working upstairs, so you two can have some privacy out here. Back in a few minutes."

"Home already? Need help with the roses?"

Ruthann almost groaned when she saw Mick Larkin in the kitchen installing the removable wooden grilles in the new bay window. "We didn't get the roses," she said as she hurried to the island that now housed a double range. She grabbed the coffeepot and turned to the sink to empty what remained of that morning's brew. It was unnerving to never know when she would run into him. Thank God he and his crew were almost finished.

"There's a place in Marlton that has some nice ones. I think the name is Goldenrod, or something like that. Pretty strange name for a nursery. Isn't that a weed?"

"I believe it is," she muttered, opening the new refrigerator to get the coffee. Usually she loved puttering around in the remodeled kitchen, where everything was so clean and in its proper place. But she resented his presence and hoped he would finish and leave. Unconsciously, her fingers pulled on the old cotton top that was fraying at the hem.

"Maybe I can take you, if you don't know where it is. It would be a nice ride, and we could even stop for an early dinner . . . if you don't have plans."

She didn't turn around to look at him. Why was he doing this? Why wouldn't he leave her alone? Hadn't she shown him that she wasn't interested? She didn't want to be his friend, or anything else.

"I think the decision concerning landscaping should be Eve's. This is her house, not mine."

He didn't answer her, and she was grateful. She didn't like being cold, yet she knew if she thawed in the least he would take it as encouragement. And she didn't want to encourage any male. She just didn't trust them after the time she had spent on the streets. Why was it that some men just singled you out and were relentless until they got what they wanted? She had spent too many years being controlled to give up even an inch of her freedom.

"Are you happy here, Ruthann?"

Her eyes closed briefly and she sighed, not caring if he heard her. Finally she turned around and faced him. "Look, Mick, you have work to do and so do I. If you'll excuse me, I'd like to get on with mine." She almost slammed the coffeepot onto the range. She needed something else to occupy her mind and her hands, and she grabbed the muffins from the morning. She would heat them and serve them with the coffee.

"I'm sorry if I offended you. My mistake."

She heard him leave the room and her shoulders slumped with a strange mixture of relief and regret. She was glad he was gone, yet she hadn't meant to be rude. What was wrong with her? Why couldn't she even converse with the man without snapping at him? She wasn't like that with the others. She knew his foreman's wife's name and the names of his children. She had laughed with the carpenters when they told a joke. It was *him*! Something about him, almost as if the air seemed charged between them when they faced each other.

But charged with what? It was a question she didn't even want to think about.

Molly sat down heavily in one of the wicker rockers. Her voice trembled as she whispered, "I don't know how much more of this I can take."

Eve sat next to her and reached out to touch her hand. "I know what you're going through, Molly. Believe me, it's going to be okay."

"How can you say that?" the woman demanded. "You're divorced. Everything you've ever worked for is lost. It's not fair!"

Eve didn't answer for a few moments. "You're right. It isn't fair. I could give you some platitudes, like If you're given lemons than make lemonade, but that won't help right now. Probably the most appropriate is, Shit happens. None of us planned for a bomb like this to blow apart our lives. But it happened, Molly. We can't change that."

"I'm trying, Eve. God, I'm trying to hold it together for the kids. But this . . . this invasion by strangers into my pain is too much to bear." She ran her fingers through her highlighted hair and sighed as fresh tears erupted. "That's another thing. I can't seem to stop this damn crying."

"You're grieving."

Both women looked out to the peaceful river. Eve allowed Molly the time to pull it together. She knew she should say something, something comforting and nurturing, yet her mind went blank. All she could feel was anger at the injustice.

It was Molly who spoke first. "How did you do it, Eve? How did you get the courage to divorce and move like this?"

Eve waited a couple of seconds while she got her thoughts together. When she answered, her words were carefully chosen. "I almost had a nervous breakdown following Jamie's death. And then this on top of it seemed like too much for one human being to carry. But I fought it, Molly. It's the only way back to normalcy, whatever that is. I got angry . . . angry at God, at Paul, at everything. I only know that when I felt like a victim, I was drowning. When I started to fight back, or at least fight for myself, I started to swim for shore."

Molly was crying openly and Eve let her, knowing that she needed this release. Eventually Eve said, "Listen to me, Molly. You have children. I don't. Your choices are more difficult than mine. Don't look to me as an example. You have two daughters to consider. I did what felt right for me. You have to figure out what feels right for you."

"I want my marriage back. I want to feel safe again. I want all of this ugliness to go away."

"It will go away eventually, but while it's here you've got to deal with it. I guess I look at it like what was normal is gone. I have to create a new normal, accept it, and get on with it. Otherwise, I'll sink again."

Sniffling, Molly said, "It isn't just the media. Last week I went into Shwering's Drug Store and I almost hit Mrs. Shwering."

Eve couldn't help smiling as she imagined Molly in a brawl with old Mrs. Shwering. "Why? What did she do?"

"It wasn't what she did. It was what she said. I thought the dirty looks were my imagination, like I was getting paranoid or something, until she said people like us had brought shame into Chelsea and the best thing we could do was leave. When I told her I didn't do anything, she went on in front of everyone about the Rotary Club and how my husband was the president and how he had resigned in dishonor. She went on and on about the notoriety and shame. . . ."

"The old witch." Eve clenched her teeth as another wave of anger washed over her. "How can she blame you, or any of the wives, for what happened?"

"If I hadn't had to wait for my daughter's prescription, I would have bolted. She actually said that if I had taken better care of my man, he wouldn't have turned to a foreign woman. Can you believe that?"

Eve was shocked. "I can't believe it."

"She's not the only one. Everywhere I go, I feel like people are talking about me. I know they stare, and when I catch them, they look away. When I took the girls to the Club for their swimming lessons, I ran into Clarice Altman and Renee Rogers. They snubbed me, Eve."

She pictured the two women from the country club. She only knew them casually, but Molly had been friends with them. "I'm sorry, Molly. It's so unfair."

"Even the kids are getting it at school now." Molly sniffled and looked defeated. "Maybe the only answer is to move too. But I just can't imagine giving up everything. I like my home. I like the school system. It's the people I want to get away from." Shaking her head, she closed her eyes and whispered, "I can't seem to make a decision—any decision. . . . I've had the divorce papers for weeks and I can't even sign them. I don't know what's wrong with me."

"Nothing's wrong with you," Eve said in a strong voice while trying to keep the anger out. "You're a good woman, Molly Kellerman. You were a good wife and a good mother. You've been placed in a horrible position, but you must realize that just because you followed all the rules doesn't guarantee a happy ending. Maybe we all took the good life for granted and this is some kind of sadistic test or something. Just take it one day at a time, and believe that in the end you'll do the right thing for all concerned. I'm sure Stuart isn't pressuring you to sign the divorce papers."

"No. Not at all."

"Then don't sign them until you know, until you *feel* it's the right thing to do. Don't let pride stand in the way."

"But how could I take him back now?"

Eve didn't answer, because Ruthann came onto the porch carrying a tray.

"Sorry it took so long," Ruthann said as she placed the tray onto the oval wicker table. "Coffee?"

Eve smiled. "Thanks. Molly? Black? Cream and sugar?"

"Cream and sugar. What do I care now?" Molly muttered. "All that counting calories garbage . . . for what?"

Eve fixed the coffee and handed it to Molly along with a blueberry muffin.

"I couldn't eat," Molly moaned.

"Try," Eve coaxed. "Ruthann made them this morning. She's a fantastic cook. I've never eaten so well in my life. Makes me a little ashamed of the way I fed my family. Paul was a meat and potatoes kind of guy, and I guess I tried to please him."

"Didn't we all?" Molly asked. Her voice held more than a hint of scorn and sarcasm, yet she did take a bite of the muffin. Swallowing quickly, she looked to Ruthann. "These *are* delicious. They remind me of my grandmother's. Now, there was a woman who could bake." She gazed out to the river. "I used to bake from scratch. Then I got so busy with the girls and their schedules . . . Maybe I wasn't a good wife or mother. Maybe I took the easy way out and—"

"Stop it." Knowing where Molly's thoughts were leading, Eve interrupted before they got there. "Being a wonderful cook doesn't make a marriage work. Ruthann's divorced." She looked to her friend and mentally apologized. It was comforting to see in Ruthann's eyes an acknowledgment, as if they'd known each other for years instead of months. Time no longer mattered. After everything they had been through and everything they had revealed to each other, she felt as if she and Ruthann were bonded for life. If she'd had a sister, she wouldn't feel closer to her than she did to Ruthann.

"I don't know what to say," Molly murmured, setting her cup onto the tray. "I used to feel sorry for someone who was divorced, and now here I am separated with divorce papers waiting for my signature." She looked at Eve and Ruthann. "Are you both glad you did it?"

Eve knew Molly was looking for direction, yet she questioned if she had the right. "It's not a matter of being glad, Molly. For me, it came down to the very last option. I had nothing left to connect me to Paul. Jamie was gone and Paul had become a stranger. There was no foundation any longer. Nothing to build upon."

"I married the wrong person," Ruthann said in a quiet, almost shy voice. "We tried for years to make it better . . . well, at least I did. I know that now, but some things can't be fixed, not when they're wrong from the beginning. It was a hard decision, and I took years making it, but I felt like I was slowly fading away. It's been hard since. Very hard. But I know, for me, it was the right decision."

"See, that's just it," Molly said. "Stuart and I had a good marriage. At least I thought it was good. He's a good father, and the girls miss him. So do I, damn it. But then I think it's just habit. I'm used to having a man around the house. Now it's so . . ."

"Lonely?" Eve and Ruthann said the word together, then tried not to laugh.

"Geez, I guess we gave ourselves away with that one." Eve chuckled and shook her head. "It *is* lonely, Molly. For me, I guess I balance that with having peace of mind."

"Me too," Ruthann piped up. "But don't rush into anything, Molly. Take your time. You deserve that, to make the right decision. Don't let anyone, or anything, pressure you into action until you're ready."

Molly smiled. "You sound like Eve. How did you two meet?"

Ruthann glanced at Eve before saying. "We met in Shop-Rite."

"Actually, it was the parking lot. The morning you called me about Susan. How is she, by the way? I tried to call but just got the machine. Has anyone seen her?" Eve hoped it was a smooth evasion, for there was no need to embarrass Ruthann by giving details.

"She's staying with her mother until the trial. Her lawyers are confident she'll get off with probation. Naturally, she's under the care of a psychiatrist. Nick Borelli. Do you know him?"

Eve shook her head.

"I've been thinking about seeing someone myself," Molly whispered. "It's just that there's been no one to talk to about this . . . until today. Thanks, Eve. You too, Ruthann. You whisked me away from the nursery like a professional bodyguard. Even Monty Clarke was intimidated."

Ruthann laughed. "Maybe that's what I should do. Bodyguard."

Molly finished her muffin and murmured her appreciation. "Eve's right. You are a great cook. Maybe you should open your own restaurant."

"Oh, sure," Ruthann joked. "I can just see it now—"

"Wait a minute," Eve interrupted. "Maybe Molly has something there. Why not open a restaurant?"

"You're kidding, right?" Ruthann looked at Eve as if she'd lost her mind. "What do either one of us know about running a restaurant?"

"I helped form a computer company. I know about business."

"Computers and dining aren't the same thing," Ruthann argued.

"It's a thought, that's all," Eve said, yet it seemed that once the idea entered her brain she couldn't dislodge it. Why not start a new business? She had money to invest. Why not invest in herself and Ruthann?

"Restaurants are a risky business," Molly said, as though reading her thoughts.

"I know. Most don't last a year. I don't think it's because the food is terrible, but more of a publicity problem. Not enough people know they exist."

"Ads are expensive, and only the more established restaurants have a large enough budget for commercials."

"That's it!" Eve exclaimed, and stood up. She began pacing back and forth in front of them as her mind filled with more ideas than she knew how to verbalize. "Listen, if we want to do this we have to jump on it now, because we have the perfect publicity."

Both women stared at her as if she truly had lost her mind.

"Don't you get it?" she demanded. "Monty Clarke. We're talking national coverage, ladies. Which means I have to find a property that's already established and make quick renovations. Mick could do it, Ruthann. Don't you think?"

"Eve, slow down. It's too much of a risk."

"Sure, it's a risk. Just like this house. Just like meeting you. C'mon. You know we can do this. Every night you prepare dinners that are delicious, healthy, and look mouthwatering. You should taste her crème brûlée, Molly. To die for."

"That's not exactly healthful," Ruthann remarked.

"So what? Healthful meals and sinful desserts. I really like this idea, don't you?"

Ruthann stared back at her. "I think you're losing it."

Eve smiled. "I need something in my life now that the house is almost complete. Why not this? We could do it. I know we could. Sure, we'll need some help getting started, and there's a lot to learn, but think of it. . . . Our own business, Ruthann. And media coverage to ensure our success. We didn't cause this fiasco, but we can certainly use it to our advantage."

She looked at Molly and almost laughed. "Remember what I said about lemons? I damn well intend to make some lemonade, and to hell with what anyone thinks. I didn't ask for this, but I know now how to turn it around."

She sat down and looked deeply into her friends' eyes. "I'm going to need your help, guys. Can I count on you?"

They merely stared back, wide-eyed with shock.

Okay, so she'd have to do a better sales job. But she could do it. She knew she could. She *felt* it.

And now she had a purpose in her life again.

CHAPTER 8

She had made love to Mick Larkin. Almost. He was working in her bedroom, running his fingers over the new trim around the door when she had become envious of the wood. She had wanted to know what it would feel like to be touched by him with such gentleness. She was the one who had gone to him and had walked into his arms, run her hands over his strong back, felt the muscles in his arms as they enveloped her, wrapped her leg around his thigh to pull him closer to her body, needing to make primal contact . . .

Drenched in sweat, she had awakened in the middle of the night, horrified that she had dreamed such a thing. And Mick Larkin, of all people! Obviously, her subconscious was trying to tell her that she had been without sex for too long.

Standing in the kitchen, in the light of day, she resolved to put it out of her mind and concentrate on *real* problems, not crazy erotic dreams. It was pathetic for a middle-aged woman to be dreaming about a man she couldn't even speak to civilly.

She had other worries. Like Eve, and her rash plunge into finding a restaurant. Eve had already contacted a business broker who was searching for an established restaurant that was on the market. She had even enrolled them both in an accelerated weekend course in restaurant management. It was all happening too fast, just as with the house. Once Eve made up her mind about something, there was simply no stopping her.

In the last week she had contacted the wives of the men involved in the scandal and had invited them over. It had turned into a group therapy meeting, a safe place to air fears and find comfort and support. Ruthann had stayed upstairs after preparing refreshments. She had felt grateful to be excluded from the kind of pain and disillusionment that was being revealed. Eve had told her that the wives were going to get together on a regular basis to meet the human need for validation of their personal experiences. She had insisted it wasn't a support group, just friends helping friends. Ruthann didn't know if Eve was codependent, or a visionary. It was scary. Part of her wanted to throw her support behind her friend, and yet a stronger part was worried.

Why did Eve feel the need to help everyone who crossed her path? And what was driving her?

The questions only made Ruthann worry more.

"I'm home," Eve announced as she burst into the kitchen. "I've asked Mick to come over for a discussion. Ron Avery has located a restaurant for sale outside of town. On Route 73, so it's close. I'm going to ask Mick to go to dinner with us."

Mick! That name again! The man was haunting her. Ruthann left the vegetables in the sink and turned around to face Eve. A shopping bag sat on the floor by the kitchen chair. "I don't get it. Why the rush?"

"I've told you. We need to move on this while we have the attention of the media. And you know what Mick told me?"

Ruthann inhaled deeply, trying to keep the impatience out of her voice. "I can't imagine. What was it?"

"The person with a new idea is a crank . . . until the idea succeeds. Mark Twain said that."

Ruthann rolled her gaze toward the kitchen ceiling. "Why, he's just a fountain of wisdom, isn't he? Ever notice that all his quaint sayings belong to others? I don't believe he has an original thought in his head."

"Ruthann." Eve stared across the room, as if she were a disapproving parent. "Why don't you like him? Every time he tries to be friendly to you, you put up an invisible wall to shut him out. He's a nice man. A very nice man."

"Then you talk to him. I'll have you know that while he was working on the house, *that's* when he'd try to talk to me. I was saving you money by not allowing him to shirk his work."

Eve threw back her head and laughed. Ruthann didn't see anything funny.

"Oh, please," Eve finally said, though she still grinned. "The man is way ahead of schedule, and you know it. His entire crew works like a swarm of bees. I have a feeling that he doesn't even need to be here to supervise his men. I think he's here so often for another reason."

She wouldn't ask. She refused to encourage this turn in the conversation.

"He likes you, Ruthann. I believe he'd like to get to know you. Though why, when you act so stuck-up, is beyond me. He must have the patience of a saint."

Eve's words hit home. She didn't know why she was putting off Mick Larkin's overtures at friendship. Something about the man sent off alarms, and she didn't like looking him in the eye. As stupid as it sounded, Ruthann felt as if Mick could see inside, and if she let him in she might tell him things, things that were better hidden. Like her dream of last night, God forbid. "I'm not stuck-up," she answered defensively. "I'm cautious."

"Cautious? You're bordering on rude. Why are you so afraid of him? Is it because you're really attracted to him?"

Ruthann blew her breath out in a derisive snort. "You're joking, right? The very last thing I need in my life right now is to be attracted to a man."

"You've said that before. Not to sound clichéd, for I know how that annoys you . . . but I think the lady doth protest too much."

"Doth she now? Perhaps she's just not interested. Ever entertain that one?"

Eve's smile widened. "I thought we could all have dinner at the restaurant to check it out. Ever hear of a place called Laveretti's?"

She shook her head. "Since I've been back to New Jersey I haven't had much of an opportunity to—"

"Okay," Eve interrupted. "Stupid question. Sorry. Paul and I went there a few times. It was nice, but I wasn't impressed. Tonight we'll look at possibilities on how we could improve it. I think it'll be fun."

"I don't see why I have to go. You and Mick can fantasize together."

"Why are you fighting me on this? Ruthann . . . this is something that we can work on together. I want you involved."

She turned and faced her friend. "Why? You don't listen to me when I tell you to be cautious. How can you risk that amount of money? Why not invest in something stable, instead of a restaurant? I don't know that I want that kind of responsibility."

Eve sighed, as though weary of the same old debate. "Look, I started a business with Paul. I know the risks. I also know that almost everything worthwhile in my life came from taking a risk and putting myself on the line. I'm willing to invest in myself, and in you. I don't have any fear about that. We can make this happen, but the key word is *we*. I need you, Ruthann. If you're dead set against this, then I'll drop it. But both of us will wonder for the rest of our lives whether or not we could have done it. I know I will."

Reluctantly, Ruthann again faced the sink. She didn't want to look in Eve's eyes and see the plea for understanding. She would never understand why Eve couldn't take the safe and secure route and live off the interest from the divorce settlement. She knew she wasn't much of a gambler. Unlike Eve, almost everything she had risked hadn't panned out. But Eve needed her, and she owed her so much. . . .

"I bought you a new outfit for tonight," Eve murmured as an added enticement.

Ruthann couldn't even get angry. Eve was so generous and thoughtful, and clothes, truthfully, had been an issue. Ruthann held a paring knife in her hand as she slowly turned back to the room and her friend, who sat at the kitchen table looking like the proverbial cat that ate the canary.

"There's no stopping you, is there?"

"You can stop me, Ruthann. Just say no."

She laughed, knowing surrender was close. "I think saying no to drugs is easier than saying no to you. You're a powerful woman."

"I'm not powerful," Eve answered. "And I don't think I'm being manipulative. I know why you're scared. But the past is over. You've got to believe that. We're not going to wind up on the streets. I won't let that happen. That's not powerful; that's believing in myself and knowing I have the ability to create my future. I don't have to depend on whims of fate, or the rise and fall of the prime interest rate. I have faith, Ruthann, in both of us. I believe we can do this."

Ruthann knew she couldn't resist Eve, and slowly shook her head for even trying. All she could do was go with the tide and hope it didn't pull them both under. "So what does this outfit look like?" she muttered.

Eve grinned while reaching into the shopping bag. "Wait till you see it. Oh, Ruthann . . . you're going to love it."

And she probably would. Surrender was that close.

Three hours later, she knew she was caught in the undertow and fighting for balance. Laveretti's was huge, far too big for amateur restaurateurs. When the four of them had walked up to the place, she had been expecting a more intimate surrounding, not this cavern crying out to be filled. At least two hundred and fifty of them—that's what the capacity sign read. There wasn't any way she could cook for that number of people. She wouldn't even know where to begin.

They were seated at a corner table, and even for a weeknight, the place was slow. Mostly couples. Mostly older. Servers were standing around idle or chatting. Once in a while, one of them would check salt and pepper shakers on empty tables, but Ruthann could see that was more out of boredom than a strong work ethic.

After they had ordered from the pedestrian menu and were sipping their drinks, Ruthann knew she had to voice her concerns. It no longer mattered that Mick Larkin had been strategically seated next to her. Her annoyance was coupled with uneasiness as she watched him socialize with Eve and Ron Avery while ignoring her as if she were a foreigner who didn't speak the language. Sipping her wine, she gently placed the glass back onto the table and looked at Eve.

"It's far too big," she announced following Ron Avery's pitch about location. "You can't expect to fill this place and keep all those employees working. And, truthfully, I would have to go to school for years to learn how to cook for a restaurant this large."

Eve nodded and looked around the room, "I know, it is

big," she remarked, then leaned closer to the table and added, "Mick, what do you think? What could we do here?"

She's not listening, Ruthann thought. She has her focus in one direction and she can't hear anything else.

"Well," Mick said as he looked out to the dining room, "you could divide it up into separate rooms to make it less open. One for smokers. One for large parties . . ." His voice trailed off as he struggled to find suggestions.

"That's possible," Eve answered, and Ruthann could see the woman's mind working overtime. "I think a main dining room is important. Seating for what . . . a hundred, a hundred and fifty people? I like the idea of separate rooms in the back. We could offer them for private parties or meeting rooms. There's a big profit in corporate catering. But what can we offer that will attract people once the initial curiosity is over? We need *something.*"

Ron Avery sipped his drink and put it back on the table. "Are you talking about entertainment? Something like a piano bar?"

"A piano bar?" Eve looked at Ruthann and raised her eyebrows, as if asking for an opinion.

Ruthann remained silent. She refused to encourage Eve in this madness.

"Okay, that's a thought, but I was thinking about something bigger, something that would attract a lot of people." Eve's gaze went from person to person, putting them on the hot seat.

Ron Avery must have felt it, and thoughts of his commission made him a bit reckless. "What about a dance club in the back? Those who have dinner first get free admission into the club."

Eve sat back and thought about it. "I don't know," she murmured. "Twenty-somethings looking to connect? That isn't the age bracket I want to target. Let's really think. What doesn't this area have that you have to go to Philadelphia to get? *That's* what I'm looking for. Something I usually have to cross the river for, deal with traffic and parking . . . all that hassle for what? The theater? Museums? What do you think, Ruthann?"

She felt everyone's attention focused on her, and she shrugged her shoulders. "I haven't the slightest idea."

"Oh, c'mon, Ruthann. Just play with it. This is supposed to be fun."

"Investing your money should be serious, Eve."

"Comedy clubs are big," Ron threw out to lighten the turn in the conversation.

Comedy was quickly rejected.

Several suggestions were brought up, and Eve dismissed each. She said she'd know it when she felt it. When dinner arrived, the four of them ate silently. Ruthann thought the entire evening was disastrous. Here was her dearest friend acting like a heat-seeking missile, searching for a way to lose her money and encouraged by two men who would profit by it. Was she the only one with common sense at the table?

Suddenly Eve put down her fork and announced, "I've got it!"

Her voice was so excited that Ruthann felt her stomach muscles tighten with dread. She'd heard that same tone before, and she knew Eve was *feeling* something.

"A jazz club," she pronounced. "A really smart jazz club with a main dining room that would include the music and a separate room without it. We could have two seatings for the sets. What do you think?"

Ron Avery's grin was wide and encouraging. "There's nothing like it around here."

Mick was nodding, as if he agreed.

Ruthann thought Eve had finally lost it. "What do you know about jazz?"

Eve sipped her wine and shrugged. "I'm not an aficionado, but I do know what I like when I hear it. And I like most of what I hear. All kinds, especially . . . what do they call it? Fusion jazz. A blend of jazz and rock. George Benson. Miles Davis. Herbie Hancock. It's sort of like classical music. When I hear a piece, I don't have to remember the composer to enjoy it."

Ruthann shook her head. "But this isn't the same. You don't know anything about hiring entertainment. How will you even know who to book? Who's available? Can you afford them? How do you even go about it? It's crazy."

Eve sat back and looked around the room, as if envisioning a different scene. "Paul and I used to go to the jazz clubs in Philly a couple of times a year. They were always filled, and it was a nice group of people. A cut above a regular nightclub. There was an aura of almost casual glamour. They didn't seem to mind spending their money for an evening out. People dressed up. The food was good. The entertainment was close enough so that everyone had a decent view. Nobody got drunk or obnoxious. I liked it. The only thing I didn't like was the annoyance of city traffic and the problem with parking late at night."

"Okay, fine," Ruthann said. "So transportation is easier, but that still doesn't solve your problem. Eve . . . you don't know enough about owning a restaurant, let alone a club. There's suppliers, staff, state and local laws, liquor boards. Good God, the list is endless and neither one of us knows enough right now to make a decision. And now you're talking about hiring jazz groups? It's impulsive madness," she muttered.

"So I'll learn. Fast."

Mick cleared his throat and everyone looked at him. Ruthann couldn't imagine what he could contribute to the discussion.

"Ahh, listen . . . In the seventies, during college summers, I used to road-manage Hugh Masekella. I still have a few friends in the business. Maybe I could point you in the right direction."

Ruthann stared at him as if he'd emerged from a spaceship. He was encouraging Eve in this insanity!

Eve's face was slowly transformed by a brilliant smile. "Somehow I felt you were going to be a part of all this, Mick. That's why it was important for you to come with me tonight," she said, and reached across the table for his hand. "Thank you for believing I can do this, and I'll need all the help I can get. You can be in charge of renovations, and would you mind helping with some of our first bookings?"

"Sure."

"See, Ruthann . . . it's all falling into place."

She felt as if she were standing in front of an avalanche,

powerless to stop the momentum. "I can't cook for a hundred people!" Why was no one listening to her?

"You wouldn't have to," Eve answered. "We'll hire a chef and you'll oversee the menu and kitchen staff. You know what we're looking for: interesting meals that are delicious and healthy, a lot of fish and chicken . . . and sinful desserts. We can even hire a manager until we know what we're doing ourselves. We'll learn quickly, because this is our future. We can do this, Ruthann. It feels right. A jazz club . . ." Her eyes seemed to take on a glazed sparkle. "I like it."

"With a big grand opening," Ron Avery added. Ruthann thought she could see the dollar signs in his eyes. He was probably deciding how to spend his commission.

"Absolutely," Eve agreed. "That's the whole point of acting so quickly. We want to take advantage of the publicity."

"Shall I talk to the owners?" Ron asked. "We could take a tour tonight."

Eve nodded as she pushed her plate away from her. "Let's do it now. I'll go with you."

Ron, sensing a fast close, wiped his mouth and stood up. He offered his hand to Eve.

Leaving the table, Eve turned to Ruthann and Mick and said, "We'll come back and get you for the tour. Keep your fingers crossed." She gave them a big smile and left.

Neither one of them said anything for at least a minute. Finally, Ruthann put her fork down and sat back in her chair. "This is total insanity. She's going to lose everything."

He didn't answer, and she turned her head to look at

him directly. "You have no comment now, Mr. Entertainment?"

She could see he was trying not to smile.

"Are you speaking to me?" he asked innocently.

"Who else is at this table? Of course I'm speaking to you."

"I just wondered, since you've made it pretty clear in the past that—"

"Okay," she interrupted before he could nail her to the cross. "We haven't exactly been friendly. All right, *I* haven't been friendly. There. I apologize. But we have to find a way to stop her."

"Why?"

She looked at him as if he were a child. "She'll lose everything."

"How do you know that? It's a pretty good idea, and there's nothing like it on this side of the Delaware."

"Don't you see? She knows nothing about it. She's caught up in using all this publicity, turning a negative into a positive thing. But she's not being reasonable. She's acting on straight emotion. Because it *feels* right!"

Mick sat back and looked out to the huge room. "Maybe it's time for Eve to put reason on the back burner."

"What's that supposed to mean?"

"I read once that life gives us plenty of good reasons for not getting and doing what we want. Most accept the excuses because they sound reasonable, but they can also paralyze us and the exciting impulse to go beyond ourselves. Do you understand?"

Frowning, she shook her head. "No."

"In your life, you probably wanted to change certain things or become something else, but you were held back from trying. Maybe it was fear, or insecurity. Whatever it was kept you in the same place, doing the same thing. And nothing was changed or achieved until you forgot the excuses and just acted."

Ruthann thought of her marriage. She hated to admit the man might be right. "But this is too scary. She could lose it all and be out on the street."

Nodding, Mick picked up his glass of wine and tasted the white zinfandel. "Everything is relative. Eve risks it all on a restaurant. Columbus risked it all seeking land. I'm sure reason told him to stay home by the fire where it was safe. If Harriet Tubman had listened to the reason of others, she wouldn't have risked her life by going back to the South again and again to help free others. Reason has survival value, but when it urges us to hold in our feelings, go with the odds, avoid all risks and stay with the familiar, it's time to take another look at how reason may be holding us back from reaching our potential. Intuition is just as important."

"You believe in intuition?" Ruthann asked, mentally reevaluating Mick Larkin. Who the hell *was* this man?

"Absolutely. I know what Eve means when she says it feels right. That's intuition, sort of an inner knowing. That's why I'm in the contracting business. When I look at a project and it feels right, I know I can do my best work. I learned a long time ago to listen to myself."

"Where did you learn it?" she asked, and realized her voice sounded shy. Was it too personal a question?

He turned and looked directly at her. Something scary

began in her belly and raced down her legs when her gaze met his wide brown eyes, eyes that were framed by thick dark lashes.

"Do you really want to know?"

She merely nodded, for she didn't trust her voice.

"I've had a number of teachers in my life, but the first was my grandfather. He was a Baptist minister, and because my mom wasn't married when she had me, I grew up with her parents on a small farm in Glassboro. I learned early about life and death, about the laws of nature. My grandfather started to teach me about the laws of the universe, at least as much as he understood them at the time. He lived a simple life, and yet was one of the wisest men I've met. He said that true wisdom comes not from adding to your learning, but from being open to it when you hear it . . . feeling it inside of you and taking it as truth. Then anything is possible. Even opening a jazz club in South Jersey."

Ruthann felt mesmerized by his voice, and she could feel herself opening to his words as the barrier she had constructed between them started to weaken. "So what should I do?" she asked. "Just surrender?"

He laughed, and Ruthann felt the sound vibrate within her own muscles. His eyes actually sparkled, and his smile . . . it made her want to smile back.

"Surrender is an old-fashioned concept," he said in a low voice while staring at the now empty wineglass in his hand. "It signifies someone being dominant, and you being submissive. When you're talking about laws of the universe, which means beyond this physical world, then you learn to bend like a willow. To sway with the changing winds, yet always come back upright. That's participation, not surrender. You claim your own power."

She thought about his words. She thought about what he had revealed about his life and his personal philosophy. Suddenly she was glad that Eve had bought her the jade silk dress, glad she had washed her hair and was wearing makeup. She was glad that Mick had been invited. She was even thankful that he knew something about jazz, and could help them. If Eve was determined to do this, then they would need all the help they could get.

And if she and Mick would be working together, it was best if they came to an agreeable understanding. It was time to grow up and accept what Eve had been saying all along. Mick Larkin was a nice man. A very nice man.

Why did that acknowledgment frighten her? Was that surrender, or participation? Only time would tell.

It was as if God had looked down from the heavens and given their little project the green light. Everything fell into place, like dominoes arranged in an intricate pattern. Sometimes the dominoes fell slowly—when dealing with the township, the liquor control board's investigation, arranging new deals with all the suppliers . . . Eve made mistakes, but more often than not, it seemed that the right people were placed in front of the trio at the right time, and it was rare that anyone could turn away from Eve's sharp business skills and optimistic spirit. Laveretti's was closed within a week. The staff was fired, according to the state law, and then rehired if they could wait until the restaurant reopened in a month. Days were spent remodeling as Mick's crew worked overtime turning the huge dining room into a smart supper club. Nights were spent in Philadelphia, listening to jazz combos, speaking with agents, and learning more about the only art form to originate in the United States. Jazz—in one way or another—seemed to consume their lives.

"I've talked to Neil Price, the artist we met last week who teaches at Philadelphia College of Art. Remember him?" Eve asked as Ruthann entered the main dining room and stepped over an electrical cord.

Ruthann pushed several swatches of tablecloth material to the side of the banquette and slid onto the soft leather. "He teaches modern art, right?"

Eve nodded. "He's agreed to let us hang some of his work, and those of his more talented students, on consignment. The only time he can meet is tonight, and I have that liquor control board thing with the lawyers. Can you and Mick go?"

Mentally and physically drained, Ruthann sighed and ran her hand over her eyes. "Eve, I don't know anything about modern art. To be truthful, I don't even like it."

"That's because you don't understand it yet," Eve said as she flipped through material. "What's your opinion? I want to go with greens and blues, but I keep thinking that white tablecloths are more aesthetically pleasing to the eye. Probably the white, right?"

Ruthann couldn't keep up with the right brain/left brain workings of Eve's mind. "Go with the white. It's safer. But look, can't you reschedule the art meeting? I really don't want this responsibility. I like watercolors, soft and tranquil, not modern art."

"Mick knows what we want. Just go with him as the official representative. Please? I wish I could do it, but this meeting with the liquor board is too important."

"Mick knows?" Ruthann tried to find him in the small brigade of workers. He was talking to one of his crew and pointing to a wall. Although he was the boss, he didn't act or dress the part. Maybe that's why they respected him so much and why all of them seemed to work so efficiently. Mick Larkin was a chameleon. He could transform and blend into any situation. Today he was wearing jean shorts and a denim shirt with the sleeves cut out. The muscles in his legs and arms seemed like sculpted marble. It was all that bike riding, she thought, and immediately scolded herself for letting her mind play with her like that. Yet she couldn't stop staring at him, thinking about all the nights that they had spent in the city with Eve. Then he was dressed like a cover of *GQ*—perfectly tailored suits, tab-collar shirts, and stunning silk ties. Women, old and young, stared at him when he walked by, for he carried himself with an almost regal air. In a quiet, understated way, he couldn't be ignored. And Mick had always been the perfect gentleman. He had old world manners— opened doors, held her elbow to guide her through a crowded club, always pulled out chairs, listened to her suggestions with undivided interest, patiently explained subjects she didn't understand.

As though reading her thoughts, Mick turned his head and looked at her. He didn't wave. He didn't even smile. When his gaze burned into hers and connected, that strange pulling sensation again started in Ruthann's belly. It felt as if the ground collapsed beneath her feet and the distance between them contracted, pulling her toward him.

"Ruthann? Are you okay?"

"Huh?" She broke the connection and blinked a few times before looking at her friend.

Eve smiled. "I asked if you were okay. You look shaken up, like a truck just missed hitting you or something."

"I'm fine," Ruthann insisted, though she felt exactly as Eve had described. Her heart was slamming against her rib cage. "Ahh . . . go with the white tablecloths. You won't have to worry about flowers or candles clashing with . . . What? Why are you laughing?"

Still grinning, Eve shook her head and reached out to pat Ruthann's arm. "We were talking about you and Mick going to the art school tonight. Remember?"

"Oh, right." Embarrassed, Ruthann didn't know how to refuse now. It was obvious that Eve had caught her. She only hoped she didn't look as foolish as she felt.

Four hours later, Ruthann not only felt foolish, she knew she looked it. There was no doubt that she was out of her element. On the ride into the city, Mick had told her that he had taken a few art courses in college and was familiar with the style of painting that Eve was looking to hang in the restaurant, but nothing could have prepared her for Neil Price's studio.

The walls were covered in nudes: nudes with three breasts shaped like beach balls, nudes with two penises, one erupting from a navel orange that vaguely resembled a nuclear missile, nudes that looked more like a demented geometry lesson in shapes. She had never seen the human form displayed in such a bizarre technique. She kept trying to concentrate on the conversation between Mick and the artist, yet her vision kept straying to the walls. What kind of mind created this stuff?

Tall, thin, dressed completely in black with wisps of white hair hanging to his shoulders, Neil resembled a pompous Ichabod Crane. He scared her more than impressed her with his speech on Fauvism, Cubism, and Dadaism. She had no idea what he was talking about, and she didn't think Eve would either. And what was with the steel-wool pads? She couldn't believe that Eve would want this stuff hanging in the restaurant. Maybe she wasn't with it, not cool enough to see how three huge boxes of Brillo pads sitting in the center of the room produced an art form that didn't hinder digestion. Was it a statement about shapes, man's obsession with cleanliness, or just three red and white boxes sitting on the floor?

"Let's look at some work," Neil finally suggested, and waved them toward a door.

Avoiding eye contact with Mick, Ruthann walked ahead of him into a room that resembled a gallery. Neil was about ten feet away when Mick whispered into her hair. "Are you okay? You look like a deer caught in the headlights."

Her spine stiffened. "I'm fine." She thought she had hidden her shock pretty well, but obviously she wasn't much of an actress, nor was there any point in trying to look or act informed any longer. Her cover was blown, and she was now lost. The best she could do was remain polite. But the Brillo pads still bothered her. How was *that* art?

It wasn't until later when they stopped into the Angel

Moon that she got her answer. Mick had asked if they could check out a blues singer his friend had told him about, and by that time, Ruthann's brain was so rattled with trying to process modern art that she'd wanted a drink.

"Okay, now tell me . . . what was with the Brillo pads?" she demanded after a quick sip on the strawberry daiquiri. Not as good as Eve's with the banana, but good. A moment of instantaneous awareness occurred when she realized that she was getting into this business of service. Every time she walked into an establishment, she scanned the place and tried to see what worked and what didn't. She was changing so quickly. . . .

Mick was laughing and didn't notice that something inside of her was slowly, almost gently altering. Like jazz and blues. Now she actually liked the music and was excited to hear someone new.

When had all this happened? When had she mentally stopped fighting them?

"Ruthann, if you could have seen your face in that man's office." Mick shook his head and again chuckled. "I swear to you . . . the muscles in my stomach hurt from trying not to laugh."

Ruthann burst into quick, appreciative laughter. "Oh, thank God. I thought it was just me. What were they doing there? I didn't know if it was some grand statement that went over my head, or if Neil had a cleaning obsession."

Mick put his drink down for fear of spilling it. "Wait . . . then you got it?"

Suddenly, Ruthann froze with indecision. What was he

talking about? Didn't he just imply that he thought the idea was also absurd? What the hell did *he* get that she didn't?

"Got what?" she finally answered, trying very hard to keep the sarcasm hidden.

He sipped his drink, then stared into her eyes. "The message."

"What message?" she demanded, and immediately felt herself fighting again the sensation of being close to this man.

Mick shook his head slightly. "Whatever it said to you. It's your message. That's what art is. It's to make you think and feel something."

"And what did you feel?"

He smiled, and Ruthann felt her resolve melting.

"I wanted to laugh, but after I looked into your eyes I was afraid you might think I was laughing at you, so I kept it inside. I want you to know, lady, I was in pain."

She relaxed and smiled back. "So what was the message?"

"For me, it was not to judge it, but to experience it. I felt silly."

"But you either liked it as art or didn't."

"It must have been a powerful piece, or we wouldn't be discussing it now. The artist was very successful."

"Because we're talking about it?"

"Exactly. How many times have you walked by a piece of art, any art, and nothing struck you? Then one will have the right color to draw your eye, a scene or a subject that seems to draw your focus? This particular person chose to artistically slap you on the back of the head, so to speak, to get your attention. Then he stirred up something inside of you, some emotion, silliness or absurdity, and then got you to think, to actually discuss it an hour after you'd seen it. I'd call that powerful."

Ruthann could feel the lines between her eyes deepen. She was thinking that hard. "So that was the point of it?"

His smile increased, and she immediately felt the sweet and seductive sensation of attraction race through her body.

"That's the point of all art forms. See, you did get it. You don't have to worry about liking it, unless you want to live with it. All you have to do is be open to it. Don't judge it. Let go and experience it."

He really did have a beautiful smile, beautiful eyes, beautiful face. . . . She had never before exactly thought of a man as beautiful. Handsome. Sexy. Manly. Yet Mick Larkin was also beautiful, and it came from inside and radiated out. Looking at him, she realized what a magnificent piece of art God had created in this man.

Immediately she stiffened. What in the world was she thinking? How poetically dumb. Mick Larkin wasn't her type, yet she had no idea any longer what her type was. Confused, she blurted out, "So why didn't you order the Brillo pads for our club if it's so powerful?"

He laughed. "Because Eve and I discussed what she wanted. The prints I chose were more like the style of Georgia O'Keeffe, and Matisse."

The lights dimmed and the combo started their set. Ruthann was relieved. Georgia O'Keeffe's work was easy. Matisse? She'd have to look that one up. She could learn. Like with jazz, she thought. Mick was right. If she opened herself to it, she just might understand the penis/navel orange/missile thing. Art, her mind corrected. It was a piece of art.

It was a piece, all right. Of what, she wasn't yet sure.

The blues singer was sensational. Her voice seemed to fill the room and evoke empathy in everyone who had suffered a broken heart. Sometimes she was sexy. Sometimes funny. Sometimes sad. By the time Ruthann left, she felt as if she had experienced a wide range of emotions. And not all of them were caused by the singer. Mick Larkin was definitely getting under her skin.

Hell, if she was honest with herself she would admit that it had first begun the day she'd met him and had taken him down to the basement of the Victorian. Ever since then she had fought it. Every time he had talked to her during the remodeling, she had tried to strengthen the wall between them. Now she could feel severe cracks in her defense. She was, in fact, standing on very shaky ground.

They left the club before midnight and walked to the parking garage. The city looked prettier at night with the lights outlining the taller buildings. There were more cabs patrolling the streets than traffic, and from an apartment window the strains of someone practicing a saxophone could be heard.

"Did you ever want to live in the city?" Mick asked.

She smiled and shook her head. "Not really. It's a nice place to visit, but I enjoy the space, the trees, the security across the river. The convenience would be nice, though. To walk out your door and do marketing, buy flowers . . . The small shops where you get to know the owners, instead of using the car for everything and trying to find it in megasupermarkets. Everything's a trade-off, I guess."

"Is it much different from living in California?"

She tensed. "How did you know I lived there?"

He chuckled. "Relax. Chill out. Eve told me."

"She did?" Ruthann was not pleased. "What else did she tell you?"

"That was about it. She said to ask you if I had any questions. So I'm asking."

Nodding, Ruthann breathed a sigh of relief. "I missed the changing of the seasons," she said. It was a safe answer.

"Were you happy?"

"No." The word popped out of her mouth before she could censor it.

"I'm sorry."

"Don't be. It was the result of my own choice."

He grinned and shook his head. Seeing that, Ruthann automatically demanded an explanation. "What? What's so funny?"

He stopped walking and looked at her. She stopped a few paces ahead and turned to see why he had paused.

"Ruthann Bucknum, you are the most intriguing woman I have ever met. I can't figure you out."

She didn't know whether to be flattered, insulted, or nervous. There was too much about her she didn't want him to know. A man like him, so refined and cultured, would never understand her living out of her car and begging for help. "There's nothing to figure out," she said evasively, and started walking toward the garage.

He caught up with her and said, "It's just that sometimes you act like a Stepford wife and then you'll come out with a statement that's so real, so enlightened, like your unhappiness in California was the result of your choices. Your still waters, lady, run very deep."

She barely heard the compliment. "What do you mean, a Stepford wife? I'm not even married." Yet how many times had she thought of herself just like that?

He threw back his head and laughed, producing a smile that was near dangerous in its kilowattage. When he looked at her, Ruthann actually felt the muscles in her legs weaken. She could sense the . . . What? Affection? It was radiating out from him and wrapping around her like a warm blanket. She was shocked to realize that she wanted to close the distance between them. She wanted to place her head against his chest and allow his arms to envelop her.

They stared into each other's eyes for what seemed like eternity. It could have been only a few seconds, but it felt as if they had somehow altered her conception of time. Her heart pumped adrenaline throughout her system as he walked the two feet that separated them.

"What was your maiden name?"

"Why?"

"I want to know who you were before you made the wrong choices, before you allowed the fear to rule your life. What was your name when you were happy, Ruthann?"

His words seemed mesmerizing, and she tried to make her brain work. "Gustofferson. Don't laugh."

He didn't. He reached out his hand and gently—oh God, how gently—traced her jawline until he rested his long index finger on her chin. "What would you do, Ruthann Gustofferson, if I kissed you now? Would you be afraid?"

"Yes." It was a mere whisper, a sound that came up from her throat in an odd swirling mixture of yearning and dismay.

"Don't be," he whispered back and smiled. "I respect you, and I would never do anything to hurt you, Ruthann. Don't you know that yet?"

There was nothing around them. The buildings seemed to disappear from her peripheral vision. The night noise of the city was replaced by a faint buzzing in her ears. Oh God, was she going to faint? And his finger felt as if it were emitting a branding heat on her chin. She might faint. She might humiliate herself and faint on Spruce Street in Center City, Philadelphia, and be taken to the emergency room and have to explain that it had been years since anyone had kissed her with more than a cursory greeting and she had never, ever, kissed anyone like Mick Larkin and then she would start crying and tell some poor ER intern her life story and . . .

"Don't you?" he repeated.

"Yes," she finally admitted, "but I'm afraid."

"Why? Why do you have to be so determined to withdraw to yourself? You aren't really living as God meant you to be if you're afraid to participate in life."

She couldn't take it anymore. She couldn't think. She was amazed that her knees hadn't buckled yet, that she was still standing. All she could do was stare into his warm brown eyes that seemed to be filled with tenderness, understanding, and compassion. She really was going to faint if he didn't shut up.

"If you're going to do it, then do it." Her mouth opened in shock. She didn't just say that. She didn't!

His hand slid through her hair until his palms cupped the base of her skull and his thumbs gently caressed her ears. "Thank you," he whispered into her mouth just before his lips captured hers.

It was soft and warm and tender, a mere grazing of skin and sensations. And she felt it race through her body, down to her toes, through the cement, and connect to the core of the earth before shooting back up and settling on his lips. When he pulled back slightly and smiled into her eyes, she muttered exactly what was on her mind.

"Oh, Lord . . ."

He laughed and pulled her into his arms. Softly running his hands over her back, he whispered into her hair, "See what happens when you walk through fear?"

She giggled like an inexperienced teenager after her first kiss. The feel of him wrapped around her was nearly overwhelming. She felt safe. Protected. Adored. And it seemed achingly familiar, as if she'd known what this felt like and had been searching for it her entire life. Or at least since she was twenty-two and kissed by Joe Moran.

"Hey, man . . . can you spare a dollar for a cup of coffee?"

They broke apart at the sound of a raspy male voice.

A street person held out his hand in supplication and Mick reached into his pants pocket to withdraw the money.

Handing the man a five-dollar bill, he said, "Get some food with that, okay?"

"Sure. Thanks," the man said, then looked down at the bill in his fingers. "Thanks a lot, bro."

Mick nodded, and the man left so quickly that it seemed as though he vanished before their eyes.

Her entire body stiffened, and she felt as though ice water had been thrown at her.

"Are you okay?" Mick asked, pushing a strand of her hair behind her ear.

She instinctively recoiled from his touch, and her heart broke when she saw the disappointment in Mick's expression. "I'm fine," she whispered, and started walking again. "It's late. We'd better hurry before the garage closes."

He didn't say anything, and she was grateful. How could she explain that her past had just slapped her in the face?

CHAPTER 9

"Something's afoot in very conservative Limbaugh-land. As we've reported, the once quiet town of Chelsea, New Jersey, was shaken to its very foundation by an explosion of truth and gunfire two months ago. *Bold Copy* was the first to expose the details when it revealed the names of the Misbehaving Missionaries who were using a struggling orphanage in Central America as a front for sex, tax evasion, and bigamy. Chelsea is still reeling from the shock of learning that the so-called Good Samaritans were none other than its most prominent citizens."

The television screen filled with the image of Doug Vansciver leaving the hospital while shielding his face with his hand. Quickly, the footage was replaced with a shot of Susan walking out of the police station with her lawyer trying to field questions. As Monty Clarke's voice droned on in the most scandalized and dramatic tones, the screen showed a quick montage of the men involved, avoiding Monty's cross-examinations.

"Besides those innocent children in Guatemala, who have been sacrificed for greed and sex, there are other victims. Victims much closer to home. For weeks, we have been trying to interview the wives, to get their perspective, and it's only recently that they have begun to talk. The only problem is we haven't quite learned anything, since they all say the same thing."

Margie Callahan was stopped in front of Shop-Rite, holding two heavy bags and trying to keep her teenage son from pushing Monty out of the way.

"I have nothing to say to you. Ask Eve Cameron."

Sally Donaldson was trying to back into a parellel parking space when Monty shoved his microphone in her face. She looked startled, then outraged. "I have nothing to say. Ask Eve Cameron."

Christine Gararra was leaving church when Monty and his faithful cameraman ran up to her and demanded to know if she had found comfort inside from the terrible betrayal of her husband. "Please move," she muttered while looking over her shoulder at a very disapproving Father Welty, who stood four steps up. "I have nothing to say. Ask Eve Cameron."

Molly actually smiled when it was her turn. "Ask Eve Cameron."

"Ask Eve Cameron."

"Ask Eve Cameron."

After three more wives gave the same answer, Monty's voice returned as the screen was filled with freeze-framed footage of Eve at the nursery, dressed in sweats and a Phillies baseball cap. She was looking to the right of the lens and almost snarling at something out of camera range.

"Who is Eve Cameron? This is the woman with all the answers? The only thing we can definitely report is that Eve Cameron, the first of the wives to have completed her divorce, has moved away from Chelsea to Montarose. She's living in a magnificent Victorian home . . ."

Pictures were shown.

". . . and is involved in some sort of business venture that appears to include a restaurant being renovated on Route 73 in Marlton, minutes away from Chelsea and its scandal."

The screen showed footage of men using a large crane to dismantle the Laveretti's sign.

"By checking with local officials, it has been confirmed that this once large Italian restaurant will be some sort of cabaret and the opening will take place this weekend. Who is this woman who seems to have thumbed her nose at the world?"

The unflattering picture of Eve Cameron returned to the TV screen.

"Who is this fiery woman? And why won't she talk? What's her secret?"

The regular host of *Bold Copy* took over as Monty's report finished, and then broke to a commercial. Before the ad could broadcast, the screen was instantly and blessedly black.

Eve placed the remote control on the desk and sat back in her chair. A satisfied smile started at the corners of her lips and quickly spread.

Looking to her left, she started to laugh but stopped herself. "What do you think?"

Ruthann was still shaking her head, as if she couldn't even conjure up the words to form an answer.

"Come on. It was perfect, right?"

"How did you know it would work?" Ruthann managed to ask, even though she still looked speechless.

"It had to," Eve said truthfully. "It was the only plan we had. The group talked about it for weeks and we all agreed to keep our dignity, no matter what he did. I just never counted on old Monty there making me look like the Mad Hatter."

Mick laughed and stood up. He crossed the small office space from his chair to Eve's desk in three paces. Holding out his hand, he said, "Congratulations. That was the best media manipulation I've ever known about before it happened. You pulled it off. Great publicity. This place is gonna be jammin' on Friday night. Hope you're prepared."

Eve crossed her fingers and looked to Ruthann. "How are we doing with the menu? Is Chaz ready?" She grimaced. "Do we really have to call him *Chaz?* He won't go for Charles? Or Charlie?"

Mick chuckled, and Ruthann shot him a glaring frown. "Oh, excuse me, and Mick isn't a nickname? What's your real name, anyway?"

"Michael."

Eve held up her hands. "People. People. Calm down. We don't have time for this. We agreed to settle all differences of opinion in a calm and quick manner. Whatever is going on between you two, keep it out of the club, all right?"

Ruthann and Mick both seemed to back down, like two fighters returning to their corners. Eve breathed a sigh of relief. "Okay, now, we have no choice but to accept Chaz's preference where his name is concerned. Who knows, it worked for Cher and Madonna."

Not getting the smiles she was hoping for, Eve cleared her throat. "However, when it comes to the menu, Chaz will defer to *our* preference. Now, have we decided on the Long Island Duckling with Japanese plum sauce?"

"Gets my thumbs-up," Mick said, avoiding making eye contact with Ruthann.

"Mine too," she told Eve. *"If* Chaz can lower the sugar content in the sauce. He keeps forgetting he's competing with the desserts."

Eve nodded. "Okay. Dinner menu is finally decided. We have French, Italian, American, Southwestern, and Vegetarian. All agreed?"

"Agreed."

Eve crossed off the menu from her list. "Okay, Mick, you hand-delivered the ads, right? They'll appear in Thursday's papers?"

"Full-page ads in the weekend entertainment sections. You won't be able to miss them."

"Perfect." Eve smiled her appreciation and picked up her schedule. Sitting back, she studied the list. "All the uniforms arrived and everyone has them. Did the jackets come for the valet parking guys?"

"We were promised delivery tomorrow. If they don't

show up with UPS, I'll call and demand overnight delivery," Ruthann said.

Eve thought about all they had accomplished in such a short time. Licenses, hassles with the health inspector, insurances, renovations, utility transfers, whether to lease or buy the building outright, and the accounting nightmare . . . When she had done the accounting for Cameron Computers fifteen years ago, it had been a simple matter of debits and credits and payroll deductions. Sixty-seven employees, a dozen suppliers, and the meticulous demands of the IRS had forced her to hire a CPA for the club.

Decisions . . . Every day she was becoming more like a professional hurdler, while she watched her money dwindle away. One of the biggest decisions was what the help should wear. She wanted to make sure that everyone was happy: management, staff, and customers. Thus, navy pants and skirts with white shirts and tiny navy bow ties were the uniform. Everyone was issued three complete uniforms, and she had even arranged for a cleaning service once a week to make things easier. It was an added expense, but she had a good staff and she wanted to keep them loyal.

"Mick, how are we doing with Jasmine?" Eve pictured the exotic singer and the man who played for her. They were a hot Philly group that was on the verge of making it big, and Eve felt blessed that Mick was able to book them on such short notice. She figured Mick had used his charm, and had possibly divulged that this opening might receive national attention.

"They're coming in"—he checked his watch—"in

about twenty minutes to set up and do a sound check. If there's nothing else, I think I'll go out and double-check the equipment myself."

Eve glanced at the list and placed it back on the desk. She looked at the two people in front of her. Good people. Good friends. "Thanks, guys. I think we have everything under control. The only thing left is to call Monty Clarke, pretend to cave in to his media pressure, and invite him to the opening for the interview."

Mick grinned. "I'd say good luck, but I doubt you'll need it. I think Monty will jump at the chance. He's already put himself on the line with this Limbaughland scandal thing. He's got to wrap it up somehow. And now you're the only answer." Not looking at Ruthann, he added, "I'll be outside if you need me."

"Thanks, Mick. None of this would have been possible without all your hard work. The club looks magnificent."

"Hey, lady . . . I'm just a soldier working under your command," he said as he opened the office door. "I wouldn't have missed it for anything."

When they were alone, Eve murmured, "He's an exceptional man."

Ruthann chose to change the subject. "When are you calling *Bold Copy*? Monty Clarke has left fourteen messages at home, and somehow he's found out this number. Ginny's taken three calls from him already."

Thinking of the very capable manager she had hired away from a club in Philadelphia, Eve said, "Tell Ginny I'm handling it, and not to speak with him again. The fewer people involved in this, the better."

Ruthann got up and smoothed her new linen skirt over

her hips. "I'll talk to her now. She's doing an orientation with the staff. She wants to know what to do with walk-ins trying to make reservations for Friday."

"We take them." Eve shook her head with amazement. "We haven't even advertised, and people are coming in off the street to see what's going on. We're going to do it, Ruthann. We're going to be a success."

"You're the success, Eve. *You've* made this happen. The rest of us are just swept along."

"Then why aren't you happy?"

Ruthann shrugged her shoulders. "I'm happy. I'm just not jumping up and down so you can see it."

Eve leaned forward and rested her elbows on the polished oak desk. "It's more than that and you know it. What happened between you and Mick? You came back from Philly two weeks ago and you've been avoiding him ever since. When you're forced to be in his company you look for something to argue about. What's going on?"

Ruthann stared at her for a few moments, as if deciding whether to talk. Finally she shook her head and opened the door to leave. "Nothing. We've got too much riding on this to let differing personalities upset the applecart now. We'll work it out, or we won't. Don't worry about it."

"Ruthann, you should know that I'm going to offer Mick a partnership. I'm forming Cameron and Company, an alliance of people I can trust. If all this works out the way we think it will, then you and Mick and I will be partners for a long time. You need to deal with whatever it is and come to some sort of working relationship."

"I said okay. I'll do it."

Eve's gaze connected with Ruthann's and held. "I know I've been busy, but if you want to talk about it I'm here now."

Ruthann's eyes seemed to fill, yet she swallowed down the threatening tears. "I'm fine. And you have enough on your plate with all this."

"Listen to me. You're important. You've worked so hard in the last two months and now is the time for you to enjoy it, but something is holding you back. Why can't you just admit you're attracted to the man? Why does that scare you so much? Hell, even I find him attractive, and I'm a confirmed divorcée . . . or whatever a divorced woman who'll never remarry is called these days. Mick Larkin is an extraordinary man, and any woman should feel flattered that—"

"He's so great," Ruthann interrupted, "then why don't you go out with him?"

Eve smiled. "We've covered this before. Because he's not interested in me. He's interested in you. More than interested, I'd say. Though why, when you treat him so poorly, I'll never know. Maybe he sees something worth it in you, beyond all the bullshit you're throwing in his face lately."

"Bullshit?" Ruthann closed the door and turned to her. "How can you say that? You don't even know what happened."

"Then tell me, Ruthann," Eve said gently. "What did

happen? Something changed you back into that suspicious, closed-off woman."

"You paint such a pretty picture that he'd have to be crazy to be attracted to me."

Grinning, Eve said, "You don't get it, do you? You're a beautiful person, inside and out. You don't even see the men that look at you when you pass. The women that admire your appearance and your skills, and want to get to know you. You're so busy being defensive, so afraid someone will see you for who you really are, that you miss it. You're just like Mick. You can't be ignored. You're two of a kind, kiddo. Neither one of you will ever blend into the crowd. He knows who he is and is comfortable with that. You can see it in the way he carries himself, the way he conducts his business, the way he treats everyone who crosses his path. He's . . . I don't know . . . honorable and balanced. You're still in some kind of denial of your uniqueness, your talents and triumphs."

She didn't get a response, but she could see that her words were at least penetrating that hard shell Ruthann had reconstructed around herself. "Damn, Ruthann . . . you should see the way you look at him. I think you're the only person around here that can't see how you feel about that man. What is it? What's holding you back? Just say it and we can deal with it."

Ruthann stood in front of the door and leaned against it. Something inside of her seemed to collapse and she whispered, "I don't know anymore, Eve. I want to believe what you say, but the truth is . . . Mick and I *are* different. He's successful. Charismatic. Open. I don't know . . . I wish I were like that, but I'm not that strong. And I can't change who I really am, any more than Mick can change who he is. Our . . . backgrounds are too different."

Disappointment surged up inside of Eve, yet she knew when to retreat. This was something she wasn't sure how to handle. "Mick doesn't have to change, Ruthann. The question is—can you?"

Biting her lip, Ruthann looked helpless as she shook her head and opened the door to leave.

Eve stared at the polished brass handle on the door and felt a wave of sadness envelop her. It was obvious how those two felt about each other. What amazed her was that it had all taken place without a single date. Unless one could call that night they went to Philly alone a date. What had happened that night to scare Ruthann so? Mick had acted hurt, then resentful, which was strange for someone who tried to be so fair. Something had struck a nerve in both of them that night.

Had they gone to bed? No. Eve shook her head and sat back in her leather chair. Leaning against the comfortable headrest, she studied the ceiling as she tried to recall the exact night. Even though they had been getting along fine then, she didn't think either one of them would've hopped into bed. They were more like two teenagers who were drawn to each other by an intense attraction, trying to do the right thing. That's why she had sent them alone to Neil's studio. She'd already seen the studio during her initial discussion with the art teacher, and she knew it would blow Ruthann's rigid mind. She and Mick *had* to have talked about it. And Mick had dropped Ruthann off after midnight. They had to have done something for hours. Whatever it was had resulted in Ruthann stealing glances in Mick's direction that could only be described as a sad longing. And Mick was now too angry with Ruthann to notice.

She closed her eyes and fervently wished that the two of them would work out their problems, but it was not her life and she was determined not to interfere anymore. She had meddled enough by throwing them together that night, and it had exploded in her face. She wasn't a matchmaker, and she didn't even know if she really believed in love any longer.

She was now a businesswoman.

She straightened, and picked up the paper with *Bold Copy*'s main number and Monty Clarke's extension. There was still work to be done.

Taking a deep breath, she picked up a pencil and used the eraser to punch in the numbers. It took four rings to be answered, and then she sat for another minute listening to an automated voice guide her through the options. When she finally heard the one that said to dial an extension if she knew it, Eve almost yelled out with frustration. How she hated these things. She swore that she would never use it in her business. People need to speak to a live person, not a machine. It was too impersonal. She didn't care how much money was saved. She thought it was technologically rude. Calming herself, she dialed Monty's extension and quickly pushed her hair back out of her eyes as she mentally cleared her mind.

This was not the time to let petty annoyances interfere with her plans.

"Monty Clarke's office."

"Monty Clarke, please." Eve held her breath.

"He's unavailable. May I take a message?"

"This is Eve Cameron in New Jersey. I believe Mr. Clarke has been trying to reach me, and I'm returning his call."

There was a moment of silence as the secretary recovered. "Yes, Ms. Cameron, and thank you. I know he'll be disappointed to have missed your call. Is there a number where he can reach you?"

The eagerness in the woman's voice would have been flattering in any other circumstance. In this case, Eve knew she only wanted to please her boss. Gossip was the motivation, and Eve was merely the helpless subject this week fidgeting under Monty Clarke's magnifying glass. The thought made her actually squirm, and she decided to use it to her advantage this time.

"Please tell Mr. Clarke that I called. I'm very busy myself right now, and I just wanted to let him know that—"

"It's very important to him, Ms. Cameron. If you could just give me a number where he can reach you, I'll page him now and—"

"Excuse me," Eve interrupted, and took back control of the conversation. "Please tell Mr. Clarke that if he wishes to speak with me again, I will grant him an interview this Friday night at eight P.M. in my restaurant. I believe from this afternoon's telecast that he knows the location."

"Friday. Eight o'clock." Eve could almost see the woman scribbling down information. "You understand that this will be a taped interview?"

Eve took her time. The woman was being pushy. She had probably picked the right business to get into, and would do well trying to intimidate others.

Feigning resistance, Eve said, "I'm not comfortable being on television. I don't like having my privacy invaded."

"Yes, I'm sure, but Mr. Clarke only does taped interviews. It's to protect everyone."

From the libel suits that probably threaten him daily, Eve thought. "All right, then. I suppose this is the only way to end this ugly period in all our lives. Please tell Mr. Clarke that this is the only interview I will give him. After Friday night, I will not discuss this again. There is no need for him to call me back. I will see him Friday. Thank you."

She hung up and let her breath out in a long sigh. The tension eased from her body and she relaxed in her chair. She'd done it. Everything was in motion. Now all she had to do was wait.

Minutes later she heard musical instruments being tuned and a smile returned to her lips. She fought the urge to run out to the stage and watch. Let Mick handle this. She would go out when Jasmine and her band were comfortable with the room. Excitement surged up inside of her as she thought of the last two months. Mick and his relentless crew of men. Ruthann and herself. It hadn't been easy, but they'd run a good race against time, had persevered, and were almost at the finish line. A few more days would tell the story. After opening night she would sit down and take it all in. Right now it would be overwhelming.

The door swung open and Ruthann gripped the handle. "Eve. Come with me. You have to see this."

She nearly jumped out of her chair. "What? What's

wrong?" she demanded. "See, I knew I shouldn't have been patting myself on the back. Something had to blow it. What is it?"

Ruthann said nothing. She grabbed Eve's hand and led her out of the office, through a hallway, and into the main dining room. Rushing past Mick and the band, Eve barely had time to wave a greeting to Jasmine before Ruthann pulled her to the entrance.

Ruthann stood in back of Eve and pointed her to the busy highway. "Look."

Eve's mouth opened with awe as she watched a sign, five feet by twenty feet, being raised high in the air by the same crane that had removed Laveretti's. Men stood underneath holding ropes to help guide it into place.

"My God . . ."

"It's really going to happen, Eve. You did it."

Tears came to her eyes and she was filled with such gratitude that speech seemed inadequate. She merely nodded and wiped at her cheeks.

Suddenly, she jumped in surprise when she heard a loud popping noise behind her. Eve and Ruthann turned around to see Mick, Jasmine, the band, Ginny, servers, bartenders, and busboys all holding up glasses of champagne.

Ginny held a silver tray with two long-stemmed glasses while Mick poured the wine into them. When Eve and Ruthann were served, he held up his glass in a toast.

"To Eve Cameron . . . who turned a dream into inspiration and inspiration into reality. Here's to the lady who made it all happen. And here's to Nirvana. May all who enter reach that glorious state."

"To Nirvana!"

A chorus of voices joined together, and Eve openly cried with appreciation. Stopping herself, she raised her own glass and drank deeply.

At that moment in time, she was already there.

CHAPTER 10

It had been Ruthann's suggestion to sit on the porch to watch the sunset. Eve was delighted with the offer, for it might be one of the last times they would be able to relax like this. After Friday night, their lives would alter and shift. Again.

Sometimes it amazed her how much she had changed in such a short time. There were nights she lay awake in bed and stared out her window into the darkened sky, just letting her mind wander. It was then she came up with solutions to problems, fantasized about the future, and revisited her past. She thought about her life, her marriage, Ruthann, that poor child conceived and abandoned in an orphanage, the restaurant, Mick, the scandal . . . and always, Jamie.

Her heart still ached every single day of her life, yet it shocked her to realize that some days she was so busy she forgot why. Then it would come to her in a wave of pain and guilt. How could she have forgotten her son for even one hour, let alone the day? Then her brain would reassure her that she was merely passing through another stage of grief. As Mick had said, she was getting whole again.

Staring out into the night, she wondered if she weren't manic-depressive. Or depressive-manic, since two months ago she didn't even want to get out of bed, let alone the house—and now she was rarely in the brand-new one she had just bought. To an outsider she might appear manic, but she knew it was inspiration. It was a challenge, but it was also like a shot in the arm. She felt *alive* again. Not like the old Eve Cameron. Now she had more energy, more patience, more appreciation. And always her mind would wander to the ultimate question.

If she was appreciative, then where was she directing that appreciation? At life? What was life, anyway? Her mind wouldn't even let her go down that endless path of questions. Was it directed at God? Hadn't she lost faith in a religious God? Weren't the scientists right in their Big Bang theory? But somehow her instincts led her back to believing that some higher intelligence must have directed that creation. She wondered what name to call it. God wasn't reverent enough anymore. That name had been used and abused so much that the word, the sound of it, didn't seem to do justice to such a power. She hadn't figured it out, and it might take her the rest of her life, but at least she had come to some peace about it. She was getting better. She felt it.

The front door swung open and Ruthann came out with two tall glasses. "Okay," she said as she handed a daiquiri to Eve, "tell me. Did I get it right this time?"

Eve smiled her thanks and took a sip. She let the frozen

mixture melt on her tongue before swallowing. "Mmm . . . absolutely delicious."

"But is it right? Does it taste like yours?"

"Yes." How many times would they go through this? Eve wondered.

Ruthann sipped hers and then shook her head. "You sure something's not off? Too much banana liqueur?"

Eve laughed. "You got it right, okay?"

A smile played at Ruthann's mouth. "Okay."

Neither woman spoke for a few minutes. It was a comfortable silence that each allowed and, in turn, received. In those minutes there was no need for words and they both knew it, for they were lost in thought as they watched the most ancient ritual of sunset.

"It's so beautiful and peaceful," Eve murmured finally. One of them always said that, or something like it. It was a respectful signal to the other that it was okay to talk.

"Look at those birds," Ruthann said, and pointed to the receding sun.

Eve watched the creatures soar with long graceful wings. "That's going to be us someday, Ruthann. Someday, we'll fly like that. We'll be free."

Her friend turned to her. "You are talking about our lives, right? You aren't thinking about trying to fly now, are you?"

Eve laughed. "You're crazy. I'm not."

"Excuse me? I was just asking because I seem to remember you being inspired once before on this very porch and we have a jazz club opening in three days to prove it. You get that look in your eye, and say in that voice, 'someday we'll fly like birds,' and sweetie, damn right I want to know what you mean. I can just see myself sky-diving, being hurled out of a plane, so you can experience the freedom of those birds. Eve, you make stuff happen. It's scary sometimes."

Eve giggled while listening to Ruthann rant. When she wanted to let go and relax, Ruthann was truly funny. "Give me a break," she pleaded, and then she thought about it. "You know, skydiving would be a good way to—"

"Stop it. Don't even let your mind go there. It was a joke."

Eve sat back and relaxed. "I know . . . but you got it wrong. I didn't make anything happen alone. I had help. Lots of help. You're a godsend, Ruthann." She sipped her drink and then sighed with contentment. The birds had flown from her view, and so she settled her vision on the stream of light from the sun that danced on the surface of the water. "Remember that first day, cleaning the old house? You said you thought we were meant to meet for a reason. I think maybe you're the one who makes things happen. You came into my life and everything changed for the better."

Ruthann made a depreciative noise with her mouth. "Right," she muttered. "I'm still not going skydiving, so forget it."

"I wasn't thinking that!" Eve protested with a laugh. "I swear I wasn't. I'm too scared for that."

"Okay, so what was the best time, the most adventurous thing you ever did?"

"Oh, come on," Eve complained. "Not again. I don't feel like playing. Can't we just sit out here and enjoy the view and the company without the trip down memory lane? We're going to be so busy from now on, and this evening might be one of the few times we can enjoy all this."

"I know," Ruthann said, "That's why we should do it now. Besides, you always fight me in the beginning and then you have fun. So knock off the reluctance and just get to it. Best adventure."

Sighing with defeat, Eve closed her eyes and thought about it. After thirty seconds, she said, "I don't know what to say. An adventure? I haven't led a very adventurous life. Unless you count marriage and childbirth. Which, if you take them to their conclusions, fits into both your best and worst category as to how the adventures turned out. There, do you want the years to date this annoying road map of memory lane? I know how important that is to you."

"Neither one counts, and I'm ignoring your sarcasm. What about your childhood? Didn't you and your friends ever go on adventures?"

Eve thought about it and grinned. "I had a friend in grade school. Ann Hegen. We were inseparable until high school. Then we sort of drifted apart."

"That's the adventure? You was robbed, sweetie. We all had best friends that went their own way in high school. Now, who's this?" Ruthann asked as a Jaguar sedan pulled into their driveway.

They both watched as Paul opened the door and got out.

"Anne and I went into spooky, deserted houses," Eve said quickly, before adding, "And this, I believe, is part of the adventure I spoke of a few minutes ago. See what happens when you live in the past, Ruthann. It haunts you."

"Stop," Ruthann whispered, trying to hold back a chuckle. "He's almost at the steps. He'll hear you."

Eve smiled at her ex-husband. "Paul. What brings you out this way?"

He was wearing the blue suit she had picked out at Boyd's and the silk tie she had matched perfectly with the material. He was obviously stopping on his way home from work. It took only moments for Eve to see that Paul looked older, not as neat, and decidedly upset. She felt an immediate, instinctive concern for his welfare, until she realized it wasn't any of her business any longer. How strange. . . .

"I need to speak with you. Hello," he acknowledged Ruthann before jamming his hands into his pockets and waiting for a response.

Ruthann nodded a greeting to Paul and then quickly rose. "I'll get dinner started."

"Thanks," Eve murmured, and watched as her friend left the porch. When they were alone, Eve invited Paul to sit down.

He took the seat vacated by Ruthann and rocked back and forth a few times without saying anything.

"Is something wrong with the company?" Eve couldn't figure out why he was there. The computer business was their last common thread.

"No," he finally answered. "I'm here because . . . Damn it, I don't even know how to say this."

She almost grinned. "Say it, Paul. You came out of your way to be here. You could have called."

"There's such insanity taking place, I don't even trust the phones with this."

"Sounds interesting." What did he want her to do? Drag it from him?

"It's not interesting! It's disgusting. And . . . and humiliating that I have to go around defending my wife like this."

She would not be goaded into an argument. She would remain calm, no matter what. It's what her brain said to do. Her mouth, however, seemed to have a mind of its own.

"I am not your wife," she said in a flat voice. "Ex-wife. And what are you defending me from, may I ask?"

"Where do I begin?" He ran his fingers through his hair and wisps of it stuck up on the side.

She fought the old urge to pat them into place, reminding herself that she was not this man's wife any longer. It was his hair, his head, and his appearance was not her concern.

"Since you're having such difficulty explaining your visit, Paul, would you like me to guess? Gossip brings you here to my home?"

"Not just gossip, Eve. People are getting angry."

She turned to face him. "Why is anyone angry because I'm getting on with my life?"

He seemed frustrated by her lack of understanding. "Eve, people are saying the real reason you divorced me is because . . ."

"Well, finish it," she said, waiting to hear the latest story.

"This is so hard, but with everything you've done in the

last few months . . . divorcing me, moving into this house, opening a restaurant, a *jazz* cabaret, for God's sake. What do you know about running a club?"

"I'm learning. I didn't know anything about running a computer business fifteen years ago, but I learned that. I do have a brain, Paul, and I know how to use it. Is that it? People are angry because I divorced you and I'm opening a club? What kind of people are these?"

"You refuse to see it, don't you? Some people think you're profiting by their misfortune. And they're not happy about it. Not happy at all."

"Whose misfortune? You and your cronies'? Is that what you call what happened? Misfortune? Like you just weren't lucky enough to get away with it for longer?"

"What about *Bold Copy* yesterday? Did you *see* yourself?"

"I thought it was pretty funny."

"Funny! You looked crazed! It was disgusting. And today that leech Monty Clarke announces that he's going to interview you at your club's opening? Tell me you're not using this mess to further your own interests."

"Of course I am. I'm not hiding that. Not any longer, anyway. Now that *Bold Copy* has committed to the interview publicly, I am perfectly willing to admit using them. Why shouldn't I have turned a negative thing into something positive? If it doesn't serve the interests of the Rotary Club, that's too bad. The wives agreed. You see, Paul, half of all the profit from opening night will be sent to that orphanage in Guatemala. No strings attached. And it will be sent in the names of the wives. That's what I'm telling Monty Clarke on Friday. That's what we want to say publicly."

He closed his eyes and blew his breath out, as though he'd been punched in the stomach. "It nevers ends," he muttered.

"Sure it will. Somebody else will screw up and make a mistake and it will catch the attention of the media, and you and I and everyone else involved in this mess will fade into obscurity again."

"Don't be so sure."

"That sounds ominous. Care to explain?"

"There are stories about you. About you and your friend. Ruthann."

The way he said Ruthann's name made her tighten with protection. "Are you going to tell me?" She actually held her breath.

"They're saying the two of you are lovers. Lesbians! I almost punched Doug Vansciver in the nuts for saying that, or whatever he has left of them after Susan got to him. Why the hell are you laughing?"

She had to put her drink down on the table to keep from spilling it. She held her hands to her stomach and laughed harder.

"You think it's funny?" he demanded. "Look at you. You still wear Jamie's clothes and you take in a strange woman and you buy a house together and then you live with her! Not just that—every time you're seen, you're with her. The two of you are joined at the goddamned hip!"

"She's my friend!" Eve managed to get out between belly laughs. "Oh, boy . . ." she finally said as her mirth subsided. "That's a good one. I can't wait to tell Ruthann."

"How can you take this so lightly? You've put yourself in the spotlight. A *national* spotlight, might I add. What do you think Monty Clarke is going to do with that on Friday night?"

"If he brings it up, I'll laugh in his face too. Paul, you were married to me. I think you know I'm heterosexual." She couldn't help it. She chuckled. It was so absurd, it was funny.

"People change."

She stopped laughing. "You can't be serious."

"Eve, you should have seen your face when Ruthann left. You followed her with your eyes until she closed the door. It's weird. It's like . . . I don't know . . ."

"Love?" Eve volunteered. "I do love her. She's as close to me as a sister, and I trust her with my life. I can't say that about too many people. But do I desire her sexually?" She tried not to smile at the ludicrous question. "No, Paul, so you can take your mind out of Doug Vansciver's gutter."

"I told you I almost punched Doug. I was defending you, damn it."

She let out a long sigh and prayed for patience. "Then thank you for that. I appreciate you informing me. Is there anything else?"

Taking his cue, he stood up and looked down at her. "I guess there's no hope, Eve? For us?"

She saw the pain in his eyes and wished she could say something to ease it. "I'm sorry" was all she managed.

He nodded and turned to leave. When he reached the bottom of the steps, he looked back. "Be careful."

"I will. Thanks." Tears formed in her eyes as she raised her hand and waved goodbye. How could she ever explain to him that she would never go back? That when she divorced him she must have also divorced her old life, because it just wasn't her any longer. All of that belonged to someone else who no longer existed.

He would never understand, and it would hurt even more.

"Are you okay? I heard the car leave."

Eve looked up at her friend. "Come, sit down," she asked gently. "There may be trouble at the opening."

"What happened?" Ruthann took her seat and stared at Eve with a worried expression. "What did he say?"

"It's really funny, when you think about it."

"What?"

"Listen, Paul wanted to tell me there's an ugly rumor being spread that you and I are having a . . . relationship."

"Huh? What are you saying? A relationship?"

Tact wasn't working. "That we're lovers," Eve said as bluntly as she could.

Ruthann stared at her for a few seconds until it sunk in. When Ruthann's mouth dropped open in shock, Eve couldn't help it—she laughed.

"You think this is funny?" Ruthann demanded. "Who would say such a thing?"

"The Misbehaving Missionaries, as Monty loves to call them. Or at least their leader, Doug Vansciver. They're just mad and frustrated, and looking to find some way to vent their frustration. I guess I was an easy target."

"What are you going to do?"

Eve shrugged. "There's really nothing to do, is there? It's ridiculous, and everyone who knows us will laugh when they hear it. I'm not worried."

Ruthann sat back and rocked furiously. Suddenly, she stopped. "What about the interview? What if Monty Clarke hears this? You know he'll find a way to bring it up. Oh, God . . ." Ruthann got up and started pacing the length of the porch. "Then he'll start looking into *my* background. And it'll all come out. How we really met—"

"Nobody knows the details about that except you and me," Eve interrupted.

Ruthann shook her head, as if saying that didn't matter. "Those shows are relentless. Look at all the lies they've told already. Right now they could be looking into my past. What if they find out I was homeless, that I couldn't find a job and was begging for money? Oh, God . . ." Ruthann hugged her waist and stared out to the river. "No matter how far you run, it's always there."

Standing up, Eve walked over to her. "Ruthann, stop this. So what if he finds out? You have nothing to be ashamed of, do you hear me? You tried everything else before that. It is not your fault that you slipped through the cracks of bureaucracy. Hold your head up. You weren't begging for money. You were begging for work."

"You don't understand. You don't know what it's like on the streets. You don't get respect for that. People give you platitudes, but not respect."

"Then you demand it. You survived a horror most people can't even imagine. That isn't you anymore. You're chained to the past, Ruthann, and you have to find a way to break free. You have to, kiddo, or it will take you down eventually." Eve ran her hand over Ruthann's back in sympathy. "And you don't deserve that. You've come too far to go back. Remember what you said to me in Jamie's room? About letting the past control me? That you either live in the present or the past, that's all there is? Why can't you practice what you preach? Why is it good enough for me, but not you?"

She left Ruthann at the railing and sat down. Rocking slowly, Eve fought for a way to break through the wall of fear around her friend. She knew about that wall. It had haunted her ever since Jamie was diagnosed with leukemia. It had slowly wrapped its possessive fingers around her mind and squeezed every time she tried to hope for a better future. Now she was again in battle with it, even though the fear was someone else's, but this time she knew her opponent. And she knew how to defeat it.

Fear. It's so very malignant, so very clever.

"You know, everybody's got something in their past that they fear or wish they could change. I do. Even Mick."

Ruthann looked over her shoulder. "Mick?"

There was the crack in the wall she was looking for.

"Sure. Nobody's perfect. Although he's as close as I've seen in many years. . . ."

"What does he fear?"

Eve shrugged. "It's his story. Ask him."

"It doesn't matter," Ruthann said.

Trying not to smile at Ruthann's transparency, Eve rocked back and forth and breathed in the evening air. This house was the best investment she would ever make.

Nothing could compare with this feeling of belonging, of really being home. She made a mental promise to never sell the place. Someday she would be an old lady rocking on this porch. The image was extremely comforting.

"It isn't real, you know."

Ruthann's brow furrowed. "What?"

"What you're feeling right now."

"Confusion? Because you're not making sense."

Eve grinned. "That fear that's taking control now. It isn't real."

Shaking her head, Ruthann turned and looked back out to the water. "It certainly feels real."

"That's because you're allowing it. You're staying in it and letting it take control."

"Oh, for God's sakes, Eve . . . not everybody is as strong as you."

Eve looked at her friend's back and wanted to hug her. They shared so much and still Ruthann didn't understand. "Listen to me, and get it this time, okay? Every single day of my life something makes me stop and holds me back from going forward. But I force myself to walk through it. For me to take control, not an emotion. That's what fear is, an emotion, and you allow it power. This house is a good example. You don't think I was afraid when I bought it? You don't think I stayed awake worrying? But I looked at all the information and made a decision. I was still afraid, but I forced myself to walk through it anyway.

"It was the same with Nirvana. I'm still scared, but I'm doing it, even if the Rotary Club of Chelsea thinks I've lost my mind and become a lesbian."

Ruthann smiled. "It sounds so ridiculous."

"Exactly. I don't care any longer what people think. It's my life, and I know right from wrong. Nobody has to tell me, or make up the rules for me. I can *feel* what's wrong or right. And so can you. You always have, you've just forgotten how to trust yourself."

"What does all that have to do with living on the streets? I'll never feel right about it. It was the most fearful, degrading time of my life."

Eve sighed, and hoped she could find the right words. "Mick happens to concur with what you said to me in Jamie's room. He agrees you can't change the past. Only the future. That it's a useless waste of time to cling to it and let it have power over you."

Ruthann turned around. "He said that?"

"Uh . . . huh. He's a very wise man."

"You two seem to have talked a lot."

"We have. You don't think I'd make him a partner in our company without learning as much about the man as possible? You may think I'm impulsive, but I'm not a stupid woman, Ruthann. We're very fortunate to have him with us now. He's been an integral part of all this. And it all started with you and this house. You changed my life, Rue . . . and all for the better. You, lady, make things happen. You just haven't realized it yet, because your self-esteem has taken such a bad beating-up since your marriage."

Eve thought about offering Ruthann her drink but decided against it. Even though Rue looked as though she could use one, Eve didn't want to lose the moment. Ruthann was listening.

"Look, you made the wrong choice in your marriage

and you stuck it out in some form of punishment or martyrdom. Then, in that state, you allowed your husband to control you, down to not being allowed to know about finances. When you finally get the courage to walk through all that fear, you wind up on the streets. I think it was because you never listened to yourself before then, and didn't act on what you felt was right."

Ruthann didn't say anything, and Eve hoped it was because she was thinking and not angry. Figuring she was in too far to retreat, Eve plunged forward.

"You don't regret leaving your marriage, even though as a result of that action you felt degraded on the streets. . . . Right?"

Ruthann thought about it for less than five seconds. "Right."

"Then it must have been the correct path to take. Do you regret meeting me, and all the outrageous decisions we've made that have brought you to this point of standing on this porch right now?"

"No. Never." Ruthann smiled, as if thinking back over the last few months.

"Wonderful." Eve's heart lightened with that smile and Ruthann's answer. "And what brought us together? Why were you outside of Shop-Rite that morning?"

Ruthann sat down in her rocker and answered, "I had just failed a job interview, and I was desperate."

"Why were you desperate?"

The words came out slowly. "I was living on the streets."

Eve felt like jumping up and yelling for joy, yet she remained seated. "So how can you be ashamed of that path?

Any more than you're ashamed of leaving your marriage? You're the lady with all the faith. It must have been the right course for you to be on at the time. You wouldn't have been there, Ruthann. We simply wouldn't have met. Who knows where either one of us would be right now if all those things didn't happen. I might have died in that house of a broken heart."

Eve turned and reached out to clasp her friend's hand. She needed her to finally understand. "You saved me, Ruthann Bucknum. I was sinking . . . fast. I have to honor whatever path brought you into my life. I'm just sorry, for your sake, that it was so hard and it filled you with so much fear. But you can triumph yet, if you can claim it for what it really was—merely a path that brought you to the present, where you are right now. That's it. In the end, that's all it really was, and you're through with it. When you do that, you take away the power of fear. And then you can really live, because finally you're free. But you're the only one who can do it. You have to walk through your fear alone."

Ruthann was staring at her with tears in her eyes. "As crazy as it sounds, it makes sense, doesn't it? If I didn't leave the marriage I wouldn't have been homeless and desperate. If I wasn't homeless and desperate, I wouldn't have been standing outside Shop-Rite that morning. And if I didn't meet you, I wouldn't be here on this porch."

She was shaking her head, letting it all sink in. "And my life is so much better here, now, than it was in California. And I'm much happier, more . . . I don't know . . . alive?"

"That's it. You just have this fear you can't let go of

yet. I know it sounds crazy for me to tell you to look at being homeless as anything less than fate knocking you on your behind, and I'm not saying that you must forget the horror that you experienced. But you can either learn to honor that experience and grow from it, or you can live in fear and let it control you the rest of your life. Those are your choices."

"Where did you learn this?" Ruthann whispered through her tears.

Eve smiled. "Mick. I told you he was an exceptional man. You should listen to him sometimes."

"Mick?" Suddenly the tears stopped. "What the hell did you two talk about, anyway?"

"Is that more than a hint of jealousy I hear in your voice?"

"Absolutely not," Ruthann protested. "Why would I be jealous of you talking to him? That's ridiculous. I couldn't care less. It's just that this kind of knowledge doesn't usually come out in ordinary conversation. It must have been one heck of a discussion."

Eve studied the shoreline across the road. "It was," she whispered back. "He helped me find some peace in Jamie's death. I will always be grateful to him for that."

"I didn't know," Ruthann murmured.

"I know. . . . He found me in the attic with Jamie's things and we talked." Eve looked to her right and playfully slapped Ruthann's thigh. "Hey, you want to hear something else? When I thanked him after our talk, you know what he said?"

"What?"

"He merely hugged me and said, 'Someday, just pass it

on.' " Eve chuckled. "Weird, huh? I thought he meant working with people who've lost children, or something like that, and I didn't think I would have the strength for it. But this is what he meant. . . . Just helping someone through our own experiences, and if we've gained any wisdom on making it through life, then pass it on at the right time."

"God, who *is* he, Eve? He's so deep that sometimes he scares me. It's like he's too good to be true."

"I know what you mean," she agreed. "He's obviously intelligent, good-looking, kind, compassionate, great sense of humor, terrific with his hands, secure with who he is . . . Need I go on?"

Ruthann was trying very hard not to smile. "No."

"And guess what's shaken this perfect man?"

"What?" The eagerness in Ruthann's voice was unmistakable.

"You, Rue. . . . He's in love with you and you can't see it. Or you're too afraid to see it."

"He is not. We don't even know each other that well." Ruthann studied the scenery and persisted in her denial. "We can't even talk to each other anymore without starting an argument."

"That's because you pulled away from him after the two of you went to Philly. Something happened that night."

Ruthann sighed deeply. "All right. So he kissed me," she finally admitted.

Eve grinned. "And . . . ?"

"And I wanted him to. *And* it was wonderful," she added reluctantly.

"I'm sorry. I don't see the problem, unless you're talking about the differences in your—"

"The problem," Ruthann cut in, "was that we were interrupted by a man begging for a dollar for a cup of coffee. It was too close to home, Evie. Like I was being told where I came from would always be an issue, it would always haunt me. After that, I just pulled away . . ."

"Rather than face your fear and walk through it," Eve finished for her. *"That's* what this has been about? You're afraid for Mick to find out you were homeless? You feel unworthy, or something?"

"Yes."

"Damn it, can't you see now how it's holding you back? Not just from facing the possibility that *Bold Copy* may tell the world—and so what?—but from really living, and participating in life. I hate to say it but, my friend, this is sheer stupidity. You're thinking like a child, not a woman. And we're talking about a secure man here, not some untrustworthy, weak, and immature jackass like Ed Bucknum who needed to build his ego at the expense of yours. Mick would never use that information to keep you down. Now . . . imagine what he's been thinking about why you pulled away."

Silence followed, and Eve was determined that she wouldn't be the one to break it. This was it for Ruthann, her moment of truth. If they had tried skydiving, it would be like getting on the damn plane. Decisions. Sometimes they require a great deal of courage. And sometimes you just do it anyway.

"Can I borrow the car?"

Eve had to bite the inside of her cheek not to smile. "Sure."

"I just need to go for a drive by myself. It used to help me in California."

"I remember you telling me. The keys are on the counter in the kitchen."

Ruthann stood up and walked toward the door. "Oh, and the chicken should be finished. I'll take it out of the oven and—"

"Go," Eve interrupted, and allowed the smile. "I can handle my own dinner, thank you."

The door had barely closed behind her when Ruthann opened it again. "And Eve?"

She looked at her friend. "Yes?"

"You really are going to have to buy something absolutely stunning for the opening. And not those boring business suits and clothes you wore when you were married. It's time to start dressing like a woman again. You're very pretty when you're out of sweats and a T-shirt, you know?"

"What?"

"Work your way through that fear," Ruthann said, winking and closing the door.

Eve stared at the painted wood for ten seconds before she burst out laughing. Damn, Ruthann was a quick student. She had certainly passed it on.

CHAPTER 11

She knew she was driving around in circles, but she couldn't bring herself to make that left-hand turn onto his street. Every time she came upon it she hesitated, yet kept on going around the block. She felt like a silly high school kid, and knew if Eve could see her she would be laughing at her foolishness. And her fear.

It's just that she had no idea what to say to him after he answered the door. She should have a plan or something, mapped out in her head before she faced him.

What if Mick was so mad he wouldn't talk to her? Then what? Tell him she just wanted to see his face and apologize?

She passed his street without turning. Again.

Come on, come on . . . she mentally prodded. *You can do this.*

As she drove through the small residential neighborhood, she taxed her brain for a plausible reason to be showing up at his door. Something about the club? The house? She could tell him about Paul's visit? That's it! She was worried about the opening because there might be trouble, and she thought he should know. Perfect!

She pressed her foot down on the accelerator, now in a hurry to see Willowbrook Lane. When she spied the green street sign, she didn't even think. She turned.

Already knowing what his house looked like from the times Eve had dropped off papers, Ruthann drove right to it. This time she wasn't staying in the car. She was getting out. Right?

Her hand reached for the door handle and stopped.

What was she doing? Going to a man's house to throw herself at him, like some woman in a soap opera? Like that crazy erotic dream? Oh God, no . . .

Walk through your fear. It was as if she could hear Eve's voice inside her head. But she was still scared. *Do it anyway.*

"Aaa . . . hhh." It was a small primal yell that prompted her to grab the handle and pull. The door opened and Ruthann hurried out before she changed her mind again. She rushed up the sidewalk to the sleek, modern town house.

Passing the landscaping, Ruthann almost groaned when she saw the perfectly manicured shrubs. Wasn't there anything that man couldn't do well? She ran her hand over her stomach, felt the smooth soft chambray fabric of her jumper, and quickly checked to make sure the sleeves of her white T-shirt were still rolled up. Did she look okay? Too dressy? Maybe jeans would have been better? But she hadn't even stopped to think when she grabbed the car keys and left. Don't think, she told herself. Knock. Pick up your hand and knock on the stupid door.

She did.

He was wearing a cream colored T-shirt, tan linen shorts with those little pleats at the waistband, and Top-Siders without socks. And those legs. Those damn cycling legs . . .

"Ruthann?"

She quickly looked up to his face. He appeared confused. At least they had something in common at the moment.

"Hi." God. What else was she supposed to say?

"Hi," he answered, looking around for Eve.

"I'm here alone." That was stupid. He could see that now. "I . . . ah, I need to talk to you."

"All right." He opened the door fully. "Come in."

She walked past him into a small foyer. There was a narrow table against the wall and a framed print above it. Matisse. She recognized that now. The keys to his Jeep were thrown on the table next to that old leather bookbag-looking attaché case.

He closed the front door and walked past her to lead her into the living room. She was impressed. Just like him, it was refined and understated in a modern, contemporary way. Copper leather furniture sat on top of a deep-green rug. The tables were of glass and that kind of copper that turns green. He could even decorate better than she could!

"What's up?"

Such a simple question. It was her moment of truth, and she didn't know how to begin. What was it again? Perspiration started to break out at the back of her neck. Paul. Something about Paul . . .

"Paul came today and we're in trouble." There. She said something.

"Who's Paul? Sit down. And why are we in trouble?"

She sank into the leather couch. And sank some more. She had never sat on anything so soft and so comfortable in her life. It must be filled with down or something. It made her want to curl up in it and . . . Oh, Lord. Mick was staring at her with an expectant expression. She needed to pull it together, or she would wind up looking like a fool.

Right. As if she didn't already.

"Paul is Eve's ex-husband, and he came today because the Rotary Club of Chelsea is angry at Eve for opening the club and talking to *Bold Copy* and so they're spreading ugly rumors about us to discredit us if they can." There, she had got it out in one breath. She sat back and waited for his reaction.

"Wait a minute," he said, running his fingers over the tiny black curls that covered his head. "You want to take that again? One crisis at a time."

She sighed with frustration. "Paul is Eve's ex-husband," she said as patiently as she could.

"I understand that. Why is the Rotary Club angry?"

"I don't know. They're ticked off because Eve is opening the club. She said they need someone to take out their frustrations on, and she made the perfect target. Yesterday's *Bold Copy* set them off, I think."

He shook his head, as if still not getting it. "And so . . . ? What kind of rumors can they be spreading?"

Oh, shit. She never intended to talk about that!

"Are you going to tell me?"

Do it anyway.

She took a deep breath. "They're saying that Eve and I are involved in a relationship. That we're . . . you know . . . gay. And it'll probably be brought up Friday at the TV interview."

He leaned forward, resting his elbows on his knees. "Are you? I never thought of it before, but it would explain a whole lot."

She sucked in her breath when she caught his meaning. "Well, I'm not. A lesbian, I mean. But if I were, I certainly wouldn't try to hide it."

"Good. On both counts." He smiled.

She loved his smile. His whole face lit up, like a delighted child on Christmas morning. She just couldn't help smiling in return. She caught herself being drawn to him again, and stopped smiling. "So what should we do?"

"Is there anything to do?"

There had to be, or she had no reason for bothering the man and sitting in his living room. What was it!

"I'm not sure," she answered truthfully. "But I thought you should know about it." This wasn't going as planned. Hell, she had nothing planned but this flimsy excuse. And she'd exhausted that. Now what?

"Well, thanks for coming over and letting me know. Can I get you something to drink?"

Okay, she wasn't dead in the water yet. "Thanks," she said in a casual voice.

"What would you like?"

"What do you have?" She really did sound like a teenager. Make a damn decision!

"Coffee. Tea. Soda. Wine." He got up and added, "Sorry I can't make you a daiquiri. Don't have the mix. I've got rum and scotch and—"

"I've already had a daiquiri tonight. Eve and I had one." Did she sound like she drank every night? "I'll have a Coke. Thanks."

"How about Pepsi?"

"Fine."

He left her alone in the living room, and she sat back on the sofa to wait for his return. Looking around, she spied pictures of his family: an older couple, probably an anniversary picture of his parents, judging from the flowers on the woman's shoulder; a young boy and a girl . . . niece and nephew? Hold it. What if they were his children? She didn't know if he had ever been married. Oh, Lord, stop looking!

Magazines were on the large square coffee table, and she leaned forward to see what Mick Larkin chose in reading material.

Architectural Digest. Time. Newsweek. Travel and Leisure. Cycling. TV Guide. It was comforting to know that he watched TV every once in a while. When she heard him closing the refrigerator, she leaned back and pushed her hair off her forehead, trying to look casual, relaxed, normal.

"Here you are," Mick said, holding out a wide glass tumbler of soda.

"Thank you." Ruthann took the glass and had to hold it with two hands as she let it rest on her thighs. He placed a brass coaster on the table, and she sighed with relief. At least she wouldn't have to do a balancing act with the awkward glass. She tried to pick it up with one hand and didn't trust the strength in her wrist to carry it to her mouth. What was she supposed to do? Hold it with two hands, like a toddler who was learning to drink from a cup? The image was embarrassing, and she had embarrassed herself quite enough this evening. She would use one hand like an adult, and take a polite sip before putting it—

"Oh, no . . ." Drops of Pepsi sloshed over the rim and spotted the beautiful copper leather. Mortified, Ruthann quickly put the glass on the coaster and stood up.

Staring at the dark stains, she wrung her hands together. "Oh, Mick, I'm so sorry. How could I be this clumsy? Quick, get a cloth or something!"

He was standing next to her. "Calm down, Ruthann. I'll take care of it."

He left her staring at the damage, and Ruthann felt tears well up in her eyes. Why was she here? What was she doing? Nothing was going as she planned. But she hadn't planned anything! All she wanted was to see Mick and explain everything, and then maybe he would hold her in his arms again and—

"Here, let me see to it," Mick said, and tried to get past her to the couch.

"No, let me," she insisted, and tried to take the dish towel from his hands.

"Look, I know how to take care of this. Just move and let me get to it, okay?" He again tried to step in front of her.

"I did it," she protested. "I'll clean it up." She pulled on the towel to make her point.

"It's Scotchgarded. I know how to do this." He pulled back, trying to take ownership of the dish towel.

"Just let go, will you, please? I'll clean up my own mess!"

He let go.

She experienced three seconds of panic as her sense of balance deserted her. Almost without knowing how, she landed in the corner of the couch, with one leg on the floor and the other dangling in the air. It was not dignified, ladylike, or even normal.

And Mick Larkin laughed. He laughed! He stuck out his long arm and continued to chuckle. "Give me your hand. I'll help you up."

She slapped it away, pushed the skirt of her jumper over her legs, and struggled to extricate herself from the soft cushions. It was like trying to rise from a vat of butter.

Knowing he would never be able to think of her as graceful, she managed to slide off the thing and stand up. She took a deep breath and said, "You are the most annoying man I have ever met in my entire life."

He merely laughed. "No, I'm not. You're just mad because you're embarrassed. You forgot about the law of cause and effect."

"That's another thing," she stated in an indignant voice as she watched him blot the stains. "You think you know *everything*. Give Mick Larkin a situation and he comes up with the perfect answer or the perfect quote. Funny, but they're never yours, Mick."

"I really didn't say everything I said."

"What?"

He didn't look up from his task. "Yogi Berra."

She had the uncontrollable, childish urge to connect her foot with his behind. Instead she picked up her glass—with two hands—and walked away from him to the opposite side of the coffee table. She drank carefully, hoping the soda would somehow put out the fire inside of her. How she would love to best him in something! Anything!

He finished cleaning the stains and balled the towel up in his hands. Sitting down opposite her, he casually threw the towel onto the table and leaned back against the cushions.

"Okay, now why don't you tell me the real reason you came here."

Her body stiffened. "What do you mean, the real reason? I told you . . . Paul and the interview on Friday." Her brain refused to function any further. Dear God, it was as if the man could read her thoughts. Was she that transparent?

He waited patiently. He didn't prod, or try to help with her confusion. It seemed the longer she remained silent, the stronger the voice inside her head became.

Just walk through it. Go on. . . .

It was too scary. How could she put herself on the line and just blurt out everything? He might think she was crazy; he might . . . *Do it anyway.* But she wasn't even sure how to begin.

Taking a deep breath, she said, "I want to apologize for the way I've been treating you. It's my problem, not yours. Eve was right. We can't keep sniping at each other with the opening in a few days. We have to find a way to settle this." It might not be much, but at least it was a beginning and the truth.

He held her with a piercing gaze that seemed to fuse her right into the soft cushion behind her back. "I agree, and your apology is accepted. Where do we begin?"

"I don't know," she murmured, feeling that intense drawing sensation pulling her toward him again.

"Maybe the best place to begin is after I kissed you. What happened?"

It felt like a direct hit, nailing her to the point. There certainly wasn't any beating around the bush with this man. She inhaled deeply, needing to take in oxygen and rationality.

"I don't know where to begin with this," she said truthfully. Her heart was beating so hard, she thought he must be able to hear it. The muscles in her stomach clenched with fear. Do it. Do it, her mind cheered. You're so close. . . .

"Should I start with my marriage and the way I allowed someone else to take over my mind and my will? Maybe I should just skip over that and begin when I came back here to New Jersey. . . . Things didn't work out the way I had thought they would and . . ." She could feel the tightening at the back of her throat, as if her emotions were trying to close off the words. Tears swelled in her eyes, yet she fought both. She had come too far now to back down. "I wound up living out of my car. Until even that gave out. And . . . that's when I met Eve. She saved me. I owe her my life."

She could feel a fat tear slide down her cheek, and she quickly wiped it away as Mick got up and walked around the coffee table. She saw sympathy and compassion in his expression, not scorn. He took a folded handkerchief from the pocket of his shorts and handed it to her before sitting down on the love seat.

Sniffling, Ruthann patted her cheek and smelled the fresh scent of Tide on the soft, ironed handkerchief. In spite of everything, she chuckled.

"You okay?" Mick asked.

She shook her head. "I don't know . . ." She held out the handkerchief in front of her. "How do you do it? How do you always do the right thing? I mean, how many men actually go around with neatly pressed handkerchiefs in their pockets today?"

Smiling, he said. "My grandfather told me a man always keeps a hundred-dollar bill in his wallet and a clean handkerchief in his pocket. Both for emergencies. Now, let's get back to what you just said. You have a unique way of condensing everything into a short synopsis. Do we have to stay with this abridged version? Or would you elaborate? Like, how old were you when you got married, and what was his name?"

Ruthann sipped her Pepsi and realized she had done it. She had told him the truth about being homeless and he had calmly accepted it. Now he wanted to know more. Encouraged, she decided to walk all the way through it this time. Maybe Eve was right. If you're scared of something, just do it anyway.

"It wouldn't have mattered how old I was when I met Ed Bucknum. I did us both a great disservice when I accepted his proposal of marriage . . ."

And so she told him her story, not sparing herself in the

narration. She told him of her marriage, her inability to conceive, her feelings of failure, the sense of drying up inside emotionally, of merely going through the motions. He listened and didn't ask questions, yet she could almost feel his compassion. He just let her talk, and she found herself telling him even more than she'd told Eve: The excitement of setting out on her own, even though she didn't have much money. The disappointment and disillusionments of getting back to New Jersey. She told him of trying to deal with the system, of panicking when she realized she couldn't pay for a room, of wandering through the airport, the utter humiliation of being asked to leave and seek out a shelter.

It was harder to explain the horrors she'd experienced during that time, most at the hands of males, but she forced herself to get it out. She felt if she could do this, if she could finally walk through this darkness with honesty, she would somehow come into sunlight again. It was as if a faucet had been turned on in her mind and nothing could stop the flow until it was completely drained.

"After they stole my purse I thought of suicide, but I wasn't brave enough to throw myself in front of a bus, and I didn't have money for anything else." She smiled sadly. "I couldn't get a job. I couldn't get help. I couldn't even sleep in a shelter. The car was the only place, and I didn't even have enough gas, or a garage, to kill myself in. If I wasn't so defeated, I would have laughed about it."

"What stopped you?"

It was the first thing he'd said in over twenty-five minutes. Ruthann stared at him and read the complete acceptance in his expression. This man cared.

Something happened to her then, something so weird, so strange, that she would later wonder in awe at the immediacy. She knew in that wonderful moment that Mick Larkin was her friend. And he would remain so for the rest of her life. It didn't matter if they never got further than that. It was so simple and instinctive. It was more than a feeling. It was a knowing.

She could trust him.

"I was sleeping in the car and, well, I guess sleeping isn't quite true. I stayed awake most of the night thinking and worrying, sure someone or something would attack at any time. Sometimes I wondered if I wasn't already dead, and this was just hell. Surely, I was paying for something I had done wrong. I came very close to losing it. Who knows, maybe I did have a nervous breakdown. . . . Anyway, every once in a while, some semblance of humanity would surface in me and I'd pull out the glove compartment just to see the light come on. It saved on the battery not to use the radio, and that light, for even those two or three seconds, would connect me again."

She realized she was putting off answering his question and got to the point. "One night, I was in the midst of a full-blown panic attack. Death seemed easier than fighting it off. At least there'd be an end to it. I grabbed for the glove-compartment door and stared into the box, desperately trying to find reason again, when suddenly a couple of folded papers caught my eye. And there was my license and insurance card and birth certificate. I looked at my picture. I read my name. I was somebody! I mattered. I belonged somewhere. I didn't know where, but I knew it wasn't huddled in the front seat of a car, terrified to live."

Mick was smiling.

Encouraged, she went on. "Funny thing is, I had been opening that door for weeks, sometimes two, three times a night, and hadn't seen them before. I thought they were in my purse when it was stolen. But there it was, on the very night I needed it. So I started believing in life again. I tried to hold on. I went on job interviews, but I knew I didn't make a good impression. I refused to let myself believe that something wasn't around the corner, something to make it through the night for. When I met Eve, I had just lost out on another job and I was desperate for money. I found the lid to a dress box in a Dumpster, and I wrote in big letters, 'I Will Work For Food.' "

She shook her head and stared at the brass dolphins that stood on the coffee table. One was large and the other very small. Mother and child. So very beautiful, so graceful, so comforting . . . "I was at the end of my rope, when this small woman comes up and hands me a bag of food and two twenty-dollar bills. She saved my life, Mick."

He was nodding. "She's a special woman, all right."

Ruthann smiled. "Tell me about it. Sometimes I wonder if she's real. When you think of everything she's gone through, her persistence in creating her own future, and the strength of that woman . . . She's a tough act to follow."

"You're a pretty formidable act yourself, lady."

Ruthann shot him a quick glance. "Me?"

Again he smiled, and her heart melted at the sight. She quickly looked away.

"Yes, you. You sell yourself short. Far too short."

The compliment warmed her inside, but she knew she

had to be truthful. It was, in fact, part of why she came to him. "I wish I could agree, but I'm realistic. I'm damaged, Mick, and I know it. I don't trust people easily. I especially don't trust men."

"That's understandable, but you have to—"

"Wait," she interrupted. "The worst part of all of it is that . . ." She paused, fighting back the tears again. It was so hard to admit this out loud. "I don't trust myself anymore. I'm still living in a state of fear. And I don't think I'll ever completely trust life again."

"Oh, Ruthann . . ."

He reached for her, yet she held him off with her hand. It was almost impossible to talk for the bitter acid rising in her throat.

"Listen to me. That's why after you kissed me, I pulled away. Seeing that man asking you for money hit too close to home. It scared me, and I pushed you away. I'll never be the same, Mick. Those experiences changed me in a way that I can't fully explain. The woman who left California is gone. I've altered somehow."

He sat back and blew his breath out in a hard rush. Shaking his head, he asked, "Is it possible you've got it all turned upside down?"

She merely looked at him. If there was another way to change this mess, she'd sure like to hear it.

"Couldn't it just be possible that you've changed, yes, but you've really changed for the better? You haven't realized it yet, because you haven't gone far enough away from it to get a true overview?"

"Eve tried the same thing. I realize I had to go through it or I wouldn't know Eve, or have the life I have now. I know all that. But it doesn't change how I feel. I'm still scared."

"You're here. And you don't look scared."

Despite how she felt, she chuckled. "You should have seen me. I had to talk myself out of the car."

"But you did it."

She looked around the living room. "I did, didn't I?"

"And I'm very glad."

Suddenly she felt shy. It wasn't like before, when she was avoiding him. It was . . . pleasing.

"Can I tell you something?"

She nodded, almost afraid to hear what he was about to say. She caught herself and tried to relax.

"The past doesn't exist."

"What?" It wasn't anything like what she thought he might say.

"Can you see it now, touch it now, smell it now?"

"I can feel it," she countered. "Sometimes."

He almost grinned. "Do you really think you can feel it, or is it just the memory of it you feel?"

"The memory, of course. It's not happening right now. . . ." Suddenly she stopped speaking. Something important was taking place inside her head. She could feel something, some clarity, shining through the darkness that had surrounded her.

Mick didn't say anything for a few moments, as if sensing he should give her time to contemplate her own words.

"The memory is just something you've stored in your head, like information on a computer disk. But it doesn't have form. It has no power, unless you choose to give it.

If the memory is just thoughts, it doesn't exist. It isn't real. It can't hurt you anymore. Whatever happened you survived it, hopefully learned something from it, and maybe it's time to let it go. You've been hurting long enough, Ruthann. And now it isn't the streets or the people who attacked you. You're doing it to yourself. There is no past. It's not real. It's gone."

"But everything could change and get bad again." She knew she sounded like a child, yet she couldn't keep the urgency from her voice.

"Honey, every single thing on this planet is changing constantly. Nothing stays the same. Nothing."

It was true. "Then I'm afraid of change."

He laughed, and threw his arm over the back of the love seat. She noticed that.

"People aren't afraid of change. People fear what something will become when the change takes place, the result of the action. And it's merely the not knowing, the unknown, that we're so afraid of, that holds us back. It isn't the change."

She stared at the dolphins. "This is too deep for me," she muttered.

He laughed again and playfully tapped her shoulder. "Are you hungry? C'mon, let's eat something. I have dinner cooking."

She immediately felt apologetic and pressed her palm down into the cushion in order to rise. "I'm so sorry. I shouldn't have gone on like that. I've interrupted your dinner."

He quickly brought his hand over her head and covered

her fingers with his warm ones. "Ruthann, I'm asking you to stay for dinner. I have enough."

She couldn't think. She was staring at their hands, his dark complexion contrasting with her own lighter one.

"Please?"

She blinked twice, as if shaking herself out of a daydream. "Okay. Sure. Thanks."

"Let's go. How does spaghetti and meatballs sound?"

They seemed to get up in unison, and she waited for him to show her the way. "Sounds wonderful. I've got to say this. . . . Sometimes Chaz's cooking is over the top. Sometimes I just want good old plain food."

He stopped and looked at her. "Well, I don't know if you'll change your mind. I don't have your gift, Ruthann. My sauce comes out of a jar."

Her smile was wide. Finally she did something better than he did. He wasn't perfect. Just damn near.

CHAPTER 12

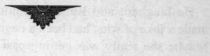

"I'm trying to impress you, you know."

Ruthann looked up shyly from her place at the table. "There's no need to. I suppose I'll admit it now. You did that a long time ago." Yet she was pleased by his admission.

He had quickly set the table using shiny black plates and burgundy place mats and napkins, with brass rings around them. She had a feeling he didn't use them very often, for they felt and looked new. When he placed smoky gray wineglasses at the top of the knives, she knew he was making a special effort. He had refused her help and had insisted that she sit down at the table and relax. That way they could still talk. And the first thing he had said again reflected exactly what she had been thinking. It was both weird and wonderful.

He boiled water for the pasta and puttered comfortably around the kitchen as he pulled together the last stages of dinner. "So then I could have just let you eat out of the pot and saved myself the trouble?"

She concentrated on him again and smiled. "Remember who you're talking to. I have eaten not just out of a pot, but out of the bloody can."

He laughed, and Ruthann couldn't believe she had made a joke of what had been a degrading time in her life. Maybe she really was getting past it. "Somehow, Mick Larkin, I can't see you eating out of the pot. It would destroy the perfect image."

She thought he would see the humor in it. But he didn't laugh.

"Where the hell did you get the idea that my image was perfect?"

She felt nailed again, as if his gaze was piercing the now flimsy shell of protection around her. "I don't know," she mumbled. "You always do everything right. I keep trying to find fault with you, and the only thing I can find is that you can't cook." She looked to the boiling pasta. "You'd better check that before it overflows."

He lowered the flame under the pot and stirred the rolling spaghetti. "Look, Ruthann, get this straight, right at the beginning here. . . . I'm just like you, a human being trying to make it through life. I love to eat out of the pot. Saves time and dishes, and it reminds me of college. I have more damn imperfections than I ever want to admit, but that's all I look at most of them as anymore—imperfections. They don't make the whole piece bad and sometimes they give it character. If they really start to bother me, I work on them until I don't notice them anymore.

But I never forget that the piece itself is imperfect. That's what makes it unique."

"See, like that," she pointed out. "How do you come up with stuff like that?"

He smiled. "I learned a long time ago that nothing anyone said to me was new. It had all been said or written down before I ever showed up. Made me have a deep respect for the wisdom of those who had come before me. That's why I quote them. Drives you crazy, right?"

She looked down so he couldn't see her expression. "Yes," she answered truthfully, and then chuckled. "I almost kicked you in the pants over the Yogi Berra gem in the living room."

Laughing, he drained the pasta into a colander. "Quotes fascinate me. Sometimes the meaning pops right out and you can hold it immediately, but sometimes it's more of a riddle and it makes you think, opens your mind to exploration. Those are the ones I love. It can take me days or months, or even years before I can finally say, 'I think I've got it.'"

"Sounds like work," she said as she watched him slide the spaghetti into a large glass bowl and pour sauce over it.

"Wisdom can come from Socrates, your next-door neighbor, the lyrics of a song, or a little old Jewish lady in Atlantic City. You just have to be open and ready to hear it." He brought the bowl to the table and placed it in the center. Satisfied with his efforts, he smiled at her. "Let's eat."

She nodded, even though her brain was still trying to assimilate what he'd said. She had the feeling that he was slowly moving toward something, and he wanted her to understand. She felt like a student, like the novice Kwai Chang Cain in *Kung Fu*, desperately trying to mentally snatch the pebble from Mick's hand.

They passed the serving dishes back and forth and ate for a few minutes in a companionable silence. Ruthann was surprised to find herself so at ease with him. When she had gotten into the car and driven over here, she'd never entertained the thought that she might be eating dinner in Mick's kitchen. It felt . . . comfortable, normal. Scared where those emotions might be taking her, she blurted out, "Was there really an old Jewish lady in Atlantic City?"

He swallowed quickly, as if surprised by her question, and then grinned like a kid who had been caught with his hand in the cookie jar. "So you really listened. That one just slipped out."

Intrigued by his answer, she went forward. "That wasn't just a metaphor? There was an old woman in Atlantic City?"

"Sometimes I used to wonder at that myself, but I swear I saw her." He twirled the strands of spaghetti around his fork and added, "I never even found out her name."

"She was that important to you?"

As if losing interest in his food, he placed his fork down and stared at her. "She saved my life."

Ruthann didn't know how to answer, or if an answer was even required. She wanted to ask questions. She was *dying* to ask questions, but something told her that this was too personal. She wouldn't pry. He deserved her respect. Instead, she broke eye contact and resumed eating.

After a few minutes he said, "Thank you."

Her eyes widened at his words. "For what?"

"For not asking, for not snooping around inside my head. I appreciate it."

She shrugged. "It's your story and your choice whether to share it. Believe me, I understand."

"You would. You, more than anyone."

"Huh?"

There was that killer smile again. If her mouth wasn't full, she would have groaned.

"Believe me, Ruthann, you're not the only one who has things in the past that they wish never happened. I have more than my share, and one day twelve years ago I almost let them take me down. That's when I met her."

She smiled and pushed her plate forward to let her elbows rest on the table. "You're going to tell me, aren't you?"

He laughed. "You look like a little kid. Don't get excited, it's not that entertaining."

"I want to hear anyway."

He took another bite of food and picked up his wineglass. Studying the wine, he said, "My parents died when I was twenty-two, a senior in college. My sister was still in high school and my younger brother was nineteen. Such a tough age for a male. I tried to help him, but Kevin was always in trouble, even as a kid. There was a strong part of him that was a rebel. He couldn't stand control, or even direction, and would start a fight as easily as talking to you. My parents . . . Their minister told them Kevin was just a bad seed, but Mom never gave up on him. She prayed and prayed, sure God would turn her boy around."

Shaking his head, he completely forgot about dinner and sat back in the chair. "After my parents both died in a car accident, Kevin went wild. Stealing. Drugs. I got him out of jail four times in fifteen months. Five years of that, of forcing him into rehab, of going to therapy with him myself, and I didn't know what to do anymore. I had just started in business when he came to me and wanted money. I knew he'd use it for drugs, so I finally said no. For the first time, I refused. Tough love, you know?"

She merely nodded, afraid to interrupt his thoughts.

"I never heard from him again. Two weeks later, I got a call from the Philadelphia police telling me that my brother was dead. Shot through the head during some drug deal in North Philly."

"Oh, Mick . . . I'm so sorry."

He nodded, as though accepting her sympathy, and then drained his glass of wine. He seemed to take a few moments to pull his thoughts together. Refilling both their glasses, he said, "I nearly lost it. I blamed myself. I was too busy, too involved with my own life, too focused on the success track. I should have been there for him, no matter what." He looked around the kitchen and added, "Did a lot of drinkin', smokin', and whorin' . . . but nothing could take away the pain and guilt. I had men working for me and depending on me. I was in charge. It was my business, and I wasn't showing up for work."

"You were grieving," Ruthann whispered as tears came into her eyes. "Surely you've forgiven yourself for that."

"In time, I did. I wound up in Atlantic City, and for the

life of me I don't know why, because gambling was never my thing. I was drinking pretty heavily, and by morning I had lost eighteen hundred dollars at blackjack." He grinned and shook his head, as if still not believing it. "Sobered me up *real* fast. You see, that was the payroll for the four men working for me. They had rents and mortgages, car payments. Like most, they were living week to week, and I had lost it all."

"What did you do?"

"I wandered out of the casino and the sun blasted me in the face, like the wrath of God sending a blinding headache. I felt like I deserved it, and then I bought a cup of coffee and sat down on one of those benches at the boardwalk that looks out over the ocean. I was trying to think of some way to end it all. So I know what you meant, Ruthann. I've been there. I finally understood Kevin. He had spent his life doing it slowly. I wanted it fast. I was sitting there trying to think of where I could buy a gun, when this old woman sits down next to me. Quiet as a mouse, so I ignored her. Never said anything for ten minutes."

He actually smiled again, only this time it wasn't quite as bright. "Then about five seagulls started flying in front of us. You know the way they hover, looking for food?"

She nodded.

"This woman says to me, 'Wouldn't you love to fly like that, to be able to be above it all and look down at everything? Maybe we'd understand it better if we weren't in the midst of it all the time.' "

Ruthann's eyes were wide. "No."

"Yes. Nearly freaked me out. I stared at that old woman

with a heavy Jewish accent, hair that looked like a shel-
lacked helmet, and couldn't believe she had said that. She
smiled at me and started talking about losing her husband
years before and how they had always come to Atlantic
City, way before the casinos were built. And then she
talked about him. . . . She told me things that morning that
blew my mind open. In less than one hour, she made me
see that the past didn't exist, that I couldn't change it.
That life was merely a play within a play, and we were the
actors. She made me question who the director and writer
and producer were. And finally suggested that I could be
all of them. That it was my choice. That it's always our
choice. It's called free will."

"You never found out her name?"

He shook his head. "She put her hand over mine and
said, 'There's my friend. I have to go.' When I tried to
stop her, she said, 'Don't forget, a great person isn't one
who never makes mistakes. A great person is one who
learns the lessons from their mistakes, picks themselves
up, and goes on. *That's* a successful human being. And the
only thing that's important is that if you've found part of
the key to living on this planet, then pass it on. That's our
purpose, and the reason for our struggles . . . to find the
way back home again.' "

"Mick . . . that's beautiful."

"She walked away, and the crowd on the boardwalk
seemed to swallow her up. I must have sat there for two
hours, thinking about everything she'd said. I kept hoping
she would come back. I kept wondering what had made
her sit down next to me, of all people, and then tell me the

exact thing I needed to hear. It was more than coincidence. It seemed almost divine."

He appeared to pull away from his musing and added, "Anyway, I finally got up, went home, and sold what little furniture and valuables I had and paid the men. Then I started over and I began reading again, like when I was in college. And listening, that was even more important. Only this time, I wasn't trying to educate my mind to make a better living. I was trying to find more little old Jewish ladies . . . and they took the form of philosophers, garbagemen, checkout clerks in Kmart, and all the writers of the major religions. There's truth all around us, and none of it is new. We only think it is if we haven't heard it before." He breathed heavily and brought the wine to his mouth. "So that's it. That's the reason for the quotes."

She took a deep breath to steady herself. "I'll never listen to them the same way again."

Chuckling, Mick placed the wineglass on the table and picked up his fork. "And now our dinner is cold. Do you want me to stick yours in the microwave to heat it up?"

He was changing the subject, and she allowed it. She pulled her plate back in front of her. "Absolutely not. I love cold spaghetti." And she ate a mouthful to prove it.

"Ahh . . . If Chaz could see you now."

She grinned. "He really is a food snob, isn't he?"

"He is, but he's also a great chef."

"We were lucky to get him."

"I think he's the lucky one. I have a feeling that after Friday night, a lot of people's lives are going to be changed for the better."

She swallowed and reached for her wine. "I hope

you're right. So much is depending on Nirvana being a success."

"Let's get back to us."

She was so surprised by his statement that she nearly choked on her wine. "Us?" she asked in a hoarse voice. "I didn't know there was an us."

"I think we're friends, aren't we? We've just spent the last hour and a half becoming intimate."

"Is that what you'd call it? It felt like opening a vein and bleeding."

He smiled. "Did it really? Come on . . . it was far less painful than you thought it would be. Right?"

"You read me too well, Mick Larkin. See, I think *that's* the reason you've irritated me so much. I always felt like you could read my thoughts."

"No one's ever said that before." He grinned. "I can't read your thoughts, Ruthann. If I could, I wouldn't be this nervous."

"You're nervous? You don't look it."

"I'm trying not to, while at the same time trying to figure out how to ask you if we could do this again."

"Eat dinner?"

"Eat dinner alone. I think once Nirvana gets kickin', none of us will have the time or even feel like eating out a lot." He shook his head. "It's going to change our lives, Ruthann."

"Mine is changed already. If I wasn't scared that Eve might lose her investment, it would be the most exciting time in my life."

"I think her investment is going to pay off very well. Try to relax and enjoy what's happening."

"Easy for you to say. You have Jasmine and her group. You know they'll be wonderful. I have temperamental Chaz and the kitchen help to worry about."

"You'll do fine. I think you're the only person in the place that Chaz has any respect for. Everyone else loves you. Almost as much as Eve."

"They do?" She was amazed to hear him say that.

"Why does that surprise you? You're a remarkable woman. You have a natural respect for a person's space and dignity. Now I know where you acquired that."

She didn't want to talk about that time anymore. Instead, it was her turn to change the subject. "What about you, Mick? Was that your parents' picture in the living room?"

He nodded. "And Denise's kids. My sister," he explained.

"You've never married?" She knew it was personal, damn personal, yet she *had* to finally ask.

His expression clouded slightly. "Once. About two years after Kevin died. It lasted about a year, and we both parted as friends. Strained friends. After that . . ." He shrugged his shoulders. "Dating and relationships. It's the story of the eighties and nineties. I guess I just got tired of it and took a sabbatical for the last few years."

"From dating?"

"From relationships. There's a kind of paranoia going on, about finding Mr./Ms. Right, a kind of shopping around while looking for the perfect soul mate. And that we're incomplete if we don't have one in our lives."

"You don't believe in soul mates? I thought you would."

"I don't believe you have just one. I read once that relationships are like assignments from God. That we're put together with this particular person, at this particular time in our lives, for a reason: to help each other and to grow individually into a more whole human being. Sometimes the growth is painful, and today we're so ready to say, 'you've made a mistake, and I'm outta here.' When the mistake might have been the very thing both people have to work through to grow. Fear is the opposite of love, not hate. So fear and our ego are what drives us away and we don't learn the lesson. Then the universe just sends someone else, and we have to repeat the process all over again until we finally get it."

"That's why so many people swear they'll never again get involved with . . . say, a person who cheats or drinks or is abusive, and then six months into the relationship they find it's the same story all over again?"

He nodded. "Like attracts like. It's scientific. It's the attraction, the energy, we're sending out. It's buried so deep that most of us aren't even conscious of it. We're attracting . . . putting out invisible energy fields that attract those things into our lives, and it's not going to change until *we* change. Until we somehow forgive and release the cheater or alcoholic or abuser, and not judge."

She blew her breath out in a rush. "Easier said than done." Shaking her head, she added, "But how do you forgive someone who's hurt you? Say the abuser. You stay in the relationship?"

"You always remove yourself from danger, but you work toward forgiveness. Not for that person's benefit. For your own. You don't deserve to carry around that heavy burden of bitterness. And feeling like a victim is a heavy burden. It was their drama, their soul play, and maybe you had a supporting role, or even co-starred in it, but once you know you've given everything you have to it, once you've learned the lesson from it, you can exit stage left not just with forgiveness, but with peace. Remember, you've participated in this stage of the play, you agreed to this on a deep subconscious level, or you wouldn't have been in the relationship. It doesn't matter if they don't get it in the end, if they don't learn the lesson. What matters is that you did. You can move forward. And that's when we alter our energy field. Now we're attracting someone into our life without the need for those lessons."

He winked at her. "Now we might meet someone who's beautiful, intelligent, and strong. Someone who is loyal and trustworthy, who has a deep respect for another's pain, who's gone through some tough soul lessons and come out on the other side. Maybe all they need to learn is how to trust again. Sounds like a good reason to come out of a sabbatical to me."

She blushed. She could actually feel it creeping up from her neck to settle on her cheekbones. "I don't know what to say," she whispered, twisting the napkin in her hands.

"Maybe you could say you'll at least look over the script and consider if you want a costarring role." He leaned forward and placed his finger under her chin. Raising her face to look at him, he smiled and added, "I have never met a woman like you, Ruthann. You're everything I just said, and so much more. And you haven't even realized it yet."

The tears stung her eyes and her throat. She didn't want to cry, yet she couldn't seem to stop. Something deep within her felt as if it was breaking apart . . . that wall around her heart seemed to be falling away faster than she could repair it. She felt like her finger was in the dike and the damn dike was disintegrating with her tears.

He brushed away the dampness from her cheeks and sat back. "Just think about it," he said softly. "Now . . . how about some coffee?"

She wanted to curl up in his arms, to cry out all the hurt and fear, to become that woman he spoke of. Instead she sniffled, wiped her face, and murmured, "Sure. Coffee sounds great."

He smiled and rose from the table. He brought his plate with him to the sink and Ruthann started to clear her own space. He didn't object, or tell her to sit down. He accepted her help silently, with merely a smile, when she brought the bowl of spaghetti to the counter.

"Do you want to save this?" she asked, suddenly shy at standing so close to him.

He looked into the bowl and sort of grimaced. "I don't know . . . I think I'll save the meatballs for my neighbor's dog and toss the pasta." He opened a drawer and brought out a ZipLoc bag.

She took it from his hand. "Here, let me."

He released the bag. "See, I won't fight you on this one."

Grinning at the memory of their tug-of-war in the living room earlier, Ruthann said, "Thanks. I'm not usually that stubborn."

"Really?" He raised his eyebrows, as if questioning her statement.

She straightened defensively. "Really, Mick. I mean it. You . . . just haven't seen my best side, that's all."

His smile lit his eyes as he put the utensils into the sink and slowly turned to her. She was standing in the corner of the counter, and he moved close to stand in front of her. He placed his hands on the counter, on either side of her, trapping her.

His face was so close to hers that she could feel his breath on her cheeks. "Ruthann Gustofferson Bucknum . . . I cannot wait to see your best side. I think, lady, you will blow my mind."

She laughed nervously. "Well, don't expect much." Oh, Lord, he was going to kiss her. She could feel it, an invisible pull of energy and awareness that was drawing her toward him.

She studied his eyes, lit with merriment and desire . . . his mouth, his lips, full and well-defined, waiting . . . waiting . . . It was her move, and she felt paralyzed.

Do it, her mind urged. But what if he thought she was bold or . . . *Do it anyway!*

She leaned forward and whispered, "I don't know what's happening. I just want you to kiss me."

The merriment left his eyes and was completely replaced with a desire so deep and so profound that its intensity shocked her. Slowly, so very slowly, he let his lips graze against her own, and she actually groaned at the sensation. His hands came up to stroke her back and gently pull her body against his.

Chest to chest, mouth to mouth, they stared into each other's eyes. It was as if she could actually feel his thirst and yearning transferring to her body, sense his thoughts of desire and hunger. It wasn't words, or even impressions. It went beyond that. It was a knowing. . . .

He captured her mouth in a breathtaking kiss that seemed to rob her of reasoning. She felt herself melting into him, wrapped in his arms, fused to his mouth, and nothing else existed but the glorious sensation of being taken away from herself and melding with him. When it ended, his fingers weaved through her hair and he held her face with such tenderness that she felt tears come into her eyes.

"To use your phrase the first time we kissed . . . Oh, Lord."

She giggled and laid her head against his chest as his arms encircled her. "I was so scared that first time you kissed me. If you only knew."

His arms tightened around her, and she could feel the beating of his heart against her breast, the deep breath he inhaled that matched her own.

"I knew," he whispered against her hair. "That's why it had to be your decision."

"Oh, Mick. Do we really know what we're doing? I'm . . . I don't know . . . I've never known anyone like you before, and I guess I'm still scared."

He stroked her hair and breathed deeply. "Ruthann, you're a precious gift that's come into my life. No matter what happens, what decisions you might make, I'll always treasure you."

She pulled her head back and looked into his eyes. He

was staring at her with an expression of loving concern. She had never seen such adoration in any man's eyes before, never directed at her.

"I'm scared because I've never felt like this with any man, Mick." She placed her palm against his cheek and tried to make him experience the new love that was surging up within her. "Now, why did you think I was scared?"

He took a deep breath and said what was unspoken between them since they had met.

"Because I'm black."

She smiled with tenderness. "How can a man that's so intelligent, Mick Larkin, actually think something so stupid?"

CHAPTER 13

She smoothed down the skirt of her white Armani suit and checked the single strand of pearls around her neck. Her auburn hair was tinted to hide the streaks of gray; her makeup was alluring and flawless. She felt . . . pretty. It had been so long since she had even given her appearance a second thought that looking at herself in the full-length mirror was a startling revelation. She actually looked sophisticated, confident, in charge. Now . . . if she only felt it.

The butterflies in Eve's stomach increased when she thought about the importance of the next six hours. Everything hung on whether or not Nirvana was a success. They were booked for both shows and almost all of the weekend. The klieg lights were set up outside in front of the blue and white Nirvana sign and moving gracefully across the south Jersey sky. The staff was as prepared as they would ever be. The refrigeration problem was handled before it turned into a disaster. Chaz's tantrum was quietly and calmly extinguished by Ruthann. Jasmine and her group had arrived and were in their small dressing room. They were all ready and waiting. . . .

Now all she had to do was deal with Monty Clarke.

Suddenly the nervousness in her stomach increased until it became painful cramping. Panic swiftly rose and settled into her nerve endings, making them tingle, before spreading inward, past her skin and muscles to grip her vital organs. In response, her body seemed to leak out tiny beads of sweat.

Television. *Bold Copy*. Millions of people. Who the hell did she think she was? It was one thing to buy the house and renovate the restaurant. It took a certain amount of daring to open a jazz club and manipulate the media. But this . . . ? This was insanity. She didn't want millions of people to see her face, listen to her voice, judge her in minutes—without even knowing her. She wanted peace and normalcy.

But what was normal?

She stiffened and immediately realized that *this* was now the new normal. Her life would never go back to being quiet. She had made a series of decisions that had brought her to this very moment.

She almost laughed when she felt the panic ease out and away from her. Her smile became more relaxed. The old Eve Cameron, immobilized in that bed, would never have lived this life. She wouldn't have even considered it. It wasn't the old Eve who had to walk out there and confront Monty. It was the woman in the mirror, the new reflection.

Eve again looked at herself closely, more objectively.

There was a peace and confidence in her eyes now. She appeared more alive, more vibrant. When did this happen? Her brain tried to pinpoint a moment when this amazing transformation occured. Was it the makeup? The hair color? Her new way of thinking? It was as if something—her will, her spirit—had been set free. And she was happy. Absolutely amazing. Considering the circumstances of the last year, she never thought she could feel like this. It wasn't even six months ago that she didn't want to get out of bed, and now . . . ?

Now she was ready to meet Monty Clarke. She had to be.

And she would not become a burnt offering to the media.

". . . so you're going on record as saying that the wives of these men *aren't* bitter? Come on, Eve . . ."

Her smile was fixed, and she hoped it hid the grinding of her back teeth. She also hoped Monty and his camera couldn't pick up the way her hands were shaking, the perspiration that seemed to pool at the back of her neck and slowly slide down the center of her spine. All she wanted was to run from this man. She had successfully maneuvered her way through his sludge of questions for fifteen minutes. She knew he would only use three out of those fifteen, and was doubly careful of her words. "I can only speak for myself and my own observations, Monty. And I don't believe any of us are truly bitter. We're only asking that we be allowed to heal any emotional, legal, and financial issues in private."

Monty Clarke leaned forward in his chair, as though to

put emphasis on his next question. "But what about the rumors circulating concerning you and your personal life? You're not bitter about that?"

She laughed and, thankfully, it wasn't forced. "Are you talking about my partner in Nirvana?" She had expected this one and was trying to play it like a game of chess. She needed to remove his rook before losing her bishop.

"Ruthann Bucknum," Monty supplied the name with a carnivore's gleam in his eyes. "There's talk that you and Ms. Bucknum have more than a business relationship."

Clever move, Eve thought, almost relieved that it was finally on the table. She'd been on the edge waiting for him to strike. "We do have more than a business relationship," she countered. "We're friends. And we were friends before becoming business partners. Perhaps you'd also like to meet our other partner, Mick Larkin. He might be better able to answer your question and put your mind at ease."

Monty looked beyond the camera and lights to Ruthann, and Eve followed his line of vision. Ruthann was standing in front of Mick and he had his hand on Ruthann's shoulder, as though making an age-old masculine statement that she was his woman. Monty seemed to pick up on it immediately. She could actually see him squirm and sensed that he was looking for another way to attack. She attacked first.

"As you can see, Monty, my partners seem to have found their own romance. . . . And I couldn't be happier for both of them. They're two wonderful people, and I couldn't have opened Nirvana without all their hard work and faith. In fact, they generously agreed to support me in donating half of all profits from tonight to the Tajumulco Orphanage in Guatemala. The money will be donated on behalf of all of the wives." There. Now what could he do?

The popular *Bold Copy* personality appeared to have taken a fatal hit. His face froze with shock upon realizing that she had disarmed him completely. He seemed to valiantly search for a way to salvage himself and recover.

"That's very noble of you," he said in a now sympathetic voice that somehow didn't ring true. He had obviously decided to change tactics. Instead of attack, he was going to praise her.

Monty turned his face toward the camera and spoke directly to his audience. "Eve Cameron, who was once the helpless victim of the actions of the Misbehaving Missionaries . . . this courageous woman has risen above the odds, rebuilt her life, despite vicious rumors, and has emerged as an angel of mercy to those poor, deprived children in Guatemala—"

"—Excuse me, Monty, but I'm not Saint Eve," she interrupted, extremely uncomfortable with his speech. "All of the wives got together and decided to take the high road on this one. There are other children involved besides those at the orphanage. We have sons and daughters with these men."

He never took his eyes away from the camera, and she had the feeling that her declaration would be edited out of the final copy.

"These wives will finish the job the Rotary Club of Chelsea disgracefully turned their backs on. Perhaps, in spite of all the betrayal, there is hope yet for all the brave victims here in southern New Jersey and in Central America. This is Monty Clarke, reporting from Nirvana."

He made the universal sign for a cutoff by slicing the air in front of his neck. "That's it," he said, ripping the microphone from the lapel of his suit jacket.

Eve expelled her breath and unclipped herself. "Don't make me out to be some saint," she repeated. "I'm just trying to get through life."

He nearly glared at her. "If I say you're Saint Eve, then the whole goddamned country will buy it. And you want to know why? 'Cause nobody gives a shit when you're happy and successful. The story's over." He jerked his head to his cameraman. "The great viewing public wants to see some poor slob whose life is more screwed up than theirs. Then they don't feel so bad. The whole country is in a fucking state of depression. And you, lady, are no longer depressed. You're simply not interesting anymore."

It was done. She wouldn't start arguing with him, not when the main dining room was almost filled. They had created enough of a disturbance. "Would you and your crew like a drink, on the house, before you leave?" No point in being ungracious now that he and his crew were departing. She stood up and waited for him.

"This story's dried up. The sooner we get out of Hicksville and back to New York, the better." He turned his attention away from her. "Joey," he called to his cameraman, "let's pack it up."

Ignored, Eve left the man to his crew and walked up to Ruthann and Mick. Ruthann wrapped her in her arms. "You were wonderful, Eve. I'm so proud of you."

"Terrific," Mick added. "You got in everything you wanted and came out smelling like a rose."

She was soon encircled by the other wives offering their support. Margie Callahan gave her a kiss. Christine Gararra hugged her. All she wanted was a tissue to wipe away the nervous sweat. A shower would be better.

"Well done, Eve."

"Congratulations. You were great."

"You did it. He's finally lost interest and we can get our lives back."

Flushed with nervousness, Eve accepted their words and yet was uncomfortable with the praise. She only wanted to put the incident behind her.

"Eve . . . Larry Kline from KWY News Six. Can you give me five minutes?"

"Georgina Mallory from Channel Three. You handled Clarke like a pro. How about giving us a shot? It'll be great local publicity for your restaurant."

Suddenly she was surrounded by Minicams, spotlights, microphones, tape recorders, and reporters from the Philadelphia media and local newspapers. She answered questions about the scandal, emphasizing that she was not the angel of mercy Monty Clarke had made her out to be. She was merely a woman trying to get on with her life, and stressed peace instead of gossip. She talked about all the women and the strides they making to heal their lives. She invited the media to stay and hear Jasmine sing. Ruthann arranged for Ginny to mingle among them offering a large sample tray of appetizers. As she was wrapping up the last of the interviews, she heard a vaguely familiar voice rise above the others.

"Hey, Eve . . . I've got a question for you. Maybe you can fool all of 'em, acting like the injured party here, but I'm the one who's lost everything. How do you feel about using this disaster to promote this joint?"

She saw Doug Vansciver weaving his way toward her, obviously drunk and spilling his drink on the way.

The crowd seemed to part in surprise and open a path, enabling Doug to walk directly in front of her. Sally Donaldson stepped forward. "Doug. Please. You're drunk and you're making a fool of yourself. Just stop."

He waved his glass toward Eve, again spilling some of the contents. "Nah . . . I think Eve's already done a pretty good job of making us all look like fools. But here she is, sitting pretty in her *new* club, and when she leaves here she'll go home to her *new* house and dyke it out with her *new* friend."

She heard a chorus of shocked inhalation from those around her. Mick immediately made his way through the crowd and grabbed the drink from Doug's hand before gripping his upper arm.

"That's enough," he stated in a strong, controlling voice. "I believe there's a taxi outside with your name on it."

He pulled Doug away toward the door, and Eve, along with everyone else, watched in shock as Doug attempted to free himself.

"You wanna call off Kunta Kinte, here?" he yelled over his shoulder. "Is this how you treat your patrons?"

Mick forcefully led Doug Vansciver through the beveled glass doors.

Silence seemed to envelop her, and Eve felt the tension

in the air as everyone waited for her to react. She turned to the crowd, smiled, and said in a positive voice, "Okay, this is opening night. Let's all get back to work. Ladies"—she directed her attention to the circle of wives that still surrounded her—"have you had dinner yet?"

One by one the group dispersed, and conversations resumed at the tables and the bar now that the scene had played itself out. Eve walked up to Ruthann and held her wrist. "Check the kitchen and make sure the servers aren't back there gossiping."

"God, Eve . . . are you all right?"

She nodded quickly and continued as though she hadn't been interrupted. "Jasmine will be on in twenty minutes, and we need to clear as many of these tables as possible. Tell them not to rush anyone." She smiled at several reporters and moved to the side as a waiter rolled the dessert cart to one of the tables. She had more than two hundred people to think about and couldn't afford to let her emotions show. Not yet. Not yet . . .

She mingled through the restaurant, stopping at tables to chat with the customers and inquire whether they enjoyed their dinner. Compliments poured back at her and she tried to make her smile genuine, yet she had to escape for a few minutes.

Once in her office, she closed the door and sat down at her desk. Leaning her elbows on the flat surface, she held her head in her hands and stared at the papers in front of her. She couldn't see the print. She wasn't even looking. Instead, her glazed eyes seemed to envision the face of Doug Vansciver. Never in her life had anyone looked at her with hate. The loathing in his expression had sent chills down her spine. Why her? She didn't even know Doug that well. Was she really just the scapegoat? He lost his marriage, his home, his practice, his reputation . . . but it was all the result of his actions. Not hers. Still, it was frightening to have anyone direct such venom at her. Tears filled her eyes, and she wondered how long she could keep up this front of strength. In truth, all her talking to herself couldn't hide the fact that she still wanted to run home, jump into bed, and pull the covers up over her head. Wasn't it just earlier that she had fought this battle inside herself? How many times could she talk herself out of it?

There was a soft knock, and then Mick came into her office. He closed the door and sat in the chair opposite the desk. "Are you okay?"

She nodded. "A little shaken, is all. That, on top of the press . . ."

"I know. I put Vansciver in a cab—forced him is more like it. I gave the driver twenty dollars and told him to take him home." Mick shook his head. "Valet said he drove here. He's still got the ticket, so we'll find out at the end of the night which one is his car and we'll leave the keys at the front. Ginny can give them to him tomorrow."

"Thanks, Mick. I'm so sorry . . . he was drunk."

"Why are you apologizing? Listen, Eve, the guy is on automatic self-destruct right now. He made a scene, and you handled it. Period. That's it." He sat back and laced his hands together in his lap. "Now . . . are you going to let this one incident, which is over, ruin the rest of your night?"

She smiled. "You know me too well, Michael Larkin. Is this my pep talk?"

"Do you need one?"

Shrugging, she said, "I feel like I need a vacation. And this is opening night!"

"Just jitters. Absolutely normal. Come one, Eve, let it go and come back with me. We've left Ruthann alone out there."

She drew in a deep breath to steady her nerves just as she heard a bass being tuned. Looking at Mick, she plastered a smile on her face and pushed herself up from the chair. "Show time. Let's not miss it."

Ruthann came in and looked at the two of them. "Jasmine will be on in a few minutes, Mick. They need you out there."

Mick raised his hand, and Eve chuckled before giving him a high five in return. "Break a leg."

When they were alone, Ruthann brushed her hair back off her forehead and sighed. "I don't know how you're doing it. I'm a nervous wreck. I swear, I wanted to slap at least three people tonight, and that jerk Vansciver was just one of them. How are you holding up?"

Eve laughed nervously. "I've sweated more in the last half hour than I did in nine hours of childbirth." She unbuttoned the jacket of her suit and started flapping the edges to create wind. "And I had to wear white. Tell me the truth, Ruthann. Do I . . . you know, offend?"

"Offend?"

"Stink!"

Ruthann laughed and walked up to her. Inhaling deeply, she said, "Like a truck driver on a nine-day run."

"What? Really?"

"Knock it off. You smell like Cabotine. C'mon, Eve,

button up and play the part. Remember, you directed all of us to this point, and if you don't get out there you're going to miss the whole thing."

Ten minutes later, she stood in the back of the main dining room and drank in the scene. Leaning against the wall, she crossed her arms over her stomach and tried to memorize everything. The room was dark except for the candles on each table and the spotlight on Jasmine. The exotically beautiful woman was dressed in white sequins that caught the light and reflected it back to the audience. Her voice was so pure that it sent out a vibration that seemed to catch in the hair on the body and resonate over the skin. She captivated her audience with a slow, sexy rendition of "Summertime." All talk ceased, even at the bar where Mick and Ruthann stood. Ruthann was in front of Mick, leaning back against his chest. He had his arm around her waist, and they both looked so happy that Eve thought she might cry.

"Excuse me. I was wondering if I might introduce myself. You were so busy earlier, and I hate to interrupt now, but I have a deadline to meet."

Hearing the low voice, she looked to her side and saw a man about forty years old with dark blond hair that was graying at the temples. He was dressed in a charcoal pin-stripe suit with a white shirt and a burgundy patterned tie.

"I'm Luke Harrelson, editor for the *Carlton County Times*. I'm also a contributing editor for *Philadelphia* magazine."

He extended his hand.

Somewhat annoyed, Eve reminded herself that this was part of her job tonight, to pacify the media, and held out her own hand. She wasn't thrilled with the county newspaper and the job it had done on reporting the scandal, but *Philadelphia* magazine? *That* was big time. "Eve Cameron."

He smiled, a nice smile that showed perfect teeth and reflected in his blue eyes. "Yes, I know. I was here earlier."

She merely nodded and looked back to Jasmine. Whatever this man was digging for, he would have to do root canal to get her to comment on Doug Vansciver.

He leaned closer to her and whispered, "I want to congratulate you on your club. This is an oasis. I usually have to go into Philly to hear decent jazz."

Surprised, Eve glanced sideways. "Thank you." Was this just buttering up? She had more than enough reason to distrust the media, and just because this one was taking a different tack didn't mean she would allow him into her head.

He just stood there listening to the music, and Eve wondered why he didn't say anything, ask any questions. She looked at him again under the cover of the dim lighting and saw that he was truly enjoying the set. Forcing her concentration back to the stage, she was determined to remember every detail. It was finally happening. All the dreaming and planning was at last realized. Yet she was distracted by the presence of the man standing next to her. What did he want? The song ended and she clapped along with the enthusiastic appreciation of the crowd.

"She's wonderful," the man said over the applause. "Do you think I could interview her later?"

Eve smiled. "I'm sure she'd be thrilled." Exposure in

Philadelphia magazine would only help Jasmine's career, and any mention Nirvana received would be a plus. "Would you be writing for the newspaper or the magazine?"

"Both. The newspaper article will appear in tomorrow's paper. The one for the magazine will be in next month's issue."

Eve nodded, again noticing how attractive the man was. And he wasn't pushy. She liked that. After spending time with Monty Clarke, Eve felt that Luke Harrelson was downright refreshing. However, she wasn't about to let her guard down.

"How did you do it? What made you decide on a jazz club?"

She smiled at a few guests and said, "It was purely inspiration. I suppose intuition is a better word. You said it yourself. You have to go into Philly for decent jazz. I studied the risks and decided to follow my instincts."

He nodded, and she noticed that he wasn't taking notes. Was this an interview, or purely conversational?

"That's a great subject. Intuition. How would you define it?"

Was he serious? What kind of interview was this? Where's the digging for dirt? The woman who's been scorned succeeding in beating the bastards who mistreated her? The poor kids at the orphanage who were used? She looked at him and saw that he wore a friendly smile and that there were lines of laughter at the corners of his eyes. Deciding to go along, she said, "I don't know exactly how to define it. I guess it's a sort of knowing without words, a sense of something valid without the need of an explanation."

"That's pretty good," he answered. "It seems you hit right on the mark with Nirvana. Good instincts."

She was surprised. "You believe in instincts?"

"I'm a reporter, remember? I probably believe in it more than most. The way I look at it is intuition takes the thoughts or desires you hold and goes out into the future to find ways for you to have them. It's all a matter of paying attention to details. What's mundane for most is essential for a reporter."

She merely nodded as the group started playing the intro to the next song. This guy was throwing her off balance. She didn't know whether to remain guarded, or relax and enjoy the conversation.

"It was nice meeting you," the man said over the music, and once more extended his hand. "Perhaps we can talk again."

She smiled and nodded. "Sure. Enjoy yourself." When their hands touched she felt the deep warmth in his palm, and it seemed to radiate up her wrist and into her arm. Even more off balance, she pulled back and held her hand to her stomach.

He walked away to the bar, and she turned her attention to the stage as Jasmine began her second song. Strange man.

Ruthann felt as if she were in a dream and she never wanted to wake up. It was so unreal. She was in love, or falling in love. She might try to hide it. She might even deny it, if asked. But the truth was too powerful to reject.

She felt his chest secure against her back, his arm lightly around her waist, and sighed with contentment. Mick Larkin. Michael Larkin. Just thinking his name made her feel like a teenager, all silly and sappy. It was hard to concentrate with him so close that if she turned around and raised her chin his mouth would close over hers. She mentally shook the thought out of her head. Not now. Not tonight. Concentrate on the music, not the man. But it felt so right to be held by him, and Jasmine's voice only made her want to snuggle into him more.

Realizing she needed more of a distraction, she sipped her mineral water and checked to make sure the servers were still catering to the customers. Satisfied, she placed her drink back on the bar and noticed a man staring at her with a hostile expression. She looked away, wondering if perhaps he was part of the Rotary Club and just angry at the world. Yet she could still feel it, the uneasy sensation that raced along her skin, and unwillingly her gaze came back to the man. He was still glaring in her direction, only now it included Mick.

And then it came to her. The man was upset because Mick was black. Her hand closed over Mick's and tightened in defense.

Mick leaned forward and whispered in her ear, "Are you okay?"

Protective now, she merely nodded, yet she started to look around the crowd. Earlier she had seen several black women looking at her strangely. At the time she hadn't connected the looks with anything more than coincidence. Now she realized it was something far more than that. It was resentment.

Confused for a few moments, Ruthann tried to figure it out in her head. She wanted to tell them that neither one of them set out to find someone outside their race. That she and Mick didn't fall in love to offend anyone. They just fell in love. She knew that it wouldn't have mattered to her what color Mick's skin was—white, black, yellow, or purple. She loved the soul of the man. It felt as though God had given her this precious, beautiful gift, and these people were only concerned with the color of the wrapping paper. It made no sense.

She knew then that this relationship, wherever it was leading, would not be a perfect one. There would always be someone who didn't approve, who would want to project their limited thinking upon them. They would have to be strong, united against such prejudiced thoughts.

A sadness settled in around her. For a few days she had been riding high on finding such a perfect love, and now it seemed as if outsiders were forcing her to face the first hurdle. And she knew, no matter how united she and Mick were, no matter how high they jumped, that hurdle would always be there. They couldn't change the world and its narrow thinking. They could only change themselves, become stronger in their bond and just accept that it wouldn't be easy. But it was worth it. Holding Mick's hand, she would walk through fire.

When Jasmine ended her first set, the applause was near deafening. Ruthann frantically searched for Eve and saw that even the kitchen staff had come out and were shouting their praise. Tears of gratitude came into her eyes as Mick hugged her.

"That's it," he yelled over the noise. "We're a hit!"

She blinked frantically to clear her eyes as she nodded. "Where's Eve?"

They looked around the crowd and saw Eve making her way to Jasmine. The two women hugged, and Ruthann could see that Eve was also crying. A waiter was standing by the stage with a tray holding a bottle of Dom Perignon and five champagne glasses. Eve broke the embrace and began pouring the wine for the group. Jasmine and her musicians, evidently more than pleased with the reception, laughingly accepted the cheers and the toast that Eve was trying to make above the applause.

Ruthann turned to Mick and pushed her glass of mineral water to the front of the bar. "I think we deserve some champagne ourselves."

Mick, still basking in the accomplishment, raised his hand to the bartender and shouted, "Bottle of your best, my good man. We're celebrating!"

A man standing next to Mick patted him on the back and reached for his hand. "You deserve to celebrate. You guys really pulled it off. This place is great. Well done."

Laughing, Mick shook the man's hand. "Thanks. All the craziness of the last two months has just paid off, right in this moment."

"Luke Harrelson," the man identified himself.

"Mick Larkin. And this is Ruthann Bucknum."

Ruthann reached in front of Mick and shook the man's hand.

"I can't tell you how happy I am not to have to go across the river to Philly to get a great meal and music that rivals any of the jazz clubs in the city. Congratulations."

Ruthann watched as Mick shook his head and glanced back to the stage where Eve and Jasmine were still talking to the singer's fans.

"All the credit goes to Eve Cameron. It was her idea. We were just swept along."

Ruthann saw Luke look toward the front of the room. "She's quite a woman, isn't she?" he asked.

Mick nodded and Ruthann said, "You have no idea. In two months she turned a casual conversation into reality. Tonight wouldn't have happened if it weren't for her vision."

Still looking at Eve, the man shook his head in amazement. "I watched earlier how she handled the media. I kept thinking . . . grace under pressure. Not many people could have managed all of that on such a night."

Even though she had just met the man, Ruthann instinctively liked him. There was something about the way he carried himself; his presence seemed to exude a calm confidence that was open and giving. He appeared to understand and appreciate all the physical and emotional energy that went into making tonight a success.

She signaled the bartender for another wineglass and then looked at Luke Harrelson. "Would you join us in our celebration?"

Mick poured the champagne into the third glass and handed it to him. Raising his own glass, he said, "I believe this one is for Eve. Cheers, Ruthann. Cheers, Luke."

They touched glasses and said in unison, "To Eve . . ."

Her feet were killing her, and she was never so grateful for the old slippers that seemed to cushion the pain. Nine hours in high heels had definitely taken its toll. As she pulled on her soft terry-cloth robe and wandered down to the kitchen, Eve's thoughts flashed back through all the events of last night. At times it felt as though it were someone else's life. She started her morning coffee and routinely opened the refrigerator. Staring into it, she looked past the food and realized she wasn't even paying attention to what was on the shelves, nor was she hungry. She flipped the door closed and walked back to the island to wait for her coffee.

Looking out the large kitchen window, her gaze fixed on the new rosebushes that were in full bloom. Still in a daze, recollections of last night once again took over her mind. It seemed like a miracle. Now that opening night was over, she marveled at their determination and stamina. Where did she get the tenacity to come up with the idea in the first place? No wonder Paul thought she was crazy. She had been a housewife for fifteen years, and when her family had been a whole unit she'd been happy and satisfied. Now she was a businesswoman again, and she had no family outside of Ruthann and Mick. Life was so strange, and this type of business was definitely unfamiliar and uncharted terrain. A lot more fun than computers . . .

It was as if thoughts of her new family made them materialize, for she saw Mick's Jeep pull into the driveway that led to the back door. They had come so far in such a short time, and last night was the first night Ruthann hadn't been home. For a moment she wondered if she was losing Ruthann, and immediately pushed the childish thought out of her head. Within minutes they burst into the kitchen carrying newspapers.

"Morning," Mick called out.

"I'm glad you're up," Ruthann added. "Wait until you read these."

Eve grinned as she observed the flush in Ruthann's cheeks. It was obvious how she had spent the night. Happy for her friend, Eve said, "You guys are just in time for coffee." She pulled out two more mugs and set them on the counter while glancing at the stack of newspapers. Her empty stomach once again filled with those damn butterflies, and she knew she couldn't read them herself.

Sighing, she pushed her hair back off her face and said, "Okay . . . lay it on me. What did they do? Did they review my personal life or the club?"

"I think it's safe to say that we're a success," Mick stated with a victorious grin.

Excited, Ruthann started flipping through the pile of papers on the kitchen table. "Wait. I know I should save the best for last, but you just have to hear this one." She found the article she wanted and looked up. "Did you meet a reporter last night named Luke Harrelson?"

Taking a minute, Eve thought back on all the names and faces she had come across the night before. Then she remembered. "I think I met him. But the strange thing was that he didn't ask me any questions. It wasn't a real interview. We barely got past introductions."

"We met him at the bar after the first set," Ruthann said, folding the paper and obviously eager to begin reading.

Mick was nodding as he poured the coffee. "He was really a nice guy. He didn't ask too many questions either, but he made it clear that he was just as impressed with you as he was with the club."

"That's funny," Eve murmured. "I didn't say much to him."

"Well, it's obvious he was observing you."

"Okay, okay," Ruthann broke in. "Let me read this. It's really the best one. He didn't dwell on the gossip, or try to make it provocative. He kept to the facts. Listen, this is how he starts: *'Nirvana is not just a restaurant and jazz club, it's a destination. You'll want to come back. Once you taste the superb five-star cuisine, experience the impeccable service and discover music that stirs your soul, you'll plan your next visit before you leave.'* "

In that moment the aching in Eve's feet disappeared, the butterflies flew out of her stomach, and that tremendous weight of responsibility lifted from her shoulders. She wasn't crazy to drag all those people into her dream. They would be safe. For the first time in a year, since Jamie's illness began, she could relax. A feeling of accomplishment and peace settled over her heart. Her future, once so bleak, now seemed as bright as the morning sun.

CHAPTER 14

"The menu says 'stuffed portobello mushrooms,'" Chaz yelled while frantically waving the menu in front of a waitress's face. "It states clearly that portobello mushrooms are handpicked and stuffed with garlic and spinach and covered with the finest cheeses. It says nothing about bread crumbs. If they want that deep-fried fast food, tell them to go to Fridays!"

Eve and Ruthann rushed into the kitchen together to witness the scene playing out between the head chef and a stunned and obviously intimidated waitress.

"Hold it down," Eve said firmly. "Your voices carry!"

Chaz shoved the menu at Eve. His face was flushed and his expression hostile. "As you are well aware, one of the reasons I was hired as head chef is because I was nominated in 1993 *and* 1994 for the Rising Star Chef by the James Beard Foundation. It is an honor I take seriously. I will *not* stuff portobello mushrooms with bread crumbs!"

Eve handed the menu to Ruthann and tried to keep her

patience. "Look, he's too temperamental for me. Can you please handle this?"

Ruthann sighed and turned to the six-foot ball of ego. "Chaz, calm down and let's talk."

Eve left the kitchen, feeling as if they were all hostage to the man's perfectionism. He was a fantastic chef, and they couldn't afford to lose him. Still, it took someone with a Ph.D. in psychology to handle him. Thank God he liked Ruthann. Eve walked back to the bar and immediately saw that in her absence Luke Harrelson had arrived and was ordering a drink. Thinking about his article, she took the seat beside him.

Eve caught the bartender's attention and said, "This one's on the house." Turning to the man next to her, she added, "I want to thank you for the review and the article. It was refreshing to read something that didn't refer to the scandal."

He smiled and held up his glass. "You're welcome, and thanks for the drink. How's business?"

Looking around the main dining room that was just starting to fill with the dinner crowd, she said, "The weekend was totally booked. Now I have my fingers crossed. Let's see what kind of business we do during the week."

"Most places are closed on Monday, so you might have an advantage. I know I didn't feel like going home and facing another TV dinner."

She chuckled. "You're kidding, right? TV dinner?"

He placed his drink back on the bar. "Don't knock it, they keep a hungry man happy. Well, not happy, but fed. And I can't see the point of whipping up a batch of tortellini and pesto sauce for one person."

Eve looked to his left hand and noticed he wasn't wearing a wedding ring. She felt sorry for him. He seemed like a nice man, attractive, intelligent. . . . Why was he alone? It was really sad that the divorce rate seemed to climb with the years. Was it their generation? What happened to the Baby Boomers? Why were they so disillusioned?

"I'd much rather come here and have Oriental Salmon wrapped in rice paper. Pesto sauce is one thing, but the Tomari ginger sauce would defeat me." He glanced in her direction and grinned. "Unless you'd care to share the recipe?"

She laughed. "I don't even know how it's prepared. We've got this prima donna chef back there who guards his recipes like top-secret government files."

"Do I sense a story in this? Culinary espionage?" His smile was teasing and his eyes were merry.

Grinning, she answered, "Don't make me insist that you leave the journalist outside when you come through the door. I think Nirvana has had enough attention from the media."

From her peripheral vision she noticed Molly Kellerman entering the restaurant. When Molly saw her at the bar, she immediately joined her.

"Eve, I need to talk to you," Molly said in an urgent voice. Before Eve could respond, Molly continued, "I'm here with Stuart. We're talking about getting back together. He's outside taking care of the car, but before he comes in I wanted to talk to you. I don't want you to feel like I'm deserting the wives, after the way you tried to help all of us."

Eve turned toward Molly, trying to keep the conversation as private as possible. "Molly," she whispered, "don't be ridiculous. Why would I ever think such a thing?" She leaned closer to her friend and added, "Listen . . . this is your life. You have to do what's best for you and your children. If you're strong enough to put pride aside and work with Stuart to heal your family, then I not only commend you but I support whatever decisions you make." She put her arm around Molly's shoulder and kissed her cheek. "I wish you guys the best. I hope everything works out."

Stuart Kellerman walked up to them and stood behind his estranged wife. He looked unsure, downright nervous, as he addressed Eve. "Good to see you again," he said shyly, putting his valet ticket in his suit-jacket pocket.

Knowing she needed to make a friendly overture, Eve smiled warmly. "You, too, Stuart. It's been a while." She saw Stuart glancing at the man beside her and introduced everyone. "Stuart and Molly Kellerman, this is Luke Harrelson."

They all shook hands, and Eve asked if they would like to join her for a cocktail before dinner. Once they were seated, the conversation became less awkward.

Stuart turned to Eve and said, "I really need to take this time, on behalf of all of us involved, to thank you. You handled it the best way possible, and tried to allow everyone to keep their dignity. I think tonight's airing of *Bold Copy* put an end to it."

"I'm just glad it's over. Maybe now we can get back to straightening out our lives. By the way, Stuart, it's good that you came in tonight. I need the address and the name of the bank in Guatemala where I should transfer the donation from opening night."

Molly grabbed her husband's wrist. "Oh, Stuart, tell them what you just heard."

Stuart shook his head and appeared sympathetic. "Nobody down there really knows about the scandal yet, and that I've resigned as president of the Rotary Club. The director of the orphanage just wrote me that there's a pretty serious measles epidemic in the area, and they've been hit bad. Whatever you're sending down there will be put to good use for medical supplies."

"Oh, no." Eve felt concern for those poor kids. "What's the quickest way I can get the money to them?"

"Unfortunately, it's not like here in the States. Wire transfers usually get screwed up and take a couple of weeks to straighten out. That's why the Rotary Club always hand-delivered everything. It just took less time. I'll call you tomorrow with the banking information. You'll need the orphanage's checking account number to try and do it properly."

Before she could reply, Luke asked, "Would it be faster to buy the vaccinations and medical supplies up here and ship them directly to the orphanage?"

Stuart shook his head. "Unfortunately, even that isn't the quickest route. You have to go through the most archaic red tape to bring drugs into the country. Even medical supplies. It could take months to get through that kind of bureaucracy."

"Then let's get on this right away, Stuart," Eve said, making a mental note to give this a priority.

One of the waiters came up and interrupted. "I'm sorry,

Eve. I wouldn't bother you if it wasn't important. We've got a problem again in the kitchen."

Her breath seemed to rush out of her body with frustration. "Is it Chaz?"

The young man shook his head. "I wish."

She stood up and smiled at the small group. "Time to go back to work. I hope you all enjoy your dinner, but you'll have to excuse me. Stuart, please call tomorrow."

She left them at the bar and prepared herself to handle the next crisis. Life certainly wasn't boring any longer.

It was fast becoming her favorite time of night, lying in bed and thinking back on her day. The moon cast a translucent light into her bedroom that eased her mind into a reflective state. She thought about Nirvana and how quickly it seemed that everything was falling into a routine. Problems arose with regularity but somehow got handled. She thought about Mick and Ruthann and felt herself smiling. They were like two high school kids who couldn't get enough of each other. It wasn't a surprise where Ruthann was choosing to spend her nights.

When she thought about the discovery of new love between her friends, she automatically thought about Molly and Stuart trying to rekindle that state in each other. What courage and strength the two of them must have to pull the edges of their torn marriage back together, despite what the rest of the world might think. She honestly believed that Molly had made the right decision. Picturing Stuart in her mind led her to almost hear his voice again describing the emergency down in Guatemala.

Measles . . . She was fifteen years old and a sophomore

in high school when she noticed red spots on her arms. When she was sent home and told not to come back for two weeks, she had felt as if she'd been given a vacation. The next day, she knew she was given a sentence in hell. Even now, as an adult, she scratched at her stomach with the memory of the agonizing itching, the high fevers that made her plead with her mother to knock her out. It had been days of torture that never seemed to end. Those poor children . . . alone, without the comfort of someone to lovingly put their arms around them and give them support. Memories of Jamie's countless fevers during his illness made her want to cry. She pictured in her mind scenes of young children in cribs and beds crying out for help, and no one answering.

A tightness started in her chest and she felt a wave of emotion closing off her throat. Tears came into her eyes and she thought of Jamie. He had grown up protected, with regular doctors to measure his weight, his height, even the size of his head. She pictured his tiny face showing surprise at being vaccinated and then turning scarlet in outrage as he screamed out his resentment. She had always felt as if she somehow betrayed his trust during those visits. Even though her intellect told her it was for his benefit to be vaccinated, it had taken days to get over the guilt. She had kept meticulous medical records on her son, never missing an appointment or even a dental checkup. Yet for all of that, he had still died.

Jamie . . . Would the pain never end?

Suddenly, her mind's eye pictured a faceless little boy alone and crying miserably in an orphanage in Guatemala. It came to her then with such swift brilliant clarity that her breath caught in her throat. The pressure in her chest was nearly unbearable, and she had to sit up just to inhale. Clutching the sheet in her fist, she heard it almost scream out in her mind. That little boy was Jamie's half brother!

Her heart was pounding against her rib cage. She could hear it ringing in her ears, pulsing in her fingertips. Part of Jamie lived on. Somewhere in a Third World country, abandoned in the midst of an epidemic, was this small link to her son. They shared the same father, the same DNA that came from Paul. Cloaked in secrecy for years, this child and Jamie were part of each other—brothers who now could never meet. She knew she had to look into this child's eyes. Would she see her son there?

Her thoughts raced furiously over the freeway of her mind. It was as if the decision was already made and she was just now discovering the road map. What airlines flew to Guatemala? Did she need shots herself? Would a passport do? Or did she need a visa? Would Mick and Ruthann be able to run Nirvana? Would Paul, if he found out, think she had completely and totally lost her mind? She didn't care.

There it was—that feeling was back again, that instinctive urging that told her she would do whatever it took to make it happen. She had felt it with Ruthann, the house, Mick, the club, and now this. . . . She *knew* she had to do it.

She was going to Guatemala.

"Is something wrong?"

Eve sat down at her desk and took a deep breath. This

would not be easy, she thought as she looked at Ruthann and Mick, seated opposite her. "Nothing's wrong. Not really. I wanted to talk to the two of you together, because this concerns all of us."

Ruthann leaned forward in her chair. "Something is wrong. I can feel it."

Mick reached out and stroked Ruthann's arm. "Maybe she just wants to talk about us. You haven't been home much and—"

"Hold it," Eve interrupted. "This is going in the wrong direction. I think the easiest thing is to just let me get this out. Stuart Kellerman came in with Molly last night. They're getting back together. Stuart said he heard from the orphanage that there's a serious measles epidemic down there and they need the money for medical supplies."

"Oh, those poor kids," Ruthann whispered.

Eve nodded. "Money transfers and even telex transfers usually get lost for weeks. That's why the Rotary Club always brought money and supplies down with them. I stayed awake last night thinking about this, and I've come to a decision. I'm going to Guatemala. Can you guys handle Nirvana while I'm gone for a week?"

Neither one of them said anything for a few tense moments. It was Mick who spoke first. "You're kidding. When?"

Ruthann seemed to come alive with Mick's question. "Who cares when?" she nearly yelled while waving her hand in dismissal at Mick. "This is insanity. You can't be serious!"

Eve inhaled deeply and tried to understand Ruthann's

bewilderment. "I've never been more serious. They need money and supplies now, not a month from now. I know this is sudden, but I can do it and be back in a week. Probably less." She looked at Ruthann's shocked expression and attempted to make her understand. "Everything's running pretty smoothly here now. Sometimes I feel like a figurehead. The only thing I'll miss is Chaz's hissy fits, and you always handle that beautifully. It's only four or five days."

"I sympathize with the problem, but do you even know anything about what you're getting into?" Ruthann demanded. "Guatemala isn't like hopping to the Bahamas. It's a Third World country, in Central America, for God's sake. Do you have any idea how dangerous this is?"

Smiling patiently, Eve said, "How dangerous can it be? I'm flying out of Miami Wednesday for Guatemala City by American Airlines. And I'm booked into a five-star hotel when I arrive. I'm following the same route as the Rotary Club. And they always got home safely."

"You've already made reservations?" Ruthann asked with disbelief.

Nodding, Eve said, "I've been working on it all morning. I'm just waiting for my visa to come by overnight express. I already have a passport."

Mick was shaking his head. "You're doing this by yourself?"

Ruthann immediately turned to him. "I'm sorry, Mick. Would you mind excusing us, please? I want to talk to Eve."

When they were alone, Eve reminded herself that she

knew this wasn't going to be easy. However, Ruthann's strong opposition was unexpected. "Why are you so upset? I'll be fine, and you two will more than manage without me for a week."

"Why am I upset!" Ruthann almost flew out of her chair as she paced back and forth in front of the desk, pausing only to make a point. "This is the most irrational, harebrained scheme you've come up with yet! Only this time, it's more than money you might lose. There's an epidemic there!"

"Measles," she added calmly. "I had them when I was a teenager, so I'm immune. I might even be able to help in the short time I'm there."

Ruthann stopped her pacing and glared at her. "You know what? You've been watching *Bold Copy* too much. Now Monty Clarke even has you believing you're Saint Eve."

She felt stunned by the anger of Ruthann's attack. "What are you talking about?"

"You get these crazy ideas and then fly off half-cocked," she exclaimed, waving her arms around. "Transform the homeless and make them into respectable members of society . . . Buy a house on the spur of the moment and spend a fortune renovating it . . . Sink the rest of your money into this place and then, a week after opening it, you come in here with another crazy scheme and desert us to fly off on some reckless mission. You don't see a pattern here? I have tried, Eve, to be the voice of reason during all this, God knows! But now I think you need professional help."

Eve was determined not to lose her patience, but it was

becoming very difficult. "First of all, calm down. Shouting isn't going to help either one of us. As for the pattern . . . all of my harebrained schemes seemed to have worked out just fine. And as far as my safety in Guatemala . . . the same person who had booked all the trips for the Rotary Club for the last eight years has arranged this one, so it's not like I'm going under the advice of a junior travel agent. You don't understand, Ruthann. I have to go."

"Oh, I understand, all right. You've lost your fucking mind!"

She blinked several times in surprise, never having heard Ruthann shout at her like that. "I'm sorry that it's something you can't understand. You've never had a child. Jamie's half brother is down there, most likely suffering in poor conditions, and I won't ignore that. I don't want our friendship to be threatened by this, but I'm going and nothing you can say is going to stop me."

They stared at each other, and Eve was almost nauseated by the unexpected clash of wills. "We're really not getting anywhere with this, so I don't see the point in discussing it any further," she said, trying to keep her emotions under check. "I'm sorry you feel so strongly about this, but so do I."

Ruthann shook her head slowly and looked at her as if seeing a stranger. "I don't believe this. It's completely irrational. And what's worse is that you won't even see it until it's too late. You simply won't listen to reason." She opened the door and added, "You know, Eve, a true friend will tell you what you don't want to hear, but don't worry. Mick and I will take care of Nirvana while you're off on your . . . little adventure. Go. Do what you want. You always do anyway."

Eve stared at the closed door and tears came into her eyes. She felt as though she had just lost her best friend.

CHAPTER 15

Everything was working out perfectly. She made her connecting flight with ease and settled into her seat in business class. Stowing her large purse under the seat in front of her, Eve finally relaxed and admitted that she'd been nervous. Really nervous. Rue had been right about one thing: This was not going to be like a jaunt to the Bahamas. This truly was going to be an adventure. The plane filled with passengers, many of them looking like they were about to revisit their native country—some short and Indian-looking, some Spanish, most an exotic mixture of both.

Eve looked out the small window at the Miami airport and realized that the feeling in her stomach had transformed from nerves into excitement. This was it. This was the point of no return. She was actually going to Guatemala, and within days she would look into the eyes of a four-year-old child. What would she find? What if there was no hint of connection? She mentally shook herself free from such thoughts. It didn't matter. Paulo Rafael Carrera was her son's half brother, and she would . . .

"Eve?"

Startled out of her daydreams, she jumped at the sound of her name and turned her head toward the voice.

Luke Harrelson stood in the empty row in front of hers, trying to keep the aisle open for the last of the boarding passengers.

Completely astonished to see him, she blinked several times, attempting to make sense out of his appearance. For a moment she felt her reality shift, as if she wasn't sure he was actually standing there. It made no sense. "What in the name of God are you doing here?" she demanded.

He looked embarrassed and smiled, almost apologetically. "I'm on assignment," he answered.

"To Guatemala?" It was too incredible! "What's your assignment?"

Now he appeared more than embarrassed. He looked guilty. "You."

"What?"

"Mick Larkin told me about your plans," he hurriedly explained. "Ruthann was actually the one who suggested that this would make a great positive ending to the series of articles we've been doing for the last few months. My editors jumped on the idea and . . . here I am. We had to pull some strings to get this whole thing together so quickly. I almost missed this flight."

She swallowed down the fury that swiftly rose within her and managed to say, "Well, you might as well have, because this is nothing less than a violation of my privacy and . . . I won't stand for it. I can't believe this! I don't want you anywhere near me, do you understand? I don't want to see you, talk to you—"

"Excuse me, sir," the flight attendant interrupted. "You'll have to take your seat now. We're preparing for takeoff."

He shifted his carry-on bag to his shoulder and moved to the aisle. "We'll talk later," he said, attempting to appease her.

"No, we won't," she answered to his back as he left business class and walked into coach. "Forget it, do you hear me?"

She sat back in her seat and stared at the airsickness bag that was sticking up from the pocket in front of her. For the first time in her life, she felt like using it. This was too much. How dare Mick and Ruthann go behind her back like this? It was manipulative, controlling, and a total disregard for her privacy. And Luke Harrelson . . . what a poor judge of character she had been there! She felt foolish to have believed that he was a decent human being. He was another media vulture, no better than Monty Clarke. He was just more clever.

She took several deep breaths, trying to fight down the bile in her throat as the plane backed away from the jetway. She didn't listen to the safety instructions and was grateful that the seat next to her was empty. She was so angry that she was afraid if anyone tried to talk to her, she would lose it and totally snap.

Time seemed to disappear after takeoff. She didn't know if she had spent five minutes staring at the gag bag, or an hour. All she knew was that she felt invaded and betrayed by people she had trusted. Yes, she was making this trip to bring the money, but she was also on a very private mission. And Ruthann had known that. To have sicced a reporter on her trail was unforgivable. Leaning her head back, she closed her eyes and tried to wipe her mind free of the mental torture. She wouldn't think about it now. She couldn't. She needed to keep her wits about her. She was about to enter a foreign country with the male version of Lois Lane five paces behind her. Unbelievable! Somehow she would have to find a way to lose him.

Soon she felt someone sitting down next to her, yet refused to open her eyes.

"Can I talk to you?"

She groaned at the sound of his voice, not caring whether or not he heard her. "Go away," she said in a weary voice.

"Listen, I know you're pissed off and maybe you've got good reason, but there was no way to let you know ahead of time. I didn't even know until late last night that I got a green light on this."

She knew he was waiting for a response, but she was determined that the only way to handle the man was not to respond at all. She would not give him an inch. "Go away," she repeated in a dull, monotone voice while keeping her eyes closed.

"Can't we talk about this? Look, I don't know what you think I'm going to be writing, but it won't be about the scandal. The editorial board was kind of embarrassed about the way they've handled the whole mess, and I think they want to make up for that. And the magazine wants to focus on the positive. I promise you I have no intentions to exploit you in any way, shape, or form." There was a pause, as if he was waiting for her to reply. "I'll even let you read my final copy before I submit it."

"Go . . . away."

He didn't say anything for a few minutes, and she tried to shut him out from her mind. She would concentrate on reaching the hotel, and envisioned herself immersed in a hot bubble bath. It would soothe her nerves and drain away her anger.

"Eve, please talk to me. This is childish."

She looked at him then, hoping that her eyes would convey the full measure of her anger. "You have no right to do this. You have violated my privacy, Mr. Harrelson. No press badge grants you permission to invade another's life. I will not talk to you, see you, or lead you to any story. Do I make myself clear?"

"I can see you're upset. We'll talk about this later."

She leaned her head back and again closed her eyes. "Go away."

She felt him leave, and she let out her breath with frustration. Typical male. Try to make a point and let them know you're serious, and they say you're just upset. He wasn't listening, and he had that irritating male reaction of pacifying the little woman. *When she calmed down?* He was also delusional. She was not going to calm down— not anytime soon. She was going to ditch him in Guatemala City and get on with her mission. Alone.

Until Eve passed through customs, Aurora International Airport seemed fairly modern in style. However, once she rolled her suitcase through the terminal, she saw the deteriorated conditions of a Third World country. There was total turmoil. People were shouting. Animals were squealing. Children were crying. She was taking it all in when she was suddenly surrounded by a pack of porters hotly contesting the custody of her bag.

Shocked, at first thinking that she was being robbed, Eve yelped and grabbed for her luggage. Not able to understand the language, she kept shaking her head at them. "I don't need assistance. Please . . . give me my bag." She watched as one small man tugged the bag from the hands of the first, who had taken it right out of her hand.

"La senora no necessita su assister. The lady does not require your help."

She looked to her side and saw Luke Harrelson speaking Spanish and trying to get the band of men to release her suitcase. Whatever he was saying seemed to work, and they eventually handed it to *him,* not to her.

She seized it from him and clutched the handle for dear life. "What was that about?" she demanded as she watched the luggage bandits move to another passenger.

"It's how they make their living," Luke said, scanning the terminal. "Do you want to share a taxi into the city? It's this way." He pointed to the right.

Eve thought for a few seconds. The scene with the porters had startled her, and Harrelson did seem to speak fluent Spanish. Still, she didn't want to depend on him for anything, nor did she want to give him an inch to use later.

"Thanks for helping me with my bag, but I think I'll go on my own." She saw the taxi sign and walked away from him.

"You're not going to speak to me? You're serious about this?"

She didn't even turn around. "Absolutely."

The taxi driver seemed to understand her hotel destination, and she settled back in an old Chevy wagon that had seen better days. Ten minutes later, she wondered if the man knew where he was going. It was impossible for her to tell if they were proceeding in the right direction, but from the scenery outside her window, she had a feeling that she was not being taken by the direct route. They crossed a bridge and she looked to the left, to a vast canyon where shacks of tin and scrap wood, squatter settlements, were huddled together and precariously clinging to the mud on the slopes. She could see children picking through garbage mounds. Disheartened, she looked away.

They passed a large military base and proceeded past homes hidden behind huge walls that were protected by barbed wire and shards of glass embedded in the foundation. What kind of people lived in such fear? When they came to an area that appeared to be a suburb—with vast green spaces, tennis courts, and the estates of private schools—Eve began to relax. At least they were driving toward the city.

Guatemala City's commercial center was like something out of a documentary showing urban decay. Bus after bus roared down the avenue, belching diesel exhaust and leaving hacking pedestrians and blackened buildings in its wake. Horns blared, trash had been dropped in the streets, and Eve wanted to roll the window up because her eyes burned from the contaminants. The sidewalks were terribly congested, with street peddler stands squeezed in every available space. There were steel bars on shop windows and armed guards at more prosperous stores. Her fingers instinctively tightened on her purse, and she made a mental note to put her money into the hotel safe until she could convert it at the bank in the morning.

She shouldn't have been surprised when the taxi driver turned away from the commercial part of town and eventually drove up a wide tree-lined street. It was truly beautiful, with hotels, embassies, restaurants, and museums. Just like any city, anywhere in the world: Those with money separated themselves from the poor. It was on this misnamed street. Avenida Reforma, that her hotel was located.

As she walked into the Hotel Camino Real, the best hotel in the entire country, she was told, Eve was focused on one thing—to take a hot bath and a nap. Exhausted from the trip and her unplanned sight-seeing tour, she walked up to the reception desk in the beautifully appointed lobby.

"Good afternoon. Do you speak English?" she asked the Spanish-looking man behind the counter.

"Yes, madam. How may I help you?"

She sighed with relief. "I'm Eve Cameron. I have a reservation for one night."

"One moment, please." He turned to a computer and looked up her name.

She was delighted to be in a modern hotel that had computers and a professional staff, was decorated with breathtaking pastel colors, and was filled with lush plants and orchids. It could have been a top-rated establishment in any major city in the States. Eve experienced a few moments of guilt when she thought of the squatter settlements on the way into the city, but she had to admit that she was more than relieved by her surroundings. Truthfully, she was a bit frightened by the squalor she had witnessed and finally felt safe.

"Isn't this a coincidence?"

Hearing the voice, her shoulders slumped even further. "Oh, no . . . I don't believe this."

He was smiling, that irritating perfect-teeth kind of smile that could have appeared in toothpaste ads. And he didn't look rattled, disheveled, and tired—which was exactly how she felt. His light blue polo shirt didn't even look wrinkled. She wondered whether he was aware that the color matched his eyes perfectly.

Annoyed with herself for noticing, she glared at him. "You followed me," she accused him. "How dare you?"

"I beg your pardon?" He appeared insulted. "I happen to have reservations. They were faxed and confirmed last night."

She ground her teeth together with annoyance and turned around to the counter. This was too much. How the hell was she supposed to lose him when he was staying in her hotel? And why did his presence rattle her so much? As a member of the press he had been in a position to take advantage of her in print, yet he hadn't. Still . . . She closed her eyes and tried to regain her composure. A bath and a nap . . . that's what she needed. She would think of an escape plan later.

An escape plan? Now she really was losing it. This wasn't "Mission Impossible." It was a simple mission of mercy. And Luke Harrelson was merely an aggravation she would deal with later.

"Can we have dinner? We really should plan an itinerary. I read in the guidebook that Chichicastenango is off the Pan American Highway. We can rent a car and drive together."

Afraid that she might slap him away like an annoying mosquito, she refused to turn around. "Go away, Harrelson. You're not wanted," It had worked earlier.

"Hey, I might start getting insulted if you keep this up."

"Get insulted," she threw over her shoulder. "And please get the message. You . . . are . . . not . . . wanted. *Comprende?*"

He actually laughed!

Eve received her room key, transferred her money into the hotel safe, and handed her bag to a porter before walking away and leaving Luke with the reception clerk.

"I'll call you when you get settled."

Keeping her chin up, she pretended she didn't even hear him. He was worse than a mosquito. He was a gnat. And if he pushed her again, she would start swatting.

Her room was lovely and modern. There was a television with U.S. programming, an excellent bed, textured wallpaper, art prints of the Guatemalan countryside, a desk with a vase containing white orchids, an honor bar, and thick terry-cloth bathrobes.

"Ahh . . ." She flopped down on the bed and sighed deeply. It was a heavenly retreat, and she intended to enjoy it. After fifteen minutes, she started to doze and finally dragged herself upright. If she didn't get up she would never take a bath, and it was a luxury she had promised herself. Fighting fatigue, Eve hung up the sundress she would wear to dinner that night and laid out her traveling clothes for the next day. Usually when she packed for a trip, she took far too much. This time, knowing she would be hauling her luggage herself, she had packed only necessities. Instead of numerous changes of clothes, she had used that space for coloring books and crayons. Two pairs of shoes were sufficient. Any more, and she wouldn't have been able to bring the small Sesame Street toys for the children.

She ran her bathwater and padded barefoot to the window. Looking out from her vantage point, she saw a lovely old city that hid its decay from the privileged. What kind of people were the Guatemalans? She had not really spoken to any. She was a stranger in a strange land. She had read the guidebook on the plane, but it had not really told her anything about the spirit of the people. She knew the Mayan culture was the foundation until the Spanish had invaded and taken over control. And now it was a mixture of Indian and Spanish, Christianity with a more primal ritual infused over it. Remembering the water running in the bathroom, she hurried back and shut off the valves. Steam covered the mirror over the sinks.

She saw a small basket containing hotel amenities. Grateful, she poured a little of the bath gel into the hot water and undressed. It was pure heaven. She laid her head back against the tub, not caring if her hair got wet. She savored the feeling of the heat entering her pores and burning away her stress. The anger she had felt earlier seemed to seep out of her and turn liquid to dissolve in the water. At that moment, the language barrier didn't matter.

The feeling of being a foreigner disappeared. Mick and Ruthann could be forgiven, and Luke Harrelson forgotten. She was finally on her way back to peace.

It was the concierge at the hotel who recommended El Pedregal as a classic restaurant. Since it was located right outside, Eve had decided to leave the hotel and experience some local culture. She dined on red snapper with fresh coriander, tequila shrimp, and crepes with cuitlacoche flowers. Sitting in a high wicker chair on a sheltered terrace amid strolling mariachi musicians, Eve truly felt as though she was absorbing the culture. She was feeling very pleased with herself for venturing out on her own, when the waiter came up and placed a margarita on the table in front of her.

Surprised, she looked up in question.

"The gentleman at the end of the bar sent this with his warmest regards."

She glanced over her shoulder, fully expecting to see Luke Harrelson and intending to send the drink back. Instead, she saw a very attractive man appearing to be in his mid-thirties with dark Latin features. He raised his own glass in greeting, and she nodded and smiled before turning around to the table. Sipping her drink, she felt flattered, and was glad that she had decided to get dressed and leave the hotel. Her cream cotton sundress was the only choice. Away from her own environment, her own troubles, she suddenly remembered those feminine feelings. She had almost forgotten what they were like. Here she was forty years old and a younger man was showing interest in her. At home, she had felt nothing, no attraction to anyone, no special feelings beyond friendship. It occurred to her that she was divorced, and single. That was it. Until this moment, she had continued to hold the mind-set of a married woman.

"May I join you?"

He stood before her—tall with an angular face, dark, wavy hair, and a smile that seemed a bit hesitant, as though he was wondering whether or not he would be refused. She remembered in the guide book reading that single women should be careful at night, yet he seemed respectable from the expensive suit and his polite bearing. She couldn't see the harm. She was in a public place, not far from her hotel. . . .

"Yes. Thank you for the drink."

His smile became more relaxed, and he pulled out the matching wicker chair. Once seated, he placed his drink on the table and extended his hand across it. "My name is Francesco Suarez. Thank you for allowing me the pleasure of your company for a short while. It makes these business trips more pleasant to share time with a beautiful woman such as yourself."

Okay, he was younger than she was and definitely smooth. She placed her hand in his and introduced herself. "Eve Cameron."

"Ahh, I guessed that you were from the States. I received my schooling at Drexel University in Philadelphia, Pennsylvania."

"I live right across the river from Philadelphia, in New Jersey! Talk about a small world."

"This must be a culture shock to you, unless this isn't your first trip to Guatemala."

She sat back and relaxed. No need to worry. He was almost a neighbor. "No. This is the first time for me. Although I've heard about it for years. I don't think any guide could have prepared me."

"Do you find it that different?"

She thought back to her cab ride through the city. "It seems very congested and . . ." What could she say without insulting him or his country?

"Dangerous?" he supplied.

Smiling shyly, she nodded. "I didn't want to say that, but you're right. Maybe because it's so different that I felt . . . a bit nervous."

He sipped his drink and sat back in the chair. "Perhaps that's just common sense. Guatemala is not the United States. You have your unrest and violence, but here it is a way of life, especially with tourists. Enjoy your visit, but be on guard, madam."

"The guidebook said something about not going out alone, that even small parties of tourists can be mugged. Is it really that bad?"

"In certain areas of the city. Outside the city . . . ?" he shrugged elegantly. "This is a poor country, unstable economically and culturally. Yet its history is very old, thousands of years before Christ."

She liked this man. He was intelligent, soft-spoken, and just looking for conversation to pass the time. "You mean the Mayan civilization?"

He smiled and seemed pleased that she wasn't completely ignorant of his culture. "Yes, the temple pyramids of Tikal, in the north, were once the tallest structures in the hemisphere until the development of office buildings in the nineteenth century . . ." He then told her of the great cities of that era, the conquest by the Spaniards, the many revolutions, the domination by the army, the assassinations of presidents, the unrest of the people.

She listened with a fascinated dismay. Was he warning her, or setting himself up as tour guide? Thinking she must be getting paranoid, she finished her drink and ordered another.

"Are you staying in the city during your visit, or are you planning any excursions?" he asked.

"I'm leaving tomorrow morning for Chichicastenango. There's an orphanage nearby that I plan to visit. How long will it take by car?"

"You are driving by yourself?" He seemed shocked.

Shrugging, she answered, "I'm a very cautious driver and I have extensive road maps. I'm sure I'll be fine."

"And you're not frightened? There are guerrilla bands that roam the countryside seeking to attack army patrols. I would not suggest you make this trip alone. A bus would be more safe."

Thinking of all the years the Rotary Club had done it, Eve sat up and straightened her shoulders. She had come too far to be frightened off now. "I'm not afraid, but thank you for your warning. I'll be very careful."

No sooner had the words left her mouth than she saw Luke Harrelson walking up to her table.

"Here you are," he said, barely glancing at her companion. "I had to pry it out of the concierge."

"What are you doing here?"

"We were going to discuss our itinerary, remember?"

She smiled at Francesco and then glared at Luke. "No. I don't remember."

Harrelson stuck out his hand and introduced himself. "Hi, I'm Luke Harrelson. And you are . . . ?"

Francesco shook his hand and repeated the courtesy.

Then, to her amazement, Luke pulled a chair from a nearby table and joined them.

"Can I buy you both a drink?" he asked, as though he had been welcomed.

She was about to tell him to leave when Francesco pushed his chair away from the table and rose. "I'm sorry, but I have an early business appointment." He shook Luke's hand again and then held hers in a gentle touch. "It was a pleasure to meet you. Thank you for the delightful conversation. Enjoy your visit to my country."

Before she could think of a single thing to say, he left as smoothly as he had appeared. Sputtering, she turned on Harrelson. "What the hell do you think you're doing?"

He held up his hand, signalling for a waiter, and said, "Well . . . at least you're talking to me again."

"I'm going to be shouting in a second if you don't explain yourself! How dare you follow me and interrupt my dinner?"

He looked at the space in front of her. "Seems to me like you've finished dinner. If I interrupted anything, it was Don Juan there. You have to be careful, Eve. You're easy prey for someone like him."

She was incredulous. "What do you know? He happens to be a respectable businessman. He even went to Drexel University." She was almost shaking with indignation. "Why am I explaining this to you for? Why won't you just leave me alone?"

He ordered a pitcher of sangria and then turned his attention back to her. "Did I really interrupt something? You were interested in that Casanova?"

"Stop calling him names. You don't know him. And no, I wasn't interested. Not like you mean. He was very nice."

"I'm sure."

"What is that supposed to mean?"

He crossed his arms at the edge of the table and leaned closer to her. "It means that this is a Third World country and your 'I am woman, hear me roar' attitude is useless down here. Males rule and women are not liberated, not like in the States. You have to remember where you are and make that adjustment in your mind."

"What the hell are you talking about?" He was really infuriating. "What adjustment? I didn't do anything wrong."

The waiter delivered the small pitcher of Sangria and Luke poured himself a glass. Sipping it, he sat back in the wicker chair. Leaning his head against it, he looked at her and smiled.

"Eve Cameron, you are one dynamic woman, but you're also foolish if you think you're invincible. You need me."

She blew her breath out forcefully through her mouth, making a very unladylike noise in the process. "Oh, right! Very clever, Harrelson. Scare me so I'll beg for the protection of a big, strong man? I don't think so."

He merely grinned, and she wanted to wipe that superior expression off his face.

"I never thought of myself as big and strong." He ran his hands over the front of his linen sports jacket. "I may weigh less than two hundred pounds, but I have covered three wars and I know something about adjusting to different cultures. I can be useful. I do speak the language."

"I have a Spanish dictionary, thank you."

He laughed. "You're not going to make this easy, are you?"

"Why should I?" she demanded. "I don't want you around me. Why can't you understand that?"

"Why don't you want me around? See, *that's* what's making this all so mysterious."

Closing her eyes, she groaned. "Oh, God, that snooping reporter's nose is twitching." She lifted her eyelids and glared at him. "There's nothing for you to report, except that I'm going to the orphanage tomorrow and delivering the money. That's it."

"There's a story in that."

"Bullshit. You could have stayed home and interviewed me when I came back. Something made you scramble around making last-minute arrangements. And, whatever it is, I don't like it. You can't just invade someone else's life like that. The media has turned into this powerful monster that no one wants to offend. But it doesn't have the right to obliterate privacy, and I'll fight you on every turn to make myself clear on that."

He finished his wine and poured another glass. "Nice speech," he said, looking directly into her eyes. "And if we were at home, I'd sit and debate the issue all night. But we're here in Guatemala, Dorothy, and you can't just click your heels to get home again if you run into trouble. You can't even converse with the people. Get real."

His condescending attitude struck a raw nerve, and she fought the urge to pour the pitcher of Sangria onto his lap.

"That's it," she announced, getting the attention of the waiter and indicating she wanted her check. She brought out her credit card from her purse and handed it over the moment the waiter came. She didn't even want to see the total bill. She wanted to leave as soon as possible.

"What? Now you're angry again?" Luke seemed surprised.

She couldn't even look at him. There was no point. After scribbling her name onto the American Express credit slip, Eve stood up and left him sitting there. "Good night, and goodbye."

She hurried out of the restaurant, determined to make it back to the hotel before Harrelson could catch up to her.

"Now, see . . . you didn't even wait for me to thank you for the drink."

She stopped dead in front of a jewelry store. "First of all, I didn't realize I paid for your drink. If I did I would have poured it in your lap."

He caught up to her and leaned his head down closer to hers. "Let's not fight again. Can't we work this out?"

She wanted to scream at him. "You won't listen to me. I want to be left alone. I don't need or want you. I can't be more blunt than that." She moved past him and continued toward the hotel's entrance.

He followed, like a lingering odor that just wouldn't leave her alone. She ignored him until she was standing in front of the elevator and waiting for it to open.

"Look, Eve, I'm sorry if you think I insulted you somehow. You may not want me, but you do need me."

She pushed the elevator button again, impatient to escape. When the doors opened, she hurried inside. So did Luke.

"Come on, Eve. This has gone on long enough. We need to talk."

Her emotions swirled inside of her like thick lava inside a volcano. Something had to erupt. "Talk? Take your macho bullshit somewhere else. I'm not buying it. I need you? You need me, and you need me for this story of yours, which I made perfectly clear from the beginning that I want nothing to do with. So now that we both know where the other one stands on who needs who . . ." The doors opened on her floor. "I would appreciate if you would get out of my way," she said while moving past him. "And out of my life," she added while the doors closed on his discouraged expression.

Dismissing him from her mind, she walked toward her room. All she wanted right then was a good night's sleep. Tomorrow she'd start her adventure. Alone.

CHAPTER 16

The weather was warm and sunny as she started off for the bank. She left her luggage with the bell captain at the hotel and planned to exchange the American Express traveler's checks for Guatemalan quetzals, then proceed to the car-rental agency. It was a good plan. Excited, knowing she would see Paulo that day, Eve was eager to begin her journey. She sat back in the taxi and tried to ignore the normal chaos on the streets. Soon she would leave the city and enjoy the serenity of the countryside. All she had to do was follow her plan.

Banco de Guatemala was situated by the post office, and not surprisingly, there was a crowd of men in front of it. She paid her fare and left the cab, checking first to make sure that the money belt she wore under her blouse was secure. She had read over and over in the guidebook that it was the safest way to carry valuables.

"Hay trato, senora."

"Puede ofrecer."

She was suddenly surrounded by men waving large bank notes at her and shouting something about exchanging her money. She might not have more than high school Spanish behind her, but she could see by their actions that these were some sort of street changers and they were trying to make her a better deal than the bank.

"No, thank you. Please let me pass."

They continued to harass her, surrounding her and making it impossible to get past them. She was starting to get frightened. Some were still shouting at her in Spanish. Others were saying something else, something she didn't need to understand. It was all said in their leering expressions and hand gestures. Panic started to rise up when she heard the laughter her confusion was generating.

"Let me go," she stated forcefully, and the men only laughed harder. She tried to push her way through them, but they banded closer together to block her way. Never had she felt such fear, for she could tell that the men thought of her as some sort of sick sport for that morning.

Suddenly, she felt an arm around her waist and she screamed, instinctively throwing her elbow into the chest of her attacker.

"Owaah, geez . . ."

Spinning around, she saw Luke bent over and clutching his chest. "What is this?" he muttered. "Payback?"

"Thank God it's you," she exclaimed, fighting tears as she heard the renewed laughter from the men.

"C'mon," Luke said, grabbing her upper arm and pulling her toward the bank doors. It seemed that they had provided the money changers with the best entertainment they'd had in days. Once inside the bank, Luke released her and took a deep breath, pushing his hair back off his forehead. "Now, who needs whom? How much more do we have to go through before you come to your senses?" He rubbed his ribs again. "That hurt."

She took off her money belt, then tucked her blouse back into her jeans. "Sorry, I didn't know. . . . But you have a point, Harrelson," she admitted. "This language barrier can be dangerous."

He looked shocked. "Are you serious? You're finally conceding that you need me?"

How it irritated her to admit it, but that scene outside had been too convincing. "Let's get this straight. I don't need you because you're a man. I need you as a translator. Period. I do not need you snooping around for a story. Now, let me change this money, or we'll never get on the road. I still have to rent a car."

His grin looked like a kid's who had just been promised a trip to Disney World. "I already rented one. It's outside."

She merely nodded as she walked away to the teller. It seemed like a fair exchange. She would put up with him, and in return his newspaper would pay for the car. Okay, so maybe she could relax around him now. *If* he understood that her privacy was paramount and he was not accompanying her to the orphanage. She'd make that point clear before they left the city.

Two hours later Eve turned her gaze away from the forest and looked down to the guidebook in her lap. If it wasn't a forest it was field after field of corn, with black beans running up the stalks. Very few towns provided any scenic relief, and the conversation between her and Luke was strained. He refused to stay away from the orphanage, saying it was the central story line for his article. The sooner they got there, the better. "It says if we follow the Pan American Highway to Los Encuentros junction at kilometer 127 we should turn right for the road to Chichicastenango."

"Hold on," Luke said, applying the brakes. "What's this up ahead?"

She saw a military roadblock and several uniformed men with guns standing in front of it. "What's going on?"

"I was reading in the paper this morning that there was some kind of guerrilla attack last night and an officer was shot. Who knows when you're in a country with this kind of civil unrest. Just get your passport and tourist card ready." They slowly pulled up to the roadblock.

Luke rolled down the window and spoke to a soldier. He turned to her and said, "They want us to get out of the car so they can search it. They're looking for insurgents. Probably the ones from last night."

It took about fifteen minutes for the group of men to search the car, go through their luggage, and interrogate them. Eve merely said her name while Luke did all the translating. Not for the first time that day, she was grateful that he was with her. Once back in the car and waved through the roadblock, she let her breath out and looked at him.

"You handled that very well. Thanks."

He glanced in her direction and grinned. "And that's only one of my many hidden talents. See? You do need me. Admit it."

"I did admit it. I said thank you. What more do you want?"

"Ahh . . . a very leading question. Do you really want to know?"

She returned her gaze to the road. "Forget it."

"What?"

"Whatever you're thinking."

"How would you know what I'm thinking?"

She could tell he was enjoying the turn in the conversation and decided to put an end to his delusions. "The contents of your mind are of no importance to me, especially your pathetic fantasies."

"Why, madam, I'm shocked. Whatever would lead you to believe that I was fantasizing, and that you were included in it?"

"Oh, just forget it," she answered, embarrassed now by the way he had turned it around.

"What if I don't want to forget it? Let's talk about fantasies. What's yours?"

"To be rid of you."

"Now, Eve . . . We've just established that you need me. I can't tell you how much I like the sound of that. I think I'll keep reminding you of it."

"See, I knew it was a mistake to tell you. I was just trying to thank you for handling those soldiers. I wasn't propositioning you."

He snapped his fingers. "Damn. Another of my fantasies blown."

She couldn't help it. She laughed. "You're absurd."

"*I'm* absurd?" He was shaking his head. "You decided

on the spur of the moment to make this trip. Alone, might I add. Do you always make decisions so quickly?"

She sat back and enjoyed the change of scenery. The forest was becoming more dense, taking on the appearance of a jungle. Every once in a while, orchids would dot the green foliage. It was really quite pretty. "No, that's a recent discovery. Ever since the scandal, something's been happening to me. Actually before the scandal—my son had just died and I guess the truth is I had a . . . a mini-nervous breakdown of sorts. I don't mean I went crazy, or anything, but I started to look at life differently. I looked at all the rules and the controls that society had put upon me and upon everyone I knew. They just didn't make sense any longer . . . not for me. So I started doing what felt right, not what sounded right. And I wasn't so afraid of change then." She stopping suddenly and looked at him. "This is not going to appear in an article. This conversation is . . . How do you say it? Off the record."

Keeping his eyes on the winding, narrow road, Luke nodded. "Got it. So what happened then? That's when you started looking to open Nirvana?"

"No. Ruthann and I met and I found my house. It seems that one thing led into another until it was opening night at the club. I know people, especially Rue, think I'm impulsive, but I'm not. I do a lot of thinking before I make a move. It has to feel right. Does that makes any sense to you?"

"Sure. You're getting in touch with your instincts. Some people would call it your soul."

She stared at him. This nosy, relentless reporter believed in soul? Before she could ask, he slammed on the brakes.

"What the hell is that on the road?"

Seeing a large tree branch, she picked up her guidebook again and thumbed through it. "I read somewhere that a tree branch means a disabled vehicle ahead. What should we do?"

"I guess we see if we can help. I'll get out and move it."

"No. That's okay. I'll do it." She opened the door and walked to the front of the car. The branch wasn't heavy, but it was wide enough to block passage. She picked it up and took it to the side of the road. When she dropped it and turned around, she was suddenly grabbed from behind.

A tiny frightened yelp escaped her lips as men started appearing from the woods. She tried to pull her arms free, yet it felt as though she were being held with steel bindings.

Bandits. They were going to be robbed!

Luke immediately got out of the car and was furiously yelling something in Spanish. The men were yelling back and pointing long rifles at him. It all seemed surreal, as if it was happening in a weird time-lapse frame. Terrified, she yelled over the pandemonium, "Luke, what's happening?"

"Be still, Eve. Don't say anything."

"But what do they want?"

"The car. Be quiet."

"The car? They can't have the car! What will we do?"

"Shut up. I'm trying to talk to them."

The man holding her jerked her arm back painfully and she shut up. This was not happening! This stuff took place in movies, not in real life!

There were five of them dressed in dirty clothes, some in jeans, others in camouflage. All seemed highly agitated, and Eve could smell the heat and humidity mixing with a predatory adrenaline coming from the man behind her. Shocked, her body felt numb as Luke was put up against the car and she was thrown forward. She landed beside him, and he took her arm and brought her close. Terrified, she pressed her side into his.

"Stay calm. Don't move and don't say a word."

She heard Luke's breath wheezing in and out of his lungs and could do no more than stare at the two men who were pointing rifles at them. The others seemed to be pulling their luggage out of the car and throwing it onto the road. Eve stared at one of the long metal barrels, seeing how the sun reflected off it, and felt a matching heat behind her from the metal of the car. It seemed to brand her skin. She couldn't think! She couldn't even react! She might be moments from death and her brain refused to function. . . .

Laughter invaded her senses and she turned her head to see the men going through her luggage. They were picking up the small Sesame Street characters she had brought for the children and tossing them to the road. "Please . . . don't."

"Eve, shut up!"

One of the men slowly rose and came in her direction. The look in his eyes frightened her far more than those of the men holding the guns. He said something in Spanish, in a low suggestive voice, and Luke groaned.

This time she didn't need a translator. From the wolfish grin and the hungry look, she knew exactly what the man wanted. Her heart, already on overload, began to slam into her chest wall. She heard its sound in her ears and felt it pounding in her hands and feet.

The man extended a sweaty hand toward her breasts and Luke moved to stop him. Suddenly a rifle butt connected with his stomach and he went down on the ground moaning. She knelt beside him, crying, and put her arm around his shoulders in protection.

"How dare you?" she shouted at the men through her tears. "We're Americans! We didn't do anything! We were bringing those toys to an orphanage!"

"Eve . . ." Luke gasped, trying to rise. "Don't make them angry."

"*No bas ala circa de la senora!* Stay away from the woman!"

A sixth man emerged from the woods, and it took only a few moments for Eve to identify him.

Francesco Suarez.

The others appeared to back away in deference as Suarez approached, and Eve slowly stood up.

"*You!* How could you do this?" she demanded. "Why?"

"My apologies," Suarez said to her, and then gave quick orders to his men. One rifle was still aimed at them, but the other men got into the car. "My intentions last night were to merely warn you off. However, circumstances have made it imperative that we avoid any further dealings with the military. And we can do that much easier by car than on foot."

Luke, standing next to her, rubbed his side and asked, "Are you part of the UNRG? The guerrilla group?"

Suarez only smiled when handed their passports. He looked through them and passed them both back to Luke. "You are a reporter, Mr. Harrelson?"

"Yes."

"Then tell your people that Guatemalans are like their national bird, the quetzal—unable to live in captivity. One day we shall be truly liberated, all of us . . . Indians and Ladinos. It may not occur in my lifetime, but it will take place. It is our country's destiny."

Eve's fear had turned to anger. "What are we supposed to do if you take our car? You can't leave us out here."

Suarez shrugged. "Your car is being confiscated by Unidad Revolucionaria Nacional Guatemalteca. When I met you last night, it was not my intention to use you. However, this morning it has become necessary for us to go north as quickly as possible. You have already passed through the main roadblock, and unfortunately there is nothing that can be done now. In a few hours a bus shall pass this way. Please consider that you have made a great contribution to our country, and your insurance would cover any losses."

"This is—is outrageous," Eve sputtered. "You can't just point guns at innocent people and—"

"Eve!" Luke's voice held a warning.

Suarez moved toward the passenger door. Before getting in, he said, "Under other circumstances, your money and valuables would also have found their way into the small coffers of the UNGR. However, I am not a thief. I am but a revolutionist who happened to have met a lovely woman last night. As you Americans say, 'God works in strange ways.' Perhaps we were put together last night for just this circumstance. *Vaja con Dios,* senora. I will remember your generosity."

Within moments of his closing the door, the car sped off down the road, leaving her staring at the dust in its wake.

"The paper is going to kill me. I've just lost a fucking car."

She spun on him. "The paper? Who cares what your paper thinks now! We're stuck out here in the—the bloody jungle! What are we supposed to do now? Oh God, they even have our maps and the guide book. We're in a foreign country with no idea how to get out of it. We have no food. No water. No idea where we are. And you . . . you just let him take the car and leave us! You told me to shut up. Maybe I could have talked to him and we could have compromised or something."

He looked shocked. "Excuse me? You didn't see the guns? What the hell did you expect me to do? Not to mention if it weren't for Miss Chatty Cathy last night giving out so much information to a total stranger . . . You might as well have asked him what model car he wanted."

She dismissed him and walked over to her luggage. Bending down, she started picking up the toys and throwing them back into her bag. "We'll just have to start walking."

"Where?" he demanded as he began gathering his own clothes. "Suarez said a bus will come by this way."

"He said a few hours. I'm not sitting here in the sun waiting for a bus. There must be a town nearby."

She zipped the large canvas bag and sat down on it. "What did I read to you earlier? We take the turnoff at kilometer . . . what? One twenty-seven? Or one thirty-five?"

"You're kidding, right? You expect me to remember?"

She wiped the sheen of sweat from her forehead and searched through her purse for the scrungee she had thrown in days ago. Finding it, she pulled her hair back off her neck and wrapped the fabric around it. There. At least she wouldn't have her hair dragging on her shoulders. "Okay, we just need a plan."

He followed her example and they both sat on their luggage in the small area of shade by the side of the road. "My plan is to sit here and wait for the bus. It's too damned hot to trek through the jungle, especially if we don't have any idea where we're going."

Her mouth already felt dry, and she looked down the road with longing. On the floor of the backseat of the car were cans of fruit juice. "I was never so scared in my life," she murmured. "I really thought we were going to die."

"Yeah, I know. I guess if it had to happen we should be glad Suarez was part of it. He seemed to have some say over the rest of them."

Contrition filled her heart and she said, "Thank you for trying to stop that man. How's your stomach?"

Luke pulled his shirt up and she saw a large red area that looked to be turning blue in spots.

"Sore," he answered, lightly touching the injured skin.

"I'm so sorry. I should have listened to you and shut up."

He looked over at her and grinned. "I never thought I would hear you say that. I never thought I would hear any woman say she should shut up."

"Don't push it, Harrelson," she said, fighting a smile. "I guess I didn't react very well. No one has ever pointed a gun at me before." She wrapped her arms around her waist and felt her money belt. "You saved us," she exclaimed, standing up and pulling her blouse up. "Look, if that man had touched me he would have found the money. Thank you, Luke. You not only tried to save me, you saved the money for the orphanage."

He looked embarrassed and dropped his own shirt back down. He didn't tuck it in. Instead, he leaned his elbows on his knees and looked down the road. "So what do we do when we find a town? We have to report the car being stolen, but what about Suarez? Do we tell the authorities?"

She tied the edges of her white blouse together under her breasts. Modesty, at this point, seemed stupid. It was too hot to bother. "I don't know," she said, pacing back and forth in front of her suitcase. "I know he's a revolutionary, but I don't understand both sides of this thing. Let's decide when we get to a town. Right now, I think we should start walking. We're not accomplishing anything sitting here."

"We're conserving our strength. This whole trek is up-hill. A bus will come along soon enough."

"Suarez said a few hours. He could be lying. Or, even if one is scheduled to come, we're in a Third World country where schedules are fairly loose and it would still have to pass through that roadblock. How long do you think those soldiers will take to interrogate every single passenger? We could be out here until nightfall, waiting."

"Your plan is to walk hours in the sun?"

"What else can we do?"

"We can stay here and wait for the bus."

"I'm not taking that chance. I'm going to start walking, and if and when that bus comes it can stop for me. But if it doesn't, I'm going to look for a town."

She picked up her bag and started off down the road.

From behind her, she heard Luke shout, "God, woman, haven't you learned anything by this? Here you are, ready to storm off by yourself *again*!"

She didn't answer. She concentrated on the winding, narrow road. Soon she heard his voice once more, only this time it sounded right behind her.

"You are the most stubborn, headstrong woman I have ever met."

She grinned and threw over her shoulder, "Remember, Harrelson, you were the one who pestered me unmerci-fully to go along on this trip. You weren't invited."

"Okay, so that must make me as crazy as you are. Damn, it's hot."

She didn't want to think about it. Already she could feel the dampness at her back and her suitcase was start-ing to feel like a ton of bricks. "Let's not talk," she said, licking her lips to bring moisture back. "We'll just waste energy."

They walked for about forty-five minutes before she suggested they take a break. Sitting on the side of the road, she swatted at the flies and mosquitoes and felt like crying, but wouldn't spare the precious liquid. If they didn't come upon a town soon, she was afraid she wouldn't make it. What in the world had she been thinking when she'd planned this trip? She should have just wired the money and been done with it. Then a vague mental picture of a four-year-old boy entered her mind and she stood up to face the road once more.

An hour later they were again sitting under the shade applying sunblock that she had just remembered was in her bag. They were both already burned, but it felt cool and soothing.

"I'm dying of thirst," Luke said in a raspy voice. "How're you doing?"

She tried to bring moisture back into her mouth, yet it felt like cotton. "Yeah, I feel like I could knit sweaters over here. Doesn't it ever rain?" She squinted up to the sun and quickly looked away. "Don't you think we should have come to a town by now?"

He had a tube sock wrapped around his forehead to catch the sweat from running into his eyes, and he wiped his face on his arm sleeve. "I'd be happy to just see another human being. I didn't think it was going to be this remote." He swatted away a huge insect. "I feel like I'm on a deserted island."

"If it were an island, as least there'd be water. I don't know how much more of this I can take." Yet she knew what he meant. Right then, it seemed as if there were just the two of them in the whole wide world.

"Well, just think about what you'll do when we get to town. That'll take your mind off it. I know I'm going to get a bath and drink a shitload of tequila, or whatever booze they've got. And a pool . . . think they'll have a pool?"

She sighed as a small warm breeze blew across her skin. "If there's a pool, I'm going to sleep in it. I've never wanted water so much in my life. God, I've never felt this hot, thirsty, or isolated."

"Survivalist training. This is like the worst kind of outward bound—"

"Wait!" She sat up straight and looked down the road. "Jesus, Luke, is that a mirage? Or can it be . . . ?"

He shot up and held his hands over his eyes. "It is!" he shouted. "It's the bus!"

She joined him, and the two of them were like children playing ring-around-the-rosy as they danced in the road. "It's here! It's here! We're not going to die!"

He hugged her until she had to pull away, and then he slapped her back. She yelped in pain from the sunburn, yet didn't scold him. She was so grateful that she would endure anything until the bus stopped.

Luke was standing in the middle of the road, waving his arms to flag down the bus. He looked like a crazed lunatic, and Eve started to laugh. "I think they see you."

"What's that say on the bus? Where's it going? Los Encuentros?"

"That's the town we were walking toward. You turn off

there for Chichicastenango. We were right! We're going to make it!"

He turned to her then and something in his eyes made her stop laughing. Without saying a word, he walked up to her and held her face between his hands. He quickly planted a firm, hard kiss directly on her lips, and she almost lost her breath in the process. Before she could recover, he picked her up by the waist in a bear hug and swung her around in a circle.

"You're right, you crazy, stubborn, impulsive woman. We are going to make it."

CHAPTER 17

"What do you mean there's no bus out of here tonight?" She sat at a small table in the tiny restaurant, the only restaurant in Los Encuentros; it was attached to the only gas station.

"Go easy on those rum and Cokes," Luke warned as he joined her at the table. "At this altitude, they're going to affect you."

"Fine. Fine," she conceded. "Now, what about the bus?"

He ordered another tequila and water and placed a piece of paper in front of her. "The bus we were on is returning to Guatemala City in twenty minutes. Another bus will come tomorrow morning that will go on to Chichicastenango. We can either go back to the capital and start off tomorrow again, or spend the night here."

Eve looked around her to the small, backward town. "Here? Where?"

Luke shrugged. "You're not going to like it."

She closed her eyes and sighed with defeat. She felt completely vanquished. "Tell me."

"There's a small inn, but it's full. The passengers of the bus already knew they were stuck here overnight. The only thing left is a barn."

Her eyelids snapped open. "Excuse me? I don't think I heard correctly. A *barn*?"

"Eve, look around you. This isn't even a town. It's more like a settlement. The innkeeper said he'll give us some blankets and we can use the community bathroom and—"

"I've used it," she interrupted. "It's . . . unspeakable."

"Then our other option is to catch the bus back to Guatemala City and get a decent room there."

"Go all the way back? Start all over again?" It wasn't even a consideration. She couldn't do it. Los Encuentros was a mile and a half above sea level, but somewhere beyond this mountain, on a plateau, was the orphanage. She was close. She could feel it. One night's delay. That's all it was. The sun was fading and the air was considerably cooler this high up, yet she just didn't have the energy to backtrack—even for a hotel room with a bath.

Her sunburn started to react to the cool air and she began shivering. "Where is this barn?"

Luke pointed down the road. "Somewhere behind the inn. Do you want to look at it before you make up your mind?"

She shook her head. "It really doesn't matter at this point. I can't go back, Luke. If I did, I'm afraid I might not try again. It's only one night. I know Chichicastenango has hotels. I've seen pictures for years. Tomorrow we'll treat ourselves to the best one. All we have to do is get through tonight."

"You're sure?"

She took a deep breath and felt slightly dizzy. It must be the altitude. Holding up her glass of rum and Coke, she said, "I'm sure. It'll be part of the adventure. Besides, we're too close to turn back."

"All right, then." He clinked his glass of tequila with hers. "Do you want another tortilla? Maybe we should bring some supplies with us. How about—"

"They're out of bottled water. That's why I'm drinking rum and Coke."

"You're kidding. No water?"

"Just the village water. I don't know about you, but I'm not taking any chances. I'm sunburned, exhausted, and sleeping in a barn. I'm not about to flirt with an intestinal disaster."

"Right." He looked around him. "Damn, it's gotten cold. The innkeeper said that at night the temperature can go down to freezing way up here in the mountains."

"Freezing?" She started laughing. Maybe it was the rum. Maybe it was the crazy day. Maybe she was losing it. It didn't even matter anymore.

"Are you okay?" Luke appeared worried.

She stopped laughing. "Tell me . . . what else can happen? We're sunburned during the day and freezing at night. After, I might add, we were robbed of our car by revolutionaries. Nobody's gonna believe this. If you were looking for a story, Luke Harrelson, you've certainly got one."

"I hear ya. Oh, by the way, I also stopped into the post office and called the car-rental agency in Guatemala City. They're notifying the authorities and they'll catch up with us tomorrow in Chichi. I said we were robbed by bandits. I didn't say anything about Suarez."

She nodded. "I'm glad. I don't think he meant us any harm. We'll just say they took the car and never spoke to us about anything. I don't want to get involved with the police here."

"I'll handle it. The car was in my name."

"Good." She held her forehead and sighed. "God, I'm tired. Let's buy some food and something to drink and then check out this barn. I need to lie down."

He paid the bill and together they bought their supplies. Each carried a string bag of food and drink, along with their luggage, as they walked through the small village. Several people stared at them, and she supposed it wasn't too often that Americans spent the night—especially in a barn.

Ten minutes later, she stood in front of the makeshift shelter and stared in dismay at their lodging for the night. It was the size of a large walk-in closet. One window allowed the last of the sun's rays to illuminate the miserable interior. Hay was stacked against the wall and a small stove was situated near the door and venting outside.

Luke opened the rusty door to the stove and peeked in. "I guess they use it to keep the animals warm."

"Great. If it wasn't so cold, I'd sleep outside. What are we gonna do now?"

He stood beside her with his hands on his hips as he surveyed the barn. "We'll make up our beds."

She raised an eyebrow. "We will? And where are they?"

He pointed to the hay. "Right there. Which do you prefer, madam? Twin? Double? Sorry, can't offer you a queen. Space is limited."

In spite of everything, she smiled. "I'm sorry, Luke. You're right. We have to make the best of this, and I've done nothing but complain."

Standing next to her, he put his arm around her shoulders and said, "Hey, you've been a real trouper. I can't name many women who wouldn't have fallen apart by now."

She glanced up at him. "Is that a sexist statement?"

He laughed and held his hands up in surrender. "I give up. I can't even give you a compliment. You are my equal, Eve Cameron. Only, don't let too many of the men in town know. They aren't enlightened yet."

She playfully slapped his hand down. "Stop it. And thank you for the compliment. Now, c'mon . . . let's see what we can do about this place. I have got to lie down soon. But first . . ." She opened her luggage and pulled out a thin rectangular bottle. Holding it out toward the interior of the barn, she began spraying. "If Coco Channel could see this, she'd turn over in her grave. Seventy bucks, and I'm using it for a barn deodorizer."

It took a half hour to clean out the shelter, pull together makeshift hay mattresses, and store their meager supplies. She had decided on a twin, since a double was out of the question. Sitting crossed-legged on her *bed,*

Eve pulled her arms into her sweater, the warmest article of clothing she had brought, and looked at her companion.

Luke was trying to start a fire in the stove, but producing more smoke than warmth, when the innkeeper appeared. He helped ignite the stove and left a small bundle of wood for the night. Luke spoke to him for less than a minute and came back into the barn with a lantern. "Not that we have any, but he wanted to let me know that they shut off the electricity at ten o'clock."

"The whole town?"

He nodded. "So if we need anything, we have to get it now."

She looked around at her surroundings and sighed. "What could we possibly need?"

He stuck his hands into the back pockets of his jeans. "I hate to bring this up, but I know how some women can be about it."

"What?"

"A bathroom."

She laughed and, in truth, was wondering the same thing. "What can we do?"

Shrugging, Luke said, "I can use the woods, but . . ."

". . . but you don't think I can," she supplied the rest of his words, "Hey, I'm your equal, Harrelson. Maybe we should have swiped some toilet paper."

"Why do you have to call me by my last name, like we're in the army together or something?"

She giggled. "I'm sorry, *Luke.* I'll try to remember." She lay down and pulled the cover over her shoulders.

"Eve?"

"Hmm?"

"I have a surprise for you."

She leaned up on her elbow, feeling like a eager child. It was pathetic. "What?"

"I just paid the innkeeper extra money for him to let us take a bath, *and* use the inn's toilet."

She bolted upright and pulled her sweater into place. "Really? Oh, God . . . a bath!"

It was his turn to laugh at her excited reaction. "Yes. We have to go now, though, before the electricity is shut off and there's no hot water."

"I'm ready. I'm ready," she chanted, slipping on her shoes and grabbing up her purse. "What'll we do about our luggage? Will they be safe here?"

"We can hide them behind the hay and bolt the door, or I can stay here while you go."

She looked around the barn while thinking that he must feel as grungy as she did, and he had been the one to secure the bath. It wouldn't be fair. "Let's hide the bags and bolt the door. You've got the stove going, so anyone who passes by will see the smoke outside and think one of us is in here. It should be okay. It'll have to be. Frankly, as long as I have the money and my passport, I couldn't care about anything else. I want a bath."

He grinned at her. "Let's do it."

They were like two little kids after their bath as they ran back to the barn with wet heads and chattering teeth. Shivering, Eve checked the luggage while Luke stirred the embers in the stove and added more wood.

"Listen," she said, rubbing her arms to deflate the gooseflesh that had popped out over her body. "We were in such a hurry that we forgot to bring any clean clothes with us. Could you like . . . turn around for a few minutes while I change? I know this is awkward and—"

"It's okay," Luke answered, rubbing his hands together. "Go ahead. I'll stay here in front of the fire and get warm."

She grabbed fresh panties, her soft cotton nightgown, and white socks. Stripping quickly, she threw on the clean garments and pulled her sweater over her head. She then rolled her dirty jeans and blouse and stuffed them in her luggage. When she was sitting on the makeshift bed, she brought the wool blanket up to her waist and called out, "Okay, you can turn around."

The expression on his face seemed to change, and Eve was suddenly reminded of that kiss on the road. She had put it out of her mind, refusing to interpret the whirlpool of emotions that had surged up inside of her at the contact.

"You look like a little girl sitting there."

His voice was low and appreciative, and Eve could only blink. Her brain was already on overload and she was not going to analyze anything tonight. Yet she studied the way his wet hair looked darker and dropped tiny beads of water onto his cheeks and shoulders . . . the way his eyes seemed more warm and intense. Realizing what she was doing, she shook herself.

"I feel like a little girl. That was the last time I went camping. Come to think of it, this isn't much different than the overnight camping trip I took with the Fireside Girls."

"You were a Fireside Girl?"

"Uh . . . huh." Why was he looking at her like that?

He left the stove and slowly came closer. Her whole body tensed, and she wished she could say that it was from the cold. It wasn't. When he reached down to her she thought she could hear her heartbeat in her ears, and held her breath in anticipation.

He grabbed his bag from behind her where she had hidden it in the hay, and her breath audibly left her mouth before she could muffle it. How stupid! Now she was projecting things! What the hell did she think he was going to do? She mentally shook such thoughts out of her head.

"Clean clothes," he stated as he unzipped his bag and pulled out white Jockey shorts.

"Right," she answered, embarrassed to have let her mind think anything else. "I'll umm . . . you know . . . give you some privacy."

She quickly turned around to sit facing the wall with the window. Her hands felt like ice, and rubbing them together to bring back some warmth, Eve mentally cursed. What in the name of God was going on? Why was she allowing her mind to entertain any thoughts of Luke Harrelson, except as a useful traveling companion? And why did she suddenly lose the ability to speak without stammering? She was an adult, not some silly girl caught for the night in the woods with her boyfriend.

Then why was it beginning to feel like that?

"Ready."

She continued to stare at the dark window. The realization was sudden and revealing, and Eve felt frozen with shock. It was so uneasy, so unfamiliar, like an old friend who had gotten you in trouble years ago. When did she start feeling like a whole woman again?

"Did you hear me? You can turn around now."

She slowly inhaled and shifted her body back toward the center of the mattress. "I want a drink."

"A drink?" Luke stopped folding his jeans and looked down at her. "For the cold? It really doesn't make you warm, you know."

"I don't care," she muttered, and scrambled to the bottom of her mattress for the string bag of supplies. She didn't want to look at his chest while he pulled that sweatshirt over his head. She didn't want to see the muscles in those legs. Unscrewing a bottle of Coke, she bit her bottom lip with determination. No way was she going to let her thoughts keep her up all night, lying next to Luke Harrelson.

She placed the Coke bottle on the ground and pulled out a small bottle of tequila from Luke's supplies.

"You don't want to mix that."

She ignored the scandalized voice behind her and unscrewed the tequila. Gulping a mouthful of Coke, she made room for the liquor and then held the glass bottle out before her. She picked up the alcohol and poured in a good amount. Satisfied, she then twirled the mixture for a few seconds.

"There."

"Eve, it's going to taste awful."

She didn't answer him. She picked up the bottle, held it to her lips, and took a big gulp. It passed her taste buds like liquid fire and immediately numbed them to the horrific experience, before descending into her stomach and radiating a sensation of unpleasant heat. Gasping for breath, Eve heard laughter.

"I told you so."

She glared at him, dressed in his sweats and throwing his bag back into the hay. "It's not funny," she managed to rasp out from her traumatized vocal cords. Crawling, with her bottle, to the top of her mattress, Eve scrambled under the cover and turned her back to him. She already felt warmer and actually wiped a thin sheen of perspiration from her forehead. She could do this. All she needed was to somehow drink this concoction and pass out.

He picked up his bottle of tequila and the lantern and lay down facing her. Getting under the covers, he said, "I don't know how that stove keeps animals warm. I'm freezing."

She held out her bottle. "This'll keep you warm."

His expression showed his distaste, and he shook his head. "Thanks. I won't desecrate a fine alcohol." Picking up the bottle of tequila, he looked at the label and added, "Maybe not so fine, but I'll still drink it straight."

She shrugged, already feeling calmer. "Suit yourself."

Neither one of them said anything. The silence wasn't strained, yet it wasn't quite comfortable either. "Thanks for the bath," she said to fill the void. "I don't think I've ever enjoyed one more."

He looked at her and smiled. "You're welcome. You know, you should wear your hair like that more often."

"Like what?" She leaned up on her elbow and felt the wet ponytail gathered behind her head.

"Back. Off your face."

No man had ever said that to her. She supposed every woman, no matter what her looks, knew that she used her hair to frame her face. Eve admitted that she wasn't any different. She thought of the thousands of dollars she had literally thrown down the drain on shampoos, conditioners, gels, mousses, hair sprays, perms . . . It was supposed to be her crowning glory! Wasn't that what she had been taught by her mother, her friends, the magazines she read, the commercials she watched? And here was a man saying that he liked it back, away from her face? And her face . . . She didn't even want to guess how much money she had spent on makeup and creams and . . . She told herself to forget it. That wasn't the issue. It was another discovery. Eve had to admit that the older her face got, the less inclined she was to expose it naked. And here sat Luke Harrelson telling her that he liked it that way, or at least something about it was appealing. He liked her. No artificial distractions. Naked.

"Are you okay? You look like you're zoning out."

She brought herself into the moment, and smiled at him. "Must be this firewater. I can't wait to tell Ruthann and Mick. Why, we can serve it at Nirvana." She took a swig and fought to catch her breath as she again experienced the shock to her system. It was only slightly less disturbing. After managing a couple of deep breaths, she whispered in a hoarse voice, "We'll call it The Wrong Turn."

He laughed at her. "To where? Nirvana?"

She was bobbing her head up and down. "Right. I don't know how you get there—meditations, chanting, ohm-ming out to the universe, something—but it sure as hell ain't this way." She shivered as a current of distaste raced through her body. "One drink and you understand why."

"Have you ever been there? Nirvana?"

She blinked a few times, wondering if she really was getting drunk. He couldn't be serious. "What are you talking about? How can you get there? I mean, don't you have to be a Buddhist monk or something?"

He laughed, not in a condescending way, but more like he was pleased that she hadn't entirely dismissed his question. They were both lying on their sides, propped up on one elbow and facing each other. She thought about what they had gone through during the day and felt, somehow, intimately connected to him.

"I think people can catch glimpses of it every now and then," he said in a low voice. "That's why we instinctively believe it's out there."

"And you've had these glimpses?"

"Absolutely. When I held my first puppy. When I hit a triple against the Freehold Lions in freshman year. The first time I made love and knew I had pleased a woman as much as she'd pleased me. Holding my daughter in my arms . . . The list goes on."

She stared at him, seeing more of the man inside. "You have a daughter?"

"I had a daughter . . . for three days."

"Three days?"

He looked to the stove and whispered, "She was born premature. We all thought she was going to make it." He brought the bottle of tequila to his mouth and drank deeply.

"I'm so sorry," she whispered. She wanted to touch him, to give him comfort, yet held herself back. It wasn't her place.

"It should have brought us closer together, me and my wife. . . . We were divorced within a year."

She felt a lump in her throat and swallowed it down. "I know what you mean. When my son got sick Paul and I sort of drifted apart. He felt guilty because of this mess down here and couldn't handle it. I thought he was deserting Jamie and me, and resented him. When I found out about . . . When I learned the truth about the orphanage, I divorced him in six weeks."

"Do you regret that?"

She shook her head and smiled sadly. "No. In retrospect, it was probably the best thing that could have happened. My life turned in a totally different direction. Truth is, I wouldn't be here in this barn if I hadn't divorced."

He waved his bottle around the small shelter. "Hey, I don't know if we can blame all this on your ex."

She lay on her stomach and, leaning on her elbows, propped her head in her hands. "The funny thing is, I don't really resent him any longer. That's weird. I guess I feel sorry for him. For all the men, really. They lost so much."

"And you didn't?"

"I lost everything before the scandal broke. My marriage was holding together by a thin thread when I heard about it. It just forced me to act." She turned her head and looked at him. "Why are we talking about this? It's depressing."

"Okay. What do you want to talk about?"

"Let's talk about you. What wars did you cover? Do you like your work?"

He lay down and stared at the rough-planked ceiling of the barn. "I covered Vietnam—the end of it—Grenada, and the Gulf War. That discussion would also be depressing. Do I like my work? For the most part. I try not to get too cynical, but it's hard when every single day stories come in over the wire about what human beings are doing to each other. Sometimes I think the world has gone crazy."

"I don't read the newspaper any longer. Sorry about that. Or listen to the local news. I'll watch the network news to find out what's going on in the world, but the rest of it . . . I feel so frightened. It's always about death and destruction. Stay tuned after this commercial break to find out what food is killing you now, what your correct cholesterol level should be. Don't eat this. Don't drink that. Stay out of the sun. Watch a burning home. A dead body in the street . . ." She shook her head. "I don't want to be brainwashed anymore."

"Is that what you think the media does?"

She raised a questioning eyebrow. "I've had close, personal contact with the media and seen how it manipulates for ratings. I guess I'm cynical too."

"We make quite a pair."

He looked at her, and she felt that same turmoil of emotions swirling around inside her as when he had kissed her and then when he'd said he liked her hair. His eyes were warm and his smile inviting. Lord, she must be getting drunk. Nervous, she said, "Maybe we should go to sleep. We have a big day tomorrow."

"Right." He turned down the wick on the lantern and the barn was cast into darkness, save for the dim orange light coming from the stove.

She removed the scrungee from her hair and fluffed it out before putting her head down. "Good night, Luke."

"Night, Eve. Are you okay? You warm yet?"

She giggled as she pulled the blanket up to her shoulders. "This is a very strange place. Hot during the day, and cold at night. But thanks for asking. You've done everything you could to make this bearable. I won't complain."

"You're cold."

"I'm not complaining."

"I have a suggestion."

She didn't want to hear it.

"We could share our body heat and—"

She laughed and pushed his shoulder. "Stop. Don't even suggest it."

Chuckling, he turned on his side to her. "No, seriously. It's a scientific fact. The military even confirmed it."

"Like I would believe the military."

"Now you sound like a revolutionary. The media is trying to scare you and the military can't be trusted. Maybe that's why you liked Suarez so much."

"Get out of here. Tell me the truth, Luke, do you trust the military? Any military? Honestly?"

"No. Not really. I've seen too much."

"Thank you. We've all been lied to, and we instinctively know it. We hear what they want us to hear, and we accept it because nobody wants to challenge something so complex and so powerful as the government. Look what's happening in this country right now. What we went through today on the road . . . I don't approve of Suarez and his methods, but I have to admire someone who takes a stand against corruption. Maybe what I'm thinking is revolutionary, to question or tune out and make my own decisions about what's real. But it's a private revolution. I'm not trying to get anyone to join."

"So . . . does this mean you don't want to share body heat? I'm confused."

Laughing, knowing she'd been caught trying to change the subject, Eve picked up her bottle of Coke and unscrewed the top. "I think I'll stick with this." She took a gulp and shivered in response.

"Gee, thanks. I'm highly insulted. You'd rather chug that swill than get close for warmth? I took a bath."

She looked at him in the subdued glow from the fireplace. His expression was open, and she couldn't detect a ploy. Part of her wanted to stay up all night and guard her emotions, yet a stronger part wanted to snuggle up against him and just go to sleep.

"If I do this, then there's no monkey business. I mean, this is for warmth. Nothing else."

He laughed. "Eve, nothing will happen that you don't want to happen. I promise."

"Well, I don't want anything to happen. I want to go to sleep."

"Then that's what we'll do. C'mere. Let's push these two together and make one warm bed."

She sat up and helped him pile hay in the small space

that had separated them. He pulled his blanket over it and lay down, using her blanket for cover. Holding it back, he said, "Your bed awaits, milady."

She smiled. "Well, at least the archaic language is correct, considering we'll be sleeping on a pile of straw."

Crawling in beside him, she tensed until she turned away with her back to him. When she breathed deeply, she had to admit that it was better and she really could feel the heat coming from his chest behind her.

"Relax, Eve. I'm not going to jump you."

"I know," she answered, yet something was holding her back. Determined to rest, she willed the muscles in her body to relax.

"There. Now, doesn't that feel better?"

"Yes," she admitted, realizing that she was exactly where she wanted to be. "Thanks."

"Does this mean the military is right about something?"

Grinning, she said, "Be quiet and go to sleep."

"No more talking?"

"No more. We have a bus to catch in the morning."

"But I liked it."

"We'll talk tomorrow. Geez, Harrelson, you sound like a little kid. Go to sleep."

"Yes, ma'am."

Silence filled the barn and Eve sighed deeply, feeling the effects of the alcohol. A warm buzzing sensation permeated her body, and she could perceive the heaviness in her arms and legs taking her deeper. Sleep was just around the corner of her lids.

"Eve?"

"Hmm?" He really was just like a child, fighting sleep every step of the way.

"It was one hell of a day, wasn't it?"

She barely nodded. "It was."

"Good night."

"'Night. . . . And, Luke? Thanks. You were my hero today."

She heard an appreciative grunt behind her and smiled.

It came upon her gently, wrapping its soft arms around her and taking her away—away from her troubles, her sunburn, the itching of the straw and the wool blanket, the cold, the man lying behind her. Time and space faded as she sank deeper and deeper, until she was warm and happy and standing barefoot in the sand. The foam from an ocean's wave ran over her feet and she felt them sinking into fine particles of sand as the cool water gently withdrew and tickled her skin. The sun shone warmly on her head and she was happy, filled with a sense of well-being. Children were laughing and she looked up to see a group beyond the waves, some riding them in to the shore. Jamie waved his hand while he treaded water, and she waved back. Her heart was filled with such love that it was overwhelming. She knew she would do anything for that child, even give up her life. She felt like a lioness as she walked the shore, filled with unconditional love.

She found a seashell and bent to pick it up. A King's Crown, with its stripes and swirls of points. It had always reminded her of one of the crowns on the Wise Men. She sat down in the sand and studied it, turning it over and over in her hands. Wet sand fell out of it and she rubbed it between her fingers. Looking at it closely, she wondered how some sand stuck to people's feet and was tracked away from the ocean. Was it wiped off, swept up and thrown in the garbage, only to have to make that same long ecological trip back to its home?

Luke sat down next to her and took her hand. Holding his own above it, he seemed to pour something into her palm.

"Sometimes sand chooses to become a pearl," he said, smiling with love.

She looked into her hand and saw a string of fine pearls. She smiled her thanks before putting them on and turning to him.

"This is for you." She blew into the shell to clean it out and gave it to him.

"I'll keep it always," he promised. "Now a part of you, your life's breath, is inside."

Her heart filled with love for him and she knew she was blessed to have found him. Luke and Jamie . . . the loves of her life.

Suddenly she heard the children yelling and she looked toward the water. Some were standing at the edge, pointing and shouting. She searched the waves for her son. All the children were dark. His blond head was not there.

"Jamie! Something's happened to Jamie!" She clutched the pearls so tightly that they broke and scattered in the sand. A piercing pain shot through her, straight to her heart. Fear grabbed her and spread out like a knife, cutting away her insides.

"He's dead! Luke, help me . . . please. Help my son!"

She turned and grabbed his shirt, but he didn't move. Then she saw that his face was gray and his eyes were dull. And he was cold . . . so very cold.

She screamed and backed away from him. He was dead too! She was alone, with no one to turn to. No one in the world loved her or wanted her or could help her. . . .

Then she felt the soft stroking of her hair. Someone's warm fingers were gently caressing her forehead and cheeks, telling her that it was all right now. She was safe. . . .

"Shh . . . it's okay, Eve. You're all right."

She heard whimpering, like a small child's, and realized it was her own. The stroking continued and she felt herself move into it, waiting for its return, wanting it. She sensed heat behind her and snuggled into it, moaning as it touched her and sent off rays of hot pleasure.

Pleasure? Eve suddenly realized she was awake and the stroking was not a dream. She stiffened and immediately removed her back and rear end from his chest and . . . and whatever she had been rubbing up against. "Oh, God, I'm sorry," she muttered. "I was dreaming and . . . I'm so embarrassed."

"Come back here," he ordered in a rough voice, and pulled her to him again, only this time she was facing him. "Look, I would feel flattered by that statement, except it sounded like—no, I know, you were having a nightmare. And, lady, if you say sleeping next to me did that, I'm gonna take offense."

Shaking her head, she felt her breath against his chest and struggled to find a place for her arm. She settled for her hip. "No, it wasn't you. I was dreaming. Crazy, stupid dream. It made no sense."

"Care to tell me about it?"

She sniffled again and said, "It was just a dream about a vacation my family took years ago."

"I was there? You were calling out to me to save somebody. Your son?"

She nodded and felt the tears come back into her eyes. "Jamie. I dreamed he had drowned. It was horrible."

He brought his hand up and stroked her hair again. God, how she missed that gesture of tenderness. Closing her eyes, she let the tears come, and she didn't know if she was crying for her son or herself.

"It was only a dream," he whispered at her hairline. "It's over now."

His fingers slid through her hair and glided over her back. She let him. It felt too soothing, too right, to protest. Soon, tiny sounds of appreciation escaped her lips, yet she still didn't censor it. Ten minutes must have passed as he tried to ease her back to sleep.

"I gave you a seashell," she murmured, reveling in his touch and thinking back to the part of the dream where he was sitting next to her. "A King's Crown."

"Did I thank you?"

She shook her head. "That's when I heard the children shouting and I knew something was wrong."

He moved slightly away and held her chin in his hand. Tilting her face up, he stared into her eyes. "Then I'll thank you now, and we can make up a whole different ending."

Lowering his head, Luke allowed his lips to touch hers

ever so slightly, as if he were memorizing the feel of them. When she opened her mouth partly in response, he deeply inhaled and deepened his kiss. Her arms automatically wound around him, pulling him closer, and together they rolled over until she was lying on her back and he was above her.

When they finally broke apart, he whispered, "You have no idea how much I've wanted to do that . . . ever since opening night. My God, woman, it was better than I had imagined." And then he held her face and kissed her again and again, taking away her breath and her reason.

Never in her life had she made sudden, impulsive love, and yet it felt like a perfectly choreographed dance between them. Touching, stroking, discovering . . . Even the awkwardness of clothing was sensuously removed. In the glow of the stove, she watched him and wondered if she still wasn't dreaming. Their bodies fit together so perfectly that they were like pieces of a puzzle finally reunited. There was no embarrassment, no clumsiness, only freedom and joy.

She felt alive again.

He told her that she was beautiful and she believed him. For that night, she believed she was a beautiful, desirable woman, capable of sharing her body and her soul with this man.

He sat with his back against the hay and she moved over him, allowing him to enter her slowly. His breath caught in his throat and she moaned with intense, deep pleasure.

They sat together in silence, save for the sound of

their breathing. He was running his hands over her body, speaking to her in a timeless language; she was tracing every inch of his face, needing to understand the wonder and reverence of the moment. Sensations, long buried, stirred inside of her, waking in response to his movements and she found tears running down her cheeks.

"Don't be sad," he whispered, wiping away a tear from her face. "Please, Eve, don't be sad about this. I couldn't take it if—"

She placed her finger against his lips to stop him. "They're tears of joy, Luke," she whispered back. "I feel . . . whole again."

He crushed her to him and she wrapped her arms around his head, bringing him to her breasts and into her heart. Frenzied, feverish, it became a primordial dance, perfected through the ages to a point of no return, to where every nerve ending and muscle participates, until it explodes in a shattering culmination of joyous energy that melds and ignites into one living dancer.

He called out her name and she threw back her head as she joined him in the final movements, rejoicing in their consummate miraculous fusion of mind, body, and soul.

Luke held her close as aftershocks continued to surprise them with pleasure. "My God, I have never felt like this with anyone in my entire life. Who *are* you, Eve Cameron?"

She slid off his body and settled in next to him, curled beneath his arm. "Shh . . . let's just hold each other for a while. I'm afraid to talk and break the spell."

He cuddled her and kissed her forehead. "I promise you. I won't break it."

She sighed with contentment and closed her eyes, finally at peace with the universe.

"Nirvana," she whispered.

"What?" His arms tightened around her protectively.

"I caught a glimpse."

CHAPTER 18

Light streamed into her consciousness and she sighed with contentment. Her eyelids fluttered opened and she glimpsed her surroundings before quickly shutting them again. She didn't want to deal with reality yet. Luke's body was next to hers, warm and protective. His arm was around her waist, and she reveled in the weight of it upon her stomach. For just a few minutes, she wanted to pretend that this was where she belonged. Her thoughts went back to the night before, and she could feel a blush creeping up from her throat. Who was that woman?

Something had been released inside of her, and she knew it was freedom. She had never been that uninhibited in her life. Not even with her husband. Then she had been playing a role, one that was expected of her. Last night there were no expectations. She had been herself.

Turning her head, she looked at Luke sleeping beside her. He seemed so peaceful and unaffected. And, even though she had thought of him as attractive, he now appeared downright handsome. Sort of like Kurt Russell. God, she sounded like a teenager! Smiling at her foolish thoughts, she resisted the urge to push his hair back off his forehead. What had taken place between them last night was so special, a cherished memory that she could relive over and over. Just thinking about it made her want him again, and she mentally pulled herself together. She had to get up and get something to eat, for both of them. That was it, she would get dressed. Find a bathroom some-where. Forget the woods. Get washed and get dressed and bring back breakfast. They still had to make a bus this morning, and it would save time.

Feeling happier than she'd felt in years, Eve carefully removed Luke's arm and placed it on the blanket. He stirred for a moment and then settled back asleep. Satis-fied, she got up and quickly changed into cotton shorts and a T-shirt. Gathering up her toiletries bag, she took one last look at the man who had helped her rediscover her-self, and left.

Eve had caught herself twice, humming and swinging the string bag filled with fruit, juice, and warm bread. She had to stop herself from picking a brilliant purple orchid and sticking it behind her ear. It was totally ridiculous to feel this good. She smiled at everyone she passed and greeted them with a cheery *"buenos días,"* feeling very at one with the world.

When she turned the corner behind the inn, she saw the barn in the distance and stopped short. It looked so small and decrepit. So primitive. She had spent the night there, with a man that she had known only a short time, the first man since she had married her husband. What would

Luke think this morning? Would he question her character? All that talk about no monkey business and she had been like a baboon in heat giving in to every one of her primitive urges. And who even said stuff like that anymore? Monkey business? If nothing else, that should have told her she was too damn old to be acting this crazy.

Finding an overturned wooden crate, she sat down with her back toward the barn. She felt suddenly embarrassed, and didn't want to face the consequences of last night. Maybe Rue was right. Maybe she did need professional help. Her actions last night had been completely out of character. What if he thought less of her for getting drunk and sleeping with him? It was the tequila. She simply wasn't herself. And what about being in a foreign country? He was her only verbal link. Of course she would form a relationship with him.

She stopped thinking, and tears started to blur her vision. In truth, she knew it wasn't the alcohol or the country. She had wanted it to happen, and had no one to blame but herself. Dear God, could she be falling in love with Luke Harrelson?

The thought made her stop crying. It was shock to discover that she was even capable of considering love again.

"Eve? What are you doing?"

She turned around and watched him walk up to her.

"Are you crying? What's wrong?"

Wiping at her face, she stood up. "Nothing. I was just sitting here thinking."

"And that made you cry?" He pulled her into his arms and kissed the tip of her nose. "C'mon, you're talking to a reporter here. What's wrong? Are you upset about last night?"

She looked up and saw that his eyes were searching hers for a helpful sign. "To be honest, yes I am."

He groaned and shook his head. "I was afraid of that. Look, tell me how you really feel so we can discuss this and deal with it immediately."

"My emotions are in an uproar now. I'm not really sure how I feel. I mean, I don't have any regrets about last night. Something very special happened for me, and I'll always be grateful to you for that, but I don't know how you feel about it. Like, do you think less of me because—"

"Stop," he interrupted. "You don't need to say anything else, and I don't want your mind to even consider more." His arms tightened around her and he grinned affectionately. "Last night blew my mind, lady. I feel so lucky, so fortunate, so blessed to have you in my life."

She was surprised by his words, and she merely stared at him.

"Okay, I know maybe that last statement was sudden. What I meant was . . . to have you in my life in whatever way you want to be. There's no pressure here, but you have to know, Eve, that I've felt this crazy pull toward you since I first saw you at the club. Why do you think I pushed so hard for this trip? Third World countries in political and social upheaval are not prime assignments. I was telling the truth on the plane, Eve. *You* were my assignment. I had to get to know you. I had to find out what this illogical attraction to a stranger was all about. The story on the orphanage was just a front. You're the reason I'm here at all."

She sniffled and smiled. "And I kept telling you to go away. Thank God you didn't listen."

"I'm persistent." He tightened his hold on her. "Now, any more questions? I don't want you to feel uncertain about anything."

All her fears disappeared. Her heart expanded and she whispered, "Just one. Are you hungry?"

His smile widened and his eyes seemed to darken with desire. "A very leading question. Absolutely."

She laughed and pulled out of his arms. Bending down to the bag at her feet, she withdrew a ripe peach. She held it up to his mouth and said, "This will have to do. We have a bus to catch in twenty-five minutes."

He took the peach and bit into it, then held it out to her. Accepting his offer, she smiled and bit into the soft fruit, feeling the juice run down to her chin. When she started to wipe it away, he grabbed her hand and pulled her to his chest again.

Lowering his head, he kissed her tenderly and whispered, "I cannot wait to get to the hotel today. I promise, I'll make up for last night."

"Last night was perfect. I wouldn't change anything," she whispered back, knowing in her heart it was true. That old, cramped barn would become a treasured memory.

The bus to Chichicastenango was an old American school bus with stiff seats and seven passengers crowded into each row. It made many stops along the way, where passengers climbed aboard, placed their machetes next to the driver, argued about the fare, and fought for a place to sit down. Women clutched chickens or squealing pigs, or nursed babies, and somehow a good number of passengers managed to doze off despite the bumping, shaking, cramped quarters and general chaos.

Eve took it all in good-naturedly. She wouldn't allow anything to shake her happiness. She and Luke joked about the conditions, and both agreed that it was a cultural experience and beat walking now that the temperature had again risen. They passed the time talking to their fellow passengers, one who spoke fluent English and told them the history of Chichi, the great marketplace for the Indians of the western highlands. He told them of the very old Maya-Quiché civilization that still had a strong influence on the people. He said that they should visit the four-hundred-year-old Santo Tomas church to see a mix of pagan and Catholic ritual, where the traditional mystical ways of Guatemala's indigenous people still visibly held sway. They would be arriving on market day, when traders from all over the region brought their goods, and he pointed out that they should wait to appreciate Chichi at peace.

Eve listened with fascination, yet soon realized that the purpose for this trip was not sight-seeing. She would visit the orphanage this day and meet Paulo. A mixture of excitement and nervousness gripped her when she thought about the meeting. And what about Luke? She knew she should tell him, yet there really hadn't been an opportunity. Would he think her foolish to have come all this way to look into the eyes of a small child?

The bus dropped them off at the center plaza of town where the market was in full swing, and walking through it reminded Eve of a medieval fair. Tables and tents were set up amid entertainers, and the commerce seemed furious. The noise level was fierce, and Luke led them away from the fair to the hotel that had been recommended by their companion from the bus.

The Mayan Inn was a tile roofed building, furnished with antiques from all over the country. It was tasteful, peaceful, and lovely. A far cry from Los Encuentros. Eve, sitting in the adjoining garden listening to marimba music while Luke made the arrangements, knew that the time had come for her to sort out her feelings and take action. Everything she had gone through in the last few days had led her to this place. The orphanage was a five-mile car trip, and Paulo Raphael Carrera was there.

"Hey, I got us a room with a terrace that overlooks the valley. Are you ready?" Grinning, Luke held up the room key.

"Come and sit with me for a minute."

"What's wrong? Did you want a separate room?"

She smiled and shook her head. "No. I have to tell you something."

He sat next to her. "This sounds serious."

"You were right when you wanted to know why I was making this trip. It isn't just to deliver the money."

"Don't tell me you're a drug smuggler," he teased.

"This is serious. At least it is for me. When I heard about the scandal, I not only found out that my husband has been having affairs down here, but one of the women had a child by him and died giving birth. That child, a boy, is living in the orphanage."

"Oh, Eve . . . And that's why you came here? To see this child?"

She nodded. "Ever since Jamie died, there's been this

emptiness inside of me that I can't fill. I knew I was grieving and that it was expected and everything, but something kept nagging at me and I couldn't place what it was. When I heard about the measles epidemic, I started thinking about Paulo—that's his name. I suddenly realized he's Jamie's half brother. Part of my son lives on, and I had to come. I know it sounds crazy. . . ."

"No, it doesn't." He pulled her into his arms and kissed her temple. "Now I see why you insisted on doing this alone. Whatever you want, Eve, I'll support you. You just tell me. If you don't want me to come to the orphanage, I understand."

Grateful for his compassion, Eve leaned her head on his shoulder and fought off the burning sensation in her throat. "I want you to come with me as Luke Harrelson my friend, but not Luke Harrelson the reporter. You can't write about any of this."

"Please. This is your personal business. I wouldn't violate you like that. And, lady . . . I hope I'm more than a friend."

She smiled and lifted her head. Staring into his eyes, she admitted the truth. "You are, and I'm glad."

He dangled a large key between them. "Then let's check out our room, get changed, and get started for the orphanage. Tonight, I'm going to treat you like a queen."

A half hour later they were driving through the rolling hills and steep canyons on their way to Tajumulco. Luke tried to talk, but she was too anxious for conversation and apologized. She just needed to get her thoughts together. They made the turnoff, and then it stood before her: long whitewashed stucco buildings connected by colonnaded passageways.

"God, I'm nervous," she muttered, clutching the door handle on the car. "I can't believe I'm finally here." She saw children playing baseball in the distance. "It looks just like all the pictures Paul took over the years."

"It's okay, Eve. You wouldn't be human if you weren't nervous. Don't worry, you've gone through too much to get here, and everything has a way of working out the way it's meant to in the end. Just let me know when you're ready."

She knew she was acting foolish, and taking a deep breath, she opened the car door. "Let's do it."

They walked up to the main building and were greeted by the director of the orphanage. He was delighted by their visit and thrilled by the donation of money.

"Your town has been very generous to us," Carlos Barrios said with a wide grin. "The children and I can't thank you enough."

Eve looked around the small office and saw pictures of Stuart Kellerman, Doug Vansciver, and others, surrounded by children. There was also a group picture of the entire Rotary Club, and she realized that those men, despite their mistakes, had done something good in this country. "How are the children?" she asked. "I heard about the measles epidemic."

Carlos nodded. "Yes. Last month was a very trying time, but we survived. All the infected children have recovered."

"It's over? I just heard about it last week."

The man smiled and shrugged. "Our mail system is unreliable at best. That letter was posted a month ago."

Luke, studying the pictures, looked at her and she knew he was trying to send encouragement. She breathed several times and steadied her voice. "Senor Barrios, I must admit another reason for my visit. I also came to see a certain child. Paulo Raphael Carrera."

The man appeared shocked and quickly looked down to the papers on his desk. "Paulo, you say?"

"I know he's my ex-husband's child. My own son died several months ago, and I would like to meet his half brother. Would that be a problem?"

"Please accept my sympathy, madam, on your loss. I did not know." He rose from the desk. "At this time Paulo should be in the courtyard with the younger children. Please . . . I will lead the way."

"Thank you. Thank you for understanding." She stood up, and Luke came to her.

Taking her hand, he squeezed it and said, "You handled that very well. Come on, let's meet this child."

They brought the bag of toys with them and followed Senor Barrios through a long corridor. He led them through a door, and Eve's heart started hammering inside her chest when she heard the laughter and chattering of the children as they played.

"Paulo!" Senor Barrios called out his name. A small, dark-haired boy pulled away from a group of children and ran toward the director.

He was so small! She had forgotten how small a four-year-old was and knelt down to put herself on the same level with him. He was looking at the director, who was speaking to him in Spanish. She recognized her name, Senora Cameron, in the conversation and held her breath as she waited for the child to turn to her.

"Buenos días, senora," his sweet voice chimed as he looked her way.

She felt a shifting of her reality, an involuntary spasm in her solar plexus, as she gazed into innocent blue eyes just like Jamie's. Her voice caught and she gulped down the thickness in her throat. *"Buenos días,* Paulo," she whispered.

She wanted to crush the child to her chest and run away with him. She knew in that instant that she would never leave him down here. No matter what it took, she would bring him back with her.

"Look what we brought for you and your friends. . . ." She unzipped her bag and showed him the toys. Luke translated for her, and she told him to tell Paulo that he could pick whatever he wanted.

The child peeked into the bag and his face lightened with surprise. *"Ernie y Bert!"* He looked up at her and then at the director. *"Por favor?"*

The director nodded, and Paulo smiled with delight as he reached in and brought out the small figures. He started to run back to his friends, but the director stopped him and said something in rapid Spanish.

The child hugged the toys to his chest and looked at her. *"Gracias, senora,"* he murmured shyly.

She merely smiled and nodded as she watched him turn and join the other children. Soon she was surrounded by tiny, excited faces and she and Luke distributed their booty.

"Senor Barrios, may we spend some time with Paulo?" Luke asked.

The director nodded. "Of course. I'll call him back."

"Wait." Eve rose and said, "I'd like to talk to you first. What is the procedure one must go through for adoption?"

"Eve . . ."

She ignored Luke and waited for the director.

He took a deep breath and said, "The . . . how do you say? The red tape in Guatemala is confounding. It would take months to process everything correctly. Besides the government, there is the formidable task of dealing with the local *cofradias* and *chuchkajaues*—the government and church leaders—and the *chuchkajaues* are the native prayer men. Paulo is part Indian, and any adoption must pass through these men first. Actually, once they give approval, the process proceeds quickly."

"How do I arrange an appointment with these local men?"

"Senora, do you not think this is impulsive? Spend time with the child. See if this is what you really want."

"He's right, Eve. You need to think about this."

She looked at both of them. "I don't need to think anymore. I've made my decision. Subconsciously, I've been thinking about this since New Jersey. All I had to do was look into his eyes and I knew it was right. The decision is made. I want to adopt him."

Luke sighed and ran his fingers through his hair. "Senor, when this lady makes a decision, there's no use in discussing it further. Can she get in to see these men?"

Senor Barrios seemed pleased and said, "I will telephone a friend of mine who is the *cofradia* of Santo Tomas. Perhaps he can see you."

Eve expelled the breath she'd been holding and extended her hand. "Thank you, senor. I can't tell you what this means to me."

Carlos Barrios shook her hand and smiled warmly. "Ordinarily, I would not support such a hasty decision. However, I see in you the belief that life continues and can be found in even the most unexpected places. Paulo's eyes . . . they are an unusual color, yes?"

Tears formed at the corners of her lids. "I see his brother in them." She looked to the group of children. "I love him already. I promise he will have a good life, and he won't forget his Guatemalan heritage."

"*Muy bien, senora.* I will see what I can accomplish with my friend in town."

He left them in the play yard, and Luke ran his hand over her shoulders. "Eve, you're sure? This is a small child. You have a business to run——"

"I'll be with him all day," she interrupted, "and still be able to put him to bed. I'll hire a nanny, someone to sit with him while he sleeps. And Mick and Ruthann really run Nirvana. I'm little more than a figurehead who pays the bills. It'll all work out." She wiped a fat tear from her cheek. "I'll make it work out."

He squeezed her shoulder. "I have never met another woman like you, Eve Cameron. If anybody can do this, you can. Now, c'mon, let's get to know your son."

She looked at him and let the tears come. Turning, she wrapped her arms around him and kissed his cheek. "Thank you, Luke. Thanks for supporting me."

"Hey, I told you I would." He shook his head. "Though this would make a great story . . ."

"You wouldn't."

"I gave you my word, but I can't help it if I'm a reporter."

"Then report on our car being hijacked."

"I'll think of something. Let's go. Look at him, Eve. . . ." They turned back to the children. Paulo was handing Bert to a little girl who got only a coloring book. "I should have brought the camera."

"We'll bring it tomorrow. Come on."

They walked up to the group of children, yet Eve's gaze was fixed on Paulo. He looked at her and smiled. She smiled back and knelt before him. "Would you like to go for a walk with us, just over there?" She pointed to a bench under a wide tree.

At the child's blank expression, Luke quickly translated for her. Paulo looked at the bench, then at an older woman who was sitting on a low stone wall and doing some sort of hand work on a blouse.

He nodded and stuck out his little hand.

Eve smiled and placed his hand inside of hers. At the soft touch, she deeply inhaled. The connection was made. She would fight city hall, the church, and Indian prayer men—whatever it took. This child was going to have a chance.

CHAPTER 19

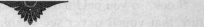

It was all very complex and Luke had done his best to explain, yet Eve felt as if she were dealing with medieval and tribal laws. She tried to keep her patience when they visited Senor Justo Guzman, head *cofradia* in Chichicastenango. They came to his house and explained their need for haste in rushing the adoption. He spoke at great length. Luke translated, telling Eve how difficult her request was but that yet all things have an answer. Luke suggested they offer a bribe. Her first instinct was to refuse. She didn't want to buy a child. Luke explained that the man would expect something for his trouble in bypassing the traditional methods, and in the end she paid for a very expensive jade horse and rider and billed it to her American Express card. The exquisite statue would remain in Senor Guzman's shop to be resold. Only the transaction, his compensation, would appear on her billing statement. She felt robbed, yet kept the sweet image of Paulo in her mind at all times. He was worth it.

By the time they got back to the hotel, Eve was hot, sweaty, and irritated. She turned on the shower and started ripping off her clothes. "I can't believe I just did that," she said for the fifth time.

"Look, so you paid three thousand dollars for a sculpture that you'll never see again. You saved yourself months of red tape. One down. Tomorrow we see the Indian prayer guy, Uman. Once we charm him, the deal is done. You have to expect this hassle if you rush these people."

She looked through the bathroom doorway into the room. "I know you're right. I just didn't expect to pay a bribe. I'm not trying to smuggle dope. I want to give a child a home. I don't know . . . I'm going to take a shower and, hopefully, I'll calm down."

"Take your time," Luke called back.

The cool water felt wonderful and the almond soap was deliciously scented. Letting her body relax, she finally accepted her actions and was determined to put it out of her mind. Luke had been a great help. It never would have even occurred to her to bribe the man. And tomorrow they would be dealing with Uman, who would act as a mediator between them and the saints and the idols. Guzman had explained to Luke that because Paulo was part Indian, Uman would contact a specific saint with active powers who could intervene in the world and set things right. She couldn't wait to tell Rue about this one.

When she shut off the water and pulled back the curtain, Luke was standing in the bathroom holding a large fluffy towel open for her.

She immediately used the curtain to cover her nakedness. "God, you scared me."

"Oh, come on. Remember, I saw you last night."

"It was dark. I don't think I'm comfortable with this."

"Hey, Eve . . . get comfortable. Your towel's waiting."

It was silly. He *had* seen her naked, even if it was in a dim light. Her figure wasn't bad, but she was no longer young. . . .

"You're being silly," he said. "And you're holding up the rest of your surprise."

"You have a surprise?" She figured she might as well leave the shower. It was obvious he wasn't going anywhere.

He grinned and wrapped her in the towel. "I do. But I'm not telling you. I'll show you." He picked her up amid her surprised laughter and carried her to the bed. Laying her down on the sheet, he said, "Turn over."

"Huh?"

"Turn over onto your stomach."

"Why?"

"Do you have to ask so many questions? Give me the towel, turn over, and be quiet. In fact, don't talk at all, or you'll ruin it."

Chuckling, she did as he asked, pulled the sheet up to cover her behind, and waited. He knelt on the bed, and she could hear him doing something yet couldn't figure it out.

Suddenly a liquid drizzled down her spinal column, and she jerked back in surprise.

"Hold still," he ordered in a soft voice. "Almond massage oil." His hands started spreading it over her back, and she moaned with deep pleasure.

"Where did you get it?" she whispered.

He laughed. "The hotel has a fitness center, can you believe that? I can't wait until the paper gets the bill. Between losing a car and massage oil, I'm gonna have to do some pretty fancy tap dancing when I get home."

"We'll figure something out," she said, and again moaned as his fingers worked their way into her sore muscles. It was so relaxing, so tender, so wonderful. A delicious slice of heaven. "All we need is a plan," she murmured.

"Shh . . . don't talk. Just enjoy this and then you can take a nap. Dinner will be brought up at seven. We're eating on the terrace."

"Oh, Luke . . . that's so . . . sweet. I don't know what I would have done without you. I really appreciate everything."

"I told you I would treat you like a queen. You deserve it."

"But what about you? You've got to be just as—"

"Eve?" he interrupted.

"Yes?"

"Will you please shut up?"

She could only laugh. She wasn't saying another word.

The church of Santo Tomas was not impressive in structure, but the ceremony taking place on the front steps amid clouds of incense certainly was. Eve, Luke, and Carlos Barrios stood reverently watching the old Indian perform his ritual. When they stopped at the door of the church, she looked to the director of the orphanage, who was translating the Indian dialect for them.

"The *chuchkajua* is explaining the purpose of the ceremony to the guardian spirits of the church and asking their blessing."

Eve held Luke's hand as they entered the old building. Platforms were set up along the aisles, and they silently followed the prayer man to the altar railing. Again, prayers were said before moving back to the center aisle. The *chuchkajua* stopped at each platform, and Carlos explained that the low wooden stands were associated with specific groups of ancestors.

Luke carried a large bag, and at each platform Eve was required to place her offering to the souls residing in each area. Candles, flowers, and liquor were left. She thought of the Catholic churches in the States and couldn't picture a parish priest allowing such a ceremony, yet it seemed quite natural here. The combination of faith, tradition, and ritual resulted in a folk religion that honored the customs and culture of the native people.

At the last platform, Carlos turned to her. "Here, the *chuchkajua* will speak to the soul of Paulo's mother and ask her blessing, then petition all the lords of all the natural forces of the Indian universe to hear his plea."

Eve held her breath and concentrated with all her will. She wasn't sure what she believed in any longer. She was certainly not a Catholic anymore. At the least, some of the things she thought now would have her excommunicated. Her faith was more private, and she was still coming to terms with God. She wasn't angry any longer. She was searching. . . .

She mentally spoke to Paulo's mother, telling her soul that she would take care of her son, love him and provide for him. That in some spiritual way Paulo was connected to her through Jamie, and they were already family. She promised that she would not let him forget his mother and his Indian culture, and that she would love him with all her heart. Closing her eyes, she asked for a mother's blessing. As added insurance, she also asked for the approval of the Indian lords of the universe—whoever they were. She didn't understand it, but she wasn't taking any chances.

"Now we shall go to Pascual Abaj. Turkaj is a stone idol located outside of the town," Carlos explained. "We'll take two cars, and when we're finished I'll return the *chuchkajua* to his home and you can continue to the orphanage."

The old Indian grinned at her, showing many missing teeth. He said something to Carlos, clearly meant for her.

Carlos said, "He tells me that your prayer was heard and accepted because your heart is open to the universe."

Eve felt a chill run through her and bowed in respect to the older man. "Please tell him that I am grateful for his help."

Carlos translated. "He says he knows that. He saw it in your eyes when he met you. He says you are a woman capable of great love and that is what will bring you through your trials."

While Carlos was explaining this to her, the *chuchkajua* walked over to Luke and bowed low before him while speaking rapidly.

She and Luke looked to their translator. Carlos seemed

to be concentrating. "He's saying something about honoring you for participating in the lesson. That your role, the part you will play, is of great importance to another soul and your sacrifice will be your glory."

"What lesson? What sacrifice? The adoption?" Eve asked.

Carlos shook his head. "No, this has something to do with Luke, specifically for Luke."

Luke seemed uncomfortable, and he bowed in return to the man. Rising, he looked at Eve and grinned. "He's probably talking about the car. I wish my boss could hear this."

She smiled back at him, and her heart filled with love. Never before had a man, any man, even her husband, made her this happy and free. Before they left the church, she offered up a quick prayer of thanksgiving—for Luke, for Paulo, for the new life she was creating.

After the visit to Turkaj, where they paid their respects to the natural forces that govern the Indian world, they gave the *chuchkajua* a large basket of fruit and two liters of premium tequila. The prayer man seemed very pleased with their gift.

"Don't you find that strange?" Eve asked once they were in the car and on their way to the orphanage. "The local guy charged three thousand dollars, and the Indian holy man didn't ask for anything?"

"Bureaucracy," Luke answered. "Guzman is probably going to have to pay off someone locally and in the state government to rush things. The *chuchkajua's* contacts have no need for a bribe."

"Thank God he liked us. Now that we have his approval, the adoption can go through. When can we tell Paulo?"

Luke smiled. "I think we're in the clear now, so you'd better do it as soon as possible. We're going to have to leave tomorrow morning for Guatemala City."

Eve chewed on her bottom lip for a few moments. "What if he doesn't want to come? What'll we do?"

"Don't look for trouble, Eve. I think that child is falling in love with you already. He followed you around yesterday like he was your shadow. Hey, you brought him *Ernie y Bert*, remember? You're his hero."

Chuckling as they turned into the orphanage, she said, "Well, I wish I had Big Bird in the backseat right now. I could sure use the help."

"Nah . . . it'd just be another bribe, and you don't have to do that for Paulo."

Minutes later they found him playing with the children, and as soon as he saw them he left the crowd and came running in their direction.

"Senora Eve!"

She scooped him up in her arms and hugged his body to her own. "*Buenos días,* little one," she murmured against his temple, inhaling the scent of him.

They walked to the same bench they had used yesterday and sat down. Eve held Paulo on her lap and said to Luke, "What should we tell him? We should wait for Carlos, right?"

"I wouldn't bring up the adoption until he got here. Look," Luke pointed to a soccer ball lying nearby under a tree. "Here, put him down and I'll play with him until Carlos gets back."

She watched Luke and Paulo and was suddenly reminded of Jamie kicking a soccer ball in the backyard. All those practices and games . . . Now here she was ready to do it all again. It would mean PTA meetings and school projects. Not to mention learning Spanish so she could help him learn English. And what would Ruthann think, bringing a child into the house? Now she would definitely believe she'd lost her mind. Yet when she looked at the laughing little boy playing in front of her with Luke, she knew all the drawbacks would be worth it.

Carlos Barrios came up and sat next to her. He grinned as several more children joined Luke and Paulo until it looked as if they had a little game going.

"He is a good man, isn't he?"

Eve smiled. "Yes, he is. A very good man." She turned to the director. "So can we tell Paulo now? We have to leave in the morning for Guatemala City."

"Yes, I think we should talk to him and prepare him for the change. I just spoke with the Migración, the Immigration Department, and unfortunately the earliest they can have Paulo's passport and papers ready is ten days to two weeks."

Eve stared at him for a few seconds, trying to understand what he was saying. "He can't come home with us?"

"I'm sorry. Already we have bypassed several important steps. This is one that cannot be hurried. The process usually takes months, and we have cut the wait down considerably. I know you're disappointed, but I have contacted my sister in Guatemala City and at the appropriate time when the papers are complete, I shall take Paulo to my sister's. She will keep him for a few days and then bring him to the airport. You shouldn't even have to leave the terminal. I promise you, he will be waiting for you, Senora."

She nodded and fought down her disappointment. What was two weeks? They would have a lifetime together. "Okay, may we talk to him now?"

Carlos called the child, and Paulo and Luke left the others and came to the bench. Eve picked him up and placed him back on her lap. "Please tell him that in the last few days I have come to love him as my own little boy, and I would like to know how he would feel about coming to live with me in America."

Carlos translated, and she watched Paulo's face for a reaction. The child merely stared at the director.

Eve became worried. "Tell him he will live in a nice house, with his own room and toys and a big backyard to play in. And I will do whatever I can to be a good mother to him."

Paulo listened intently and then looked up at her. *"Mi madre?"* he whispered hopefully.

Eve gulped down the lump in her throat. *"Sí,"* she whispered back.

He climbed up onto her legs and wrapped his arms around her neck, hugging her tightly.

Luke stood with his hands on his hips, grinning like a fool. "I do believe we have a family here," he announced. "Congratulations, Momma."

CHAPTER 20

"We would have heard, right? If anything was wrong? They must have made their flight."

"I'm sure we would have heard if anything happened. Luke would have called us." Mick reached over and squeezed Ruthann's arm. "Honey, stop worrying."

Ruthann supposed it was silly to be nervous, yet when Eve had left they hadn't been on the best terms. Sitting on the porch, she rocked back and forth while wondering how Eve would take her news. "I hope we get to see her before we leave for the club."

"We have plenty of time, Rue."

She looked out to the river and sighed. For days she had been worried about Eve, wondering if she was still upset with her, how she had taken Luke Harrelson showing up in Miami, what had happened in Guatemala. . . . She had driven poor Mick crazy with her anxiety and—

Her thoughts were interrupted by the sound of a horn.

"She's here," Mick announced.

Ruthann stood up as a car turned into the driveway. "*They're* here," Ruthann corrected. "Luke's with her. I guess she can't be too mad."

"Take a look at that smile on her face," Mick said as they walked toward the steps. "She looks pretty happy to me."

Eve opened the car door and yelled, "Ruthann! I missed you!"

The two women came together on the front lawn and hugged each other.

"Oh, Eve . . . I missed you too. Thank God you're okay. I'm sorry I got mad. . . ."

She felt Eve's arms tighten around her. "I'm sorry too. Let's forget it, okay? Everything turned out fine. Better than fine. *Great!*"

She pulled back and looked into her friend's face as Mick and Luke started talking. "What happened?" Ruthann whispered. "You look . . . I don't know, ten years younger than when you left."

Eve appeared embarrassed. "It must be the tan. Wait till you hear how we got it. Revolutionaries hijacked our car in the middle of a jungle! Can you believe it?"

"You're kidding, right?" Ruthann was horrified.

"I'm not kidding, but we made out fine. We walked for a couple of hours and then caught a bus, and then spent the night in a barn."

"Mick . . ." Ruthann called over her shoulder. "Did you hear this? They were hijacked in the middle of a jungle!"

"It might have been the best thing that happened to us," Luke said, and laughed at Mick's confused expression.

"What *did* happen?" Ruthann whispered to Eve. "You look great. You both look great."

"We'll talk later," Eve whispered back, and winked.

"Uh . . . oh, I can't wait to hear this."

"Let's go into the house," Eve suggested. "I have some news."

The guys carried the suitcases in and Eve and Ruthann, still with an arm around each other's waists, followed. Once inside, they gathered in the kitchen, and after pouring iced tea for Eve and Luke, Ruthann asked, "Okay, so what's the big news?"

"I've adopted a little boy," Eve announced with a big grin. "Paulo Raphael Carrera."

Ruthann, standing next to Mick, leaned against him. "Paul's son?"

Eve nodded. "He gave up all legal rights when he placed him in the orphanage. Once I looked into Paulo's eyes, I knew I couldn't leave him down there. I want him to be with me. He's Jamie's half brother, and he's family."

Mick put his arm over Ruthann's shoulders and brought her in closer to his side. "You're going to take all this on now, at this time in your life? Have you really thought—"

Ruthann nudged him. "Hey, I learned the hard way," she interrupted with a laugh. "When this lady makes up her mind there's no use in trying to talk her out of it. Congratulations." She left Mick and walked over to Eve. Kissing her cheek, she said, "So what . . . do we have a baby shower, or something?"

Eve laughed. "Paulo is four years old, and I really haven't the faintest idea what's hot for kids now. Sesame Street was my era. Power Rangers?"

"Barney," Luke suggested, and they all groaned and laughed.

"We have some news too," Ruthann said, walking back to Mick and slipping into his arms.

Luke and Eve were sitting at the table and looking at her with expectation. All she had to do was say it. Mick must have felt her nervousness, and he tightened his hold on her shoulders.

She took a deep breath and said words that she never thought would come out of her mouth.

"We're getting married. Me and Mick."

Eve yelped and got up so quickly that her chair fell over onto the floor. She ran across the kitchen and hugged them both.

"Oh, I'm so happy for you guys! I *knew* you were meant for each other! When? When are you going to do it?" She hugged them again and pulled back suddenly. "Talk about showers? A bridal shower! At Nirvana!"

"Hold on," Ruthann said with a laugh. "There won't be time. We're getting married on Thursday."

Eve looked stunned. "Four days from now?"

Mick, shaking Luke's hand, said, "Neither one us wants to wait. We're that sure this is the right decision."

Eve backed up and ran her fingers through her hair. "Four days! God, we've got to get flowers, music, food. Food! We'll get Chaz to cook—he likes you, Rue—and we can hold the reception at the club. I need something to wear. *You!* You need something—"

Laughing, Ruthann grabbed Eve's hands and held them firmly. "Calm down. We've made all the arrangements. We're going to a judge's office. It's going to be very small. Just Mick's sister's family and you. You will stand up for me, won't you?"

"Of course I will. I'm honored, but Rue . . . why not have it at the club? We have a private dining room. Mick, you can ask your friends and we can make this a real wedding reception. My wedding present. Please?"

Ruthann looked at Mick. "What do you think?"

"You won't have to do anything, I promise. I'll take care of it. You two just show up," Eve said as an enticement.

"Honey, whatever will make you happy," Mick said, and pulled her into his arms again.

She looked into his eyes and could feel the love coming back at her, surrounding her with warmth. "Well, I think we have something to celebrate. Why not?"

"Great!" Eve almost jumped up and down with eagerness. "This is so wonderful. I can't believe it. The two of you getting married. Do you have a dress yet, Rue?"

She chuckled and shook her head. "No, I was waiting for you to get back and help me with that one."

"Tomorrow morning we'll go into Philadelphia. And we won't come home until we've found the perfect wedding dress."

Luke stood in back of Eve and slipped his arms around her waist. "Is there no end to your energy, woman? Ever hear of jet lag?"

Eve unconsciously covered Luke's arms with her own. "Oh, come on. Guatemala is on Central Time. There's no jet lag."

"Ahh, it looks like that was some trip. Is there something else you want to share?" Mick asked with a knowing grin.

Suddenly Eve seemed to be aware of her position and Mick's deduction. A blush appeared, and she looked down for a moment. "Well, I guess you could say that I'm not mad at either one of you for sending this man after me."

"But you should have seen the chase she gave me. It wasn't easy winning her over. Not until guerrillas jumped out of the jungle and stole our car." Luke hugged Eve tighter. "I'd do it again . . . for this."

"Really? I thought you were kidding! Revolutionaries?" Mick asked. "What happened?"

As the men started talking about the incident, Eve eased out of Luke's arms and motioned for Ruthann.

"We'll be on the porch," she said to Mick, who was merely nodding, totally transfixed by Luke's story.

"Male testosterone," Eve whispered as they walked toward the front of the house. "It's like telling tales in front of the tribal fire. They won't even miss us."

When they were on the porch, Ruthann sat down in her rocker and looked at her friend. "Okay. Now tell me everything."

Eve took her place beside Ruthann and rocked slowly while staring out to the river. "I'm glad to be back," she said, and breathed deeply. "Though it was one hell of a trip . . ."

"I'm waiting," Ruthann answered. "Patiently, I might add. What happened down there? You and Luke?" Eve seemed bashful, and Ruthann grinned. "Out with it, Evie."

"I think I'm falling in love," she whispered in disbelief.

"Oh, Eve, I'm so happy for you. Luke seems like a wonderful man."

"He is," she agreed. "He's loving and . . . and I guess that's the only thing that matters. Besides that, he's also funny, intelligent, supportive, strong, sexy. The list goes on, but it's more than that, Rue. When I said I was having a love affair, I didn't just mean with Luke."

"With Paulo?"

There was a pause.

"With myself," she said, and laughed as if she still couldn't believe it. "I know it sounds corny, and I don't care. The only way I can explain it is that when Luke saw me as whole, as being fine, lovable, just the way I am, I saw it too. I felt like a whole complete woman for the first time."

Eve lifted her chin, gazed at the sunset, and inhaled the summer's breeze. "I love him, but I'm not in love with him for his ability to keep me feeling good about my self. That's mere romance, and he can't do that indefinitely. I wouldn't put that burden on anyone. I'm in love with him for the gift he gave me, of being able to see that woman as myself and accepting her—faults and all."

Eve turned and stared at her. "I know it sounds nuts, Rue, and Zenned out or something . . . but for the first time in my life I'm acting the way I want, thinking what I want, believing what I want, loving the way I want, and I've never been happier. And I'm not hurting anyone along the way. It's incredible!"

"I know what you mean," Ruthann whispered as tears came into her eyes. "That's how I feel with Mick. I never expected to experience that kind of love. It transcends everything I've been taught about it. It doesn't mean I have to keep him at my side for the rest of my life, that without him I wouldn't survive intact. Even if he left, he couldn't take that gift with him. It's mine now, and I'm the only one who can put it again into someone's back pocket while they walk away, or allow someone to control me by manipulation, like Ed did."

She shook her head, as if trying to put it all in perspective. "Why were we taught that it was so wrong to think well of ourselves, Eve? If we don't, we're always looking outside of us for the answer, the magical solution, the perfect lover. In the end, it always seems to disappoint us anyway. There's a big difference between humility and denial of who you really are. You can't find real love *out there* until you experience it . . . well, in here." She touched her left breast, then wiped away the tears that were streaming down her cheeks. "Mick made me see that. Once I knew it and accepted it as real, I wasn't so afraid to love, and trust loving again. It's so weird, so incredible, that this is happening to both of us at the same time. Maybe this is why we came together, Evie. To support the other one along the way, so we don't think we're going crazy. . . . 'Cause this ain't the way the world thinks, you know?"

Eve smiled and once more deeply inhaled as another breeze came up from the river and gently caressed their skin.

"You know what I think?" she asked, again studying the sunset. "I think I was crazy, at least a form of it, for most of my life, probably since I was a kid. And what's more, I think the majority of people alive right now are insane to some degree. Look at what's happening in the world around us, and what we allow to happen because we're so afraid. Is that how we're supposed to live? Enjoying life for brief moments, and then returning to fear? Not for me, not anymore. I know what this is like, this peace. I remember it from when I was young. I'm finally starting to feel whole again. Sane. Remember what it was like on a Saturday morning, when you did your chores and opened the door and ran outside to play, to discover what the day held for you? Remember what that felt like? To truly enjoy life? God, it was wonderful, climbing trees, being sane. Sometime after that, little by little, I started to take on what the rest of the world thought, their beliefs and their fears and their judgments, and I became just like everyone else, a functioning, though slightly insane, robot that stopped climbing trees. I survived life, but I can't say that I enjoyed it, at least not like when I was sane. Until now. Now I have that feeling back again, and I finally figured out down in Guatemala what it was."

Eve turned away from the sunset and looked at Ruthann intently. "Joy. I know what it means now to enjoy life again. To live in joy. If you call that crazy, Rue, then I really am the Mad Hatter."

They looked at each other and experienced a moment of awe, when two people recognize that they will be friends forever. When they know that time, space, distance, or death can't keep them apart. They are, and always were, eternally connected.

Under a canopy of white wisteria, Ruthann and Mick vowed to always hold each other in love, to respect and honor one another, and declared before God and humanity their commitment to live as one.

Mick was dressed in a dark summer suit, looking joyous and handsome. Ruthann wore a delicate white silk sheath dress, unadorned except for the pearls at her neck. Her red hair was pulled up into a French twist with tiny sprigs of baby's breath attached. She carried a bouquet of white calla lilies as she quietly and sincerely made her wedding vows before the small gathering of family and friends. Eve stood next to Ruthann in her white Armani suit, holding a single lily and dabbing at her eyes to stop the flow of tears.

Ruthann felt it was a precious moment, when heaven and earth came closer together, and she knew it would be lovingly etched into her memory.

The reception that followed couldn't have been more perfect. The private dining room was tastefully decorated in green and white, with bouquets of summer flowers on each table. Jasmine provided the music, and Chaz outdid himself with the food. Mick's family and friends accepted her wholeheartedly and without question. Even the staff got together and presented them with a card that everyone had signed, and an exquisite crystal sculpture of two swans with their necks intertwined, making them one.

She felt so happy, so blessed, as she and Mick danced and mingled. It was like a fairy tale, one that she thought only others might experience. Even Luke and Eve, inseparable since they had come home, seemed to be caught up in the magic.

In the end, she pulled Eve aside and looped her arm through her friend's as the reception wound down.

"How can I ever thank you?" she asked. "Everything was perfect."

Eve tightened her hold. "I'm glad. You deserve the best. And I think you have it in that man. He loves you so much, Rue."

She looked across the room to where Mick was horsing around with his nephew. "I honestly think we'll make it, Eve. This time around I know what love is and how to take care of it."

"I have a surprise for you," Eve said, leading her to Mick.

"What? You've done so much."

"Well, this is the finishing touch to your wedding. Come on," she prompted, making her stand next to her new husband.

"Michael Larkin, your bride awaits you," Eve announced.

Mick turned around and smiled at her, filling Ruthann with even more love.

He came to her and slipped his arms around her waist. "And I thank God for her life every morning when I wake up." He kissed her soundly on the lips.

Everyone clapped, and Eve cleared her throat. "Lovely as that speech was . . . there's something else outside."

She led everyone to the back door and opened it. In the parking lot behind the restaurant was a white Mercedes limo.

"This car will whisk you and your bride to the Presidential Suite of the Ritz Carlton Hotel in Philadelphia." She looked to the rest of the crowd. "I feel like Robin Leach, but how else was I supposed to say it."

Everyone laughed, and Mick hugged her. "This is tonight?"

Eve shook her head. "This is for now. Both of you. Out of here, and into the limo."

"Will you be okay with the club?" Ruthann asked, having planned to stay until they opened for business.

Eve grinned. "Not to worry. Taken care of."

"Who's going to clean up—"

"Taken care of," Eve interrupted.

Mick looked out to the parking lot. "What about my car? How will we get back tomorrow morning?"

"The limo driver will return at four P.M. tomorrow afternoon," Eve answered with a triumphant grin. "Late checkout. And your car . . . ?"

"Taken care of," Luke piped up, looking very much like a pleased conspirator.

After giving him a look of pure love, Eve turned back to them. "Now . . . is there some reason why the two of you are still standing here?"

She hugged Eve and said, "I love you, lady. Thanks."

Exactly a half hour later they were issued into the Presidential Suite.

Now, this time, she knew what a marriage was intended to be. He was her husband and, for the first time she knew what it meant to be a man's wife, to be his partner, his equal in love and in life. It filled her with a deep yearning to unite with him, to fuse together their commitment to each other.

"You looked beautiful today," Mick whispered, his breath tickling the skin right behind her ear. "My wife. I like the sound of it."

Ruthann smiled and felt her blood thicken with desire as it raced through her body. "I feel beautiful. Thank you for that."

"You're finally feeling what everyone else has known. Watching you flower and bloom," he said, running his fingers up her arm, "has been an extraordinary experience."

Standing at the large bed and holding her second glass of champagne, she leaned back against him and felt the warmth of his skin through the sheer-silk nightgown. Rachelle Farrell's pure voice was filling the suite, and she caught her breath as Mick's fingers placed the thin strap of her gown over her shoulder.

Gently kissing the back of her neck, he murmured against her skin, "Thank you for coming into my life, Ruthann."

Her head fell back onto his shoulder. "Oh, Mick . . ."

He moved slightly to take her glass while sliding the other strap down her arm. Her gown puddled at her feet. When he closed the breath of distance between them and pulled her once more against him, Ruthann gasped at the searing naked contact.

"This is so powerful," she breathed, watching his hand move over her arm. His dark skin slowly, tenderly, stroking her lighter one. The contrast only added to it.

"I know," he whispered, touching her almost with reverence. "I've never wanted anything as much as I've wanted this marriage. As much as I've wanted you . . ."

His lips now followed his hands, and she moaned with pleasure. Turning around, she stood before him and pulled the baby's breath and pins from the twist at the back of her head. She dropped them to the rug and ran her fingers through her hair to bring it back to her shoulders.

"You are so beautiful," he murmured.

"I am honored to be your wife, Michael Otis Larkin. You are an extraordinary man, and I do love you . . . with all my heart." She grinned. "Even if your middle name is Otis."

He laughed and crushed her to his chest. When she raised her head, she was still giggling like a young-hearted girl. He lowered his mouth and took her laughter, changing it in an instant to the desire of a woman.

She pulled him even closer to her body, needing to feel his intensity and substance as it surrounded her with love. Never had she experienced such joy in another human being.

Bending, Mick picked her up and carried her the few feet to the bed. He laid her down and stood beside it, staring at her in the fading light. Their hands reached out to connect, and his voice was hoarse when he spoke.

"I plan to honor you and respect you for the rest of your life, Ruthann Larkin. When we're old and gray and move slower, I want you to remember this moment and feel beautiful and loved, knowing that in my heart I will always see you like this and want you as much as I do now. I have never, ever, loved anyone the way I love you. You're the light in my life, and I feel so fortunate to be your husband."

Tears came into her eyes, and she pulled him down to the bed. Cradled into his shoulder, she wrapped her arms around him and sniffled. "I have waited a lifetime for you. Thank God you showed up."

He raised himself on his elbow and pushed the hair back off her forehead in a tender caress. Lowering his face to hers, he whispered, "The wait is over. We've both come full circle," right before his lips claimed hers in a deep kiss.

They were two souls who recognized the sacredness of their union, knowing it was the closest two human beings can become to each other. Every emotion, every feeling, was exchanged from body to body in a holy communion of intimate sharing, while their hearts fused together into one pulsing unit, creating a stunning explosion of pure love that swept them into their future.

CHAPTER 21

Eve looked at the wall clock in the kitchen and started worrying. Luke should have been home by now. He had left the club when she did, following behind her in Mick's Jeep. She had made the light on Route 73. He hadn't. That was two hours ago. Where was he? And what was he doing at four o'clock in the morning? She had called the paper, thinking he might have stopped at the office for something, but had only connected to his voice mail. Had he decided to drive Mick's car to his apartment instead of coming to her house? Her earlier phone calls had gone unanswered.

She shook her head. No, he would have called if he'd changed his mind. Something was wrong. She could feel it. Maybe the Jeep broke down. Maybe he was in trouble. Looking at the phone on the counter, she again fought the urge to call the police. No sense in creating trouble if it was only a broken fan belt or something. She would wait a while longer. And pray . . .

She changed into the new black nightgown and robe she had bought in Philly with Ruthann. It seemed like an act of faith. If she got changed and waited for him, then it was demonstrating that he was coming to her. She paced the house, looking out to the dark street every time she passed the front windows.

Nothing.

Something was wrong. Even though she tried to push the thought out of her mind, she knew Luke wouldn't do this to her. He was too considerate to leave her hanging for—she looked at the clock—now three hours. Five o'clock in the morning.

She didn't care if she sounded like a foolish woman. She didn't care if Luke would look like a foolish man. Enough was enough. She picked up the phone and dialed the police.

After the dispatcher answered, Eve cleared her throat and said, "I'm sorry for bothering you this late, but I'd like to know if you've had any reports of an accident or a breakdown involving a black Jeep. I was expecting someone three hours ago. He was following me and got caught at a red light on Route 73. That was the last I've seen him."

"This person's name?"

She mentally apologized to Luke if he was caught at some all-night gas station without a phone. "His name is Luke Harrelson. He's a reporter, an editor, at the *Carolton County Times*."

"One moment, please."

Eve continued to pace with the portable phone at her

ear as she was placed on hold. What could be keeping him? She closed her eyes and prayed that he was all right.

A man's voice came on the line. "Can we have your name, ma'am?"

Startled, Eve paused for only a moment. "Eve Cameron. I'm . . . I'm a close friend of Mr. Harrelson. As I told the woman, he was following me in his car and caught a red light. I've been waiting since two-thirty and he hasn't shown up. I know it's silly, but I couldn't think of anyone else to call." God, was she rambling?

"Ma'am, could I have your address?"

"My address? He's not here, that's why I'm calling."

"We need your address for the records."

"Oh, right . . ." She gave it to him, and listened as he said that they would get back to her. Hanging up the phone, she felt a bizarre mixture of dread and ridiculousness. Luke was a grown man and had certainly proved that he could take care of himself. Shaking her head at her own silliness, she opened the freezer and took out a bag of Irish Creme coffee. She would make cappuccino. When Luke finally arrived, she was sure he'd have a story to tell, and she wanted to stay awake. But why didn't the police ask her what year the Jeep was, or want a description of Luke? It was weird.

Listening to the whooshing of the machine as it whipped the froth, she heard her doorbell ring and ran to the front of the house. In the back of her brain she realized that Luke never used that door. He always came around to the kitchen.

She unlocked the huge wooden door and flung it open. "Thank God, I was so . . ." Her words trailed off as she saw two policemen standing on her porch. Every muscle in her body became weakened. Her heart pounded furiously in her chest and her legs and hands started shaking.

"Ms. Cameron?"

She nodded. "What's wrong? Why are you here?"

"Can we come in?" They both looked grim.

She stood to one side and allowed them entrance into her living room. "Is Luke all right? What happened?"

"Ma'am, you might want to sit down."

"Tell me!" She knew her voice sounded shrill, yet she couldn't stop it.

"He was involved in an . . . an accident on Hartford Road—"

She clutched the edges of her robe together. "Is he all right?" she whispered. "Where is he?"

"Ma'am, I'm sorry. The Jeep was forced off the road and he hit a tree head-on. He died instantly."

She felt as if she had been hit between her eyes. She must have staggered, for the police officers moved quickly to help her into a chair. "He couldn't have died," she whispered, staring desperately into the face of one of the men. "He was behind me. I saw him . . ."

"I'm sorry. I know it's not any consolation, but we have the person responsible. The strange thing is, he's claiming he was only trying to stop the owner of the car. Mick Larkin. It appears that this is all mistaken identity."

"Mick Larkin is black! How could it be mistaken?" She ran her fingers through her hair, desperately trying to keep her hold on sanity. This isn't real, she kept telling herself. This can't be happening. It can't . . . !

"Doug Vansciver said he was having a problem with Larkin and—"

"Doug Vansciver!" Eve stared at the man in disbelief. "*He* did this?"

"He claims Larkin had him thrown out of your club several times last week and he wanted to even the score. He said he only wanted to force Larkin off the road. Mr. Harrelson was in the wrong place at the wrong time. I'm sorry. Is there someone you want to call? Someone to stay with you?"

She thought of Ruthann and Mick. Dear God, it was their wedding night. Shaking her head, she said, "No, thank you. I'll be all right."

"You're sure?"

She merely nodded. She felt numb, void of all feeling and reaction. She stood on unsteady legs and walked them to the door. "Thank you for coming and telling me. Have you notified the paper?"

"We called them right away. Tomorrow, we'll send someone to get a statement from you. Do you know where Mick Larkin is? He's not answering his phone or door."

"He was married today. He'll be back tomorrow afternoon."

"Okay. Vansciver is in custody for driving under the influence and, at the least, manslaughter. He won't be walking away from this one."

She had no comment. After thanking them again, she closed the door and shut off the light. She moved like a robot through the house, turning off lights, pulling the plug on the cappuccino machine. When she was in her bedroom, she removed her robe and got into bed. Pulling the covers up to her chin, she stared at the darkness surrounding her and felt it once more enter her body and pull her down.

The pain in her chest was almost unbearable, and she whimpered like a wounded animal, huddled beneath covers and waiting for someone to make it better. There was no one. No one could take this pain away. No one could make it all disappear.

"Luke." She whispered his name into the night, wanting it to carry out to him, needing to connect with him again. . . .

Oh God, she couldn't take this pain. Not again. A sound emerged from her mouth, a mournful wailing of grief, and she found herself screaming out to him.

"Luke!"

The tears erupted from her ducts like a fountain of sorrow, and she didn't try to stop them. Her body convulsed in sobs and she felt herself drowning in a deep, dark hole of anguish. Her mind replayed scenes of her and Luke together in Guatemala, in the barn, at the orphanage, at the wedding . . . Over and over she saw his loving face before her, laughing, supportive, filled with desire. . . .

It wasn't fair! It was cruel! Why would God take him? Why would God put him in her life and then take him away just as she trusted loving again? What was this? Was it a cruel way of telling her that she couldn't love? A thought settled in and gripped her heart, twisting it painfully.

Everyone she loved was taken away.

They found her twelve hours later in bed and staring at the wall. From a distant place in her mind, Eve heard them enter her house and call out her name, yet she didn't possess the strength to answer.

Ruthann burst into the bedroom looking radiantly happy, and yet Eve continued to be paralyzed with grief. This time she knew down deep that she simply didn't possess the energy to pull herself out of it.

"We're back," Ruthann announced. "It was beautiful, Eve. What's wrong? Are you sick?"

She merely stared at her.

Ruthann sat on the edge of the bed. "We went to the town house and Mick's car wasn't there, so we figured we'd come here. Eve, what's going on? Say something."

"Luke's dead," she whispered, forcing the words past vocal cords that were raw from hours of crying.

Ruthann stiffened. "What are you talking about?" She turned toward the door and yelled for Mick.

He entered the bedroom hesitantly and stood next to Ruthann. She looked up at him. "Eve just said Luke is dead."

"What?" Mick stared in disbelief.

Eve smiled sadly. "He's gone, Mick. Doug Vansciver ran him off the road and he died instantly. That's what the police said last night."

"My God, you've been alone?" Ruthann demanded. "Why didn't you call us?" She gathered Eve into her arms and held her tightly. "Oh, Mick, what are we going to do?"

Mick placed his hand on Eve's shoulder and said, "I'm so sorry. I can't believe this. Vansciver was looking for me. I wouldn't allow him into Nirvana last week. We didn't want to say anything to you, but I did tell Luke. That must be why he wouldn't stop. Vansciver was looking for me, not Luke. It should have been me. . . ."

Eve pulled away from Ruthann and shook her head as she sniffled back the tears that just wouldn't stop. "Don't say that, Mick," she muttered, and wiped at her nose. She tried to keep her voice steady, wanting to assure him, yet it was hopeless as fresh emotion slammed into her. "It—it shouldn't have been either one of you. Vansciver was drunk, and . . . angry. The police have him in jail. But it won't bring Luke back. Nothing will. He's gone. Oh, God, he's gone. . . ."

She covered her face as the racking sobs returned to carry her back into that dark hole. She was tired. Her will had been broken. She had put up a good fight in the last year, but it was over. All the positive thinking and good intentions in the world didn't have the power to change it. For the rest of her life she would carry this within her. It would be like a stone in her shoe that she could never get rid of, a constant reminder of what happened when she dared to love.

Two days passed, and yet she had little memory of them. She stayed in bed, not even taking a shower, until Ruthann forced her to get up and get dressed for Luke's funeral. It had been impressive, as far as funerals go, and well-attended. Eve had sat in the back with Ruthann and Mick, not even touching the casket. A strange thing happened at the funeral that she hadn't told anyone about, and never would. It was too . . . intimate.

Luke started talking to her in her head.

For a few minutes she thought she was having a nervous breakdown, that part of her brain was making up the dialogue. Isn't that what schizophrenia was about? But she could hear the laughter in his voice, the love in his words, and it started to urge her out of the depths of darkness.

She had been staring at the copper casket when she'd suddenly heard a chuckle in her head. The sound of it had startled her out of her numbing grief.

C'mon, babe . . . you really don't think I'm in there, do you?

She had looked around her to Mick and Ruthann, to see if they too had heard anything. Their faces revealed only sorrow.

Hey, lady, I'm not there, okay? That's only a body, a shell that kept me grounded. It's gone now, useless. But that's not me. and, down deep, you know it.

As crazy as it felt, she started talking back in her head.

Luke? Where are you?

There was a pause, and she held her breath as she waited. When her answer came, it was soft and loving.

I'm where you placed me. In your heart and in your memory. I'll always be there. You'll never be alone. Remember the seashell from the dream? Ask Mick about it.

No matter how hard she tried to question, nothing more came and she walked through the rest of the funeral in a daze. When they got back to the Victorian, she sat out on the porch and stared at the river, playing the dialogue over and over in her head.

Was this it? she wondered. Was this what being crazy meant? Hearing dead people talking to you? Okay, so she had taken some pretty heavy hits in the last year and maybe her brain just couldn't absorb this last one. But, damn it, it had *felt* like Luke. No matter what any psychologist told her, she knew she would always believe what she had heard.

"Eve, do you want something to drink?" Ruthann stood at the door and smiled sympathetically.

"No, thanks. I think I'll just sit here awhile." She rocked back and forth, thinking at least she was in a good place to lose her mind. She was home and safe. "You don't have to baby-sit me, Rue," she said, and smiled back at her. "I'm okay . . . I think. I just don't have any interest in anything anymore."

Ruthann came out onto the porch and looked down at her. "It's just what you need. You've been pushing yourself ever since I met you. There's nothing wrong with a rest."

Eve nodded. "Thanks for taking care of the club. I'll get back there soon. Just not right now. I'd bring everybody down."

"Take your time. There are a few things we should discuss, though. A lot of people have called and I've taken messages. There was a call from Carlos Barrios about Paulo and—"

"I forgot," Eve interrupted, and stopped rocking. "I can't bring that child here. Not now. Not like this . . ." She looked pleadingly up to her friend.

Ruthann nodded. "I'll take care of it, but don't you want to call and tell them when you'll be ready?"

"But I don't know when I'll be ready—for anything! I can't do any more, Rue. I can't take on any more now. How can I bring a child here and play momma? I'm scared to love anyone. They all die!"

"Eve, you're just being emotional. You didn't make anyone die. Not Jamie, and not Luke. Both were out of your hands."

"Then it's a curse. You should be grateful you married Mick and are away from here."

Ruthann placed her hand on her hip. "What if I told you that Mick and I decided to move in here with you? He's putting the town house up for sale."

Eve stared at her. "Why? I'm not afraid to be alone. I don't even care anymore. Live your own life, Rue. It's too short to spend it playing nanny to a grown woman." She ran her hands over her eyes. "I just need some time and some rest. I feel . . . old."

Ruthann sat down next to her and grabbed her wrist. "Don't do this to yourself, Eve. Take your time, and grieve for Luke. I know you loved each other. You could see it in both your faces. But do you really think he would want you to withdraw from life? He loved you too much for that."

"I know you're right. He doesn't want it. I just don't know how to change it. Not now, anyway. Call Senor Barrios back and explain things, please? Tell him I'll contact him soon. I can't do more than that right now. I don't want to disappoint Paulo. God knows, I don't . . . he was so excited. But I can't do this until I pull myself together, Rue."

Ruthann nodded and stood up. "Okay. I'll handle it. We have to take off for the club now. You'll be okay?"

"I'm just going to sit here and watch the sunset."

Two nights later she was sitting in the same place, watching the sun set over Philadelphia. She didn't know

what time it was or what day it was. There was sunrise
and sunset. Just one cycle of time that had passed. She felt
rooted to the rocker, for it seemed to ease her pain and
soothe her fears. She was home and safe. Nothing could
happen here. If she stayed where she was, she couldn't be
responsible for anyone else getting hurt. She had enough
guilt to last the rest of her life. If Luke hadn't been involved with her, he never would have been in Mick's car.
He would be alive.

*Silly woman, stop it. You're doing this to yourself. No
one else blames you. My time was over. That's it.*

She pushed his voice from her head and rocked harder.
She wanted this guilt. It made her feel that there was a
reason for all the pain. Otherwise, she would lose her
mind at the injustice.

"How would you like some company?"

Startled, Eve jumped at the sound of Mick's voice. He
came out onto the porch and looked at her with compassion.

Needing the presence of another person, Eve waved toward Ruthann's rocker. "Sit in your wife's chair. Where is
she? I haven't seen her all day, and I didn't even hear her
come in last night."

Mick sat down and leaned back against the thick cushion. "She'll be home soon," he said in a casual voice.
Then it changed suddenly to that of one trying to help another. "I've got something that might cheer you up." He
reached into his pocket and brought out a small box.

Handing it to her, he added, "Luke went with me to
pick out the wedding rings, and he ordered this for you. I
just picked it up today."

Her hands trembled as she held the black velvet box, too afraid to open it.

"Go ahead. He had it designed especially for you, and paid extra to make sure all the details were perfect. He even put a rush on it. This really meant a lot to him, and you should have seen him in the jeweler's—he was so excited. You know what he was like about details, but then, what do you expect from a reporter, huh? He couldn't wait to give it to you and see your reaction."

Inhaling deeply, she slowly opened the box and her breath caught in her throat. Inside was a small gold seashell, a King's Crown, attached to a fine gold chain. Her finger trembled as she touched it, and tears filled her eyes.

"Oh, Luke . . ." she whispered, clutching the exquisite charm in her fist and turning to Mick. "This is what he meant. He told me to ask you about the seashell. Oh God, Mick . . ."

"He did? He told you about it? When? That's weird. He swore me to secrecy."

She shook her head. "It doesn't matter. I know what this is about. I had a dream in Guatemala and . . ." She stopped speaking, and a chill ran down her spine. "Mick, I dreamt that I was in Mexico and Jamie was swimming and Luke was with me. I gave him a shell, a King's Crown that I had found in the sand, and then Jamie was drowning and when I looked at Luke . . . he was cold and lifeless. He was dead!" She started crying deeply. "It was a terrible nightmare, and I woke up to Luke holding me and soothing me. That's . . . when we made love for the first time."

"What a fitting gift," Mick said in a low, thoughtful voice.

She placed the chain around her neck and held on to the seashell. That small act made her feel closer to Luke. "Mick, what do you believe about death?" she asked in a tiny voice that sounded like a child's as she sniffled away the tears. "I know we talked about it in the attic that day, about Jamie, but do you believe all the religious stuff we were taught?"

"Heaven and judgment?" Mick smiled. "Maybe heaven. Though not angels sitting on clouds and playing harps. I read once in a book that dying is akin to having been in a stuffy room where too many people are talking and smoking, and suddenly you see a door that allows you to exit into fresh air and sunlight. This passage also said that we are here to visit, to learn lessons, but not to remain. That death isn't a curse. It's a gift from God, calling us back to where we really belong."

"That sounds nice," she murmured, and again wiped at her damp cheeks. "But what about all the pain? It sounds stupid, but I don't want to let him go, any more than I wanted to let Jamie go."

"But you never lose them, Eve. Maybe the physical body is gone, but that wasn't what made Luke Harrelson the man he was. That was just his space suit, the vehicle he used to get from one place to another. It kept him grounded against the pull of gravity. What made him breathe in and out? What made him think and then respond to those thoughts? What force was that?"

"I don't know."

"Okay, whatever name you want to call it—God, soul,

energy, whatever—it was something he never really gave much analysis to, right? It was just there—keeping him alive, reminding him to breathe. He never saw it. You never saw it. But you both knew it was there. Just like it's in every plant and animal. That animating force of life doesn't die. It can't. It existed before birth, and it exists after. It's eternal."

"I don't get it. I mean, I think I know what you're saying but—"

"All right, how about this? Don't think of Luke. Think of yourself. Who is it who breathes, without thought? And when you do think, who is the thinker of the thoughts?"

"I am."

"Can you physically touch the part of you that is the 'I am,' the thinker behind the thoughts?"

"Physically? No."

"Well . . . that's where and what Luke is now. He is totally the thinker behind the thoughts, without the burden of a space suit that people admire or ridicule, or that breaks down many times until it eventually gives out."

He smiled at her. "Some say that we've got life and death all mixed up. People are filled with happiness when a soul is born and it has to travel such a long distance, go through so many trials, so much pain, and it begins dying the moment it attains life. What's the opposite of death?"

"Life," she answered.

"No, the opposite of death is birth. If dying is like taking off a tight shoe, and finally being released from pain and returning to who we really are, the 'I am' presence, then why do we cry for that person? Cry for yourself, Eve, but don't cry for Luke. If he could, he would tell you that it's just silly."

She stared at him, hearing Luke's words in her mind, telling her that exact thing. Was it possible? Was Luke's love eternal?

Her voice was a mixture of fear and awe. "Mick, remember when we told you and Rue about all the weird things we had to go through for the adoption? Remember me telling you about this old Indian prayer man, the *chuchujua*, or however you pronounce it?"

"Right."

"After the ritual in the church, this old man comes up to Luke and bows in front of him. Carlos translated and told us that the man was saying something about honoring Luke for participating in a lesson, that the part he played was of great importance to another's soul, and something else . . . that his sacrifice would be his glory. Luke thought he was talking about losing the car!"

Mick continued to stare at her. "So you think this Mayan priest was talking about the future? That Luke would die?"

"I don't know," she whispered, clutching the gold seashell in her hand. "God, there's so much I don't understand." She looked out to the sunset and sighed deeply. "Why is it so damn hard, Mick?"

"Maybe because we wouldn't learn the lessons if it was easy."

"But what lessons? Come on, how much do we have to learn before we're happy?"

"I'll tell what I was told. Until we learn all about love

and forgiveness, there will always be another lesson waiting."

"But I loved Luke. I really did! And I don't blame him for dying. It wasn't his fault."

"Whose was it, Eve?"

She chewed her bottom lip for a few seconds. "Doug Vansciver's," she said, knowing she was avoiding the place where Mick was heading.

"But who do you really blame?"

She didn't say anything, only continued to stare out to the fading sun. Finally, she couldn't stand the silence any longer and said what was in her heart.

"God. I blame God."

"Then that's where you have to start to forgive. It's not an easy lesson. I know. I was there myself."

"What did you do?" she asked, desperate to pull the stone out of her shoe.

"I worked through the anger and fear. And I came to peace when I realized that forgiveness is an act of love for yourself, to stop the pain and guilt that you never should have carried in the first place. There's no point in being angry with God, because God doesn't recognize your anger, only love. The opposite of good isn't evil. Doug Vansciver wasn't evil. He was wounded and disconnected from that 'I am' presence, or his soul, whatever you want to call it. His act of violence was his desperate attempt to connect on a physical level. Right now he's disconnected to anything positive within himself, so he strikes out at others. If you believe that God is loving and incapable of seeing you as anything but whole and perfect the way you are, then your anger serves no purpose, except to make you, in the physical body, fearful."

She was crying again, knowing in her heart he was right yet not knowing how to accept it.

"Honey, I've got to get to an appointment. An addition for a house over in Medford. Are you okay? I know this is some heavy-duty stuff we're talking about, and we can continue tonight if you want."

She nodded, and wiped the tears off her cheeks. "I'm so sick of crying," she muttered, and then suddenly chuckled. "Luke would tell me I'm being foolish. He was so amazed by my energy. Now I feel like an old woman when I walk up the stairs."

Mick stood up and kissed her cheek. "Just don't give up, Eve. It will get better. In every moment the universe is renewed over and over again, and you're part of the universe. It will happen for you. Be patient with yourself. There's always another chance to start over again. It's your choice when, where, and how."

She stayed on the porch until it was dark and the street-lights came on. She thought about Luke, and she thought about Mick's words. She thought about herself. And she thought about God. Her heart was only slightly lighter, and she finally got tired of thinking at all, so she got up.

Entering the house, she wondered if Ruthann had come home and left for the club without checking in with her. Poor Rue, the joy of her wedding being overshadowed with grief. Eve resolved that when she was stronger she would make sure that Mick and Ruthann had a proper honeymoon. And she would also make sure that they didn't move in with her. They needed to start their own life.

Exhausted from doing nothing but sitting, Eve changed into her terry-cloth robe and was standing at her bedroom window, lovingly touching the seashell, when she heard the back door opening.

"Eve? Where are you?"

"Up here in my bedroom," she called out, and looked back out to the starlit sky. She remembered the night Luke had arranged dinner on the terrace of their hotel room in Chichicastenango. They had been looking up at the stars when he'd wrapped his arms around her and confessed he was falling in love. She had been so happy, so grateful. . . .

"Eve?"

She turned and saw the silhouette of Ruthann standing in her doorway. She was holding the hand of a small child. It couldn't be! She must be seeing things!

"Senora Eve?"

That voice! That tiny, precious voice . . . "Paulo?" she asked in disbelief.

He came running to her, and she grabbed him up and held him tightly to her chest, turning around over and over again. She pulled back to see his face and kissed him soundly. "How did you get here?" She looked to Ruthann, and Mick, who had joined his wife at the doorway.

She asked only one word. "How?"

"Ruthann decided yesterday to bring him back, and I made a few phone calls. It happens that an old college roommate works for the State Department, and when I told him the story, he said the administration could use some good publicity. The rest, as they say, is history."

"I left last night for Miami so I could get the first flight out this morning. We didn't even have to leave the terminal. Carlos Barrios's sister was waiting with Paulo. We caught a flight in forty-five minutes for the States."

Ruthann walked into the room and Eve shifted Paulo onto her hip. "You did this alone?"

"She insisted," Mick said, and walked up to his wife. Putting an arm around her shoulders, he kissed her temple. "She's quite a woman."

Still carrying Paulo, Eve came up to her, and Ruthann held her face in a sweet gesture of love. "You saved my life. It was the least I could do."

Those stupid tears came back, and Eve merely sniffled them away. "I love you, Rue. Thank you."

Ruthann swept Paulo's dark silky hair back from his tired eyes. "This kid's wiped. He'd never been on a plane before. And this language barrier, Eve. We've got to get someone to help out."

"I have the name of a nanny who's bilingual. Luke found it for me. I'll call tomorrow," she said, kissing Paulo's round cheek and watching his weary smile.

"Where are we going to put him?" Mick asked. "I guess I should have got something ready."

Eve walked over to her bed and gently put Paulo down. "He's sleeping here tonight. With me." She looked at her friends and smiled proudly. "I'm his mother."

A half hour later Paulo was put in his pajamas, given milk and Ruthann's special muffins, and tucked into the large bed. Eve was beside him with her head on the same pillow, softly singing him to sleep with the "Mockingbird Song." As his long eyelashes fluttered for the last time before sleep, she inhaled the clean scent of his breath and studied his beautiful face.

It was like a miracle. Love once again penetrated the scars around her heart, and she prayed for his safety. She had to forgive God. She had to believe that Luke's reason for living had been fulfilled, even if she didn't understand it. She wanted peace again. She needed it for this precious, innocent child.

Gently, so very gently, she kissed his nose and whispered what was swelling up within her heart.

"Welcome home, my son."

CHAPTER 22

Ruthann watched Eve playing with Paulo and sighed deeply. Something was still wrong with Eve that had nothing to do with grieving. It wasn't that she didn't show love to the boy. She did. And Paulo seemed happy, yet every once in a while he would look at Eve with such an expression of sadness that Ruthann's heart would break. Maybe it was something that only she could detect, having lived with Eve for almost a year.

A black and white soccer ball came rolling to her feet and she heard Paulo call out to her.

"Auntie Rue!"

She laughed and kicked it back in his direction, just as Carmelita came out from the kitchen and announced that Paulo's lunch was ready. Eve lifted him up in her arms and tickled him, making the child bend over with giggles, as she brought him to the house.

"Eve, can I talk to you?" Ruthann asked as she walked toward the kitchen door.

Eve sent Paulo in with his nanny and turned to her. "Sure. What's up?"

"You tell me," Ruthann answered. "What's happening . . . or not happening, to be more accurate."

Shaking her head, Eve grinned. "I don't know what you're talking about. You're not making any sense."

"Are you happy? Have you regained that sense of wholeness, of peace, that you had two months ago when you came back from Guatemala?"

Eve's shoulders slumped. "Why are you doing this? Isn't it enough that every time we sit out on that porch you get me to take trips down memory lane? I'm doing the best I can. Paulo's happy. I'm happy. What more do you want?"

"I want you to be that woman again."

"Look, I've dealt with Luke's death. I've even accepted it as part of some greater plan that I am kept miserably in the dark about, I might add. I've surrendered, Ruthann. Isn't that enough?"

"No."

"What more can I do?"

"Stop being afraid."

Eve stared at her. "What do you mean? Afraid of what?"

"Afraid of life. You think you're happy? Even your son knows you're not. You should see the way he looks at you sometimes. If you don't stop this, you're going to make him afraid too."

Folding her arms in front of her chest, Eve said, "I don't know what you're talking about."

"You're overly protective of the child. You watch him like a hawk—"

"He's four years old!" Eve interrupted defensively. "In a totally different environment. I have to watch him."

"When Mick took him to the Phillies game on Wednesday, you paced so much I thought we'd have to replace the carpeting. You almost had an anxiety attack until that child was back in your sight. You're afraid, Eve. You're afraid to trust, afraid to love totally again. What's worse is that you're afraid of life."

Eve walked away a few feet in anger and then stopped short before turning back. "Of course I'm afraid of life. Every time I totally love someone, something happens. Something bad."

Ruthann walked up to her. "Let's go in and get our purses. I'm taking you somewhere."

Eve backed up. "Where? I can't go now. Paulo—"

"Paulo is well cared for by Carmelita," Ruthann interrupted. "He'll be taking a nap soon anyway. Get your purse."

"Why? Where are we going?"

Ruthann started walking into the house. "I'll tell you when we get there. Come on. You're wasting time."

"You have lost your fucking mind!"

Ruthann laughed, and Eve thought she might actually hit her. She was that angry.

"You drag me into the car and refuse to talk to me for twenty minutes until we pull up at this rinky-dink little airport in the damn pine barrens, no less. And then you sit here in the car and tell me that we're going *skydiving*!

You're the one who's crazy, Rue. Take me home. I may be a little afraid of life, but I'm not suicidal!"

She watched Ruthann continue to laugh, and Eve could feel her blood pressure rising. "Does Mick know about this? Does he know that you intend to get up in a plane and fling yourself out into thin air? Does he know his wife is certifiable?"

Ruthann was laughing so hard that she kept waving her hand to make her stop ranting. "Please . . . don't. If I'm going to wet my pants, then let it be after I jump and am on the way down."

Eve shook her head and stared out the window to the small airport. "This is ridiculous. I'm not doing it."

Ruthann calmed down, took a few deep breaths to steady herself, and said, "Why aren't you going to do it? Because you're afraid?"

"Of course I'm afraid! Who wouldn't be?"

"What about all your talk about fear and walking through it? Damn, Eve, for weeks I heard your voice in my head saying, *Do it.* And then the fear would intensify and I'd hear you nagging me, *Do it anyway.* What about that? Wasn't that real? Wasn't that how you made things happen? Was all that a lie?"

"That works when you're talking about your life, your relationships, your work, not jumping out of a damn plane to prove some stupid point!"

"That you're not afraid of life? Come on, what can happen? They make you jump tandem with an instructor. Just do it, Eve. Do something you're afraid of and you'll have conquered your fear forever. Mick says it all originates from our fear of death. You're not just afraid of yours, you're afraid that everyone you love is going to die. Well, we are. Someday. But not today. Live right now, Eve. Look it right in the face and tell it to go screw off. You're not buying in to it today. You'll have taken back control of your life."

"I won't survive it!" she nearly screamed. "I'll die of a heart attack!"

"Back to being afraid to climb trees, I see. Feeling like a Stepford wife, are you?"

Eve nearly sputtered, "Find me a tree and I'll climb the damn thing, if it'll make you happy. But I'm not jumping out of a plane!"

"I never figured you for a gutless wimp. I used to have this good friend, Eve Cameron, who wasn't afraid to take chances, who had learned how to really live life and make things happen for the better. She taught me that life was filled with endless possibilities and it was up to me to make things happen. All I had to do was walk through my fear and take control of my destiny. But now you're too chickenshit to follow your own advice."

"I beg your pardon?" Eve demanded. "Chickenshit? I am not a coward."

"You heard me." Ruthann opened the car door. "Come on. If you're too paranoid, too spineless, to do it yourself, then you can watch me."

Ruthann got out of the car and slammed the door. Eve followed, also slamming her door. "I am not paranoid or spineless," she called out to Ruthann, who was ignoring her and walking toward the small office. "I have survived the death of my son, a divorce, Monty Clarke! The jungles of Guatemala, a . . . a guerrilla attack, and the death of a man that I loved! All in one year!"

Ruthann stopped short and turned around. Eve almost walked right into her.

"Then what in the name of God makes you think you won't survive this? Fear. That's all it is. Let me give you back your own words: It isn't real. It's just an emotion. The only power it has is what you give it."

Eve stared at her friend as the truth came slamming back at her, rendering her speechless. They stood for endless moments in silence, until Ruthann spoke.

"Are you coming with me?"

Eve's breath sounded ragged as it left her mouth. Her palms were sweating and her heart racing. "If I die—"

"You're not going to die."

"But if I do, you'll take care of Paulo?"

Ruthann impatiently looked up to the sky. "Eve, I love you and I love that kid. He's the child I never had. You think you're his mother? Well, he's got two." She looked back at her. "Now, will you shut up about dying, and just do it? I can't make you, no matter how much I want it for you. You're the only one who can decide how you want to live the rest of your life. Remember, Eve, you said we were going to soar."

"See, if I knew this," Eve said, walking past her toward the office, "I would have stopped at 7-Eleven for coffee that morning, instead of Shop-Rite. I've created a monster, with a mouth on her that won't quit."

Ruthann caught up with Eve and put her arm over her shoulders. "Think of all the fun you would've missed."

"This is fun?" Eve demanded as they neared the door.

"Wait . . . you'll see."

She initialed and signed a stack of papers that released Fearless Freefalls from any liabilities in the event of her death, however small the possibility. It was crazy and reckless, and she was on automatic pilot as she flipped through the pages and scribbled her name. After forty-five minutes of ground instruction, they were suited up and taken into a small two-engine plane that Eve was sure must have been built during World War II. Four others, besides her and Rue, were making a jump. They, however, were an experienced team; they were practicing hooking up together on the ground before entering the plane. Numb with dread, Eve watched them as she waited for her instructor to join the group.

Joe was young, had impressive credentials, and was the master instructor—probably given to the most fearful students. They had made a good choice. In the last hour she had used the bathroom four times.

Ruthann appeared scared, but it was more excitement than fear. Her instructor seemed a bit older; he was tall and joked around a lot. Eve couldn't even make her lips form a smile.

"Okay, here's the way it's going," Joe yelled in front of the sliding door to the plane. "Three of you," he pointed to the team, "will sit on the seat at the back. Bryan, you and Ruthann will sit on the floor. Ruthann between your legs. I'll sit next to you, with Eve between mine. Then you," he pointed to the smallest and thinnest man on the team, "will sit between Eve's legs. Once we hit thirteen thousand five hundred feet, I'll slide the door open, look down, and spot us. I'll give the pilot instructions and then the four of you guys will jump first. Then Eve and I, and then Bryan and Ruthann. Got it?"

Everyone else gave him a thumbs-up sign. Eve could only nod as the jumping team climbed into the plane. This wasn't happening! How in the name of God had she let herself be talked into this?

After Ruthann and Bryan got in, Joe sat on the floor with his legs open wide and patted the space for Eve. With the bindings, straps, and harness, she felt as if she were playing Twister as she struggled to get in and sit down. She supposed there was some order to it, but it seemed as if everyone's legs were crammed into a small space, and when the last member of the team got in and sat between her legs . . . well, it was a good thing she wasn't claustrophobic or she would have jumped out at ground level.

Joe slid the door closed and the plane began moving onto the runway. She tried to keep her mind blank, to avoid thinking of what she was about to do, but everyone started yelling over the noise of the engine.

"First jump?"

"You'll love it."

"Perfect day. You're lucky."

"Nothing to be afraid of. You're gonna fly like a bird for sixty seconds at two hundred miles an hour until you pull the cord. It's a blast."

Joe started running his hands up and down her arms and over her shoulders. She was sitting up against his chest in a very intimate position, and he leaned his head forward and said in her ear, "You're going to be fine. Take some deep breaths, relax, and remember your instructions. Arch your back now, while I tighten your harness."

The roar of the engine was intense, and Eve thought she might throw up as the plane gained altitude. She refused to look out the windows, to see the earth and safety receding.

"Look at your altimeter," Bryan yelled at her and Ruthann while tapping her wrist. "See how it's rising as we do?"

She merely nodded, incapable of speech. She looked through the goggles on her face to Ruthann. The woman was grinning with excitement, like some adrenaline junkie.

She had lost her natural mind. That was it. She had crossed that thin line. It was the only explanation for wearing a jumpsuit, goggles, and a helmet, sitting in an old plane between a man's legs, with a stranger between her own, and preparing to hurl herself out into the universe. Her gastrointestinal tract started rebelling—upper and lower.

She closed her eyes and prayed to God to watch out for her. When she left this plane, she begged to be caught in the arms of some wandering angel and—

"Look," Bryan yelled, and tapped her arm again. "There's Atlantic City on the right and Philadelphia on the left. You can see across the whole state!"

She opened her eyes, saw both skylines in the distance, and groaned. She was not meant for this! These people were thrill-seekers. They enjoyed the sport. She was trying to overcome fear. Couldn't Ruthann have found a fire walk? Hot coals on the ground sounded like a breeze compared to this.

"Okay, we're almost there," Joe yelled, and slid open the door right next to her. There was nothing, _nothing,_ between her and the intense wind that came rushing into the small cabin!

Eve thought she might soil herself.

"We're doing it! We're really doing it!" Ruthann yelled over the engine noise, and held her thumb up in a victory sign. "Remember, Eve, everything we've ever done has brought us to this moment. This is it!"

Eve was so scared, she couldn't even find her thumb. How the hell was she supposed to remember to pull the cord?

"I can't believe I'm doing this. . . ."

"What?" Ruthann yelled. "I can't hear you."

"I said," Eve yelled back, "I can't believe I'm doing this. When we get back on the ground, I'm either going to kiss you or knock you flat on your butt."

Ruthann laughed. "We'll both probably be on our butts. You can kiss me later. And think, Eve, this will make the best _rocker_ yet!"

Thinking of the stories they told each other on the porch, Eve shook her head and tried to grin. If nothing else, if she did survive this it would make one hell of a rocker.

Joe suddenly leaned out of the plane, and since she was harnessed to him, she was forced to follow. Cold wind slapped at her face, and she almost lost her breath and her mind as the upper half of her body emerged from the plane! It was sensory overload, and she couldn't even force her mind to function. Instinctively, she grasped at anything to hold on to as Joe yelled for the pilot to turn right. The plane banked and she thought she was falling out. Terrified, she closed her eyes and was about to call the whole thing off, when Joe leaned back into the plane and she came inside with him.

"Okay, guys, ready! Go! Go! Go! Go!"

Everything happened so fast. The jumping team climbed over her legs and stood on the little ledge under the door. She didn't even see them jump. She was in an alternate reality. Never in her life had she felt such gripping, paralyzing fear.

Eve looked at Ruthann. Their gaze met and held with such intensity that it was almost as if they didn't need words to communicate. Telepathically they sealed their love for each other. No matter what . . .

She forced her cramped legs to slide toward the door. It was the bravest thing she had ever done in her life. She settled her feet on the ledge and her behind on the floor. Joe urged her forward until she was balancing between his legs to stay in the plane.

"Remember," he yelled into her ear, "I'm right behind you," and unlocked the death grip of her hands from the door. "Grab your harness," he yelled, and put her hands to her chest. She clutched the thick belts and nearly fainted. It was like sitting on top of a flagpole two miles high! Death seemed easier than this.

Do it, her mind urged, but she was too terrified to move a muscle.

"Okay, Eve . . . We're gonna rock back and forth and on the count of three I say go. Just fall forward. Arch your back when we get out there, like you did in practice. Look at your altimeter, and when we reach fifty-five hundred feet, we pull the cord."

Falling eight thousand feet in sixty seconds!

Don't look down, she told herself as the wind whipped at her, yet her eyes couldn't help staring at the tremendous distance she would have to travel. Thirteen thousand, five hundred feet above the earth! It was her moment of truth, when she would either surrender and trust or give in to a faceless enemy. *Do it anyway . . .* Flashes of everyone she loved crossed her brain, until she saw herself as she was when she came home from Guatemala. She wanted with all her heart to be that woman again. A woman who trusted herself and lived in joy. Despite everything life threw at her, she couldn't give up. There was still excitement and satisfaction in accomplishing goals, especially raising a little boy. A hard life doesn't take those things away. We only choose to let them go. The wind ripped at her face and she nearly lost her breath. Okay, what other platitude could she think of? What doesn't kill us makes us stronger?

Fear gripped her again, squeezing at her torso, and she suddenly heard a strong yet loving voice inside her head.

I'm here for you . . . I'll always be with you. Don't be afraid. We're a good team, you and I. I'll catch you in my arms.

She almost sobbed her relief at Luke's words. Immediately her muscles felt like liquid, giving no resistance, and her mind stopped functioning. There was nothing left but trust. Trust in the power of love.

"Here we go," Joe yelled, starting the rock. "One, two . . . *Go!*"

The sound that came out of her mouth as she gave herself over into the unknown was raw and primal and instinctive.

"*Oh, G-G-Goddd . . .* "

EPILOGUE

"Can you believe it, Evie? That was almost forty years ago. You should have seen yourself. I never saw such terror in anyone in my whole life. You looked death right in the face and won. And when you landed, you loved it so much that you demanded they take you up again." Ruthann giggled, coughed, and then sighed as she looked out at the sunset that was almost over the horizon. She rocked back and forth, though much more slowly now. But what could she expect? Over eighty years on this planet had taught her acceptance. "When Paulo and Karen bring the children tonight, let's tell them that one. Those kids love our stories. Is Paulo bringing the paperwork for the new club in London? How many does that make now? I can't remember. Hard to believe we own so many. . . ."

She looked to her friend and wondered if Eve had fallen asleep. "Evie? Wake up. We should go in now. You were right. I am getting cold."

There was no response, and Ruthann pulled her hand

out from beneath the afghan and reached for Eve's arm to wake her. It was cool, and fell lifeless to her side.

Ruthann gathered her energy to pull herself forward and look at her. "Eve, get up," she commanded. "Wake up!"

She shook her shoulder with as much force as she could muster and watched in horror as Eve's head rolled to her shoulder like a rag doll's. *"Mick!"* She screamed her husband's name and then fell back into her chair.

A snowy cap of white hair topped his head, yet he still walked erect and proud as he left the bird feeder he was fixing and came to the steps. "Why are you screaming, woman? They can hear you in Philadelphia, and my hearing is—"

"Get up here," Ruthann commanded, and pulled herself upright. She steadied herself with the arm of her chair and looked down. "Mick, I think Eve's . . . I don't know what happened. Check her for me, honey. Please. . . ."

Mick slowly walked up onto the porch and bent over Eve's body, checking her wrist and her neck for a pulse. He looked up and smiled sadly. "She's gone, Rue. I'm sorry."

Ruthann clutched her husband's wool sweater and hung on. "No, she's not. She wouldn't die on me! We were talking about skydiving that first time, and she didn't answer me and . . . and then I looked at her and she . . ." Tears filled her eyes and she raised a shaking hand to wipe them away. "Oh God, Mick . . . what am I going to do without her? I don't think I can take this. Not now . . ."

Mick eased her back onto her rocker and Ruthann reached out and held Eve's hand in her own. It was quickly losing its warmth, and Ruthann only held tighter, wanting to postpone the final moment of release.

The tears rolled down off her cheeks and onto her chest, yet Ruthann barely noticed. "We would always sit here and talk about our life. Best Christmas. Best dancer. Best . . ." She shook her head at the futility. Bending forward, she brought Eve's hand to her cheek and inhaled the faint essence of the beautiful person who had shared her life for the last forty years.

"The only question we never asked was the last one in the game. Best friend . . . It was the only one that never really needed an answer. What will I do now, Mick? Without her?"

He knelt down between them, placed a hand on Eve's knee and one on his wife's. "You love her enough to let her go," he whispered. "You set her free."

She felt herself being pulled away from Ruthann, weightless and light, soaring at a great speed toward a radiant light in the distance. There was no pain, no doubts, no fears . . . only a tremendous sense of total peace.

"Mom? Over here. We've been waiting for you!"

Jamie! And standing with his arm around her son was Luke, both smiling and holding out their hands to her. Her thoughts seemed to explode with luminous joy, and she rushed to join them.

Enfolded in complete love, she looked back one last time and watched the final rays of the sun recede over the horizon before turning toward the brilliant new sunrise.

She had finally, ultimately, come home.

There is no end.

A Thinker, A Thought

As sure of me as your fear, for what you have to face
Just going through the motions, trying to keep pace
Along the way I test you . . . see if you make the grade
Time's your only captor on the path that you have laid
Your heart is beating fast, why continue this life that's led?
The present doesn't last; the past trapped in your head
You hold the lock and key; I give you the light to look
What is given along the journey should equal what you took
Some lessons may be simple, while others take time to get
Gazing into the dawning day, remembering . . . the sun also sets

—Jim Hahn

Acknowledgements

Kris Flannery . . . for her help, insights and, after reading this manuscript, challenging me to walk my talk. The time we shared was special. I shall never forget our Fearless Freefall Adventure. Skydiving with my daughter became my ultimate rocker —so far.

Deshune Compton . . . for his friendship and his encouragement during the writing of this book. Thank you

Adele Leone . . . my agent for the past twelve books. Our relationship was always more than business. My acknowledgement and friendship remain constant.

Joe Giantonia . . . master skydiving instructor. My life was literally in his hands for three minutes and he brought me safely back to terra firma, not on my behind, but on my feet. In those moments, my vision of life altered and will never be the same.

Jim Hahn . . . my own "adopted" son. Watching him identify the thinker behind his thoughts and discover his gift of poetry was a true joy.

Jeanne Tiedge . . . my editor, for believing in this project and helping to make it a better book.

Vernon Edwards . . . for not only teaching me, but also demonstrating, the freedom of living in joy.

God . . . for everything.

THROUGHOUT THE NEXT YEAR, LOOK FOR OTHER
FABULOUS BOOKS FROM YOUR FAVORITE WRITERS
IN THE WARNER ROMANCE GUARANTEED PROGRAM